UNTIL DEATH DO US PART

THE DEADLY WOLDS MURDER MYSTERIES
BOOK 3

JACK CARTWRIGHT

CHESTNUT PRESS

ALSO BY JACK CARTWRIGHT

The DCI Cook Murder Mysteries

A Winter of Blood

A Secret to Die For

The Wild Fens Murder Mysteries

Secrets In Blood

One For Sorrow

In Cold Blood

Suffer In Silence

Dying To Tell

Never To Return

Lie Beside Me

Dance With Death

In Dead Water

One Deadly Night

Her Dying Mind

Into Death's Arms

No More Blood

Burden of Truth

Run From Evil

The Deadly Wolds Murder Mysteries

When The Storm Dies

The Harder They Fall

Until Death Do Us Part

The Devil Inside Her

UNTIL DEATH DO US PART

The Deadly Wolds Mysteries

PROLOGUE

She had waited her entire life for this day. It would be a day she would never forget. A day she *could* never forget. Yet for all the wrong reasons.

Her skin tingled with the significance of the day, her body alive to every sensation, from the wind caressing her half-up-half-down hair to the goosebumps stirred by nerves that fluttered like a caged bird in her chest. Today was the most important day of her life. Since she was a little girl, watching princess films on a Saturday morning, she had waited for every second of it. Now, finally, *finally*, it was happening.

It wasn't quite everything she'd dreamed of. But it was close enough.

The sky oscillated between a brilliant azure and lingering white clouds. Her dress was a simple gown with a long-sleeved, plunging lace bodice. At the time, it had seemed an elegant and sophisticated choice, but the lace was beginning to scratch at her wrists. She would get through the day, regardless. Nothing could spoil it.

The man in front of her, her lovely Lucas, was not quite the tall, gallant prince that had romped through her childhood dreams, but his large, brown, puppy-dog eyes stared down at her, awash only with love as the officiant announced the promises of marriage.

Nancy felt the weight of every eye in the field on her, standing at the front of the aisle beneath the ornate, wooden wedding arch. She made a conscious effort to lift her chin and to stand on the right side for the photographer to capture her best features. Mixed in with the birdsong, unaware of the significance of their melodies that morning, was the occasional sniffle from a family member or close friend. Sure, it had been Nancy's dream to marry inside a grand, stately home with chandeliers aplenty and decorative balconies, or even a castle, which would not have been unreasonable, considering Lucas's family money. But she had to admit that the smell of freshly mown grass and the subtle scent of wildflowers created a deep sense of peace and comfort that she had always associated with her soon-to-be husband.

The rustic mill, with its ancient water wheel, was far more suited to their wholesome and grounded relationship. Lucas had brought so many things into her life that she had never expected. But they had turned out to be exactly what she needed. And as she gazed back at him without a single doubt as to her decision, the officiant declared them man and wife.

"You may now kiss the bride."

Lucas's face broke into a wide smile that seemed to ease the tension of the formalities. Like a wave breaking, their audience spilt into a chorus of applause and whistling as Lucas bent to plant a gentle, loving kiss on Nancy's lips. She turned to face the crowd and threw her right arm into the air, holding up her bouquet in triumph. Everybody bent as one to collect their packets of biodegradable confetti, and hand-in-hand, Lucas and Nancy skipped down the aisle of garden chairs in a flurry of red, green, and blue snowflakes.

While the guests prepared to follow the newlyweds back to

the watermill, Nancy and Lucas shared their first private moment as a married couple.

"No backing out now, Mrs Coffey," he whispered into her ear, pressing his cheek against hers.

"That's fine with me, Mr Coffey," she replied.

"You're mine now," he said, planting a kiss on her forehead.

At this, Nancy pulled away sharply. It was more of an involuntary twitch than a purposeful movement, a reaction to some long-lost memory she had tried to forget. But it had surfaced, just for a second, just in that moment of playful possessiveness. She swallowed and touched away a bead of sweat on her brow.

Lucas looked at her, concerned. "You okay, love?"

She shook her head dismissively, and the laugh she emitted was empty. "I'm fine."

"I didn't mean to—"

"It's fine," she said. "Honest."

He shook his head and bit down on his lower lip. "Pinch me."

"What?"

"Pinch me," he said again. "Tell me I'm not dreaming."

She placed a hand on his chest and leaned into him for one more kiss.

"It's not a dream, Lucas," she whispered.

"And this place. Is it what you wanted?" He took her hand gently. "I know you probably wanted something more like Lincoln Cathedral—"

"It's perfect," she insisted and squeezed his hand with a reassuring smile, appreciating the warmth of his body against the dampness of the grass from yesterday's storm. "I wouldn't change a single thing."

"Come on, you two," said her father from the end of the aisle, clapping as if he were herding his sheep across the field. "Lead the way. You can talk all you like after today. And trust me, the novelty wears off."

"I'll tell Mum that," she called out, then smiled up at her new husband. "Shall we?"

Nancy and Lucas Coffey led the wedding party along the small path from the ceremony field to the converted outbuildings where the wedding breakfast would be held. It was their first act as a couple, and she was in no rush to let the day pass.

They had chosen Stockwith Mill for its romance, its history, and its timelessness. With strong links to Lord Tennyson, who penned the poem *The Miller's Daughter,* the venue was everything they needed and more. Nancy and Lucas had even included the line, 'Her heart would beat against me, in sorrow and in rest,' in their wedding invitations.

But they had chosen the venue too, for its one proud guarantee: *to make your wedding day truly memorable*.

And memorable it would be.

Nancy and Lucas led the way along the path as though leading a swarm of bees. Conversations buzzed behind them, natterings about the ceremony, the touching vows, the moment the sun had broken through the clouds just as Nancy had walked down the aisle. Now, they were all looking forward to the next thrills of the day — the speeches, the wedding breakfast, and the toast to the bride and groom.

"After you," Lucas said as they reached the narrow bridge beside the water wheel. Despite the serenity of the scene, the river raged beneath them, frothing and gargling as it entered the mill pond. And just like the water's journey, the excited guests passed over the wooden bridge one by one, then spewed into the open courtyard where the catering staff were waiting with trays of champagne, and calm was once more restored.

The photographer, a ferret-like man who clearly refused to succumb to hair loss and had opted for a comb-over, had run ahead to snap the couple as they crossed the bridge. He scuttled around, capturing moments, planned and candid, and somehow never seemed to be in the way. Nancy, for one, could have done without the click of a camera every three seconds during the ceremony. But nothing could spoil her day. Not today.

"Nancy! Nancy, over here," he called from behind the camera, like paparazzi calling to a celebrity from the other side of the street.

She smiled politely and caught Lucas offering her a wink to diffuse her frustration. That was why she loved him. One look at Lucas could dissolve any negative emotion in her heart. He held her hand, kissed it once, and together they turned to face the ferret. With Lucas by her side, she was invincible. She beamed a bridal smile, uncompromised, honest, and a true reflection of the day.

The master of ceremonies, Ethan St Claire, had come to stand at the doors to one of the outbuildings, a long stable like structure.

"Ladies and gentlemen," he called. "Might I invite you all to take your seats?"

He was a jovial man. The sort who seemed born to bellow announcements at guests unruly and otherwise.

As the guests began to filter inside, the photographer pulled Nancy and Lucas aside.

"Just a few photos beside the water?" he said. "While your guests take their seats?"

"Lovely," Lucas said cheerfully, and he led Nancy to the mill pond bank. He put a loving arm around her waist and turned their backs to the pond so they faced the photographer, and Nancy summoned that smile that seemed never to be far away.

Had she known the smile would be her last, she might have refused.

"Beautiful," the ferret said as he changed between two cameras, crouching, standing, and even using a small step to gain height. "Gorgeous," he said between clicks, hopping between feet as though standing on hot sand. "Now turn to face each other, if you will."

Nancy turned to face Lucas, raising her arms to his neck as though they were dancing. "Today has been the best of my life," she said honestly.

"It isn't over yet," Lucas replied with a grin. "Let's get this lot fed and watered, then you and I can slip off to—"

Playfully, she slapped him, then feigned being shocked at the very idea.

"Lucas!"

"What? I'm only saying what every newlywed husband thinks," he said. "Anyway, if you don't drag me away from the bar at a reasonable time, it'll be days before I'm capable."

She laughed and reached up to kiss him, noticing, for the first time that day, an uneasy quiet had fallen upon the place. A single moment without birdsong, without the rush of wind through the leaves, as though nature itself had silenced, or the world had stood still.

The guests had been ushered inside, their constant chatter stifled by the heavy barn doors. Even the photographer's incessant clicking had ceased.

She turned to face the ferret, wondering why he wasn't capturing photos. But there was a look on his face that just wasn't quite right. His finger had stilled above the shutter button and his pale skin was revealed as, slowly, he lowered the camera.

Nancy's first reaction was to check her dress for wardrobe malfunctions, but everything was as it should have been.

She turned to her new husband, only to find that he too had followed the photographer's gaze, between them to the mill pond.

And then she saw it, and that wonderful silence she had moments before savoured was broken by her own shrill scream.

CHAPTER ONE

George took a deep breath and welcomed the salty sea air that filled his lungs. This was how an Englishman was supposed to enjoy the sea, he thought, with a fresh wind blowing, flicking at his trouser legs and threatening to lift the paper-wrapped chips from his lap.

The sand scuttled beneath him, shifting the shape of the dune that protected the small coastal town of Mablethorpe from the harsh North Sea winds. The near-straight coastline stretched north to south in his peripheral, continuing for what seemed like forever. There were few distractions to such natural beauty, and only one he allowed to occupy his mind.

His wife.

Grace by his side, whose beauty far surpassed the wild beaches before them.

"We used to do this," she said. "Me and my husband. We always said that, when we were old, we'd spend our days looking out at the sea together."

George took a moment before replying. He never enjoyed hearing her speak about him in the third person. It reminded him that, in her reality, the man sitting beside her, and her husband were two different people. There was no pain like it, knowing that the woman he loved most in the world didn't even recognise him.

"We used to say that, too," George said quietly. "My wife and I."

Her deterioration was increasing. The doctors had said it might gain momentum. But even still, there was little pleasure in being forearmed and forewarned.

She sat beside George, not on the old, wooden bench dedicated to a man called Henry, who had apparently always loved this place but in a wheelchair. Just as George had been getting used to her middle-stage symptoms of anxiety, disorientation, and forgetting her train of thought halfway through a sentence, her dementia had progressed. Her hallucinations had increased, and she often asked to speak to her parents, who had been dead for decades, or old childhood friends George had never even heard of. Last week, a nurse at the home called him at work because Grace had become aggressive and pushed one of them away as they tried to help her into a chair. After two worrying falls, she'd been confined to a wheelchair full-time. She'd also started to have trouble swallowing and seemed to be thinning before his eyes. She'd barely touched the chips.

It was for those reasons that George had driven them to the seaside. He wondered if Grace had known, the last time she had paddled in the sea or swam, that it would be her last. Or whether the day had passed, forgotten, without momentousness.

"Why do you have all that bloody junk in your car?" she asked.

Grace had asked the same question numerous times on the drive over, to which George had provided the same answer each time. The drive over with Grace had been a slow one. He had driven carefully, aware of his precious cargo, avoiding any sudden braking that might dislodge the jam-packed furniture. He had read once that even just a box of tissues alone on the back seat was enough to cause a serious injury in a car accident.

"I'm moving house," explained George for the fifth or sixth time that day.

"Is that right?" Grace said. "Where are you moving to, then?"

"On," George said, throwing a particularly salty chip into his mouth.

Grace huffed. "I know *on*," she said. "I know you're moving *on*, but where are you moving on *to*?" George grinned. She spoke as though he was a petulant schoolboy. It was one of her newer character traits. The old Grace had so rarely spoken harshly, even on the days he deserved it. But she was different now in so many ways, and a sharp tongue was a new addition to her personality.

"I'm moving to the Wolds," he said slowly. "I've already been there for a few months, actually."

"The Wolds," Grace said. "Very nice." She paused as though double-checking what she was about to say was true. "I grew up in the Wolds, you know?"

"Yes," George said. "I know."

"How do you know that?" she said, turning on him suspiciously.

George swallowed, not out of fear of the small woman sitting next to him, but to water down the lump in his throat. "I just supposed so," he said. "You seem like a woman from a pretty little village where everyone knows everyone else." He turned to her and winked, but it did little to quell her suspicion.

"How's that then?"

"Well," he said, imagining Grace in one of the rolling, wildflower fields, "the Wolds are slightly wild sometimes, like you. They're a haven for rare flowers, like you. And the Wolds is an Area of Outstanding Beauty, and..."

"Yes?"

"Well, I think you are outstandingly beautiful, Grace."

She rolled her eyes. "Oh, you're a charmer, are you?" But George noticed her softening to him.

"Would you ever like to go back there?" he asked.

"Where, dear?"

"To the Wolds," George said. She was less and less able to keep up with conversations these days, forgetting the topic of discussion or what she had only said a few seconds earlier.

"Oh, I suppose so," she said. "One day."

"What about this weekend?"

"This weekend!" she repeated with a laugh as though it was the wildest suggestion she had ever heard. "Oh no, not this weekend. I can't run away with some strange man to the Wolds for the weekend. What would my husband say? This weekend, I tell you..." She trailed off.

"Why not, Grace?" George asked. Now, he did sound like a petulant schoolboy, his voice high and whining. He had been renovating the house for the past few months. Any time he wasn't at the station, he could be found hammering and screwing and varnishing. Or at least running to and from the DIY store with some new renovation in mind. After making the spare bedroom liveable for Ivy, he had moved on to the rest of the house. And it had all been for her. For Grace. It gave him some control over an uncontrollable situation. Part of him dreamed, with every loose hinge he fixed in the house, he was fixing Grace's broken mind. "Grace?"

She was staring out to sea; whether she had forgotten his question or simply ignored it, he wasn't sure.

"I wonder if you'd recognise it," he said, more to himself than to his estranged wife. "It's changed a lot, Grace. I painted all the walls apricot white, your favourite shade. I fixed all the cupboards and painted them blue. I tightened any loose pipes in the bathroom and relayed the floors. I even fixed the roof." He laughed, remembering the silliness of it, a man his age climbing along the old, loose tiles, hammering them into place. "And I'm sorry, but I had to replace the furniture. No offence to Alice and Frank, but their taste in home decor had a lot to be desired, to put it kindly."

"Alice and Frank," she laughed and said dreamily, "strange. Those are my parents' names."

"See, I thought about buying everything from scratch," George continued. "Because I couldn't bear the idea of moving everything from here to the Wolds. To leave our Mablethorpe home empty. Because that would be like moving out. Like leaving our marital home. Like leaving you just to be alone again." He took a deep breath again, hoping for some sea-faring strength from the air. "But I decided it was time. Time to move on. To move everything from Mablethorpe to the Wolds. At least then, all our furniture is together. That dresser your sister bought us when we were married. That hideous fruit bowl from that market in Lincoln we bought as a joke." He laughed joylessly. "Because everything else has moved on, so why not me? Everything else is gone now, isn't it, Grace? Your parents, my parents. Even you, Grace. You're gone from me, aren't you?"

He turned to look at her, watching for a reaction, a twitch of her lips or a narrowing of her eyes, just something to show that he had gotten through to her, that she recognised his voice — her husband's voice — and the pain that lined it.

"Look at that boat," she said, squinting at the horizon.

George shook his head and rubbed his brow, dabbing at the corners of his eyes with his thumb and forefinger, which came away moist with early tears. He followed her gaze to the horizon.

"Looks like a fishing boat to me," he said, his voice cracked and tired.

They sat for a while in a silence with which lifelong companions are often comfortable.

Then George's phone began vibrating on the wooden seat where he had placed it beside his thigh. Grace startled in shock. "Those things," she said angrily. "I don't like them."

"I'm sorry," he said, seeing the number. "I have to take this." She watched with a scowl as George lifted it, pressed the green button, and placed it to his ear. "Hi, Tim," he said over the line.

"George," he said. "There's been a situation. Are you free?"

George watched the clouds move tirelessly across the sky. After lunch with Grace, he had planned on returning to his house in Bag Enderby and adding a final layer of varnish to the dresser he had painted and coated in Grace's childhood bedroom. It was how he spent many of his Saturdays recently. That was when he wasn't working on an investigation.

George sighed. "Not really, Tim," he said. "What is it?"

"A body," he said. "At Stockwith Mill."

George recognised the name of the place. It was not far from where he lived, and he drove past the sign to the mill almost daily. He continued watching the clouds. Part of him wished he shared their indifferent patience, allowing themselves to be blown hither and thither with the changing winds. But George was and always had been a man of action. He would fight against the winds of change for as long as he was able. And in the times when change was inevitable, he would, at the very least, keep himself busy. He felt Grace's stare on the side of his face, neither wanting him to leave nor asking him to stay — as indifferent as a cloud.

"Give me an hour, Tim," he said, smiling apologetically at his wife. "I'll be there."

CHAPTER TWO

When Ivy pulled up to the scene, Stockwith Mill held an eerie quiet one wouldn't expect of a popular wedding venue on a Saturday afternoon. She parked on the driveway outside a right angle of farm buildings and noticed the distinct lack of wedding clues — no tapping of teaspoons on champagne flutes, no incessant clicking of photographs. In the middle of the Wolds, with the nearest village over a mile away, surrounded only by tree-lined fields, rolling country roads, and old stone bridges over ancient streams, all Ivy could hear was birdsong and the primal, reassuring thundering of water.

She followed the sound and discovered a decommissioned water wheel. A rush of water from the field on higher ground flowed beneath it to the mill pool behind her. She marvelled at it, in awe of the energy.

A small, wooden bridge provided passage across the rushing water, and she stood upon it to peer down into the pond.

And then she saw it.

A dead body, bloated and pale and resembling an old plastic bag, caught in the reeds. She understood the disquiet of the place now. It was the dark silence that followed death, the stillness that followed the loss of life. Of course. She recognised it. She'd experienced it many times before.

"Help you?"

The voice came from a man she hadn't noticed approaching. She turned to face him as he stepped from the old mill. At his feet trotted a long-haired border collie, well-trained and more interested in having a sniff than the newcomer.

"Detective Sergeant Ivy Hart," she said, holding up her warrant card for him to see. The man seemed tense. His friendly face displayed worry lines, and he hunched his wide-set shoulders halfway to his ears with apprehension.

"Ethan St Claire," he replied. Then he turned to the dog as though having forgotten his manners. "And this is Molly."

Ivy smiled, and perhaps unprofessionally, she could not help but reach down to stroke Molly behind the ears; her fur was thick and wiry and stirred a familiar calm in Ivy. She looked around, her hand still resting in the thick forest of the dog's neck.

"You're the owner?" Ivy asked.

"I am," he clarified. He was in his forties, Ivy guessed, and she imagined that owning and running such a peaceful and breathtaking venue had inspired a very pleasant life. Up until now, that was.

"I was under the impression that a wedding was taking place," she said. "I saw the cars in the car park up the road."

"There is," he said and nodded at a pair of closed barn doors across the courtyard. "They're all inside. I thought it would be best to keep them away from..." He trailed off, but his eyes flicked to the body that floated in both their peripheral visions.

"You thought right," Ivy said. "We'll be cordoning off the scene soon. But, seeing as I have you alone, could you tell me what happened?"

He ran a hand through thick, salt-and-pepper hair not dissimilar to Molly's. "I'm not quite sure," he started. "I was inside, helping the guests to their seats, pouring champagne for the speeches. They had just returned from the ceremony. The bride and groom were outside having photos taken while everyone settled down. And then I heard this...this *scream*. It was horrifying."

"You heard the victim?"

"No," he said, holding up a hand to admit the misunderstanding. "No, I heard the bride. She must have seen it when they were taking photos. So I rushed outside. She was crying, and the groom was leading her away, and the photographer was just standing there staring at it."

"It?"

"Him," Ethan said, nodding at the body and then second-guessing himself. "It is a him, isn't it? I haven't really had a closer—"

"Where do you hold the ceremonies, Mr St Claire?" Ivy asked, enticing him from the bloated corpse for fear of losing the conversation.

"In the field," he said, gulping and pointing past the small bridge that crossed the flow of water. "We have a wedding arch up there, and we put out chairs for the guests."

"Then they all walk back here to the reception?" Ivy asked, looking around the courtyard.

"Exactly," he said. "In there." He nodded at the thick, double barn doors on the opposite end of the courtyard.

"And they're all in there?" Ivy asked. "Are any of the guests missing?"

"I...well, I don't know. I haven't exactly done a headcount," he said with an unsteady laugh that faded quickly once the look on Ivy's face told him there was nothing funny about it. "You think he's a guest?"

"Well, he's dressed in a suit and tie," Ivy said. "Hardly seems like a coincidence, does it?"

"I suppose not," the owner said, frowning. "I can do one? A headcount, I mean."

"I think that's a good idea, Mr St Claire. Thank you." She ruffled Molly's fur one more time, turned her back on the pool of water, and headed towards the double barn doors. "Shall we?" she called over her shoulder.

Ethan followed her with heavy steps that seemed accustomed to the uneven ground, sure-footed and steady. He pulled open the heavy door, allowing Ivy a generous view of the venue inside. Although a few heads turned, their welcome did little to stir the guests, who seemed lost in their own conversations, thoughts, and worlds.

Whispered voices hummed like crickets, heads twitched, and sobs erupted. Always the centre of attention on her wedding day, Ivy spotted the bride immediately; she sat at the bar, choking on her own despair, easy to spot. People were huddled around her, one topping up the whiskey glass in her hand that she clutched like a safety blanket, another wiping away the tears that smudged her mascara that rolled down her cheek like the river beneath the water wheel.

"That's the bride," Ethan whispered in Ivy's ear, like an assistant aiding his boss at a party.

"You don't say," she muttered. "Which one's the groom?"

"Bloke in the floral waistcoat," he answered, nodding towards a short, bear-like man who stared helplessly at his new wife with wide, red eyes, hovering at her side with a hesitant hand on her shoulder.

"And the photographer?" Ivy asked, but she spotted him as soon as she spoke, a tall, mousy man sitting and staring at a wood knot in the authentic barn floorboards, his fingers caressing an untouched flute of champagne. His camera hung limply around his neck, like a dunce sign. He looked in no mood to capture this particular scene.

And Ivy could see why. Nobody knew quite how to behave, and so the room was a strange hybrid of wedding celebrations and mourning. A soft, romantic soundtrack played in the background.

The servers continued with the charade, undoubtedly fuelled by some rule shared by hospitality and showbiz alike, that the show must go on. They carried canapes on a tray, offering them to haunted guests who either shooed them away or took a bite that Ivy doubted they even tasted. Another topped up the guests' rapidly depleting drinks. Most of them were still sitting in their assigned seats at round, decorated tables; a few fiddled with the nametags on their plates with anxious fingers.

Ivy wasn't sure where to start but figured the groom appeared the least hysterical of the witnesses, but before she could head towards him, the barn door opened behind her. She turned to face the two PCs, who she had called to meet her at the venue.

Campbell, a strong female who was growing on Ivy with every passing day, entered first. She took in the scene and offered Ivy a subtle grimace.

Byrne's approach, however, was far less subtle. He was in his mid-twenties, with more intelligence than refinement.

"Bloody hell," he muttered, straightening his jacket. "The bride won't forget today in a hurry."

CHAPTER THREE

George parked beside Ivy's car and admired the gorgeous old brickwork. To his right, a pair of large doors were open, allowing a view of the congregation inside.

It was a sombre sight, reminding him of a funeral he had attended, where the deceased had requested that everyone wear bright summer clothes. He strode across the courtyard towards his colleagues, who were standing just inside the door, clearly not even noticing his arrival. They appeared to be in the middle of a heated debate.

"Alright, alright?" Byrne said, wringing his hands.

"It's unprofessional, Byrne," Ivy fumed. "A man has died. Show some respect for God's sake."

"You need to think before you speak," Campbell spoke up.

"Hey," he said, turning to her like a betrayed sibling. "Thought you were on my side?"

"Alright," Ivy sighed. "Thank God nobody heard you." She jabbed an index finger his way. "Just watch your tongue, okay? Emotions are high."

He clenched his jaw. "I know," he said quietly.

"That includes you, Campbell. You're not out of uniform yet."

Campbell blinked as though unsure how to react to being scolded. "Yes, sarge."

George was close enough to feel the heat emanating from the conversation, but he thought it best not to push it further by asking for information. Ivy seemed to have closed it off in her own way, as harsh as George felt it was. Instead, he approached cheerfully with a "Now then. Beautiful day for another weekend of work, is it not?"

"How's it going, guv," muttered Ivy.

In turn, Campbell and Byrne replied with weak smiles, nods, and brief replies of, "Guv."

"What have we got then?" he asked quietly.

Ivy stepped up. "A body in the pool over there," she said, nodding in its direction. "Looks to be male. Otherwise unidentified. The guests are all inside at the reception." She nodded towards the barn doors across the courtyard. "The bride and groom spotted the body when they were having photographs taken about an hour ago. I've already called the FME and CSI. Doctor Saint and Katy Southwell are on their way."

"Are we sure that's necessary?"

"He has a head wound," Ivy explained. "Better to have them here and not need them than to delay things further. I'm sure the owners of this place would appreciate the urgency."

"You're sure about this, are you?"

"If I wasn't sure, I wouldn't have made the call, guv."

George took Ivy's word for it, not rushing to examine the body before it was necessary. In his experience, water-damaged corpses were some of the ugliest to witness, and forensic evidence was often scant.

"Any guests missing?" George asked.

"The owner, Ethan St Claire, is doing a headcount as we speak. No one has said anything, though."

"And nobody recognises the victim?"

"I don't think anyone's had a chance, guv," Ivy said. "Aside from the happy couple and the photographer, the owner was the only other person to see the body. As far as I can tell, he had the good sense to keep them inside. They all seem pretty shaken."

"You would be, wouldn't you?" George said, and the memory of his and Grace's wedding, when they'd had their photos taken by the chapel doorway burst into his mind. "Happiest day of your life. Ruined." He took a breath and clapped his hands once, rallying them all from their own musings. "Well then," he continued, "let's meet this happy couple, shall we?"

With that, he strode across the floor of what might have been a converted stable or a barn, his colleagues catching up with his long steps. A few heads turned, and some leaned into their neighbour, presumably to begin the gossip trail. It seemed that only the openly weeping bride clutching her whiskey at the bar understood the severity of the situation.

Therefore, George reverted to the more subtle way of capturing wedding guests' attention, a long-held tactic in such scenarios. He grabbed a nearby empty champagne flute and a teaspoon and stepped onto the raised stage at the front of the room. He tapped the teaspoon on the glass, so it created a sharp and ringing *ting ting ting*. At this, the curious guests turned to face him; a toast was familiar of all the unexpected things that had happened today. They seemed to welcome it. Even the bride and her fawning husband stopped their fussing to hear what he had to say.

"Good afternoon, everybody. I am Detective Inspector George Larson. I'd like to apologise for the inconvenience and thank you all for your patience. I won't insult you by concealing the truth. Your patience has earned you far more respect than that. But, an incident has occurred, and we must, for now, at least, treat the circumstances as suspicious. For your own safety and comfort, I ask that none of you leave this room. If you need to use the facilities, which I understand are in the next building, then one of my team will escort you."

"You what? You can't lock us up in here," a man whose bald head had a greater shine than his shoes called out.

"I can, and I am," George told him flatly. "We are treating the entire venue as a crime scene. We will need to speak with all of you individually."

"Is this some kind of wind-up?"

"While we are doing so," George said, regaining the audience's attention. "I'd like to thank you again for your patience. We will do everything we can to move this day on, one way or another. Nobody wants to keep you from leaving for longer than necessary. But before I proceed, I have one question for you all."

Here, George paused for dramatic effect, much like a priest might pause before asking if anyone present knows of any just cause why two people should not be married.

"Does anyone have anything to say? Anything at all."

"Yeah, this is a bloody joke," the bald man called out.

George ignored him and allowed the silence to linger, resting his eyes briefly on every face visible in the room. He knew his colleagues at the doorway were doing the same, watching for any slight movement that might betray guilt, suspicion, or a secret. But nobody spoke, choosing instead to hold their peace.

"Alright," George said eventually. "In that case, please persevere with us. We'll try to be as efficient as we can. We'll need to take statements from you, and we'll need to implement measures to protect the scene and yourselves."

"Ourselves?"

"The last thing I want, sir," George said, "is for somebody to see something that might keep them awake at night." He glanced down at a fragile-looking woman whose eyes were as wide as saucers. "It's a sensitive and emotional occasion. I'd like to keep those emotions at bay where I can." He wondered if anybody had ever stood on this stage and not offered a toast to the newlyweds. He thanked them all, then stepped down and made a beeline for Ivy.

"Anything?" he asked.

"Not that I noticed. They all seem quite in shock, but that's to be expected, I suppose."

"In that case, call a dive team. We're going to need that body removed from the water ASAP."

"Already done, guv," Ivy replied, and George took a second to appreciate the woman who barely came up to his shoulders, a small and efficient force if he'd ever seen once, not unlike a white snooker ball.

"Good," he said. "Good. Byrne, Campbell, start interviewing the guests. Find somewhere private to do it. I want to know what they saw. If they noticed any strangers at the venue who didn't look like wedding guests, anyone who seemed out of place. If there's anything they think we should know, make sure they tell us."

"Yes, guv," they said in unison, which George noticed they were doing more and more so these days.

"And, Byrne," George said, at which the young PC turned to face him. He looked different to how he had two months ago when George had met the lad — more filled out, harder, as though he'd been working out. "I'm looking for a collection of statements that all say the same thing. If one of them goes into detail, I want to know. If one of them omits details or tries to make a joke, I want to know. And if one of them asks too many questions, I want to know."

He nodded. Then with a "Yes, guv" and a swift glance at Ivy, Byrne headed off with Campbell to further disrupt the day.

"Think that's wise, guv?" Ivy asked. "Sending those two, I mean."

"Oh, I think we can loosen the leash a little, Ivy," he said. "If Byrne chooses to wrap it around his neck, then so be it."

CHAPTER FOUR

George watched with dread as a diver dragged the floating body to the side of the mill pond, where two other men could help lift it from the water. It was one of those tasks that, no matter how delicate they tried to be, was hard to achieve with any ceremony. He imagined this was one of the easier jobs for which they were called out. Considering most of their workdays consisted of diving in algae-filled, fast-flowing rivers in search of human remains or searching the silt and mud for a discarded weapon they might only identify through the touch of a wetsuit glove, removing a body from a near-clear pool of relatively shallow water was probably a breeze.

George could see clearly enough the man's congealed wound. The torn skin had turned white, but the cleft was more of a rich crimson so that the overall effect resembled the colour palette of the wedding flowers and centrepieces inside.

"Now then, George," said a familiar voice at his shoulder. He turned away from the dive team to face the familiar dark-haired man he had not noticed arrive. Doctor Saint dabbed at his forehead with an old-fashioned, monogrammed handkerchief. It was not a hot, sunny day, but the growing humidity was a sign of an incoming storm.

"Peter," George said, shaking his hand. "Good to see you again."

Although George and Peter Saint had worked together many times when George had lived in the Wolds with Grace ten years ago, they had only worked together once since his return to the area.

Saint set down his leather bag and turned to face the body that was being carried onto a gurney behind the ambulance. "What have we got then?"

"We don't really know yet," George admitted, walking towards the body. "The bride and groom found him in the pool just over an hour ago."

Saint puffed out in response but didn't comment on the obvious downer on a happy day.

Ivy busied herself as the two men stood at the gurney. If she found it difficult to see the dead bodies in Pip's mortuary once she had cleaned them up, Ivy would find it almost impossible to witness the bloated and distorted remains they had pulled from the water. George could not speak for Saint, but he, for one, was happy not to do the obligatory bend on aching knees in order to inspect the body.

"Well, this body has been in the water for more than just a few hours, George," said Saint, opposite him. "I'd say at least twenty-four."

"A whole day?" clarified George.

"Yes. Look, he's started to bloat, which suggests he wasn't recently killed. The water has, in part, preserved him. It must be quite cold in there." He nodded at the pool. "But rigor mortis is already easing off."

"Can you give a time of death?" George asked, and Saint grimaced as though weighing up whether his estimation would truly help an investigation going forward until eventually deciding that it was better not to guess.

"Afraid not, George. All I can say is more than one day but less than two." With his gloved hands, he rolled the man onto his side, then peered up. "How was he found?"

"On his back, over by those reeds," Ivy said.

"On his back?"

She nodded.

"Well," Saint said, "he didn't die there, and he certainly hasn't been on his back for twenty-four hours."

"What do you mean?"

"I mean," Saint said, presenting the side of the man's torso, which had the appearance of a huge bruise, only richer in colour. "When we die, our body goes through several...phases, if you like. The first is known as algor mortis. It is the body cooling to its surroundings."

"Hence the preservation?" George asked, to which Saint nodded.

"After that, we have livor mortis," Saint continued. "Gravity's effect on blood."

"So, he was lying on his side?" Ivy asked, and again, Saint nodded.

"Livor mortis takes around an hour to get going. It is well-established after three to four, and by six to eight hours, it is well and truly set."

"So, if the body is moved after eight hours..." George began.

"The effects of livor mortis would still be evident in the original position. We had a case a few years back in the city. A young man's face was the colour of beetroot. The rest of his body was the colour of fried cod."

"Thanks, Peter. I'll be skipping my fish and chips on Friday."

"Turned out to be a sex game gone wrong," Saint continued. "Though, to this day, I can't fathom what type of game it was."

"Each to their own," George said, glaring at Ivy's childish smirk.

Saint, who was unnaturally tall and whose jacket cuffs stopped a good four inches from his wrists, stood up from where he'd been leaning over the body. "I'll need a few minutes."

"Take all the time you need," George said gratefully. He looked up at the sound of tyres on gravel to see Katy Southwell and her team pulling into the quickly filling-up car park. "We'll leave you to it," he said, gesturing for Ivy to follow him.

"Thanks, George. For now, all I can tell you is male, late twenties, dead for one to two days, and certainly not in here."

George nodded his appreciation and walked around the private ambulance to greet Katy Southwell who was rapidly climbing from her car, already offering instructions to her team to close off the area and construct a tent. For someone who worked with people who were already dead, to whom the worst had already happened, he respected her sense of urgency.

"George," she said, turning suddenly to him as though he were another member of her team. "What have we got?" she asked, shaking his hand and then Ivy's.

"Male, late twenties, dead one to two days," he relayed. "Saint is just doing his examination. The body was found in the pool here," he said, pointing to the body of water. "However, livor mortis suggests he died elsewhere. Might be worth doing a toxicology report?"

At this, the owner of the venue, who George had not noticed watching the procedure with eagle-like eyes, stepped forward.

"Toxicology?" he repeated. "Is that really necessary? There's nothing wrong with this water. It comes straight off Raymond's Hill. Flows all the way down, it does."

"I'm sure it's very fresh water," George said. "We just need to cover all bases."

This seemed to do little to reassure the man, who wrung his hands anxiously. "Just...it doesn't look good for business, does it?"

Again, he ran a hand through his hair. "A dead body, I mean... *bloody hell.*" At his feet, the border collie whined as though emitting the distress of its owner. "How do you think this looks?"

But George could not respond before yet another car entered the car park.

He heard the owner mumble, "Christ," in despair. "What now?"

It was a police car, ferrying the uniformed officers Ivy had called to assist. She stepped forward, taking charge of them, then began ordering them to close off the road and the venue as a crime scene. One of them, she sent inside to make sure no guests left or entered the reception.

While Ivy rallied the troops, George took the opportunity to crouch down and hold out the back of his hand to the dog, who sniffed it and then licked it gently. Accepting the invitation, George ran his hands through the collie's thick, wiry fur. "What's his name?"

"Hers," said the owner distractedly. "She's Molly."

George ruffled Molly's ears. He'd always loved dogs, especially hearty, working dogs like collies, who could endure a good, long walk and then settle for a night in front of the fire.

"I always wanted a dog," he said calmly. "But my wife is allergic."

"There're pills for that," the owner said, somewhat incredulously, as though unsure why they were discussing pet care only a few metres from a dead body.

"I suppose. But still, didn't want to put her through that." George stood slowly. "And your name?" he asked, holding out his hand. "I don't believe we've been introduced."

The man looked slightly shocked at his inhospitality, and he stopped scanning the usually peaceful courtyard that had suddenly become somewhat of a circus. "Sorry," he said, shaking George's hand. "It's Ethan, Ethan St Claire."

"Well, Ethan," George said, looking around and eager for the chance to escape the madness. "You say the water flows from Raymond's Hill?" The man nodded, and George gestured to the tiny bridge that crossed by the watermill. "Why don't we go for a little walk?"

CHAPTER FIVE

Molly followed George, and George followed Ethan St Claire from the pool of water upstream towards the mill. Crossing the charming little bridge that connected the venue and the ceremony field, he could absolutely see the old mill's appeal as a wedding venue. It was beautiful. Not only did the mill provide an impressive yet rural image, but small details added to the rustic aesthetic — the wildflowers along the stream, the commitment to rosy, reddish wood, and the gaps in the shrubbery that perfectly framed the stunning views of the Wolds beyond.

"So, how long have you owned this place?" George asked as the two men walked.

"About five years now," he said. "The people who owned it before had it for generations. Used to be a working water mill, you know, back in the day."

"You seem quite proud of it."

"I am. My wife and I quit our city life to move here. We just fell in love with the place."

"And do you only host weddings?" George asked. "Or do you cater for other events, too?"

"Yeah, we do all kinds of things," he said, expertly navigating the larger puddles of muddy water as though he knew the route well. "But mostly weddings." He looked back, eyeing George's brogues, which kept slipping in the mud. "What about you? You local?"

George hesitated. "Somewhat," he said.

The man laughed. "Somewhat?"

"I'm from Lincolnshire," George said. "Just north of Lincoln. But we lived out here for a while before moving to Mablethorpe. My wife's local. From Bag Enderby."

"Why did you move away? I can't imagine ever leaving this place."

"It's all part of the job," George said, trying to avoid the muddiest puddles as best as he could. "If you want to climb the ladder, then you have to do these things. You have to make sacrifices."

"And were the sacrifices worth it?"

George pondered the question and grimaced when he thought of Grace and how different life could have been had they not made the move to the coast.

"Who knows?" he said, rather ambiguously.

Ethan nodded, clearly sensing that George was unwilling to delve into his personal life.

"I fell off the ladder when we moved here," he said. "And good bloody riddance to it."

"I can't say I'm not envious," George said, stepping over a large puddle. "Shame about the rain. Aside from putting in an ugly footpath, I don't suppose there's much you can do, is there?" he asked, changing the topic.

"Had a downfall yesterday. Not ideal, but we can't control the weather, can we?"

"No," George said. "I suppose we can't."

They had reached the top of the field, which had a slight incline that would offer an expansive view over the venue if not for the line of trees that lined the stream.

"This is as far as we can go," said Ethan. "The stream continues up through the farmer's fields, but this is our boundary."

They had stopped at another pool of water that lay before the boundary fence. George peered over the edge, noting an overflow pipe that could just about fit a child, but definitely not a grown man. The other end of the overflow pipe poured excess water into the stream that wound through the property, eventually feeding the decommissioned water wheel and the mill pond.

"So, if our victim entered the stream before this pipe," he said to the owner, speaking aloud but to himself, "then he wouldn't have been able to get through this pipe. He would have been stuck in this pool."

"Suppose so," Ethan replied.

"Which means he either went straight into the mill pond or entered the river somewhere between the lower end of this pipe and the water wheel," George said.

"I doubt he floated down the river, Inspector. It's only a few inches deep," Ethan mused, eyeing the many roots, pebbles, and loose branches that created small dams in the waterway. "Look at all that. He would have got stuck at some point."

George nodded politely but disagreed.

"Right. Except..." he said, crouching down to inspect the area of flattened grass on the riverbank, marking the high water level. "If there had been heavy rainfall recently, say yesterday, that might have dislodged the body from the roots. Right?"

"Right," the owner said slowly. "You know, that has happened before. We'll find foxes and badgers and whatnot after a storm in the mill pond."

George stood up straight once more and turned to face the field, hoping for the view to give him some perspective. "Was anybody here yesterday?" George asked. "Another wedding, maybe?"

"Another wedding?" the owner laughed. "No, one or two per

week. Takes that long to prepare for the big day and then clean up. Then we have to schedule days to keep on top of the gardens and the footpaths."

"So, nobody was here?"

"No. I mean, we had the rehearsal. Usually, do that the day before the wedding. Gives the wedding party a chance to see the venue, know where to stand, where to walk, and all that."

"Who was here?"

The man puffed his cheeks, trying to recall. "To be honest, we usually let them get on with it, you know? Normally, it's the bride and groom, of course. The parents come mostly for support. Then there are the bridesmaids and the groomsmen. There could be others, but it's normally those. Oh, and whoever is doing the officiating."

"No one else?" George asked.

"Not that I know of," said the owner. "But really, you'd have to ask the bride's mother. She was the one in charge."

"Did you see anyone yesterday who *wasn't* a part of the wedding party?" George asked, his stare serious.

The man gave it some thought, but then he shrugged. "I don't know who was part of the party or not. But everyone that came through *that* car park," he said, pointing at the mass of cars in the distance, "I sent them up to *this* field for the rehearsal."

"And can people enter the field from anywhere else?" George said, squinting his eyes to scan the periphery.

"I suppose so," he said. "If they can climb a fence or jump the stream, but I don't see why they would."

"What's that way?" George asked, pointing to the opposite corner of the field.

"Hagworthingham," said Ethan. The owner spun around. "North up that way is Bag Enderby. Then, the A16 to the east. And eventually, Horncastle over there to the west." He finished his circle and rubbed at the stubble on his chin. "It's unusual though, isn't it? Out here in the Wolds? I mean, in small villages like this, it's as safe as you can get. Those kinds of things don't happen here."

George laughed at his own private joke. He had been in the Wolds for less than two months and had already seen his fair share of small-town drama with its fair share of crime, deceit, and violence.

"If I told you the truth about small villages, Ethan," he said, looking out at the peaceful, rolling hills, "you'd move back to the city in a heartbeat."

CHAPTER SIX

George led the way back from the field to the courtyard, spurred on by the list of tasks and potential happenings developing in his mind. He navigated the puddles, crossed the little bridge, and strode across the car park straight up to Ivy, with the owner and the dog following in his wake. She was talking to one of the catering staff, a long-haired teenager in a white shirt, black waistcoat, and opulent, purple tie.

"Ivy," he said, still three feet away from her, "I want you to check all local guest houses for names that are *not* on the wedding party list."

"Sorry," Ivy told the young lad, then closed her notepad and turned to George. "You don't think he was invited, guv? If that's the case, then why is he in a shirt and tie?"

"I think he showed up at the wedding rehearsal yesterday. But if we don't have a guest missing, that means he wasn't on the guest list."

"Well, actually, guv," she said. "We did a head count of all the guests, but there's one missing."

"What's his name?" George asked.

"Uncle Pete."

"Uncle Pete?"

"That's his name on the guest list and his table card. I guess that's how everyone knows him. He wasn't in his seat, so I asked if anyone had seen him, but nobody has all day."

"And nobody has left or entered that reception while I've been gone?" Ethan asked.

"No," Ivy said sternly. "Though a few of them are keen to get away from the circus."

"How are we doing with the search of the property?"

"I'm expecting more uniformed officers shortly. The few that arrived are helping Byrne and Campbell take statements. The sooner we get the guests on their way, the better."

"Right," George agreed. "Do we have a description of this, Uncle Pete? A last name?" he asked.

"We're working on it," Ivy reassured him. "As you can imagine, emotions are high, and the last thing we want to do is let the bride's imagination run away with the idea that the man she saw floating in the mill pond was her uncle."

"Fair point," George agreed. "How do we know he's her uncle and not the groom's?"

"The seating plan," Ivy said, then gave him a wink. "The families aren't integrated."

It was a fair response, and as much as George was keen to press on, with nearly a hundred guests to deal with, all with access to social media on their smartphones, it was best to err on the side of caution.

Ethan St Claire edged closer, aware that he was interrupting but keen to say something.

"Look, I know this is serious and all, but do you know how long it's going to take? Think how it looks. My venue swarmed with police the whole day. Are we even allowed to keep them locked up in there?"

George turned to Ethan St Claire. "A man has died," he said. "Possibly murdered. Another man is missing. I don't like it any more than you do, and of course, they are free to leave. We can't keep them in there. But it goes without saying that those who fail to cooperate will put themselves under scrutiny."

"Right," Ethan replied, nodding.

"We're doing what we can," George assured him. "I'll wager that every person in that room has a smartphone, and whilst my team are requesting they maintain a level of decency, it wouldn't take much for your venue and my team to be under a rather crummy spotlight. Is that what you want, Mr St Claire? Because I certainly do not."

"No," the man said solemnly.

"Just let us do our jobs, Mister St Claire, and with any luck, we'll all get through this unscathed."

In the man's eyes, George witnessed his thought process as he oscillated between the two options.

"I hadn't considered that. I'll be in my office if you need me," he muttered eventually, and the dog sitting patiently at his side followed him as he strutted across the courtyard to the main house.

George turned back to Ivy, who had her own information to relay. "They're taking the body away," she said. "I just wanted to wait for your say-so."

He glanced over at Doctor Saint, who stood talking to the two paramedics somewhat casually.

"If you've got what you need, they can take him away," George called out. "I think we've got all we can for now until we get more from Pip."

He caught the eye of one paramedic and gave a nod that they were okay to leave. In turn, Doctor Saint held up his hand in a static wave of goodbye and walked over to his car. The dive team was packing up and stripping out of their dry suits.

"I'm guessing they didn't find anything?" he asked Ivy.

"Not a thing," she replied. "They did two sweeps of the pond. If there was anything to be found, they would have found it."

"And Southwell's team?" he asked, noting the white tent they had erected as a base for their equipment.

"Sadly not," Ivy said, sensing they were at a loss until they either found the elusive Uncle Pete or had a description of him.

"Come on. As soon as that body is out of sight, I want to start releasing the guests," George said, walking towards the barn doors. "In the meantime, I'd like to meet the bride."

"Guv, might it be an idea to see if anybody recognises him?" Ivy asked, to which George was horrified.

"What? Are you suggesting we ask the guests to have a quick peek? Do you realise what they're going through in there?"

"Not all of them. But, maybe we could identify somebody who isn't as emotionally invested as the immediate family."

"The answer's no, Ivy. I know what you're trying to do, and had it been some other occasion, then I'd agree. We can't lock them in there, but I'm going to do my damndest to prevent anyone from seeing that body. The last thing I need is to be accused of being insensitive or...incompetent. No. We'll treat this as we do any other homicide. Now, let's get this done."

Once again, their entrance went unnoticed save for a few glassy-eyed looks that were, at least in part, a result of the free-flowing alcohol, which was a shrewd move on Ethan St Claire's part and one for which George was grateful.

The bride was sitting at the bar clutching her whiskey, and George wondered how many refills she'd had. From the way she stared into space while tears rolled freely down her cheek, no doubt processing her *magical day*, he guessed someone had topped up the glass more than once. He beelined for her, edging between the tables, when a woman stepped into his path.

"Mr Larson," she said, blocking his way.

"Mum, don't," said a young man following closely behind and tugging her shoulder, trying to steer her away. With him came an older man who looked like his future self, with shockingly similar features, only with greyer hair, a thinner face, and more lines on his brow. "Let the man do his job."

George took a moment to appraise the woman whose hat was clearly a recent and expensive purchase and the young man's three-piece suit.

"You must be the groom," George said.

He nodded apologetically. Unlike his wife, he had retained a firm grip on his emotions. His cheeks were rosy with stress, and he ran his sweaty hands through his styled hair. The woman who was his mother had sharp, determined features, a long nose and pursed lips, which, along with the blue and purple feather-patterned dress, gave her a rather peacock-like appearance.

"I'm sorry, but no," she told her son, then turned to George and held his gaze easily. "I think there's something you should know, Mr Larson."

CHAPTER SEVEN

George led the groom and his parents out of the barn, leaving Ivy to watch the door, leaving Byrne, Campbell, and the uniformed officers to continue interviewing the guests. They sat at the white patio chairs and tables outside. It was a space for smokers to share a light and a story. George imagined that it had never been used to host a police interview, but needs must.

As though by instinct, the three of them sat together on one long bench. Parent, son, parent. It was an interesting dynamic, George thought, that he could read in one of two ways. The first would identify the parents as caring and protective. The second would conclude that with all the trials and tribulations that come with raising a child, the parents had drifted apart. Whether the son was the glue that held the parents together or the wedge that drove them apart would remain to be seen.

George pulled up one of the single chairs and sat opposite.

"I apologise," George said. "I didn't catch your names."

The mother spoke before anyone else had a chance. "Beatrice Coffey," she said, raising the sound of the Y at the end of her surname as though purposely differentiating it from the hot beverage. "This is my husband, Daniel Coffey," she said, repeating the surname as though it was one with which George should already be familiar.

Her husband was a shorter, older man whose anxieties frothed beneath a slightly trembling and furrowed brow.

"And this is my son, Lucas Coffey, the groom," she said proudly, her voice cracking at the end as though realising that today would never be a point of pride for anyone.

George smiled at the young man between his parents.

"Despite the unforeseen events, might I offer you my congratulations?"

"Thank you," the man said, then took a large mouthful of the champagne he had carried outside. He had a thick mop of brown hair that appeared to have a red tint when the sun broke through the clouds, which, along with his rosy cheeks, gave him a confident appearance. It wouldn't surprise George to learn that he received an education at Oxford or Cambridge and excelled in team sports.

"So, Mrs Coffey," George said, leaning forward, "what is it that you wanted to tell me?"

"It's nothing," Lucas said.

"It *is* something," Beatrice snapped at her son. Then she shook her head dramatically and said, as though to herself but making sure George could hear, "I knew this was a bad idea. I knew you should never have—"

"Mum, please," Lucas said, his voice whining as though tired of making the same defence over and over again.

"That family," she said, looking at George. "I mean, don't get me wrong, Nancy is a lovely girl. A *lovely* girl," she repeated, touching her son's hand. "But you should have known, Lukey, that marrying into that family would only bring chaos. And look! My God, you're only married for two minutes, and there's already a death in the family."

"A death in the family?" George repeated. "Are you saying that you know who the victim is, Mrs Coffey?"

"No," Lucas said. "She doesn't know. She didn't even see the bloody body."

"Then where is he, Lucas?" she said. "Have *you* seen him all day?"

George looked at Daniel Coffey, hoping he could provide some clarity, but he simply watched the proceedings as though watching a vaguely interesting TV show.

"I'm sorry," George said, interrupting the bickering. "Who is it that you're talking about?"

"Uncle Pete," Lucas said, sighing.

"Ah," George said.

"I haven't seen him all day," said Beatrice. "It *has* to be him. Though, why nobody's brought it up, I don't know."

"It could be anyone, Mum. Isn't that right, Inspector? We don't know who it is yet."

"That's right," George said. "We can't make any assumptions. But I am keen to know why you seem so convinced, Mrs Coffey."

He made sure to lift the Y so as not to antagonise her.

"He was at the rehearsal yesterday," said Beatrice. "And, well, there was an...altercation, let's call it."

"An altercation," repeated George.

"It was nothing," insisted Lucas.

Beatrice laughed. "Nothing? Perhaps it was nothing to that family. Perhaps they act like that all the time. I told you, Lucas, I told you this was a bad—"

"What exactly was the altercation, Mrs Coffey?" George interrupted.

"Well, they only ruined the day, didn't they?" Lucas rolled his eyes but stayed silent. "They did, Lucas," she said, even though her son hadn't voiced his opinion. "We were practising the cere-mony," she explained to George. "Who walked where and where everyone stood; you know how it is."

"Sure," George said, despite not having attended a wedding in some years. In his day, weddings had been a lot less performative. Just a pub rented out for the afternoon with a few close friends and family.

"And then halfway through the ceremony—"

"The *practice* ceremony," Lucas confirmed.

"Yes, halfway through the ceremony, they got into a fight!"

"It wasn't a fight, Mum."

"It was almost a fight," she said. "A very heated argument, wasn't it, dear?"

Daniel Coffey seemed surprised to be put on the spot, but he swallowed, nodded, and added in a gruff voice that seemed rarely used, "Yes, very heated."

"Who's they, Mrs Coffey?" George asked. "Who got into a fight?"

"Rory and Pete," she said, as though George should know who those people were.

"Uncle Pete, you mean? And Rory...?"

"Wetherford," she said, shocked, and added dramatically in a hushed tone, "*the father of the bride*."

"I see," George said. "And what were they arguing about?"

"God knows," said Beatrice. "God only knows what that family—"

"*Mum*," Lucas said.

"Oh, come on, Lucas," she said. "Look around you. Look what's happened. This is meant to be the biggest day of your life, and they've ruined it. They're rough," she explained to George. "Nancy is lovely. I have no idea how she's so lovely, coming from that family. But that family is bad news. They're not from the same...stock. Not good enough for our Lucas, you mark my words."

George moved on before she could go into a more explicit insinuation of the families' different class levels, a topic for which he had little time. "And this altercation," George said, "did it esca-late? Was there any physical altercation?"

"I would say so," said Beatrice. "Punches were thrown. It was all quite barbaric."

"Punches were *not* thrown, Mother," Lucas said. He squirmed a little in his seat. "Rory grabbed Pete's collar, that's all. It was nothing."

"And you have no idea what this was about?" George asked.

He was asking Lucas, but Beatrice answered. "Like I said, God knows. Could be anything." But George watched her son, who averted his eyes.

"Very well," George said.

"But that's why Pete's not here," explained Lucas. "Not because he was *murdered,*" he said, emphasising the ridiculousness of the word and turning to his mother. "He was uninvited, that's all. They just didn't want anyone to make a scene today."

At this, Beatrice laughed as though her son had told the funniest joke she had ever heard. "Didn't want to make a scene? Well, look how that worked out." Then, she grew serious and turned to George. "I just thought you should know, Mr Larson. If there's anywhere you should start in your investigation, well, I'm not telling you how to do your job—"

"Mum, please."

"But I would start with that family," she said, then sat back, flinging her hands up as though she had said all she needed to say.

Lucas rubbed the skin between his eyes, and George empathised with him and the future difficulties that come with dealing with opposing families.

"Thank you, Mrs Coffey," George said slowly. "I'll keep that in mind."

"That's all I ask," said Beatrice, rising to her feet. She glanced at her husband. "Daniel? Are you coming?"

"Yes, dear," the groom's father replied faithfully. He flicked his eyebrows up at George apologetically, then led his wife back to the reception, holding the door for her.

Lucas, however, lingered, and George took the opportunity to speak to the man on his own.

"How is she doing?" George said. "The bride?"

Lucas laughed and ran a sweaty hand through his greasy hair. "Well, let's just say we won't be consummating the marriage tonight, that's for sure."

George didn't laugh at what he assumed had meant to be a joke.

Lucas coughed. "I'm sorry. She'll be fine," he said. "She's just in shock."

"And to be clear, you have no idea what the argument was about between Rory and Pete?"

Again, Lucas hesitated and avoided George's eyes. "Just brother stuff, you know how it is. Weddings bring it all out, don't they? Family histories, long-standing disagreements. Everyone says you should have the wedding that you want but then spend two years telling you exactly how to have it. Who they want there. Who they want to speak. Who they *don't* want there. Sometimes I wish..."

He hesitated and looked around the courtyard, his eyes finally landing on the mill pond and the white suits that were crawling all over the banks. Then he downed the rest of his champagne and left the empty glass on the patio table.

"Sometimes I wish we'd just gone away and done it on our own. Just me and Nancy," he said. "But hindsight is twenty-twenty. Isn't that what they say?" He fingered the glass, rolling it between his fingers. "The amount of people that told us to enjoy the day, that it would fly by, and how we should savour every moment."

"I only wish I could make this easier," George told him. "The ambulance has left. We can start releasing people as soon as they've given a statement. It might not be the party you had planned, but at least you'll be able to get on and make the best of the day."

"Make the best of the day?" he replied.

"May I offer you some advice, Lucas?" George asked, to which Lucas nodded. "Comfort your wife. Take her home, feed her, and have someone else deal with all of this. Just look after her." George cleared his throat. "She'll remember that. Make a good memory. It's never too late to make good memories."

CHAPTER EIGHT

"Mr Wetherford?" George asked as he approached the man who had not moved from the bride's side all afternoon. He was a tall, burly man with thinning hair and a thick, dark beard that he rubbed at with agitation. The bride seemed oblivious to George's presence, unaware of anyone or anything else in the world other than her own misery, as she continued to swirl her whisky as if the amber whirlpool she had created might give an indication to her future.

"That's me," he said, looking George up and down. "I wondered when you'd get around to me."

"I'm Detective Inspector George Larson. I know this is a difficult time," he said, glancing at the man's devastated daughter. In his peripheral, George sensed Beatrice Coffey's peacock-sharp stare boring into the side of his face. "But I was hoping I could have a word?"

Wetherford hesitated, glancing between his daughter and George as though deciding his priorities, but eventually accepting that there was nothing he could do for her at this moment that might right any of the wrongs. "All right," he said. "Just a quick one." He squeezed his daughter's leg. "You be alright, love?"

The bride nodded but didn't look up.

"I'll make it as quick as I can," George said, hoping it might somewhat ease the moment.

Wetherford followed George outside to the patio furniture that was fast becoming a makeshift interview table.

Wetherford, however, took the opportunity to use it for its intended purpose. He pulled out a cigarette from his pack and lit up, taking pleasure in that first drag with a sigh not too dissimilar to those George gave off when he eased himself onto his sofa at the end of a hard day. He offered the open packet, and George waved it away with a shake of his head.

"Mr Wetherford," started George.

"Rory, please," he said, exhaling two great plumes of smoke through his nostrils. "No need for formalities."

"Rory," George said, "I'm trying to get an idea of what happened here before I arrived. Do you understand?"

"Of course," Rory said, not without an obvious disdain either for George or the force in general.

"First of all, one of your guests is missing. Your brother, I believe? Peter?"

"Oh," said Rory, his face darkening. "No, he's not missing. He wasn't invited." He spat a rogue piece of tobacco from between his lips.

"He was on the guest list," George said. "He's on the seating plan, too."

Wetherford thinned his lips.

"They drew up that seating plan weeks ago. My brother, Inspector, was uninvited. Yesterday. Too late to draw up a new plan. I'm sorry if that confused your..." He waved a hand around the scene, his eyes flicking from one of Southwell's team to another. "Investigation."

"I see," George said. "And may I ask, why was he uninvited? Was there some kind of problem?"

The look on Rory's face suggested it was a topic he'd rather not discuss. But the man gave pause, cleared his throat, and took another drag on his cigarette.

"We had an argument," he said simply.

"What was it about?" George replied.

Rory laughed. "Can I ask a question, Inspector?"

"That depends on the question," he replied.

"None of this is news to you, is it?" he grinned. "I saw you talking to her."

"Her?"

"The nosey old cow my daughter has the pleasure of calling her mother-in-law. Beatrice."

"I have spoken to her, yes."

"I'm sure she told you all about it, didn't she? I'll bet she loved every minute of it. Spiteful bitch."

George sat back and crossed his legs. "I'm not one for idle gossip," he said. "I'd rather hear it from you, Mr Wetherford."

"She never liked us. *Beatrice Coffey*," he said, imitating the way she had said her name with surprising accuracy, as though he had practised it in the mirror. "We never were good enough for her precious family." He scoffed. "Well, not much she can do about it now, is there? There was no stopping those two from getting married. However hard she tried."

"I appreciate that adapting to new in-laws is tough, Mr Wetherford. But that is not the question I asked."

Again, Rory's face darkened. "Family stuff," he said. "We were arguing about family stuff."

"What family stuff?"

He clenched his jaw. "*Private* family stuff."

"I appreciate that, Mr Wetherford," George said. "But as you might have noticed, I'm currently conducting the investigation of a dead man. And in such investigations, details are paramount. Do you understand?"

"Tiffs between me and my brother have nothing to do with

your investigation." He blew a smoke ring and watched it disperse.

"A tiff, was it?" George said. "I heard it became quite physical."

Again, Rory laughed a malicious laugh that seemed reserved for Beatrice Coffey. "Oh, I bet you did."

"I heard that you grabbed your brother by the collar. What surprises me, however, is why you would have such an altercation the day before your daughter's wedding. It must have been quite serious, no? To have been worth disturbing her wedding rehearsal? You seem quite close to her. Surely you wouldn't risk upsetting her."

Rory performed an entire inhale and exhale cycle before replying. "Do you have brothers, Inspector?"

"No," George said. "I have a sister in Exeter, but I can't say we're very close."

"Well, allow me to enlighten you?" Rory said, leaning forward. "Brothers fight. It happens. You know how it is." He glanced at George's crossed legs. "Or maybe you don't. But testosterone is a powerful force. It builds up. Encourages competition, you see. And men have to expel it sometimes. That's all. No big deal."

"If it's no big deal, Mr Wetherford, why did you go to the length of uninviting him from his own niece's wedding?"

Rory sat back once more. "Like I said. Family stuff."

"And have you seen him today? He didn't, for example, decide to turn up to the wedding despite being uninvited?"

As though the thought had not once crossed Rory's mind all the blood drained from his face in a second, as the possibility entered his mind. "No," he said gently and thoughtfully. "What are you saying? Are you suggesting—"

"I'm sorry to ask, but did you, for some reason, see the body in the water? Maybe before we arrived."

"Why on earth would I want to see—"

"Curiosity, perhaps?"

Wetherford shook his head in disgust.

"I haven't left my daughter's side. The fella that runs the place—"

"Mr St Claire?"

"Right. Him. He ushered us all inside. Plied us with drinks and advised that we stay there until you arrived. To be honest, I thought we'd have been allowed to go home by now."

"Mr St Claire was right to do so," George said. "Can you imagine if he had allowed everyone to have a look? Can you imagine how upset some of the people would have been? Not to mention the damage to the crime scene."

"I see," Wetherford replied. "When you put it like that."

"There's no easy way to say this, but the body we found, Mr Wetherford, has been dead for more than one day and less than two. Whatever happened to him happened yesterday."

Rory frowned as though genuinely unsure whether to interpret George's statement as an accusation or a suggestion to prepare for the worst. "No. No, not Pete. It can't be him."

"I would like you to call your brother, Mr Wetherford, and find out exactly where he is. And I hope I don't need to emphasise the urgency."

At this, Rory Wetherford rose and stubbed out his cigarette in the sand-filled flower pot.

Lucas Coffey's empty champagne glass still stood in the middle of the table, which gave George an idea.

"I'll bear that in mind," Rory spat.

But before Rory could turn his back on George and return to the bar, George called out.

"One more thing, Mr Wetherford."

Rory threw his head back as though praying for strength and turned around. "You know my daughter is in there grieving the wedding day she'll never get back? And I should be in there grieving the thousands of pounds I spent on it. So, *what*?"

"How old is your brother Pete?"

"How old is he?"

"It's a simple question, Mr Wetherford."

Rory sighed. "He's two years younger than me. So forty-six." He waited for a reply that George didn't offer. "So? Is that it?"

"Yes, Mr Wetherford," George said. "That's all." And as Rory turned and walked away, George waited until the man's hand had gripped the barn door before he added a comment that he hoped would stick, "For now."

CHAPTER NINE

George, Ivy, Byrne, and Campbell gathered in a circle in the centre of the courtyard. The sunlight was softening, and the shadows elongating.

It was the time when the guests should have been enjoying the party. The speeches should have been done, the first dance should have been danced, and the bouquet should have been tossed. But of course, there would be no music that evening. There would be no first dances or cutting of cake or stolen glances across a dance floor.

There would be only a quiet, late-night processing of a tragedy.

"So, what have we got?" George said, mirroring how he would begin an incident room meeting. His hand even twitched at his side, as he would usually tap his pen against the board at this point.

"Just talked to the officers conducting the search," Campbell said, shaking her head. "Nothing."

"Katy Southwell's team have been around every inch of the mill pond," Ivy added. "No sign of anyone being anywhere near it. No trampled grass, no footprints, no anything."

"That makes sense," George replied.

"And we still don't have a positive ID," Ivy said. "So, all in all, we're no better off than we were when we got here. Most of the guests have given statements and have been sent on their way. There's just a few of the immediate family left."

"Good," George said. "I'm glad the crowds are beginning to disperse."

"Guv, we've got nothing except a pile of statements to go through."

"Did anybody stand out to you?" George asked Byrne and Campbell.

"Not really, guv," Campbell said. "They were all a bit bemused. They came for a wedding. Next thing they know, they're being shut up in there and questioned by police."

"We should have had somebody identify the body," Ivy said. "We've missed an opportunity there."

George shook his head.

"All in good time, Ivy," he muttered, and Ivy sighed in despair. "Peter Saint thought the victim was in their late twenties, and if I'm honest, I tend to agree."

"So?" she said.

"So," George continued, "according to the bride's father, our mystery Uncle Pete is forty-six, which suggests our victim A wasn't him, and B was not on the guest list. Also, when I spoke to Ethan St Claire, he suggested there was a heavy downpour yesterday."

"Again," Ivy said. "So?"

"What happens when we get heavy rains?" he asked.

"Car accidents," Byrne said without thinking.

"True," George said. "What else happens? What happens to the rivers and the lakes?" He waited for a response but received nothing of the sort. "And streams?"

"The water rises?" Campbell said tentatively.

"The water level rises," George said. "Southwell and her team haven't found anything on the banks of the mill pond because the body didn't go in there. It entered the water upstream. Somewhere between here and the little pond at the top of the property. He must have snagged on some roots or rocks or something. Then the rains came and washed him down into the pond. If it hadn't rained, he'd probably still be there, hidden by the tall grass and the bushes."

"What are you saying, guv?" Ivy asked. "That the body is unrelated to the wedding?"

George grinned.

"This whole place is surrounded by fields," Byrne said. "Could've been anyone walking past."

"It's private property," Campbell said. "They'd have to climb a fence."

"And did you see the body?" Ivy asked. "He's wearing a suit. Hardly hiking gear, is it?"

"Does wearing a suit mean he was attending a wedding?" George asked, pleased to see the interaction taking place.

"You don't think it's a bit coincidental," Ivy said, "that a dead body turns up on the same day as a wedding?"

"There's no point debating what we don't know," George cut in, sensing the rise in temperaments. "We can't assume anything at this stage. Right now, the guests' witness statements are all we have. So let's go through them. If somebody knows something, then it might be apparent in their statement. Byrne, Campbell, can I task you with that?"

"Guv," Campbell said.

"First things first, I want to find Uncle Pete. Ivy, did you check nearby guest houses for anyone who is not on the wedding list?"

"I haven't had a second to, sorry."

"We can do that, guv," Campbell said, and it didn't escape George's attention that she had inferred that she and Byrne formed a little partnership. It was small progress but far better than the bickering he had witnessed in the previous months.

"Thank you," he said. "Then start writing up those statements. Collate them into a narrative of what exactly happened here this morning. Understand?"

"Yes, guv," Byrne said for the both of them.

"What about me, guv?" Ivy asked, to which he winced at the task he had for her.

"Find whoever deals with PR at the station, will you?" he said. "Set up a press conference."

All three members of his team groaned.

"The press, guv?" Ivy said. "Really?"

"I know, I know," George said. "Believe me, I don't relish the thought. But there were over eighty people in there with smartphones who have taken pictures all day to upload to social media. They may have demonstrated some sort of restraint while they were here, but now? People love to gossip. I'd be surprised if this isn't already all over Instabook or whatever it is. We can't keep that under wraps. There's no law against it."

"There might not be a law, guv. But there is such a thing as common decency."

"A dying resource," he countered. "I want to get ahead of the game. I want to make a statement before the media gets hold of this and turns it into something it's not."

Ivy groaned but accepted her defeat gracefully. She stepped away to make a call, leaving Byrne and Campbell to return to the station to begin their tasks. George was enjoying a moment to collect his thoughts when Katy Southwell stepped up beside him, removing her white gloves to signify that her role at the scene was coming to an end.

"We've collected the water and done a general sweep of the area, but until we process everything, there's not much else we can do," she said. "So, I think we'll be off."

"What about upstream?" George asked. "I think there's a chance our victim entered the water further up."

"It's not deep enough, surely."

"Not now, it's not," he said. "But yesterday, that water would have been raging."

"The rain," she said, eyeing her team, who were busy packing the flight cases.

"That could take a while. We'll need to set lights up," she said. "But just to set your expectations, if it rained hard enough to carry a body down the stream, any evidence would have suffered."

"I realise that," he told her. "And I'm grateful for your help."

"Grateful?" she said suspiciously. "Grateful, as in you're genuinely grateful for us being here doing our jobs? Or grateful, as in you have something else to say?"

He grimaced. She was astute, and he admired that. He took the glove from her hand and then walked a few steps to the patio furniture.

"We're torn," he said. "If the victim washed down the stream, then there's a good chance he wasn't even a part of the wedding."

"Right?" she said slowly. Using the folded glove, he picked up the champagne glass that Lucas Coffey had left behind and held it up to the sky. "Inspector Larson, I do wish you'd just come out and say it."

He nodded, accepting her need to press on. But he had a point to make.

"If the victim was not part of the wedding party, then my list of suspects grows from eighty-odd to the entire population of Lincolnshire." He turned and held out the glass for her. She opened a clear evidence bag from her pocket, clearly seeing where he was leading her, and he dropped it inside. "Most murder victims know their killer. Which is faster, eliminating eighty wedding guests or the entire county?"

"You want DNA?" she said.

"I do," he replied. "With any luck, there will be something on the body. A hair, bodily fluids, something."

"Every glass?" she asked.

"Every glass," George confirmed. "Identified and tagged. The good news is you've got the seating plan to help you. There were eighty-three guests, plus the bride and groom. So I'm going to need eighty-five identifiable DNA samples." He looked at the glass in the bag. "Let's start with this one. Belongs to the groom."

He held the glove out for her, and she took it with obvious reluctance.

"You do realise it's a long shot?" she said, snapping on the glove. "The chances of there being any DNA on the body are seriously low."

"I agree," he said. "But low chances are better than no chances."

"I'd better get to work then, hadn't I?" she said. "That's if I want to get home this week."

She strode off and called to her team to stop packing up.

"Katy?" he shouted after her, and she glanced back, too professional to ignore him. "I am, you know?"

"You are what?" she said.

"Grateful," he replied. "I'm grateful."

"Grateful is fine," she replied, handing the glass to one of her team. "Hopeful? Now that's a different story altogether."

CHAPTER TEN

"All done. Local press will be at the station in a couple of hours," Ivy said as Byrne and Campbell's liveried car turned out of Stockwith Mill. George watched them go, feeling a sense of pride in the two. "Are you sure they can handle it, guv?" Ivy said, following his gaze.

"They'll be fine," George said. "If they can't make a few calls and go through some statements, then they might as well start looking for new careers. Better to know now."

"So that's still your plan for them, is it? To keep them on the detective path? You don't think they'd benefit from a few more years in uniform?"

"I think they've shown promise," he said, frowning and turning to look at Ivy. "Don't you?"

"I do. I do," she said. "Don't get me wrong. It's just..."

"Just what?"

"Well, I was in the force for ten years before I was made DS. It's a big step, that's all."

"They'll do their time as detective constables. The difference is they'll work for me and not Tim Long. You don't begrudge them careers, do you?"

"No, but—"

"Campbell joined when she was nineteen, so it's been ten years for her. Anyway, it's not like the plain clothes route is a step *up*. It's more of an adjacent road. You know that better than anybody."

"Sure," Ivy said. "But I think we both know it's not Campbell I'm worried about."

"I understand your concerns, Ivy, but he's really trying. I'll admit that when I first met Byrne, I saw a downtrodden guy who just needed a chance. But he's more than that. He's more capable than I expected. I thought he would need much more guidance, to be honest."

"But why *them*, guv? Why two officers that you met on your first day here? Why not look around the station and see if there's anyone more...detective material?"

"Because why *not* them?" George said. "Besides, I quite like them."

Ivy scoffed. "So it's an instinct?"

"*You* were an instinct," George said as he made his way towards his car. "And look how lovely you turned out."

He unlocked his car and appraised the scene one more time.

"I should prepare for the conference," he said. "Are you alright to wrap things up?"

"What about the bride and groom?"

"Send them home," George told her.

"Guv, don't you think—"

"All I do is think," he cut in. "It's a curse of the job." He leaned on the car roof. She seemed so small in the courtyard alone. Southwell's team were lugging flight cases across the little wooden bridge, the caterers were loading their van, and Molly, the collie, was sitting beside the front door to the house, indifferent to the comings and goings. "We've got everyone's statements, have we not?"

"We have," she said.

"And CSI are all over the scene."

"Right," Ivy said as two white-suited individuals walked past her and through the barn doors. "Where are they going?"

"Glasses," George said.

"Glasses?" She gazed after them. "DNA? There were eighty-odd guests here."

"Eighty-five, to be precise," he said. "Of course, there's always the photographer and the catering staff, but I doubt they were here yesterday during the rehearsal."

"What happened to the chances of the victim being unrelated to the wedding?"

"Okay, I tell you what. I'll deal with the eighty-five guests who we know were here. I'll process them, I'll talk to the pathologist, I'll see if there's a DNA match. I'll see if we can link the body to the DNA of one of the guests. And if there's not -If I can elimi-nate every one of them from our enquiries, then you can take over." He grinned at her. "And you can interview the rest of the county. How does that sound?"

"Not great," she said, matching his grin. "Maybe I can ask tweedle dum and tweedle dee to do it."

"One day, you'll realise, Ivy," he said, "that to everyone out there, we are the enemy. It doesn't matter how much good we do. We're the enemy. Who would you rather go up against, eighty-odd guests or the rest of Lincolnshire?"

"Point taken," she replied, clearly still unconvinced.

"The fact of the matter is, Ivy, that we cannot do a damn thing until we have an ID. We can't make an arrest. We certainly can't interview anybody. Not in any official capacity, anyway."

"So what next, then? The pathologist won't be ready for us until tomorrow. We can't expect to ID him from his DNA until the morning, and that's if he's even on record. What do you want me to do when I'm done here? How do we move forward?"

"The way I see it, we have one man who was here yesterday who we haven't spoken to."

"Uncle Pete?"

"Right," George said. "Why don't you find him? Find out where he went when his brother asked him to leave. See if he'll tell us what they were arguing about."

"What are you going to do?" she asked, and he watched her reach for her phone.

"I'm going to talk to the press," he told her. "I want to get them on our side before this whole thing erupts on social media."

"Erm, guv," she replied, holding her phone in the air.

"What is it?"

"I think you'd better see this. Campbell just sent it." He strode over to her, recognising the tone of her expression. "She must have been looking it up while Byrne drove them back."

"What is it?" he asked again as he drew near, and she handed him the phone. A video was playing, and the scene was instantly recognisable. The sound was off, but subtitles played over the video.

Oh my God, someone literally just died at this wedding, and the police have locked us in. Help?

"We could find out who posted it," Ivy suggested.

"And then what?" he said, handing the phone back to her. "We can't lock somebody up for posting on social media."

"Actually, guv—"

"This changes nothing," he said, turning back to his car, then stopping to face her again. He jabbed a finger at her. "If anything, it only proves my point."

"What point was that?"

"That we're the enemy," he called out as he opened his car door.

"So this is war, then?" she toyed with him.

"It's going to be a battle. The wedding party, the media, and the rest of the bloody country will be against us on this one," he replied as he climbed into his car. "But fear not!" He hit the button to lower his window and winked at her, pleased she was on his side. "I haven't lost a battle yet, and I don't intend to start now."

CHAPTER ELEVEN

A muggy heat that often builds before a storm still clung to the air. The last few months had been a series of hot and sunny days interspersed with the occasional onslaught of cooling but disruptive rain. Homes, businesses, and livelihoods were still recovering from the biblical floods that had hit the area on the first night George arrived in the Wolds, and as he stood on the police station steps, half a dozen local reporters below him, he felt those first teasing drops of rainfall.

Focusing on the crisp, white paper in his hands, George took a deep breath, as a singer might before a performance. He blinked at the flash of a camera — just one. It was nothing like the big city press conferences that showed on the news. But this was not London, and George was not standing outside Scotland Yard. They were small-town, local journalists, and their lack of determination to become more than that was painstakingly clear. Of the six reporters, four were busy typing into their phones, and the others held their microphones half-heartedly as though blaming George's procrastination for their aching arms. Still, that one camera flash left a white glow in his vision for a few seconds until it faded, and he returned to focus.

Of all the jobs the force had asked of George, more than patrolling a high street on a Friday night, inspecting a dead body with the insufferable Doctor Pippa Bell, or even telling a victim's loved one about their tragic loss, talking to the press was the one he hated the most.

Despite talking to strangers intimately and sensitively almost every day, George was, at heart, a shy man. He had learned to grow past it. But in moments when he had to stand in front of a crowd and make a speech, the shyness that had haunted him since childhood was painfully and shockingly exposed. It wasn't only the public speaking that unnerved him, but the long-held conflict between press and police. Two forces that should work together often failed to do so, not in small part due to the media manipulating his every word into a narrative of failure to do more for the public. Not out of genuine concern, George understood, but to spin the most sellable web of lies possible.

He could see them now in his peripheral, capturing a photo of George standing alone and sombre on the police station steps. George cleared his throat and spoke loud enough to be heard, but quiet enough that the reporters would have to hold their microphones close. If he had to earn his keep, then so would they.

"Earlier today, we discovered the body of a yet unidentified man not far from here in the south of the Wolds."

"Where?" one of the reporters called out, but George ignored him.

"I can disclose that the body was discovered at around twelve-fifty p.m. And we believe the victim died sometime between twenty-four and forty-eight hours ago."

"Victim?" said one of the reporters.

George cringed internally. He'd had less than twenty minutes to write and practice the release with Tim, and it was by no means fool proof.

"The man was found with a substantial head wound. However, we do not yet know whether this was an attack or an accident.

We are treating the incident as suspicious until we know otherwise."

"Are you saying there is a killer on the loose in the Wolds?"

George looked up sharply. "No," he said. "We are keen for the media not to misinterpret what I'm saying. We have a body and we are treating the incident as serious until we know otherwise."

"So, do you have a suspect?" asked another, rallied by the first reporter. "Are they in custody?"

George moved on. "We're calling for any witnesses who saw anything suspicious in or around the Hagworthingham area yesterday. Or, if you have any concerns about a missing loved one, please get in touch. Thank you," George said, nodding his head humbly.

His sign-off was met with a rally of questions.

"Was the body found at Stockwith Mill?"

"How old is the victim?"

"Was this a premeditated murder?"

George chose the easiest of the three. "We believe the man to be in his late twenties," he replied. "Although we cannot be certain until we have identified the individual."

"Is this connected to the body found at St Leonard's Church last month?"

"What? No," George said. "That was an entirely different investigation—"

It was the same gum-chewing reporter, who again grinned at George's snap response. "Is there a reason, Inspector Larson, why there seems to be an increased number of suspicious deaths since you transferred from..." He glanced down at his notes. "Mablethorpe?"

"I'm not sure what you're suggesting or insinuating," George said, his jaw clenched.

The man held up his hands in faux defence. "I'm just saying, this place seems a bit Midsomer Murders lately." To the mutterings and laughter that followed, he nodded, adding, "Am I right?"

George stepped forward. "As you know, or maybe you don't," he said, with a pointed look at the gum-chewing reporter, "depending on your level of research, we recently merged the major crimes unit here with other stations throughout East Lincolnshire. That is why there has been an increase in the number of serious crimes being reported from this station. We are simply covering major crimes over a larger area of land."

"And yet," said the reporter, "your last three cases took place within ten miles of here."

George paused. Somehow, this reporter already knew as much information as George himself. "Do you have a question?" George asked, his eyes dark.

"I have many questions," he said.

"Well, I can't release anymore at this time," George said. "Thank you." He turned to leave, but the reporter was far from finished, and as George folded his piece of paper and walked back into the station, a firing question marked his every step.

"Is it true the body was found at a wedding, DI Larson?" he asked. "Is it true that videos of your attempt to contain said wedding are going viral on social media? Is it true that your department does not have the resources to deal with the current crime spree?"

At this, George stopped in his tracks, ready to spin around and argue against the ridiculousness of calling his last three investigations a crime spree. And perhaps he would have, had it not been for Tim staring at him through the window, shaking his head. Whether out of warning or disappointment, George couldn't be sure. Either way, the distraction was enough for his temper to abate. He waved for his team to follow him to the safety of the yard, where they gathered in the privacy of the fire escape stairway. Tim Long walked behind them, clearly deciding on the tone of his feedback.

"God, what was that guy's problem?" Byrne started as soon as they were out of earshot.

"A crime *spree*," Ivy said, rolling her eyes. "Bloody hell, half of those investigations were cold or failed investigations from decades ago."

"Look," Campbell said, holding up her phone. "Thirty views of the most viewed video from the wedding. *Viral?*" She scoffed. "Viral, my—"

"I appreciate the support," George said. "But we knew what to expect. We did what we set out to do and put the investigation out to the public. Right, Tim?"

DCI Long looked on silently, staring at George as though deciding in real time whether to offer more carrot or more stick. Slowly, he began to nod his head.

"Yes, you're right. We needed to get ahead of this, and we have." He met George's eye. "But this isn't good, George. We can't have this spiralling into a bigger story. I want this investigation closed quickly and without fuss. No more barn fires, no more digging up bodies in the middle of the night, no more standoffs on church towers. You hear me?"

George kept quiet, silently fuming at the suggestion that during forty years of police work, it was not his goal every single time to solve investigations quickly and quietly. Of course, it was. But when his investigation uncovered flaws in historical investigations, things became complicated. If finding justice meant getting his hands dirty, he would run into a burning building, grab a spade, or climb a church tower if need be.

"Yes, guv," Ivy said so that George didn't have to.

With that, Tim nodded, taking Ivy's word as enough, and he turned to climb the steps. He opened the door but paused there as if his point hadn't quite been made.

"This needs containing," he said to George.

"I think that horse has bolted, Tim," George replied. "However, I think we can play the game. If all eyes are on us on this one, then instead of seeing that as a negative, let's turn it into a positive."

"A man died, George," Tim said. "Where's the positive in that?"

"It's an opportunity," George replied. "An opportunity to show the county exactly what we can do. Let's show them where their taxes go. I mean, other forces are in the news for far worse reasons. Officers abusing their positions, corruption, falsifying evidence. Christ, Tim. If we make a few headlines as a result of doing our jobs, then as far as I can make out, that's a good thing."

"You and I have very different ideas of what constitutes a good thing," Tim replied. "But I hear you."

"Of course, if we're going to make a big show of our accomplishments," George began, to which Tim's eyes narrowed suspiciously. "Then we could do with a larger team."

"A larger team?"

"I mean, we can handle things, just the four of us," George said. "But from a PR perspective, a few more bodies would make us far more efficient as a team."

"A few?"

"Oh, at a minimum," George said. "We've got eighty-odd wedding guests to work through, and that's even if the body is linked to the wedding."

"He could have just been a local lad," Ivy added. "In which case, we'll need to go door to door in the area. That's quite time-consuming."

"A week or more," Byrne added, much to George's surprise. "I mean, imagine if this is on social media all that time—"

Tim raised a hand to silence the young PC.

"I get it," he replied, then turned to George. "Why do I feel like I walked into a trap?"

"A trap?" George replied. "This isn't a trap. This is reality, Tim. You want us to work faster? Give me more bodies. Live ones, preferably." He pointed to Byrne and Campbell. "These two need to be out of uniform. Plus, I'll need someone in the office full-time to research and coordinate. Plus, it wouldn't hurt to bring in two more detectives so we can pair off and cover more ground."

"Just…" Tim said, his agitation showing through his calm exterior. "Just keep things moving, and we'll speak about this later. But do not, and I repeat, George, do not give the media a reason to turn this into something else." He eyed the team as if trying to read their expressions. "If that happens, the deputy chief constable will be reducing the size of your team."

"I hope you'd fight our corner, Tim," George said. "I can't operate with a smaller team than I've got."

"I wasn't talking about these three," Tim replied, gesturing at Ivy, Campbell, and Byrne. "He'd reduce the team by one. You." Having made his point, he turned away to head up the stairs to the first floor, but he stopped once more and jabbed a finger at himself. "And before you ask, that would be on *my* recommendation."

CHAPTER TWELVE

George slumped into the kitchen chair. Somehow, that single ten-minute press conference and the subsequent conversation with Tim had drained more energy from him than an entire night patrolling the streets of Lincoln city centre. He closed his eyes and took a lungful of air, which was pleasantly full of the soft scents of Ivy's cooking. She was an excellent cook. She used spices he had never heard of from local markets he had never been to. It was a far cry from the pasta pesto he had been making himself every night. While she cooked, she hummed along to some song that played on the kitchen radio. It was modern music, of which George had long ago come to terms with his lack of understanding. Her mood had noticeably improved in the last few weeks. However, there had to be an underlying train of thought she was dealing with. Separating from her husband and leaving her children in Mablethorpe was a weight she was carrying well, but he knew her better than most.

"Is it bad that I'm glad you're getting a divorce?" he said, grinning to show he was joking. She stared wide-eyed but said nothing. "At least I get to enjoy your cooking."

There were only so many times they could discuss Ivy's

personal life with earnestness. More and more frequently, he was able to touch on the topic in a light-hearted manner, hoping to coax some truths from her. Her private life was, of course, none of his business, but he couldn't help probing. It was his job to encourage people to speak, after all.

"If it means you're eating something other than pasta pesto every night, guv, then I'm glad too."

"Now we're roommates, don't you think you should start calling me George? At least at home?"

She smiled as she ladled something steaming and colourful onto his plate.

"Never, guv," she said, placing a plate on the table. "That would be like calling my dad Geoffrey."

He grinned at her as he took the plate but internalised his response and wondered if she realised she had just aligned him with her father.

"You seem happier," he said cautiously to her back as she returned to the stove. "Don't you think?"

"Yeah," she said, carrying her own plate over to join George at the table. "I feel happier." She shrugged. "Or, I feel lighter, at least, if that's the same thing. I feel like the burden of just making a decision about Jamie was weighing me down. Even more so than the actual act of leaving. Does that make sense?"

"Yes," George said. "I think the idea of taking action is often harder than the action itself."

She held up her water glass in a *cheers to that* gesture, took a sip, and then began eating. The flavours burst into George's senses as if he had eaten a firework.

"My goodness. This is amazing, Ivy," George said, staring down at the plate. "What is it exactly? Some kind of rice?"

"Moroccan couscous with roasted vegetables, chickpeas, and almonds."

George moaned at the specific deliciousness of it. Ivy insisted not only on eating healthily but on sitting at the kitchen table rather than on the sofa, another small detail for which he was grateful. That was the thing about living with someone else; sure, he had a little less privacy, but there was also a social standard to which he had to keep. It was good for him. For one, he was no longer plagued by bouts of acid reflux. He had forgotten what it was like to have a woman in the house, and he didn't mind it at all.

"I just hope you are dealing with it," he said after a moment of silence. "Jamie, I mean," Ivy said nothing while he licked at his teeth. "I just hope you're not holding it all in, and it's all going to come out at once." Ivy continued to chew on her food, almost determinedly, as though holding back a specific thought on the tip of her tongue. "I know," George said. "I'm one to talk. I know I'm doing the same with Grace."

Ivy looked up at him. "As long as you know that, guv."

"We're both on a journey that is, for better or worse, going to end in a crash. Let's just hope it hits us at different times," George said. "We've got a team to run. We can't both be mentally unstable. Perhaps we should schedule it in each other's calendars. You can take Mondays to mourn your marriage and I'll take Wednesdays to mourn..." He loitered there for a moment, unsure how to finish the sentence. "Well, to mourn."

Ivy laughed, releasing the tension they both shared. "How is she?" she asked with the same caution George had shown. "Grace, I mean."

George swallowed a particular spicy mouthful. "Fine," he said.

"How was this morning?"

He nodded, looking at his food. "Yeah, fine. Really...fine."

"Was she in a better...mood?"

George put down his fork. "Ivy, please."

"You have to talk about it, guv."

"I know. I know I do. But I don't feel like it, okay? Not right now."

Ivy relented, and they ate on in a lingering silence, on the outside at least. His mind was a riot of memories and regrets.

"She didn't know who I was again," George said eventually. "She said that she and her husband had always planned on sitting by the sea as an old couple. *Her husband*, Ivy." He looked up. "*I'm* her bloody husband." Ivy pulled a sympathetic grimace but knew not to interrupt. "I asked if she wanted to come here to see the house, you know? I thought it might help. I thought maybe…" He swallowed hard. "Maybe if she saw her childhood home, it might trigger some memories. She might see what I've done to fix it, and maybe she'll remember me. Remember…something."

George looked around the room. He wasn't sure exactly what had stirred his more manic approach to home improvement in the last few weeks, whether it was some subliminal attempt at control, a way to prove to himself he was still able-bodied, or if it had been little more than a distraction. But reminders of his hard work existed all over the house, in the repaired light fixtures, the fixed door hinges, the multiple-coated paint jobs, and reams of sandpaper. Numerous times, Ivy had caught him in his pyjamas finishing a little job in the middle of the night.

"The house looks great, guv," she said. "Grace will love it, I'm sure. She's still the same person. On some level, she'll understand what you put into it. But there's no rush to make it perfect."

"Isn't there?" he said quietly. "She can't walk anymore, Ivy. I drove her to the sea then had to put her in her wheelchair today. Her motor functions are closing down. She's not just a forgetful version of Grace anymore. She's becoming someone that not only doesn't recognise me but someone I don't recognise." He sighed.

"Or perhaps you don't want to recognise her that way?"

He nodded at her and took a sip of wine.

"She's like a different person sometimes. She's got all these new personality traits she never used to have. She's sharper and speaks more harshly. Bitter."

Ivy raised her eyebrows. "Grace? I can't imagine Grace talking harshly to anyone."

"Yeah, she told me off for answering my phone." Ivy laughed, and George wrinkled his nose. "Could be worse, couldn't it?"

She shrugged. "I suppose so."

He felt ashamed of the lump in his throat and used a long gulp of wine as cause to peer through the window at the dark shapes in his garden — the newly painted, old shed and stacks of timber beneath a tarp. He dabbed at his eye discreetly.

"I guess part of me..." George struggled through, embracing the opportunity to speak candidly. "Part of me, and I know it's naive, Ivy, I know it's ridiculous, but part of me thinks that maybe if I can save this house, bring it alive again, it might return her to me."

Ivy leaned across the table and squeezed his hand. "I don't think that's ridiculous, guv," she said quietly. "I think you miss your wife, and you want her back."

"But she isn't, is she? Coming back, I mean."

To this, Ivy did not have a reply, at least not one that would help anything.

"You know, I'd do anything to feel like you right now, guv," she said. "You miss your wife, and here's me smiling at my newfound freedom. I've disrupted my children's lives, my life, my husband's...and for what? For happiness? Will I ever find it? Or should I have stayed put and just got on with it?"

"Well, I can't answer that for you, Ivy. None of us can change the past," he said. "But maybe we can do something about our futures."

"Like what?" she asked.

"Not just ours. But Byrne's and Campbell's, too. And whoever else we can get on the team. I want to...I want to hand something down to you all. I want to be remembered for something."

"Guv?" Ivy said as if she'd read something in his tone that wasn't there.

"If I died tomorrow, what would people say?"

"Sorry?"

"If I died tomorrow, Ivy. You heard those reporters. You heard what they said, the questions they asked." He shook his head. "It shouldn't be like that. They shouldn't be prodding for cracks in our investigation." He poked the tabletop with an index finger. "When people know we're working on an investigation, I want them to know it's in safe hands. I want them to have confidence in us. I want their backing. I want the support of the community."

"And how do you suppose we achieve that?" Ivy said. "You said it yourself. We're the enemy."

"We're the enemy," he repeated and heard his voice fade to nothing.

"You can't fix the world," she said softly. "People die. People... do bad things. And it's our job to bring them to justice. When we're done, we move on to the next and the next after that. Then we retire, and nobody even realises we're gone."

"You sound like me," he said. "Thirty years ago."

"That's because I am you," she replied with a wink. "Only younger, and prettier, and smarter—"

"And that's what's troubling me," he said thoughtfully. "A man is found dead close to twenty-four hours after he was killed." He set his fork down and swallowed the food in his mouth. "Yet nobody has reported him missing." He took a sip of wine and rinsed his mouth. "When I die, I want to die here. At home. But if you don't realise I'm missing, then I will have seriously underestimated my impact on the world."

"What are you saying, guv?"

"I'm saying," he replied, a little more jovially, pleased to have found a direction for the investigation, "that our victim knew somebody and that somebody hasn't said a word." He grinned at her. "And I want to know why."

CHAPTER THIRTEEN

Much as George and Grace had assumed roles within their marriage, so too had he and Ivy, within whatever their relationship had become. She made the evening meals whilst he prepared the morning coffee. So when Ivy awoke in an old, grand, four-poster bed in the master bedroom of Grace Larson's childhood home, it was to the aroma of freshly ground beans carrying through the house. Although she had insisted many times that George should be the one to take the master bedroom, seeing as it was, in fact, his house, George insisted on sleeping in Grace's room. He didn't explain why. But Ivy supposed that he felt closer to her there. Perhaps even closer than he felt when he was with her these days, with her mind the way it was.

In truth, the way that George spoke about loving Grace had been a key part of her decision to leave Jamie. She didn't know that kind of love. Not anymore. The idea of growing old with Jamie seemed like a trap set by society, something that she should want but never would. The thought of spending the rest of her life with him filled her with dread.

Such dark thoughts often hit Ivy in the minutes after she woke up, before she had even rolled out of bed, before she decided to start her day. She'd stare up at the handmade, ornate wooden posts and admire the patience and care somebody had put into their handiwork and wonder why she should move at all. But the thing for which she got out of bed was hope. Hope for change. Hope for a happier life for her children. For them to have happier parents. Hope for a different, if not better, life.

"Morning," she said to George when she entered the kitchen.

He was just adding milk and sugar to the coffee that he handed to her.

"Sleep well?"

"Beautifully," she said. "They don't make beds like that anymore, do they?"

George chuckled. "You mean, with a lumpy, old mattress and woodworm? No, Ivy, they don't."

His negativity masked the positive undertones, and she smiled inwardly.

"So, what's the plan for today?" she asked without reciprocating his question, having been woken up at two a.m. by him searching for something in the garden shed.

"Well, if we're to make progress, then we'll need to attend the post-mortem and pray for some DNA results," George said. "Let's see what, or rather who, we're working with here. And let's hope that press conference achieved something and that someone has some information for us to go on."

Ivy sipped her coffee. "Like what? Someone whose loved one is a notorious wedding crasher?"

George tilted his head at her sarcasm. "Someone who hasn't seen their loved one for two days, maybe?"

"Then expect a call from half the country. Hell, I haven't seen my own loved ones in two days."

"But you would be missed. Someone would notice you're gone. A missed day of work, a missed social event. Someone must know that man. Someone must miss him."

"I suppose," Ivy said. "But to be honest, guv, I'd put more hope on the DNA results. There are a lot of lonely young men out there for whom going AWOL for a few days isn't exactly headline news." She took another big sip, savouring the taste and caffeine boost. "What else is on the agenda?"

"Let's see if Byrne and Campbell have found anything looking at nearby guest houses. Then we'll have to look through all the guest interviews and see if a picture of whatever the hell happened yesterday develops. I didn't get to meet the bride yesterday. I'd like to see what she has to say, too. I didn't want to impose too much on her yesterday. Hopefully, she'll be in a better state today." He peered into the garden as he spoke as if he was reciting his ambitions to a secretary taking shorthand. "And we should start looking at nearby CCTV. See who was taking the buses nearby. Taxis, too. A man in a suit shouldn't be too hard to miss."

"Would it be that strange? Stockwith Mill is a wedding venue."

"Right, hosting a wedding he wasn't invited to, remember? The victim wasn't on the guest list. So, I doubt he got a lift. There was no one missing except Uncle Pete, and we've agreed the body wasn't his. The victim was a younger man."

Ivy puffed her cheeks. "That's a lot to do, guv."

"You're right," he said, grabbing her coat from the back of a kitchen chair and handing it to her. "Ready when you are, then."

"What about breakfast?"

"Oh, I've already had it," he said, swirling his car keys on his finger.

She sighed, poured her coffee into a travel mug, and pulled on her coat.

"I suppose I'll pick something up on the way," she muttered to herself as she followed him out. "A cold meat slice from a petrol station. Maybe a Mars bar."

"You weren't expecting breakfast in bed, were you?" he replied as he climbed into his car. He waited for her to follow suit.

"Maybe I should order some fresh fruit and bring you a platter with the morning papers."

"The fruit sounds good," she replied. "But not the papers. God knows what they're going to say today after the press conference."

A single low-hanging, grey cloud cast its sprawling shadow across the rolling fields, the winding roads, and the endless hedgerows.

"Well, whoever it was," George said, his hands tapping the wheel to match his racing mind, giving Ivy the impression he had been awake for far longer than she had been, ruminating on his theories. "Why would he murder someone at a wedding rehearsal?"

"It could have been before the rehearsal," Ivy said.

"Well, alright then. But why there? Why not somewhere private?"

"I think it's safe to assume that the attack wasn't premeditated. If your theory about the heavy rainfall washing him down the stream is true, then he died on the property or was at least carried there from elsewhere," she mused. "Which begs the question, what was he doing there? If he wasn't invited to the wedding, then what was he doing there? And what did he do to provoke such an attack?"

"As ever, we're looking at this all wrong," George said, guiding the large saloon around a tight bend. "We need the basics before we do anything. First and foremost, we need an ID. We need to establish a link from the victim to the wedding party. When we have that, we can start conducting interviews."

"And if we can't find a link?" Ivy said. "Or if the links all prove to be alibied? What then?"

"Then I hand over to you," George replied. "We question family and friends. We establish a timeline of the victim's movements. We follow the process."

"Follow the process?" Ivy said with a laugh. "Guv, I've never known you to adhere to any formal processes in all the time I've known you."

"Well, I—"

"You talk a good process, guv. And you start off on the right lines. But more often than not, you…"

"I what?"

"Deviate," Ivy said. "You deviate from the process."

"I may flex the boundaries, Ivy, but do I or do I not always get a result?"

"You do, guv. You…flex…the processes," she replied, merely to prevent an argument, no matter how light-hearted it might be. "Tell me, when you conducted those interviews at the mill, was that following strict procedures outlined in the legislation?"

"I'm sorry?"

"You know. The patio furniture you used to speak to the groom and his parents, as well as the bride's father. I didn't see a second officer with you. I thought it was protocol to ensure a sound witness attended any interviews."

"It is," he said, then cleared his throat. "And they were not formal interviews. They were what I would call testing the water. They were preliminary conversations."

"But you couldn't cite them in a court of law, right?"

"Ivy, have you a point to make in all of this, or are you still upset about missing breakfast?" he said. "Do I need to stop at the petrol station so you can pick something up?"

"I would rather chew broken glass than eat from a petrol station, guv," she replied. "And no, I'm not making a point. I am merely highlighting a recent incident during which you *flexed* the processes to suit your needs."

"Not my needs," he said. "The investigation's needs. There's a difference. Had that body been discovered at any other time, when a wedding was not taking place, things would have been very different. But as it stands, we've got a newlywed couple who have had their day ruined. We've got eighty-something guests with access to social media, which, by the way, we've already seen the result of, and, as a result of my flexing the processes, we've established conflict."

"Conflict?"

"Conflict," he said. "Between the bride's family and the groom's. Most notably, surrounding the groom's mother and the bride's father."

"What was he like?" Ivy asked. "Rory Wetherford?"

George contemplated the question. "He was reserved," he said. "In some ways. And vaguely threatening in others. Threatening enough to start a fight with his brother at his daughter's wedding rehearsal, at least."

"And you think his brother might be the same?"

"Well, Beatrice Coffey sure seems to think so."

"Who?"

"The groom's mother," George said. "She's one to watch."

"Do you think she's hiding something?"

"Her? No. She would have given me a rundown of every one of the Coffeys given half a chance. She's opinionated, that's all. She was peacocking," George said, smirking at the memory of her feather-print dress. "Literally."

"Sticking her nose in?"

"She doesn't like the marriage, apparently. Thinks her son married beneath him. Wanted me to keep an eye on the Wetherfords, claimed that they're where the trouble is."

"Do you think that's what the fight was about? Family pride?"

"Well, if it was, then it didn't exactly make the right point, did it?" George said. "But for what it's worth, no, I don't. I think it had to be more than that. I don't think Rory Wetherford particularly enjoyed proving Beatrice Coffey right. I think it had to be something pretty bad for him to ask his brother to leave the rehearsal and not to show up the next day."

"Like what?"

"Like the opposite of pride, Ivy," he said, pulling into the police station car park. "Shame."

He parked, and Ivy mulled over what he had said. Shame was everywhere: in every family. Jamie had done plenty in the past that she had been ashamed of, as had her children.

As had she.

In fact, the word shame seemed to trigger something inside her. She was a mother, and she had abandoned her children to their father.

"You okay?" George asked, rousing her from her thoughts as they strode towards the station's rear entrance. "You've gone quiet."

"What about the owner?" Ivy asked. "Ethan St Claire? Surely he saw something?"

"I think he was worried about the image of his business. I don't think he knows anything we don't. But if your question is whether or not I trust him..." George said, stopping outside the incident room just before the squeaky floorboard on its threshold. "Then no. Not one bit."

He took a deliberate step so that the creak was particularly loud and then entered the room to find police officers of varying ranks and teams scrambling to look busy, including their very own PC Byrne, who almost fell off his chair in an effort to pull his feet from his desk. Campbell, however, rushed over as though she had been waiting for George to arrive all morning.

She held the headset of her desk phone, out of which came the gentle but maddening hold music. Her palm was pressed firmly over the mouthpiece.

"Morning, Campbell," George said. "You seem bright-eyed and bushy-tailed this morning."

"Morning, guv," she said, holding up the phone. "Turns out that press conference was worth it after all."

George eyed the headset, then peered up at her, his eyebrows raised in question.

"Somebody saw something?" he asked. "If that's the case, then I'd urge you to invite them in—"

"No, not that," she said, thrusting the headset into his hand. "It's Uncle Pete. He wants to talk to you."

CHAPTER FOURTEEN

"This is DCI Larson," George said. He stood at Campbell's desk while his team listened in. "To whom am I speaking, please? Is this Peter Wetherford? Nancy Wetherford's uncle?"

"Yes," said the man on the other end slowly. "This is Pete, Nancy's uncle."

"Well, it's good to hear from you," George said. "We were looking for you yesterday."

"Worried about me, were you?" he asked, then his tone sobered. "I saw the news."

His voice fell somewhere between gruff and cheery, as though he could have masked the question as a joke if needed. But George sensed the underlying tension. Otherwise, it was decidedly average, with only a slight local accent, not particularly memorable.

"As I'm sure you know by now, there was an incident at your niece's wedding yesterday. We actually thought it might have been you."

At this, Pete Wetherford scoffed. "I wasn't even at the bloody wedding," he said.

"No, I did notice that," George said. "So, what's the purpose of the call? Do you have any information that might help our investigation?"

"Probably not," he said in a quiet tone, to which George found himself undeniably unconvinced.

"Then why did you call us?"

"I want to know what happened, don't I? It's all over Facebook that something happened."

"If it's gossip you're after, I might suggest you call your brother?"

Wetherford was silent for a moment, then said, "I thought it was better to call you lot. Get a proper account of what happened, you know. My brother has been known to spin a yarn or two."

"Well, that's very responsible of you," George said. "But we don't usually provide updates of live investigations to any member of the public who calls in claiming to be somebody we're looking for. Maybe it would be best to get the details from your brother."

"No," said Wetherford sharply, as though worried about George hanging up. "Look, we're not talking, alright? I just wanted to know what happened." He paused. "I need to know who you found."

"Who we found?"

"The *body*, for God's sake. Who is it?"

"That's what we're trying to find out," George said slowly. "Why? Do you have any ideas about who it might be?"

"No," said Wetherford, quickly. "Of course I don't. Just imagine it from my perspective, Inspector. Your entire family goes to a wedding, and this tragedy happens. I'm not really in a position to call them up, am I? I'm just trying to find out what happened."

"Why don't we start at the beginning? What happened between you and your brother?" George asked. The insinuation was clear. If Wetherford provided George with some information, maybe he'd reciprocate.

But Wetherford just laughed over the line and, in a voice reminiscent of his brother's, he said, "I don't see how that's any of your business."

"Oh, I do," George said. "I certainly see how it's my business. I'll ask you to put yourself in *my* shoes for a second, if I may. I am called to a crime scene where the body of a man has been found. One guest is missing from the guest list. That is you, by the way. And I have also been informed, by multiple guests, I might add, that you had a huge argument with your brother at the rehearsal the previous day. The day after the wedding, after my press conference, you call me, innocently probing for information about what happened at the wedding. I'm sure you understand now why it is my business?"

The other end of the line was silent save for Wetherford's fury rasping across the microphone.

"It was family stuff," he said. "The argument with my brother. Family stuff."

"What family stuff?"

"It's private."

"Your brother was willing to talk about it with me," George lied.

"He's not my brother," said Wetherford. "He's my stepbrother. And if he had told you what the fight was about, then you wouldn't be asking me right now."

George changed tact. "The man we found is in his late twenties, we believe. He was killed, possibly from a blow to the head, between twenty-four and forty-eight hours ago. Does that mean anything to you?"

"No," said Wetherford. It was a solid *no*. An emphatic *no*. "Look, I just saw the press conference and wanted to know what happened. I figured it might look suspicious, you know, me not being there. I wanted to clear the air. That's all."

"That's very generous of you," George said. The conversation could have ended there, but for some reason, Wetherford stayed on the line. He had more to say, it seemed. Or perhaps more to find out. "Why weren't you there?" George said softly. "Why did you miss your own niece's wedding?"

"Like I said, Inspector. Family stuff. Surely you understand that? Nothing to do with your investigation."

It was George's turn to laugh. "In my many, many years of experience, *family stuff*, as you call it, is directly related to my investigation, one way or another."

"Not this time," Wetherford said.

"I highly doubt that. Why don't you tell me what it was all about? And I can be the one to decide?"

"No, thanks."

"Maybe you'll change your mind. Where can we find you?"

Wetherford didn't reply.

"If you can give us a phone number where we can reach you. If Rory Wetherford is your step-brother, then do we even have your name right? Are you Peter Wetherford..." But Wetherford had already hung up. "Get me his phone number," George said immediately, turning to his team.

"Already done, guv," Campbell said, tapping at her computer. "Looks like it's a payphone in Skegness."

"A payphone?" Byrne said. "I didn't know they still existed. Thought they'd all been turned into book swaps and mini discos."

"Why did he call us at all?" Campbell asked. "Even from a payphone?"

"He said he saw something had happened on Facebook and called in to find out what it was."

"Why not just message one of his relatives?" Ivy asked. "Why call us?"

"You know how stubborn people can be," Byrne said astutely. "If he and his brother were in a fight, maybe he wouldn't want to let him know that he had been interested?"

"Then why call from a phone box?" Ivy said.

Byrne shrugged. "Maybe he doesn't have a phone."

"Oh, come on."

"It happens," he insisted. "People go off-grid. They don't like technology. Don't trust it. My nan never had a mobile and never got up to answer the landline because it was always scam callers or heavy breathers."

"Heavy breathers? What are they?" Campbell said, to which George waved his hand to move the conversation on.

"You don't want to know," he assured her, then beckoned for Byrne to continue.

"If you wanted to see her, you had to go round her house, knock on the door, and have a cup of tea. Old school, you know?"

George looked between Ivy and Campbell, who appeared as unconvinced as he was.

"Want me to look at CCTV around the phone box, guv?" Campbell asked.

"No," George said. "It's a waste of time. He's used a public phone for a reason. He'll be a mile away by now, in any direction. No, let's move on. Peter Wetherford, who, until further notice, remains to be known as Uncle Pete, is alive. What does that tell you?"

The team had nothing.

"It tells us," George said, "that we don't know anything. Anything at all. We thought he was Peter Wetherford. Now he's back to being Uncle Pete. What else don't we know?" Despondency spread like the coronavirus throughout the team, and it was down to George to provide the vaccine. "We know that Rory Wetherford and Peter argued: that's what we know. And we know that Peter is alive and somewhere near Skegness." Byrne's eyes tracked George's movements as he stepped slowly around their little space. "We know that our victim died sometime during the day of the wedding rehearsal. That doesn't mean it happened during the rehearsal."

Campbell's head remained upright, and her eyes were alert.

"Will the pathologist be able to give us a more accurate time of death?" she asked.

"I hope so," George replied.

"And a murder weapon?"

"Again, let's hope so. It's not like the TV shows. There are often too many variables for them to provide objective facts. We have to rely on their experience and probability," he replied, sensing she was clinging to hope. "What about Katy Southwell? Has she been in touch?"

"I called her this morning, guv," Byrne said. "She said to give her an hour, and you'll have the results."

"Good." George finally took off his coat, draped it over a spare chair, and then settled down at his desk to mull over the pockets of missing information.

"Guv?" Byrne said tentatively.

"Yes, Byrne?" he replied.

"If we don't make any progress, do you think Detective Superintendent Long will reject your request for a larger team?"

George smiled back at him.

"Tim Long has been in this game for as long as I have," he replied. "He knows how it works. He knows that we can spend days or weeks searching for a breakthrough. But when that breakthrough comes, an investigation can gain momentum very quickly. That's when we need resources." He drummed his fingers on his desk, deep in thought. "Mark my words, Byrne," he said. "We'll find that breakthrough. We'll find it if it bloody well kills me."

CHAPTER FIFTEEN

After rejecting Byrne and Campbell's insistence to make the coffees, George returned from the station kitchen with a tray of weak instant brew and handed a cup to each of his team.

"Thanks, guv," Campbell said, sounding more than a little surprised. She accepted her cup and sat back in her chair while Byrne typed up the witness reports from the day before.

"Not exactly detective inspector behaviour, is it, guv?" Ivy remarked as he handed her one of the cups. "Making coffee for us?"

"Ah, you know me, Ivy," George said, taking a hot, watery sip. "We're in this together, aren't we? Besides, there's nothing like waiting for a kettle to boil when it comes to thinking time."

It felt indulgent for George and Ivy to sit there chatting, enjoying the quiet before the storm. There was always a risk that Tim would walk in and find them in a less-than-heightened state of urgency. But so what? It wouldn't be long before the first rumble of thunder rang out, and when it did, George would be the first to stand in the rain.

And ring out, it did.

It came in the form of Campbell's desk phone, and she

answered it immediately. George didn't need to hear Katy South-well's voice on the other end to get a gist of the conversation. Campbell's replies were enough. She typed almost aggressively into her computer, making notes as she listened, her eyes widening at what she heard.

"Yes…okay…sounds good… thank you, Katy," she said before hanging up. She paused for a moment as if deciding where to begin. "Results are in," she said, in a similar manner to a game show host. George rose from his chair, taking his place at the whiteboard and waiting with a marker pen, poised for action. "Ryan Eva," announced Campbell, and George wrote the name in block letters in the centre of the board.

Byrne also typed furiously as though the two were in some kind of gaming competition.

"How sure is she?"

"She has a DNA match," Campbell said. "Ninety-nine-point-nine per cent chance of it being accurate."

"Well, we have a fact at last," George replied. "What have we got on him?"

There was silence as Byrne and Campbell processed the information on their screens, making sure it was one hundred per cent correct before relaying it to George.

"Bloody hell. He's a convicted child abuser," Byrne said as Campbell nodded her agreement. "Looks like he served nine years in His Majesty's Prison Whatton in Nottinghamshire." He peered up from the screen. "He was released seven months ago, guv."

George wrote the information as it hit his ears.

"That opens things up," he said. "Not just any old wedding guest, was he?"

"Doesn't look like it, guv," Campbell said.

"Next of kin?" George asked.

"The only contact listed is an Ian Eva. I'll print his details for you," Campbell said.

"What about his victim?" George asked. "Or victims. Is this a revenge attack?"

He liked getting the information in real time, putting Byrne and Campbell's research skills on the spot and forcing them to be quick and precise. During this investigation, more than any other, he would be watching their every move, ensuring they were ready for the next step in their careers.

"Yes. Melissa Hale. Lives in..." Campbell said, clicking.

"Spilsby," finished Byrne. "From what I can see, she gave evidence at his trial. She was thirteen at the time."

"Does she live alone?" George asked, not wishing to leave room for imaginations to run riot.

"No," Campbell said. "There are two other people registered at that address. A Sandra Hale and a Mark Hale. From their ages, it looks like they're her parents."

George frowned at the board. "She was thirteen at the time, and he was inside for, what did you say, nine years? That makes her..."

"Twenty-two," Campbell said.

"Any information on the parents?"

"Nothing on the mum," Byrne said. "But the dad has a previous for assault."

"Against who?"

"Doesn't say. I'll do some digging."

"Alright," George said, stepping back to gather a first impression of the board. They had gone from having nothing to having a solid basis for an investigation. "Where's Ryan been staying since his release?"

"A bedsit in Skegness, guv," Campbell said. "I'll send you the address."

"Skegness? Coincidence, maybe?" he said and walked over to his desk, downing his now lukewarm coffee in one. "Ivy, with me. You two," he said, turning to the remaining members of their small team. Too small. "I want everything you can find on Ryan

Eva. Where did he spend his time? Who did he work with? And where? And most importantly, why was he in the vicinity of Stockwith Mill two days ago? What's his connection to the wedding? Check social media, phone records, everything. If you need a warrant, just make a request, and I'll back you up."

"Yes, guv," they said in unison.

"Good," he said, turning to Ivy with a glint in his eye. "We have a breakthrough. It's time to get our hands dirty."

CHAPTER SIXTEEN

An empty crisp packet rolled passed the front of George's car as he drew up outside Hawthorn Court, as inland as could possibly be with a Skegness address. He and Ivy shared a few moments of silence before she caught his eye. Her look said it all, but she verbalised it anyway.

"What a hole."

"We can't all live in pretty little cottages in quaint little villages, Ivy," he replied. The buildings were a combination of large, functional houses and two-storey flats, presumably what the architects back in the seventies thought to represent modern living.

"Yeah, I know, but if this is all you can afford, then at least bloody look after it," she said. "My house isn't exactly perfect. It's small, it needs work done to it, and yeah, we need new windows. But I make sure the grass is cut, and the windows we do have are clean. There's no rubbish on the drive, and there's definitely no graffiti on the front door. It's a matter of pride, right?"

"Or shame," he countered, referencing their earlier conversation.

But he had to admit, she had a point. Everything that had

once been painted was now peeling, including the white wooden front door and the balcony railings that connected two flats on the second story. The building's only redeeming feature was its classic red brick walls, but even those had been graffitied in places.

"The people that live in these places have, for the most part, been released from prison. They've often lost touch with society. They don't know how to pay bills, for example. They wouldn't know how to use the internet or Bric-Brac—"

"Tik-Tok," Ivy said.

"Right, whatever it's called. But do you see what I'm saying? Do you think that cutting the lawn is at the top of their list of priorities? Or washing the windows, for that matter? They're just happy to be free and want to lead normal lives; at least, we have to assume so until they put a foot wrong. Places like this are a stepping stone for them. Nothing more. We're not here to judge."

"No, I know." She looked across at him. "I do. I get it."

Of course, it was not the first time George and Ivy had been called to buildings like this one. In their line of work, visiting such homes was not uncommon. Although working in the Wolds, these days, more often than not, the homes they visited were as charming as their surroundings.

"Just remember," he said. "The primary purpose of our visit is to—"

"Get an insight into Ryan Eva," Ivy finished. "Yes, I know."

"Well, good," he replied. "I just thought I'd mention it before—"

"Before I go off and start making accusations about Ryan Eva's past?"

"Well, as long as we're singing from the same song sheet," George said with a sigh. "Shall we?"

"If we must," Ivy said, taking a deep breath as though savouring the fresh air inside George's car before venturing into the flats.

George double-locked his car and checked the windows were up before making his way towards the peeling, white door of the red-brick building. He stopped at the door to listen for any sounds inside, but heard nothing, and so he gave his usual two knocks on the door.

A burly, unshaven, middle-aged man came to the door wearing a coffee-stained white tank top, beneath which a mass of chest hair sprawled. He scratched his stomach as he opened the door and waited for George and Ivy to introduce themselves with an icy stare.

"Good morning," George said, as pleasantly as could be. He held up his warrant card. "My name is Detective Inspector George Larson. This is my colleague Detective Sergeant Hart."

The man moved his icy stare between them as though it wasn't the first time he'd found two detectives on his doorstep but still impatient to find out why exactly they were there.

He nodded a greeting but said nothing.

"We're here with regards to Ryan Eva. Is this where he lives?"

"Who?" said the man, the question coming out as more of a bark.

"Ryan Eva," Ivy repeated, annunciating every syllable with clear condescension.

"S'pose it is," he replied as if daring her to continue. And, of course, Ivy dared. "If you can call it living." He nodded up the stairs behind him. "His room's up there."

"I'm afraid there's been an incident," she said. "Perhaps we can come inside?"

The man looked Ivy up and down slowly. Then, staring straight at her, he yelled, "Edward!" Ivy did not attempt to hide her actions as she wiped some of his spittle from her cheek.

From upstairs came a flurry of footsteps, and over the man's shoulder, a pair of dirty, white trainers appeared on the stairs.

"Yeah?" a young man's voice said quietly. "Who is it?"

"Where's Ryan?" the elder of the two men asked, still staring at Ivy, who stood her ground, staring back with more than a little contempt on her face.

The young man bent to look through the front door. He glanced between George and Ivy on the doorstep. "I ain't seen 'im. Why? Steve? Who's that?"

"He's not here," Steve said, and, with a final glare at the two of them, he went to close the door. Before George could react, Ivy had already put her foot between the door and its frame. He stared up at her, a look of confusion forming amidst the outrage.

"We know he isn't here. He was found dead yesterday," she said flatly, varying from George's original tactic. But he had admitted to bending processes to suit the situation himself, so he could hardly pull her up on adapting to hostility. "I think it's best if we come inside. Don't you?"

The man looked between Ivy's foot and her face with something akin to hatred.

"Got a warrant, have you?"

Dealing with individuals like the man at the door was simply tiring. They knew the law as well as George or Ivy and would pull every card from their sleeves to create delays and make an investigation difficult.

Ivy leaned in. "Oh, I could get a warrant," she hissed. "I could bring a whole team of officers here. I could overturn this place, rip up the floorboards, empty the cupboards, search this place room by room and drawer by drawer. Is that what you want me to do? Because, you know what? I'll make damn sure I find something in your room, and I'll make damn sure it results in you breaching your parole terms. You'd be back on A-wing crapping in a bucket before you've had a chance to call your two-bit solicitor. So get out of my way, get back to your hovel, and if you want my advice, stay there."

Steve and Ivy stared each other down for what George felt was an unnecessary amount of time. He rolled his eyes and went to speak just before the man said, "Dead, you say? How?"

"I'm afraid—"

"Yeah, yeah. You're not at liberty to discuss a live investigation," he said. "Edward, show them Ryan's room, won't you?" He lingered on Ivy for a few more uncomfortable moments.

"Alright," he said, timid and obedient like a shy child.

"And Edward?" Steve said, his eyes roving across Ivy's chest. "Make sure they don't take anything."

Steve ground his teeth as though chewing gum and turned away from them to return to wherever it was he had come from. Only when he was gone did the young man named Edward tiptoe down the remaining stairs. He couldn't have been much older than twenty, although he could have passed for younger if it wasn't for the revealing lines on his face, the wrinkles between his brow and around his eyes that suggested the man had seen and experienced too much of life to still be a teenager. He had thinning, blonde hair and oversized front teeth that George imagined could allow for a very charming smile given the right circumstances. Each time he spoke, it was so quiet that George wished the lad had a volume button.

"Is that true? Ryan's dead, is he?" he said, wringing his hands. From his accent, George placed him as a southerner. Somewhere on the outskirts of London, possibly.

"I'm afraid so," George said. "Sorry."

The man's eyes moistened at the news, and he gulped down what George imagined was a lump in his throat.

"I'll show you his digs," he said, turning to the stairs, his voice steady.

"Thank you," George said, holding out his hand. "After you."

Ivy was still staring down the hallway where Steve had disappeared. Her eyes narrowed, and her lips pursed as she ran her tongue across her teeth in disgust.

"Come on," he told her following Edward upstairs. She remained still. "Ivy, you can't take it personally."

At this, she laughed, although she didn't seem to find the

comment amusing. "Easy for you to say, guv. You don't have to deal with men looking at you like you're either a piece of meat or something on the bottom of their shoe."

"I'm a police officer, Ivy. I have been for forty years. Of course, I've had to deal with men looking at me like I'm something on the bottom of their shoe."

"But not like a piece of meat," she said, following him up the stairs.

"You can't start vendettas against everyone who looks at you the wrong way. That's just the job."

She didn't reply, which George translated as her finding at least a sliver of truth in his statement, however much she would deny it.

Edward led them along a dingy, grey-carpeted hallway that apparently hadn't seen a lick of paint since Tony Blair had been in charge. There were half a dozen doors, all of which were closed. But as they passed one, the stench that emanated from within suggested that it was the shared bathroom. However foul it may have been inside, no doubt it was far better than what they were used to.

Edward led them to the door at the end of the corridor on the right-hand side, and for some reason, he knocked, perhaps out of habit. Then, perhaps remembering the news that George and Ivy had delivered, he twitched and pushed down the handle. The door creaked open, and Edward stood there, unwilling to look inside.

"No lock?" George asked.

"Busted," he replied.

"Does that often happen around here? Is there a maintenance service?"

"I think so," Edward said. "But nobody's got nuffin' against Ryan, and he ain't got nuffin' worf nickin'."

George stepped into the room and could see that for himself. It was nearly empty, except for a single bed, a single dresser, and a

single desk that had no chair. The room had been painted an aggressive red over what appeared to be textured wallpaper. The carpet
was a blend of seventies reds and browns in kaleidoscopic patterns
that began to shift when George stared at them for too long.

He walked around the room and opened the dresser. Inside
were two t-shirts, two pairs of jeans, and a pair of trainers at the
bottom. In the drawers were four or five pairs of underwear and
four or five pairs of white socks. The bed was perfectly made, and
the pillows were placed at perfect right angles so precisely that
they might have been measured with a ruler.

"This is it?" George said, turning to Edward. "This is all he
had?"

Edward shrugged, leaning on the doorframe. "Yep. Guess he
was one of the minimalists. S'what they call it, ain't it?"

"That's what well-off people call it," Ivy said. "This is just
called being poor."

Edward snorted in an attempt to laugh. "Tell me about it," he
said. "None of us have much here, except what we got from
Nick." He pulled at the gold belcher chain around his neck. "My
dad's," he said by way of an explanation. "But Ryan didn't have
nuffin' like that."

"So you were friends?" George asked. "You and Ryan?"

Edward shrugged. "S'pose. More like allies, really. Place like
this, everyone needs an ally."

"What was he like?"

Edward frowned. "What do you mean?"

"Well, what was his personality? Was he a nice guy?"

"Look, I know what he did if that's what you mean. I know
why you're here. But I've got to be honest. I never saw that side
of him. He was alright. Kept to himself, sure, but he never had
nuffin' bad to say 'bout no-one." Edward kicked at the loose
carpet in the doorway. "Most people here treat me like a knob-
head. Push me around, you know? But Ryan was alright."

"Why do you think we're here, Edward?"

"'Cause of what he did, ain't it? Because of...his past?"

"No," George said. "We're not parole officers. We're detectives, Edward. We're investigating his murder."

Again, Edward exhibited another of his gulps.

"When was the last time you saw him, Edward?" Ivy asked.

Edward breathed in and out, his eyes looking up at the peeling ceiling as though remembering. "Fursday," he said. "What was that, couple o' days ago?"

"Three days ago," George said. "Today is Sunday."

"So yeah, free days ago. It was just out here in the hall. Bumped into him on his way out, didn't I?"

"Did he say where he's going?"

"See a mate, I fink," said Edward. "Didn't say who."

"What time was this?"

He blinked hard. "About four-ish. Four-firty? Summink like that."

"How long have you and Ryan known each other?" George asked.

Again, Edward leaned heavily on the doorway as though searching through his memories was an act of physical exertion. He closed his eyes. "Must be getting on for seven months now. I've been here for about nine, summink like that. He came here a couple of months after me. Just had his tag removed, didn't he? 'Bout a month ago, now. Had a little celebration, we did. Couple of beers, you know?"

"Congratulations," muttered Ivy, running her finger along the desk, which was spotless.

George studied the room a final time but found nothing that might tell them much more about Ryan Eva, except for the fact that he was certainly not a materialistic man. Or, at least, he couldn't afford to be.

"Thank you," George said, extending his hand to shake and

offering a contact card. "If anything else comes to mind, do get in touch."

Edward hesitated before shaking the man's hand as though distrust was ingrained in his psyche, but eventually, he took it and shook. It was the very definition of a wet lettuce.

"There is one more fing," he said before George and Ivy could leave. He glanced once at the broken lock. "I didn't fink about it at the time, but there was a man here. It was on fursday, just after Ryan left. I didn't think about it at the time. Standing outside the door, he was."

"And did you speak to him?"

"Well, yeah. I asked if he was one of Ryan's mates, and he said he was. But we aren't supposed to have mates over, are we? I didn't even know he had any friends."

"What did this man look like?" George asked.

Again, Edward squeezed his eyes shut as though dipping into his memories was a painful experience.

"Tall?" he said, although he made it sound like a question, and George imagined that, to such a short man, everyone appeared tall. "Brown hair, I fink. He looked...well, out of sorts, let's say."

"And what was he wearing?"

"I dunno—"

"I need you to think, Edward. This could be important."

Edward made a show of staring up at the ceiling, crinkling his nose.

"He had baggy cloves on. Jeans and that. New trainers. Clean they were. That's what they say, aint it? To judge a man on his shoes?" Edward looked down at his own shoes self-consciously — tattered, old, white trainers coming apart at the seams. "Anyway, I went back to my room, and by the time I came out again, he was gone."

George glanced at Ivy, who was making a note of the loose description.

"And that was the last time you saw him, was it?"

"Well, yeah," Edward said, then reddened. "Look, I didn't say nuffin' 'cause I didn't want to get involved." He leaned out of the door, looked both ways, then returned. "Stick your hooter where it ain't wanted round here, and you're likely to get shivved. Know what I mean? I ain't done all that time in stir to get cut up when I get out."

"No, quite right," George told him. "And I can assure you, your words will be in the strictest confidence."

Edward gave a nervous nod, and George found Ivy staring at him.

"Well, you've given us a lot to think about, Edward. Thank you," he said, and like a fifteenth-century servant, he backed out of the room.

"Tall with brown hair and loose clothes?" Ivy said. "Or should I say *cloves?*" She mimicked Edward's accent and grinned.

But George was lost in thought. He opened Ryan Eva's wardrobe again.

"What is it, guv?" Ivy asked, coming to stand beside him. "Didn't have much, did he?"

"He had a suit, Ivy," George replied. "Which is a darn sight more than our friend Edward has. The question is, why was he wearing it?"

CHAPTER SEVENTEEN

Through the windscreen, the council housing bore an uneasy quiet. It wouldn't have surprised George to see tumbleweed roll past. Instead, the same crisp packet he'd seen earlier bumped across the road in search of a nook in which to rest.

"So," Ivy said, resting her head against the headrest, processing what they had just seen and heard, "someone broke into his room two days before he died. Hardly a coincidence, is it?"

"No signs of a struggle, though," George said. "And Edward said that he was out at the time."

"Right, but whoever broke in didn't know that."

"You don't think so? What if they were watching him? What if they waited for him to leave?"

"But why?" Ivy said. "Not like there was anything there to steal, was there?"

"Unless they stole whatever it was they were looking for," George said cryptically. "What I'm more interested to know is why someone bothered breaking into his room seven months after he'd been released."

"What do you mean?"

"Well, say someone wanted to hurt Ryan for something he did before he went to prison. If they felt that strongly about it, why wouldn't they act on it as soon as he was released? Why wait around for months before doing anything?"

"Maybe they didn't know he was out," Ivy said. "It's not like they put it in the papers, is it?"

"No, but the prison service has a duty of care to inform the prosecuting officer, who in turn has a duty of care to inform the victim."

On that thought, he clicked the screen on the car's centre console and put a call through to Campbell's desk phone. As reliable as a lighthouse, she answered immediately.

"Guv," she said by way of a greeting.

"I need the address of Ryan Eva's victim," he said, straight to the point.

"Melissa Hale?"

"Right. Melissa Hale," George repeated, getting the hint that it was best to use her name.

"So, you think his murder is connected to his attack on her, then?" Ivy asked as Campbell busied herself, flicking through papers and clicking a mouse to search for the address.

"Let's just say that I think it's a scenario worth investigating," George said. "You heard what Edward said. He didn't know anyone. He didn't have any friends. That doesn't mean he didn't have enemies. Melissa Hale would have received a courtesy call. If she did, then who knows who else she might have told. People close to her. People who have been harbouring a grudge against Ryan Eva."

"People like her father," Campbell said over the line.

"What's that?" George said.

"We've been looking into him while you've been gone. Melissa Hale's dad has a record for aggravated assault."

"Yes, you told us that when we were there—"

"Against Ryan Eva," Campbell added, which surprised George enough to make him stop and think.

"Well, that figures," Ivy said. "If someone ever did that to Hattie, then I'd be up for assault, too."

"I've got it, guv," Campbell said. "Melissa's address. It's an address in Fulletby."

"Fulletby? That's—"

"Within spitting distance of Stockwith Mill," Campbell cut in, clearly hoping he had made the same connection.

"Send it across to Ivy, will you?"

"Already done," Campbell said. Ivy checked her phone, nodded, and immediately began tapping into the car's navigation system. She hit enter and the map positioned itself.

"It's thirty minutes from here," she said.

"Good," he said. "Is there anything else we should know before we head there, Campbell?"

"Only a bit of background stuff," she replied. "Ryan Eva had a position in a local abattoir. Just outside Willoughby."

"Jesus," Ivy said. "Straight out of prison and into a death zone. What a life."

"Anything else?" George asked.

"That's about it. He was on a GPS tag until about a month ago. Part of his parole terms. We managed to gain access to its tracking history, but it doesn't give us much. We know that he only went from his address to work every day. Occasionally, he'd stop at the shop down the road, but that's it."

"Okay," George said. "Remember to look at local bus timetables. That man could definitely not afford a car, and Stockwith Mill is in the middle of nowhere, too far to walk from here. He would have had to get the bus."

"Will do."

"Good. And I want someone to look into nearby security cameras. Local businesses might have some."

"What about doorbell cameras?" Ivy asked.

"No, we'll never get the warrant to access footage from private cameras thirty minutes drive from where the murder took place. We'd need a real reason."

"You mean, like a murder, guv?" Ivy said.

"I mean, a reason such as valid evidence that whoever killed Ryan Eva came here. So far, all we've got is a third-hand account of the victim from a convicted criminal with the disposition of a kitten."

"Someone broke into Ryan's bedsit on Thursday, guv. Surely that's—"

"We don't know that somebody broke into his bedsit, do we? The lock is broken, but Edward couldn't tell us when the damage happened." He paused to give her time to digest the information. "Edward saw somebody in the hallway outside Eva's room. That's all."

"Yeah, but come on. The lock's broken, and Eva's been murdered."

"Circumstantial," George told her. "Until we can prove that whoever Edward saw last Thursday actually did the damage. If you want to request a warrant to go knocking on doors, be my guest. But trust me, a judge isn't going to sign a warrant unless we can put a bit more meat on the bone. And before you suggest we prey on the local residents' good nature, look around. Does this strike you as the sort of street where the neighbours would be keen to talk to the police? I'll bet that half the occupants are either stoned or drunk, more than half of them will be falsely claiming dole, and the rest of them have more than their fair share of stolen goods. If you enjoy having a door slammed in your face, then go for it. I'll wait in the car."

"Christ, guv. And you call me judgemental. You should be a politician."

"I'm not being judgemental, Ivy. I'm exercising experience," George told her. "If anyone has a doorbell camera in this street, you can bet your life it's not to stop them being robbed. It's so they can see when us lot come knocking so they can stash their gear or leg it out of the back door. We're the enemy, remember? And this," he said, pointing to the street through the windscreen. "This is the bloody front line." Ivy clearly wanted to say something but held her tongue. "Campbell, contact local businesses. There's a betting shop and an off-licence up the road."

"How do you know that?" Ivy said, peering into the distance to where a small group of teenagers were hanging around outside some shops.

"There's always a betting shop, and there's always an off-licence, Ivy. Just like at least one of those kids will have either a bag of weed or a knife on them. We're not in the Wolds now."

"I've found the row of shops you're talking about on Google Maps," Campbell said. "There's a pet shop and a chippie." George waited for her to scroll along the street. "And there's a betting shop and a corner shop."

"That sells alcohol?" George asked, and Campbell's smile was evident in her response.

"That sells alcohol," she said with a sigh.

"Good. We might get lucky. We're looking for a tall, middle-aged male wearing baggy clothing heading towards Ryan Eva's bedsit sometime last Thursday."

"I'll put Byrne on it, guv," she said.

"That'll do."

"Any more of a description?" Campbell asked.

"Tall with brown hair," Ivy replied. "We won't be able to identify him from the footage, but when we do finally catch up with whoever it is, we should be able to place him at Ryan Eva's bedsit. That'll give us a line of questioning he won't be able to ignore."

"And what's more," George added. "It'll give us some meat on the bone. We can start requesting warrants."

"Right," Campbell said slowly, as though writing down the

rather useless description as she spoke. "How was Ryan's apartment, anyway?"

"Well, it's not so much an apartment as a room in a house," Ivy said. "Some neanderthal answered the door—"

"Is he worth looking into?"

"No," George said, with a sideways look at Ivy. "I don't think he's involved. Didn't seem to care about Ryan at all."

"What about the Edward bloke you mentioned?"

"He was friends with Ryan, or more accurately, the closest thing he had to a friend."

"What did he have to say about Eva?" She sounded nosy, and had it been anybody else, George would have told her to wait for the debrief. But her intrigue was healthy. She was keen, and he didn't want to quench that thirst.

"Only that Eva kept to himself and that he was a nice guy."

"A nice guy?" Campbell repeated.

"That's what he said. That Ryan was alright."

Campbell gave an indistinctive, unimpressed snort.

"What?"

"Well, I just don't know if Edward is a reliable character witness," she said. "He is, as you said, a convicted criminal. He's also quite vulnerable."

"Now, who's being judgemental?" George said. "For all we know, Ryan *was* a nice guy. He was going through a process of rehabilitation. He served his time. Who are we to cast aspersions?"

"I suppose you're right,"

"Listen, we, of all people, have to trust in the rehabilitation process. Otherwise, we might as well sentence every criminal to life and bring back the death penalty."

Neither of them replied.

"What will you do now, guv?" Campbell asked.

George started the car. "We're going to see Melissa Hale," he said.

"So, you're not following up on the wedding guests, then? You're taking it wider. I thought you were keen on eliminating the guests."

"I *am* keen on eliminating the guests," George replied and couldn't help but smile at Ivy, who also recognised the deviation in strategy. "I'm following up on a lead. Sometimes that means bending the procedures and admitting when you're wrong."

CHAPTER EIGHTEEN

George drove through the two stone gateposts and parked outside a double garage that many would have considered large enough to be a house in itself. Further up the driveway was a sage-green Volvo XC40, an everyday family car. George wondered if there was something a little more special hidden inside the garage, perhaps under a cover to keep the paintwork fresh.

He appraised the house, which, although large, would have made a wonderful family home. He admired the lancet window above the front door, the impressive chimneys, and the neat row of shrubs beneath the symmetrical downstairs windows. When George turned off the engine, all he could hear was birdsong, the subtle hum of a tractor in a nearby field, and Ivy's soft breathing.

"Not bad," she said, leaning forward to peer up at the house through the windscreen.

"Must be a bugger to heat," he replied.

"Christ, that's the sort of thing my mum would say."

"Well then, your mum speaks common sense," he replied, turning to her. "You should listen to her more often."

They climbed out of the car and breathed the fresh air.

"Coming from a man who lives in a house older than time

itself," she said. "Have you felt the gale that blows in through the cracks in my bedroom window?"

"Your bedroom now, is it?"

"Oh, you know what I mean," she replied. "The walls are nearly two feet thick with not a shred of insulation, the radiators are hotter than the sun but do absolutely nothing to heat the rooms, and the front door was put on right about the time King James signed the Magna Carta."

"It was King John," George said. "And he didn't sign it."

"What?"

"He didn't sign it. He allowed his wax seal to be used, but he didn't sign it."

"You're missing my point."

"Can I help you?" a voice called out, cutting the history lesson short.

A middle-aged man walked around the side of the house carrying a bucket of what appeared to be compost waste. He was dressed well in what George would have called country attire — smart olive trousers, a Tattersall shirt, and a Barbour gilet. He stopped beside a row of three compost bays beside the garage and emptied his bucket into one before approaching them, his bucket swinging by his side.

His brown hair, though tightly curled, was indented by a receding hairline as if somebody had taken a razor to the centre of his head.

"Mr Hale?" George asked when he was just ten feet away. The man nodded cautiously, and George let his warrant card fall open for him to see. "My name is Detective Inspector Larson. This is my colleague Detective Sergeant Hart. We wondered if we might have a few words."

He eyed them both and then his bucket as if deliberating on whether or not he should invite them inside.

"About?"

"Ryan Eva," George said flatly, studying the man's face.

The man's lip curled as soon as George spoke Eva's name, and his whole body seemed to swell as he took a deep breath.

"I don't have anything to say about Ryan Eva," he replied and then turned to leave.

"He's dead," Ivy said bluntly.

The man stopped in his tracks, turned his head to them, and paused for thought.

"Good riddance," he said eventually and continued on his journey.

George stepped forward, calling, "Are you not curious how it happened, Mr Hale?"

The man stopped again and set the bucket down on the ground. He turned around slowly. "I'll wager there were more than a few who had it in for Ryan Eva. It was only a matter of time before one of them caught up with him."

"Ryan was released seven months ago from Prison Walton. Were you aware of that, Mr Hale?"

He paused to chew on the inside of his mouth. "My daughter told me, yes. And you can stop with Mr Hale, okay? My name is Mark."

"Have you seen Ryan recently, Mark?"

He scoffed. "As I'm sure you're more than aware, Inspector…"

"Larson," George told him again.

"Inspector Larson, right. Ryan Eva is not permitted to come within one hundred yards of my daughter or any of my family. So no, I have not seen him, nor would I have wanted to."

"Ryan is not permitted to come to you," George said. "But did you go to see him?"

"Why on earth would I go to see the man who…" He glanced at the end of the driveway and lowered his voice to a hiss. "Why would I want to see the man who assaulted my daughter?"

"Come on, Mark," George said. "I think that's obvious, don't you?"

"Oh, I see," he said, a wry grin forming on his face. "You think I had something to do with it, do you?"

"We're not accusing you of anything, Mark. We are at the beginning of our investigation. I am just trying to understand Ryan's movements before he died."

"Can I give you some advice?" Mark said.

"I'm not really in the habit of taking—"

"Knife crime is up, fraud is up, sexual assault is up. Why are you wasting your time with cretins like Ryan Eva? Save your time, Inspector. That's my advice. A man like that won't be missed. You hear me? Not by you, not by me or my family, not by anyone."

"I'm sure you understand, Mark, that we have an obligation to investigate every murder, whoever the victim. Ryan Eva served his time. He was a free man."

"An *obligation*?" Mark said, stepping forward. "And where was your *obligation* when my daughter was being assaulted by that freak? Where was your *obligation* when he followed her home? When he groomed her into trusting him and then dragged her through the fields and..." He glanced around again. "And raped her? Where was your *obligation* to stop that from happening in the first place? To stop men like that from being on the streets? From being allowed near women, near children?"

"I'm very sorry about what happened to your daughter—"

"I don't need your apologies," Mark spat. "And neither does Melissa. She needs justice. We all do, seeing as your lot have apparently given up on getting that for us; someone clearly took it into their own hands. Well, you know what? Good on them. So, no, I have not seen Ryan Eva anytime recently. He would know if I had because I would have knocked him into next week if he'd come within a thousand yards of my daughter ever again."

George paused, watching Mark Hale's chest rise and fall with fury.

"Well, now he never can, can he?"

"No," Mark said, a smile growing on his face. "He can never

touch her again, and I can sleep easy at night knowing that monster is in a cold, dark grave."

"I have to say, Mr Hale, you're not exactly helping your position."

"If I had wanted to kill Ryan Eva, I would have done so when I had the chance. When his neck was within my grip. But I didn't. For better or worse, I did not kill that boy. I let him go. But if you do find the man who killed Ryan Eva, let me know who it is, won't you?" He leaned in close to George. "Because I'd like to shake his hand."

Mark and George stared each other down for a few quiet seconds. Mark's cold gaze insisted upon his innocence, and George's struggled to interpret his response. But that long stare was cut short by footsteps growing louder on the driveway behind them.

"Dad?" said a voice, female and concerned. "Dad, what's going on?"

Mark broke the eye contact to look over George's shoulder and say, "Nothing, honey." Then he frowned. "What are you doing here? I told you to call me."

"It's fine, Dad. I wanted the fresh air."

"It's not fine," he said, clearly comfortable raising his voice in front of strangers. "You call me when you finish work, and I'll collect you. You hear me?"

"Alright, fine," she snapped, then repeated, "what's going on? Who are these people?"

"Nothing and nobody," he replied. "They were just leaving."

"No, we weren't, actually," George said, turning to face the girl who he assumed was Melissa Hale. "Melissa?"

"That's me," she answered.

"You leave her out of this," Mark said reaching for George's arm. George stared down at his hand until his grip loosened and then fell away. Mark's voice lost its strength. "She's been through enough."

Melissa had short, blonde hair pulled back into a ponytail that only just managed to stay contained by a hair tie and a collation of hairpins sticking out like a corgi's tail. She was small and pretty, with large, dark eyes, and she stood slightly hunched, as though tired from a shift at work as a waitress, judging by her black shirt, crimson waistcoat, tie, and metal name badge.

"We're here to talk about Ryan Eva," George said. "I'm sorry, I know it's—"

"Don't you dare," Mark said, marching forward to stand between George and his daughter. "Don't you dare force her to talk about that man."

"It's okay, Dad."

"The hell it is. They have no right."

"Dad, please." She pushed her father out of the way so she could ask George, "What's going on?"

A lot could be conveyed in a look, an expression, and George did his best to reassure her, to comfort and ready her.

"Ryan was found dead two days ago," he said, and to his surprise, Melissa's eyes welled up at the news. Or perhaps it was just the mention of that name. Ryan Eva. The name that had most likely haunted her for nearly a decade. She swallowed. But when she spoke, her voice was strong. Defiant.

"What happened to him?"

"Sweetheart, don't—" Mark started.

"He was found at Stockwith Mill," George said, overriding her father's objections. "Do you know where that is?"

"What are you implying?" Mark said.

"I'm not implying anything, Mr Hale. I'm simply trying to understand the situation."

"I've heard of it," Melissa said, shaking her head.

"You heard her," Mark said, putting an arm around her shoulder. "She doesn't know the place. So, if you don't mind—"

"*Dad*," Melissa said, saving George from having to put him

back in his box again. "Dad, can you just give me a moment with them?"

"What? No."

"Please," she said. "Just two minutes. Why don't you go inside and make us a cup of tea?" She softened with his expression. "I'll be fine. I can handle it."

He looked at her in disbelief, then slowly removed his hand from his daughter's shoulder, and with one last glare at George, he headed back to the house, snatching up his bucket en route. Soon enough, however, Mark Hale appeared at the living room window, his arms crossed, watching their interaction with a keen eye.

Melissa seemed to notice, too, because she turned her back on the house so her father couldn't read her lips.

"He came here," she said quietly.

"Eva?" George said. "He came here?"

She nodded. "Last Thursday. When Dad was at work."

"What time was this?"

"Just before five," she said. "I remember worrying that Dad could come home any moment and..." She hesitated.

"And what, Melissa?"

She took a deep breath. "And lose his temper."

George moved on before Melissa could realise the suggestion of her words. "What did he want? What did he say?"

"He just said he wanted to talk to me."

"And did you?" Ivy asked softly, who had remained silent and watchful until now. "Did you talk to him, Melissa?"

She nodded. "Just for a bit. He wanted to apologise. He said he *needed* to apologise, that he was making amends."

"Did he do anything..." Ivy struggled to find the right words. "Inappropriate? Did you feel threatened?"

"No," Melissa said, almost defensively. "No, not at all. It was a shock to see him. Of course, it was. But I knew he was out of prison. Someone called me last year to let me know that he had been released. And he kept back. He didn't come too close. I didn't feel unsafe."

"How long did you talk for?"

"Less than five minutes," she said. "It was just like he wanted to get the apology off his chest."

"How did it end?"

"He promised me something."

"Promised you what?"

"He promised..." Again, she turned away to swallow, frowning as though confused by her own emotional reactions.

"What, Melissa? What did he promise?"

"That he'd leave me alone. That I wasn't to worry," she said. "And that I'd never see him again."

CHAPTER NINETEEN

George drove along the winding country lanes, lost in thought. He took turns faster than he had when he'd first moved back to the Wolds, becoming accustomed to their dips and peaks like a farmer learning his body of land and the seasonal rhythm. He routed a call through the loudspeaker in his car, which rang out.

"Guv?" said that recognisable voice on the other end.

"Campbell, how's it going?" George said. "Things are moving. Give me an update, will you?"

"Byrne found something on CCTV. Hold on. I'll let him tell you."

They heard a rustling over the line, as though the handset was brushing past leaves. Then the background noise of the incident room entered the call, and Byrne's voice said, "Alright, guv?"

"I hear you have some kind of update for me, Byrne," George said.

"Yes, guv. I got in touch with those shops on Hawthorn Court," he said. "The pet shop came through. Said they were always getting their windows smashed and yobbos gobbing all over their front door, so they had to get them installed."

"Charming," George said.

"The system is cloud-based, so they were able to give me the login details. I've got a tall, brown-haired man walking past the shop towards Eva's bedsit."

"Did he force entry?" George asked. "Did the camera reach that far?"

"Eva's front door was right on the limits of the second camera. But it captured the whole thing. He didn't exactly break in. He lingered by the doorway for a few minutes, and when someone walked outside, he talked to them on the doorstep for a few seconds. They held the door open for him so he could enter the house. He looked shady, for sure."

"Any facial recognition?"

"We're running it now, guv, but nothing so far. You know what these systems are like. The cameras were set up to focus on the shop. Everything we're interested in is all blurred and grainy."

"What time was this?"

Byrne paused, then said, "Ten past four. He walks past the shop at four-oh-eight and arrives at the house at ten-past. He hangs around for three minutes and then enters the house. Then he leaves eighty minutes later, at five thirty-eight."

"*Eighty* minutes?" George repeated.

"Yes, guv. No idea what he was doing all that time."

"Did anyone else enter the house during that time? From four-ten to five thirty-eight, when the intruder was there?"

"They did, as it happens," Byrne said. "A few people in and out. You can't identify anyone, though."

George looked over at Ivy, deep in thought.

"Can we identify his clothes? The intruder's, that is?"

"It's hard to tell," he said, and George imagined him squinting at the image on his computer screen. "But maybe tracksuit bottoms and a hoody. Why?"

Ivy answered for him. "Doesn't exactly sound like something Mark Hale would wear, does it?"

"He might have been trying to fit in," George said. "You'd

stick out like a sore thumb walking around Hawthorn Court in corduroys and a Barbour jacket."

"You think it was Mark Hale?" Byrne asked over the line.

"I think it would make sense," George said. "The way he talked about Ryan. He clearly loathes him. Maybe he found out that Ryan had come to see Melissa. Maybe he wanted to finish what he had started last time he assaulted the lad."

"But Ryan wasn't home."

"Well, maybe if he was, then we would have been investigating Ryan Eva's murder a few days earlier."

"Wait, you said ten past four on Thursday?" Ivy said. "Melissa said Ryan went to her house just before five. That's where he was going, guv. Ryan had left to go to speak to Melissa."

"Which means Mark Hale couldn't yet have known that Ryan had met Melissa."

"Wait, when did Ryan talk to Melissa?" Byrne asked.

"Just before five on Thursday," Ivy repeated, deadpan.

"But wouldn't that break his restraining order? Surely, he's not allowed anywhere near her."

"One hundred yards, to be exact."

"So, he was willing to break his parole terms? He risked going back to prison? Why?"

"To apologise, apparently. And to promise that she'd never see him again."

"Well, he could've *shown* her that," Campbell said, the vitriol clear in her voice. "By not making her see him again. He had no right to turn up on her doorstep and inflict his apology on her. It's selfish."

"I agree."

"It's enough to trigger a trauma response," Campbell said. "How did she seem?"

"Shaken," Ivy said, "but surprisingly understanding. More understanding than I would be. To be honest, she seemed almost philosophical about it. Maybe even sad to hear of his death."

"Very mature," Byrne said.

"Or naive," Campbell added. "What did her dad think of it?"

"Oh, he doesn't know," George said. "And I imagine he would go after Ryan if he found out."

"Well, maybe that's exactly what he did do," pointed out Ivy.

"What was he like?" Campbell asked.

"Angry," George said. "And protective. Didn't like us speaking to Melissa alone."

"Well, that figures," Byrne said.

"She was *sad*? It doesn't make sense," Campbell said, fixating on this one point.

"It's not expected," Ivy said. "Doesn't mean it doesn't make sense. We all have different reactions to things. None of them are the right way to react, particularly."

"Yeah, but what he did... I mean, it was sickening."

"How do you know?" George said.

"I've been reading the original report." She paused. "I read Melissa's statement."

"And?" George said.

Campbell took a deep, unsteady breath. "He was eighteen, in his final year at college, and she was thirteen, in her first year of high school. He'd been following her home for a few weeks, keeping his distance at first. But then he started to catch up with her and talk to her, asking if she had a boyfriend, telling her she was pretty, that he liked her."

"Grooming her, you mean?" Ivy said.

"Something like that, yeah. It continued for months. She'd go a different way home or tell him to leave her alone, but he didn't. He got obsessed. He tried to hold her hand and hug her goodbye, but she kept running away. He freaked her out, and she was too scared and shy to tell anyone. She didn't understand exactly what was happening."

"She was a child, for God's sake," Ivy said, seething after hearing the story. From a male perspective, George found it best to remain objective under the circumstances. There was a guilt, he found, that all men carried on behalf of the few that sullied their name.

"Then, one day, things escalated. She was about halfway home when he stopped her and tried to kiss her. She pushed him away, and he became violent. He grabbed her arm and dragged her into one of the fields off the lane, not far from her own house. In the safety of her own neighbourhood. He took her beneath a tree in the bushes, held her down, and...well, I don't need to go into detail, do I?"

"No," George said before anyone could say otherwise. "No, that won't be necessary."

"According to her statement, he kept her there for hours. It got dark, and her parents grew concerned. They eventually went looking for her, along with some local friends and neighbours."

"And?" Ivy said.

"And that's how they found him. Pinning her down beneath a tree. They had him bang to rights. They had Melissa's statement, her parents' statements, the neighbours, plus the DNA. They even used the GPS on his phone to place him at the scene, in case the statements and DNA weren't enough. He had no chance."

A grim silence followed as the team processed the story. They were investigating the murder of a rapist, giving him the same level of respect and dignity in death as they had law-abiding citizens.

"Feels wrong, doesn't it?" Byrne said. "Like we're defending him or something."

"We don't need to be doing this for him," Ivy said quietly. "There is a murderer out there. And even *if* Ryan Eva deserved it, which I'm not saying he did, then it is still our duty to find and arrest them so they can't do it again."

"Hear, hear," George said. "Any other updates?"

Campbell sighed. "Yes, two things," she said. "Pippa Bell says she's ready for you."

George checked his watch. Dr Bell had had nearly a day to examine the body. With any luck, she would have something tangible for them to go on.

"We'll see her now before we come back. Tell her to expect us, will you?"

"Will do," Campbell said.

"And what was the other thing? You said there were two more updates."

"Ah, yes," she said. "Melissa's statement also mentions an Adam Potter. He was Melissa's boyfriend at the time, so we looked into him. He was a bit older than she was when the attack happened. Fifteen, I think. According to the report, he went after Ryan when he was out on bail. Jumped him in the street. Beat the living daylights out of him."

"Was this before or after Mark Hale assaulted Ryan Eva?"

"Before," Campbell said. "But there was only a day in it. Ryan had just got back from the hospital when Mark Hale went over to his house and did the exact same thing."

"Almost seems coordinated," muttered George.

"I don't know, guv," Byrne said, "I think a lot of people wanted to beat the hell out of Ryan, and the two men closest to Melissa made sure they succeeded."

"So, we've got two men with strong motives and a history of assaulting Ryan Eva," Ivy outlined.

"It's not the motive that's the problem," George said. "If we're going to make an arrest, we need evidence to keep them in custody. For that, we need a murder weapon, means, an opportunity, time of death, and DNA. We need facts."

"Right, guv."

"Byrne, build a profile on Adam Potter. We're going to need to talk to him sooner or later."

"Yes, guv."

"Campbell, find out where Melissa works. We need to talk to her again, preferably without Mark Hale breathing down our necks. I get the impression she has more to say. From her uniform, she works at a restaurant or a hotel. It was too formal for a pub. And she walked home, so it must be walkable or on a bus route. Ring around. I'm going to want you to go and see her later."

"Yes, guv."

"But first, I have a job for you to do together." He paused, wanting to convey the weight of the task. "It's a step up for both of you." And as though talking to himself, he added, "I just hope you're ready for it."

CHAPTER TWENTY

Ivy and George paused before the familiar double doors. As usual, Ivy took a few deep breaths to prepare herself for what lay inside — in this case, Ryan Eva. George, however, prepared himself for the *living* body behind the door, namely Dr Pippa Bell, especially considering that the last time they had met, she had slammed the door in his face. George reached up to press the buzzer. But, before he could, the large door to the pathology lab swung open.

"You took your time," Pip said, opening the door fully for them. "Come on, come on. I haven't got all day, have I?"

Pip stomped back into the lab, leaving them more than a little bewildered. She was already dressed in her scrubs, ready to go, which was a far more professional look than her usual attire, which often comprised a grunge band t-shirt which was too-long, baggy jeans, and heavy, black boots that wouldn't look amiss in either a techno club or on the feet of hippy protesters marching down Whitehall.

George and Ivy dressed in their scrubs in silence, George considering how he might survive this interaction without damaging a professional relationship, and Ivy considering how she would do so without fainting. When they were ready, they took another second to prepare themselves before entering the morgue itself.

"It'll be over before you know it," he told her, focusing on Ivy's anxieties as a distraction from his own.

Ivy was the one to open the heavily insulated door into the morgue, and she did so as an alcoholic might introduce him or herself. But she stopped only two steps in at the sight of Ryan Eva beneath a thin, blue sheet on a stainless-steel gurney. Pip waited by his side; her head cocked to one side as if intrigued by Ivy's reaction.

"Now then, Pip," he said casually.

"Alright, George," she said, her Welsh accent thick and strong and somehow comforting in a room filled with the stench of death. "Making quite a habit of this, aren't you? Were the Wolds always this exciting before you turned up?"

"Ah," he replied. "Been reading the papers, have you?"

"Just the cartoons," she replied. "Usually, anyway. Unless something catches my eye." She grinned playfully, a sign perhaps that her cold welcome was not a reflection of her mood. Or maybe she was luring him into a false sense of security.

"Well, I wouldn't believe everything they say," he told her, as guarded as he could be.

"Oh, I'm quite selective about what I read and who I listen to. Besides, they paint you in a decent light."

"Is that right?"

"They say you're what the area needs."

"I'm not sure if I can take the credit," George said. "The area needed a strong team focused on major crimes. That's all. Whoever headed it up was always going to be the one in the spotlight."

"They also say that crime is getting worse. Even out in the Wolds."

"Bad things happen everywhere, Pip," George said. "The population is growing, that's all. As far as I know, the ratio of suspicious deaths per capita hasn't risen. Not like burglaries or drugs."

"Well, clearly, you are paying attention," said Pip. "A few months ago, this might have been dismissed as a hiking fall gone wrong." She gestured at the lump beneath the blue sheet.

"What, a man dressed in a three-piece suit? At a wedding venue on the day of a wedding?"

Pip shrugged. "I've seen some pretty suspicious deaths go through as worse. If there's no evidence, there's no evidence, and if there's no resources to find it..."

"Well, we know he wasn't there on a hike," George clarified. "His name is Ryan Eva. He was recently released from a stint at His Majesty's pleasure."

"So? Criminals can be hikers too, you know? What's the connection to the bride or the groom? Or is this the groom?" She grinned again, clearly toying with him. But he was in no mood for light-hearted japes. And even if he was, doing so while standing beside a dead body seemed a little unsuitable. He put the humour down to her spending all day every day surrounded by death, which almost certainly affected an individual's psyche.

"I don't know if there is a connection to the wedding yet," George said. "That's what I'm here to try and find out."

"Okay then," she said, seeming happily intrigued. "Well, I do have some information for you." Pip removed a red pen from her breast pocket, which she often used in the same way a professor might use a stick to point to a blackboard. "First up, cause of death," she said. "Despite the head wound, this man drowned."

"Drowned?"

"Judging by the water in his swollen lungs, the debris in the trachea and the bronchial tubes."

"So, it wasn't the head wound," he said aloud but to himself.

Pip eyed him for a solid three seconds before replying. "He was probably unconscious when he entered the water." She shook her head. "But he certainly wasn't dead."

"We're working on a theory that he entered the water at a shallow stream. Doctor Saint suggested he was there a while due to the livor mortis."

"That makes sense," Pip agreed.

"There was a heavy downpour that day. We think the water rose and carried him downstream to the mill pond where he snagged in the reeds."

Pip listened intently, considering her response.

"I can see nothing to suggest otherwise," she said. "In fact, it's a solid theory."

"Time of death?"

"Dr Saint was right on the money," she said, then muttered quietly, "But I did manage to narrow it down a little to between twelve and two p.m. Friday afternoon."

"The day before the wedding," George said, nodding. "You're right. That is exactly what Doctor Saint said."

"Makes your job a bit easier then, doesn't it?" said Pip. "You can narrow it down to just the wedding party."

"Perhaps," George said. "Perhaps not. Somebody could have followed Ryan to the venue."

"Other hikers, you mean?" Pip said with a wink.

George scanned Ryan Eva's body, specifically his head, and more specifically, the large dent on the right side of his skull. Ivy had been quiet this whole time, and George understood why. It was a difficult sight for anyone to see — the concave of a man's skull: it was never supposed to look that way. It looked unreal, uncanny, even for someone with as much experience as himself and without Ivy's weak constitution.

"It was done with a palm-sized round object," Pip said. "I'd guessed a rock, which was confirmed when I sent a sample to Katy Southwell." She held up a plastic bag from a table by the side of the gurney. "I found traces in his congealed blood. Katy Southwell has confirmed that it's limestone. She said she'd send you over a report."

"Doesn't help much," Ivy said, her voice thick with nausea. "The whole area is covered in limestone."

"We can still match it to the venue," George said, "to be sure that he was killed there and not moved there after being killed somewhere else. Anything else, Pip?"

"Yes, signs of a scuffle," she said, pointing to scratches on Ryan's arms and face. "Which also confirms the rock theory. If I were to hazard a guess, I'd say he was fighting someone, and they grabbed a rock to finish the fight with a blow to his head."

"What are the signs?" George asked, hoping for skin under the fingernails to DNA that they could use to close this investigation quickly.

"Bruises and plenty of them, all over his arms and legs and some on his face," she said, pointing to a faint blue circle on Ryan's cheek.

"The man travelled through a bloody watermill," Ivy said. "I wouldn't be surprised if he had a few bruises."

"You said he was killed upstream, and then his body floated down the next day, right?"

"But Ivy's right. You should see the power of that water. I'm surprised he doesn't have broken bones, too. They could've been from that journey."

"Impossible," said Pip. "For bruises to form, you need a beating heart. Blood coursing around the body. Think of them as puddles rising from the groundwater of blood flowing around the body. Basically, George," she said, reminding them of something that they should already know, "a dead body can't produce bruises. However violent the after-death circumstances. These bruises had to be made before he died, and I know bruises. They are small and precise, from a fist or kicking feet." Pip looked into George's eyes. "There was a scuffle," she said certainly. "And whoever he was scuffling with grabbed onto the first thing they could find to finish the job."

She swung her arm up and down as if to punctuate her statement.

"I don't suppose we can tell if they were right or left-handed, can we?"

Pip shook her head.

"Not with any deal of certainty," she replied.

"Thank you, Pip," George said.

With that, George turned to leave, nudging Ivy as he did. Pip crossed her arms and watched them leave.

"I have a question, Sergeant Hart," she said. Ivy slowly turned around, keeping her gaze solidly on Pip rather than the body beside her. "Why do you bother to come in here every time? If you clearly can't stand it? I mean, look at you. Your knees are weak, your stomach is most likely churning, and I'll bet you have a cold sweat on your back. You can barely stand up. It won't help me if one of these days you faint or unload your breakfast on the floor, you know. It'll be me who has to clear up the mess."

George turned to her, also curious, although he thought he knew the answer. After all, he would never leave Ivy to do this alone, especially not with Pip.

"This is my job," Ivy said calmly. "Besides, I just love spending time with you."

Pip laughed out loud, like a muted stab of a horn.

"Flattery will get you everywhere," she said pulling the sheet back up to cover Ryan Eva. "Don't think of them as people."

"Sorry? Isn't that a bit disrespectful?"

"No," Pip said. "Think of them as a gift from the dead. Something they left behind for us to take care of. Something we can use to bring them justice." She rested her hands on Ryan Eva. "Something to be cherished."

"I'll bear that in mind," Ivy said.

"What did he do, anyway?" Pip called across the room. "You said he was in prison. What did he do?"

"He raped a thirteen-year-old girl," Ivy told her flatly. "Now, maybe you can see why I find it difficult to cherish his remains."

CHAPTER TWENTY-ONE

Campbell pulled the car up outside an end-of-terrace house on the outskirts of Louth. The house was narrow but charming, with a cream porch with hanging baskets on either upright and a neat row of dog violets beneath the single downstairs windowsill.

Byrne sat in the passenger seat beside her, squirming like a small child in need of the bathroom.

"I really, really don't want to do this," he said. "Why are *we* doing this? Why not him?"

When the two of them were seconded to DI Larson's team, she had seen Byrne as the opposition. Someone to put down where possible and who would be looking to do the same to her.

But as the weeks rolled by, she was beginning to like him. He wasn't a threat, not to her anyway. He was like the little brother she had hated during her teenage years and came to love in adulthood.

She rolled her eyes, practising her newfound patience, then turned to face him. "He's testing us. He's trying to see if we've got what it takes. If they're going to expand the team, that means opportunity. That's what you want, isn't it? You want to progress, don't you?"

"It is," he said. "Of course it is, you know that. I just...I don't know if I'm comfortable doing stuff like this. I mean, you know what I'm like. I'm bound to say something wrong."

"Just think before you speak."

"I do," he said. "Stuff...just comes out. I can't help it. I just end up saying the wrong thing."

"Do you know what?" she said. "When I first met you, when we first worked with Larson, I bloody hated you. I thought you were a moron."

"Eh?"

"Sorry, but it's true," she said. "But over these past couple of months, I've started to see through that. I've started to like you."

"Really?"

"Don't get carried away. I said I've *started* to like you. You've still got some work to do."

"Right," he replied.

"And now we've been given an opportunity to really show him what we can do, and what do you do? You fall to pieces."

"I'm not falling to pieces," he said. "I just don't want to mess it up. You say this is a test. *Every day* is a bloody test. Every day, I'm up against you. Always the first to answer the phone, always the one with the right answers." He jabbed at his chest with an index finger. "I've got the right answers, too. I just don't feel the need to impress Larson every second of every day. I know I can do the job. I've wanted this for as long as I can remember, but I'm always on the back foot."

"Well, get on the front foot, then," she said.

"I don't want..." he started, then took a breath. "I don't want competition. The world is hard e-bloody-nough."

"What?"

"I don't want competition. I don't want to feel like every single thing I say or do is being scrutinised by you or him or DS Hart."

"What are you saying?"

"I'm saying," he said. "I'm saying that I've had your back since day one. It's about time you had mine. If the team is going to get bigger, then it'll be you and me who have to really step up to the mark. I don't want to fight for it. I want it for you, and I want it for me."

"Do I really make you feel like that?"

"It's not about how you make me feel," he said. "We're not at school. The guv said that we're the enemy, right? That everyone out there has a dislike for us."

"He has a point—"

"Yeah, well, imagine having that at work as well," he said. "And at home. Imagine having the need to fight in every aspect of life."

"And that's why you say the wrong thing?"

"And that's why I say the wrong thing," he agreed. "Because I just want to have a part of my life where I can be myself instead of trying to be someone I despise."

"Bloody hell, Byrne, I think I'm going to cry."

"Ah, sod you," he said, and he reached for the door handle, but she leaned over and stopped him.

"Alright, alright," she said. "I hear you. Maybe I have been a bit hard on you. Maybe I have gone out of my way to impress Larson." She cleared her throat. "And maybe I have shone a crappy light on you sometimes."

He said nothing, and she studied his profile. His jaw was square, and his beard was neatly trimmed. He was by no means a large man, but there was strength in his rounded shoulders and full chest.

"So, you're not a nerd then?" she asked, which raised a smile. "I thought you enjoyed quiz nights and sci-fi. If you had told me you were attending a Star Trek convention, I wouldn't have been surprised in the least."

"Star Trek?"

"Well, come on. I mean—"

"Look, I do enjoy a good quiz night. I like having somewhere

I can go and be the best at something. Somewhere where people don't really know me." He looked across at her. "I also enjoy having a few beers. I enjoy watching the football. I enjoy listening to the music I grew up with. I enjoy playing the guitar."

"*You* play the guitar?"

"Since I was a kid, yeah."

"Well, that surprises me."

"Why? Because you thought I was a nerd?"

"No, I just didn't have you down as a musician," she replied. "I still think you're a nerd."

"You do know that music is just maths, don't you?"

"Eh?"

"It's maths," he said again. "Firsts, thirds, fifths, sevenths, diminished fourths. It's all maths. It's all relative to the root note."

"You've lost me," she said. "But I'll take your word for it and retract that statement. You're not a nerd." She gave his shoulder a playful squeeze. "Bloody hell, Byrne."

"What?"

She retracted her hand and smiled back at him.

"Nothing," she said. "Anyway, PC Byrne, soon-to-be DC Byrne, the guv gave us a job to do."

"Can I ask you something?" he said, to which she simply nodded. "Can you call me Liam?"

"Liam?"

"It's my name," he said. "It'd be nice if you could use it."

He climbed from the car and seemed to stand three inches taller. He walked over to the front gate of the property and stared up at the house, and Campbell found herself staring after him, admiring his shoulders and his lean waist. She climbed out and closed the door, then came to a stop a few feet from him.

"Alice," she said. "Mine's Alice."

"Alice? How didn't I know your name until now?"

"Because you didn't ask," she replied as she shoved the garden gate open. "And I wasn't just going to tell you, was I?"

"Why not?"

"Because then, we'd be friends," she replied as she marched up to the front door, calling back over her shoulder. "And as a rule, I don't befriend nerds."

CHAPTER TWENTY-TWO

The scene at Stockwith Mill was very different from the previous day. An eerie quiet lay over the courtyard and the mill pond like a still morning fog. Lingering pieces of police tape along the driveway flapped in the breeze in place of wedding ribbon.

Before George had even pulled onto the driveway, the office door was flung open, and Ethan St Claire was striding across the driveway. He didn't look threatening — which would be difficult with those rosy cheeks and kind eyes — but he did seem agitated.

"Inspector Larson," he said, his voice conveying an unwelcome shock at seeing them again so soon. "Your team finished up last night, didn't they? I thought this nightmare was over."

"It is, for the most part, anyway."

"No sign of that Uncle Pete fella?"

"The investigation is still live, so I'm afraid I can't divulge details," George told him. "But there's something I wanted to check out for myself."

"Oh?" said Ethan, visibly disappointed. "Anything I can help with?"

"No, thank you," George said, pulling his coat around his chest and burying his hands in his pocket as though preparing to enjoy a casual afternoon stroll. "Would you have any objection to us taking a walk up to the field and having a closer look at the stream?"

"No, should be fine. Won't be long, though, will you?" Ethan said, clearly straddling the line between wanting to dismiss them from his property and wanting to seem like a team player.

"We'll be as quick as we can," George replied, doing his best not to commit.

"Alright," Ethan replied, and he watched as Ivy and George walked past his open front door towards the little bridge. Molly the collie waddled out, sniffing at the air as dogs do, her tail wagging as though she recognised their scent. "She'll probably follow you," Ethan called out, his hands on his hips. "Is that alright?"

"No complaints from me," Ivy replied, bending down to scratch the dog behind her ears, and together, the three of them crossed the little bridge and walked up into the field.

The footpath was uneven following the rain, but Ethan and his wife had done a grand job of making it passable, cutting a fresh route through the grass to one side.

Seeing as this was Ivy's first visit to the field, George took the chance to relay the information he had gathered before. He started at the pool in the top corner of the field. Once they reached it, he stepped back so Ivy could see the child-sized pipe that served as an overflow from the pool into the stream that wound through the property, past the defunct waterwheel, and into the mill pond.

"Too small for Ryan Eva," she said, stating the obvious.

"Which means," George said, walking east to where the pipe fed out to a smaller stream filled with tree roots and branches, "the body had to have entered the water from this point onwards."

"Not exactly a clear route, though, is it?" she said, kicking one of the larger branches that would easily snag a piece of clothing.

"Unless there was a downpour. Ethan said it's happened before that all sorts will wash up after heavy rainfall. Even if Ryan's body did get caught here, the higher water levels would've released him."

Ivy nodded and went to look further downstream. George followed and wondered if she was thinking the same as him as they followed the grassy bank. As usual, she was.

"No rocks here," she said. "If Ryan Eva and his attacker had a struggle by the water, there aren't many rocks nearby that they could've grabbed in the moment. A clump of grass maybe…"

She trailed off, coming to a patch of grass closer to the water-mill. Molly had indeed followed them up from the mill and was currently sniffing at an innocuous patch of grass. Like a hunter tracking its prey, Ivy bent down to touch it.

"What is it?" George asked.

"I don't know," Ivy said. "Just looks flatter here, doesn't it? Or am I imagining it?"

"Maybe," George said, joining her. "There might have been a struggle here. That would fit Pip's theory."

"Not *all* of Pip's theory," Ivy said, still scanning the ground for even one rock amongst the grassy bank.

As Ivy was talking and pacing, George was busy kicking off his shoes and taking off his socks.

"What we really need…" she said, turning around and stopping in her tracks. "Guv?" she said, her voice somewhere between a laugh and genuine concern. "What the hell are you doing?"

George bent on one knee, rolling up his trouser leg before switching to do the same thing to the other. He pulled both up to just below his knees. "Detective work," he answered with a wink, then plunged into the shallow river. The water came up to the middle of his shins and was icy cold, which, combined with the bed of sharp stones beneath his feet, made for quite an unpleasant experience.

"Now I've seen it all," Ivy said, tugging her phone from her pocket. "Can I get a photo for the others?"

"Don't you dare," he said.

"Ah, come on. It'll be good for them to see how real police work is done."

George opened his mouth to reply, but his toe connected with something alien to the tiny stones.

"Smile," she said, but he ignored her.

He unbuttoned his shirt sleeve and rolled it up to his elbow, then plunged his hand into the river and winced at the prick of cold. Molly stood at the bank and barked at his reaction, as though warning him of the madness of it. But then his fingers closed on it. A palm-sized rock that had been smoothed by decades — perhaps centuries — of flowing water. Being careful not to slip on the mossier stones, he turned around and found Ivy holding her phone up, either videoing him or taking photos.

"Never mind that," he said. "Bag. Now."

Smiling, she pulled a clear evidence bag from her inside pocket and, holding it open, reached out for him to drop the stone into it. She turned it over and around as though expecting to see blood or hair on it, but such hope was naïve. Life was never so kind.

"I'm not saying it was that one exactly," George said. "But let's assume that the scuffle had already let them into the water before the attacker was able to reach a rock with which to hit Ryan Eva. Let's send that off to Katy. See if she can match the style of stone to the granules in his head wound."

"But it's smooth, guv," Ivy said. "Surely we'd need a rock with rough edges."

"Ah," he replied. "I was hoping you'd say that." He reached a hand out for her to help him climb out, and the grass was pleasantly soft and warm comparatively. "That rock was half-buried."

"So?"

He held his hand out again, the hand he had plunged into the water.

"Feel it."

"What?"

"Just feel it, will you?"

She ran her fingers over his skin, then rubbed her forefinger and thumb together.

"Grit," she said.

"Grit," he agreed, beaming. "Even if we found the exact rock, the chances of getting anything off it to use as evidence are minuscule and almost certainly arguable.

"So what use is it?"

"It means we have a theory, Ivy. When whoever it was picked up a stone to bash Ryan Eva with, they also collected the grit. The sand." He smiled at her. "That's what was in his head wound."

"Alright," Ivy said, placing the rock in her endless rain jacket pockets. "But don't you think someone would notice one of the wedding party walking around here soaking wet?"

"That's if it *was* one of the wedding party," George said. "Remember, we still can't rule out that this was an outsider. Someone who had nothing to do with the wedding at all. For now, I'm more interested in what the hell Ryan Eva was doing here. How did he get here? Did somebody follow him? Did they know he was going to be here?"

Ivy looked around. "I don't know."

"I know you don't know, Ivy. I don't know either. That's why we need evidence," he said, allowing the automatic to-do list to stretch out in his mind. "I want local CCTV to track his movements. That means road cameras—"

"He didn't have a car, guv, remember."

"Bus cameras then. How would you get here? Taxi records. Get onto Campbell. Tell her to check everything she can think of. I want to know his movements on Friday morning."

"Byrne and Campbell are dealing with the family," Ivy said.

"Anyway, they're already building a profile on Adam Potter and finding out where Melissa Hale works to go talk to her. I don't think we can put them on this as well. Getting hold of all that CCTV could take days."

"You're right," George said. "You know what we need, Ivy?"

"A bigger team, boss."

"We need a bigger team," he replied, pulling out his phone.

The call rang six times, and George thought it was going to ring out before it was answered. Whether or not it was projection, he imagined the man looking at George's name on his screen and purposefully waiting to answer it as part of some stupid powerplay.

"George," Tim said eventually. "How are you getting on?"

"Slowly," George replied. "Which is why I'm calling."

———

Campbell knocked four times, twice as many as George. She felt it gave more urgency to the situation and set a precedence of control. On average, she thought that the door was opened twice as fast as a result, and indeed, the door was opened in a matter of seconds by a middle-aged man wearing a white t-shirt and jeans. His hair was receding, and his moustache reminded Campbell of an eighties TV show. But behind his silver-framed glasses were kind eyes that flicked between her and Byrne innocently.

"Can I help you?" he asked, as if he had expected one of them to speak first.

"Ian Eva?" she asked.

"I am," he said, stretching the words out to guard his initial reaction.

"My name is PC Campbell, and this is my colleague, PC Byrne. We wondered if we might have a word."

"Well, I—"

"Is your wife home?" she asked. "It might be best if we speak to her."

"I don't have a wife," she said.

"You are Ian Eva, though? Father of Ryan Eva?"

"I am. But his mum isn't around anymore." He seemed to be gaining a sense of the purpose of their visit. "What is this about, please?"

"We would like to talk to you about your son, Ryan. May we come in?"

The man's expression dropped like a stone in water. But he stiffened his resolve and turned his back on them. He waited by the open door and ushered them inside.

He gave the impression that this was not the first time he had opened the door to police officers. He knew what to do and the game he had to play in the situation. "Should I make tea?" he asked.

"No, thank you," Campbell said quickly, to which Byrne agreed.

"Of course," Ian said, pointing them to the first door on the left that led into the living room. The house was something between a family home and a bachelor pad with its oversized TV and minimalist log burner. But it lacked the features that made a house a home. There were no photos on the mantlepiece or useless trinkets that may have been given as Christmas gifts or bought on family holidays. Instead, there were only artistic, black-and-white photos, presumably taken with the collection of vintage cameras on the bookshelf. Nobody could guess that this man had a son, at least not from his house.

As soon as Campbell and Byrne sat on the sofa and Ian Eva took the armchair, he spoke. "What's happened? What's he done?"

He had got straight to the point, and Campbell decided to give him the same grace in return. "Mr Eva..." she said slowly, knowing that this was as important a moment in her career as it was in his life. She tried to steady her voice, but it had a slight shake to it, like the vibrato of a violinist's fingers. "I'm sorry to tell you that your son, Ryan, was found on Saturday afternoon."

"Found? What do you mean, he was found…?"

"He's dead, Mr Eva," she said softly. "I'm sorry."

He stared at her quizzically.

"Dead. Ryan is dead. My Ryan," he said. It was not a question, just a statement of fact, as though he knew it was true before she had confirmed it. Byrne shuffled uncomfortably next to Campbell but thankfully stayed silent.

"Yes," she answered. "I'm afraid so." The man's eyes were as dry as a desert, but his jaw was clenched as tight as a vice, as though keeping them so demanded every last ounce of his energy. "I realise this is a lot to take in—"

"What happened?" he said, cutting her off, and she noticed a crack in his voice.

"We're looking into the cause of death," Campbell said. "But we can tell you that he was found in the mill pond at Stockwith Mill." Immediately, the man's eyes raised in recognition.

"Stockwith?"

"Do you know it?"

He shook his head dismissively. "Well, yes, but…" His voice petered off. "I'm sorry. I'm just finding this…"

"It's okay," she told him. "You take your time."

"Stockwith Mill. It's not far from here. I drive past it all the time."

Campbell didn't reply, but she knew exactly how far away it was.

"But he's out in Skeggy. He doesn't drive."

"Like I said, unfortunately, I can't provide any specifics."

"But he was killed." Again, there was no question. "It wasn't an accident, or…"

"We're treating the death as suspicious."

"So, what do you want from me?"

"Well, as his next of kin, we're obliged to tell you."

"Right," he said.

"And I'm sorry to say, but we do have some questions we need to ask."

"Questions?" he said. "Look, I don't know what he was doing there. I don't know how he could have got there or why he would have wanted to. I don't know what help I could possibly be. I don't know what to tell you."

"You could tell us where you were," Campbell said quickly. Too quickly. As soon as the words left her lips, she regretted how quickly she had spoken them.

A terrible silence followed, like the silence before a storm.

"I'm sorry?"

"It's a formality," she said. "I just need to know where you were so we can eliminate you from our investigation."

"You need to know where I was," he repeated quietly.

"Like I said..." She was floundering, and she knew it; her heart beat fast. She struggled and failed to pick up her voice. "We just need—"

"How dare you," Eva said, slowly rising to his feet. "How dare you come into my home and tell me that my son has died and then, in the next breath, accuse me of killing him?"

"That's not what I—"

"You're all the same. You see the name Eva and jump to conclusions. Well, let me tell you..." He took a step forward. Campbell prepared herself for some kind of outlet from the man — verbal or physical. But before he could finish, she noticed a shape in her peripheral rising.

Byrne took a step forward, placed the flat of his hand against Eva's chest, and spoke calmly. "Mr Eva, please sit down."

The two men stared at each other. Campbell had never realised how tall Byrne was. She hadn't even noticed him until they had started with Larson a couple of months ago.

Slowly, Mr Eva relented and sat back down in his chair before throwing his head into his hands. Only then did Byrne take a step back, and he remained standing for the duration.

"Mr Eva," Byrne said, his voice strong and confident, "during each of our investigations, we follow the same processes. Once we've identified the victim, we talk to those closest to him or her and determine their whereabouts at the time of their death, and to gain a better understanding of the victim's last few days."

"The victim?" Eva said as if the word had a sour aftertaste.

"We need to develop a timeline of the events leading up to his death, sir—"

"Sir?"

"You would be helping us with our investigation if you told us where you were that afternoon. My colleague was by no means accusing you of anything. But you have to understand that should we identify your son's killer, Mr Eva, his or her defence lawyer, will be looking for holes in the investigation."

"Holes?"

"Areas we haven't covered. Questions we haven't asked," Byrne said. "It wouldn't take much to convince a jury of reasonable doubt. In which case, whoever is responsible for your son's death could walk free on little more than a technicality."

"What? All because I wouldn't tell you where I was? Give over."

"But what if everyone we spoke to had the same response? Imagine how that would look."

"We need to ask the questions, Mr Eva. We're not accusing you. We're merely building an investigation," Campbell said. "We're on your side."

"She's right," Byrne added.

Perhaps it was something about the presence of a man's vocal resonance, but Byrne's words seemed to calm Ian Eva.

"I just can't believe he's gone," Ian said, no longer trying to repress his tears. "He just got out. He just got the chance to start his life again." He looked up, not at Campbell but at Byrne. "I know my son isn't perfect," he said. "But he had nine years of rehabilitation. He bettered himself. I saw it in him. He didn't deserve this."

"I agree with you," Byrne said. "Ryan did his time and deserved a fresh start." He sat down before him, elbows on his knees. "That's why we're investigating his death. That's why we're going to find out who did this to him. And that's why, Mr Eva," he said slowly, "we need to know where you were on Friday afternoon."

CHAPTER TWENTY-THREE

The feeling had only just returned to George's feet when they reached the first-floor corridor of the police station. Ivy headed straight to the incident room to begin looking into developing CCTV evidence of Ryan Eva's movements on Friday morning. George, however, kept going to the very end of the corridor. He paused at the last door on the left where a gold-plated plaque read, *Detective Chief Inspector Timothy Long*.

He knocked twice and waited for Tim to respond. Given the tone of the phone call, he felt it best not to kick the hornets' nest any further.

"What is it?" came the eventual response.

"Oh, George," Tim said, as though he hadn't been expecting him. "Come on in."

George entered the room and sat down opposite Tim without a word; then, fearing he was presenting a moody silence, he said, "Thanks, Tim." So that was what their friendship had become, a back-and-forth of loaded silences and an overthinking of every single word.

"How's the Stockwith Mill investigation going?"

George took a deep breath as though he was about to blow up a balloon of information.

"We identified the body as belonging to one Ryan Eva. He was released from prison seven months ago, so his DNA was on record."

"What did he do?" Tim asked.

"Sexual assault against a minor." Tim raised his eyebrows, but, to his credit, he chose not to interrupt. "Campbell and Byrne have informed his next of kin. Ivy and I have been to see the victim of that sexual assault, Melissa Hale. She said Ryan had contacted her before his death. So that's one lead. Plenty of motives from her, her father, and her ex-boyfriend."

"Anything else to go on?"

"The wedding party. We believe Ryan was killed during the wedding rehearsal that took place the day before his body was discovered. Doctor Bell confirmed the cause of death as drowning, but he also had a nasty wound to his head. The theory is that he was knocked unconscious and subsequently drowned."

"Anything to substantiate that theory?"

"As it happens, yes. DS Hart and I have just returned from the crime scene. We think we found where the body entered the water."

"Evidenced?"

George shook his head.

"There looked to be evidence of a scuffle on the bank, and we found pebbles in the water, any of which could have been used as a weapon," he said. "But any DNA would have been lost, and if Katy Southwell and her team had discovered anything on the bank, we would have heard by now."

George finished his monologue and allowed Tim time to process the information, hoping that he could analyse the situation independently without needing to explain it in further detail.

"Why was this man-."

"Ryan Eva," George added.

"Right. Why was he at the wedding rehearsal?"

"We don't yet know," George said. "But he was wearing a suit."

"To the rehearsal?" Tim said. "Rehearsals are usually informal affairs."

"Sorry?" George said.

"They're informal. These days, anyway. It's not like when you and I were married, George. People don't make an effort, do they?"

An image of Grace all those years ago moved across George's mind. How wonderful she looked.

"George?"

"Sorry?"

"I asked if anybody recognised him?" Tim said.

"Of course. Only seen by the bride, the groom, and the photographer," George said. "Thankfully, the owner of the mill is a sharp chap. He managed to keep everyone inside the bar area where the wedding breakfast was due to take place. All eighty of them."

"But you didn't ask anyone to have a look?"

"What? No, of course not." George said.

"Surely you had the perfect opportunity to find out who he was and what he was doing there-."

"Who should I have asked, Tim?" George replied. "The bride? The bride's father? Christ, they were all emotional enough as it was. Imagine the backlash I would have got if I'd had asked a member of the public to have a quick lookie-loo at a dead body? It was hard enough keeping them off social media."

Tim nodded, then shrugged.

"I suppose," he said.

"I had to make a call, Tim. I know what I could have done, but under the circumstances, I felt that protecting the guests from seeing the body and protecting us from social media was the most appropriate path."

"And he wasn't on the guest list?" Tim asked. "This, Ryan Eva."

"No."

Tim frowned, relaying a confusion George himself felt. "Next steps?" he asked.

"We're gathering Eva's movements on the day he was murdered, how he got to the venue, when, and who was there when he arrived."

"You'll need access to CCTV and ANPR cameras. You'll also need to track his phone," Tim said while George nodded along.

"Exactly. That's why, as I said on the phone, I need more bodies."

"What about Byrne and Campbell? Aren't they holding up?"

"They're focusing on Melissa Hale. And they're great," George clarified. "That's why I want them on my team full-time. I want them out of uniform. It's not a promotion, so you won't have to clear it with whoever holds the purse strings. I want them to move sideways, from PC to DC. They're hungry, Tim. They have potential."

"But?"

"But they're human. They're not robots. As good as they are, we can only do so much. Jesus, I've got the media all over this. If we drag our heels, they'll all over us. I need bodies to do the groundwork."

Tim sat back as though giving it a long, hard think. "I don't know," he said. "Are they ready for the move? Campbell, maybe. She's been in the game for a while. She's confident. Everyone knows that. But Byrne? I'd hardly even heard of him until two months ago when you took him under your wing."

"Well, that's your loss. He has potential, Tim. You know how it is. Good officers get lost in the politics, in the gossip, and in the assumptions people make before they can prove themselves. Some people just need to be given a chance."

"And has he stepped up to that chance?"

It was George's turn to offer a loaded silence.

"He's got potential, Tim," he said honestly.

"Is that good enough, George? I'd be happy to recommend a more experienced officer. Someone who might be looking to move into a major crimes career path. You said it yourself; the media are all over this. One wrong move by any one of you, and…"

"If you're asking if he's experienced enough never to make a mistake, then no, he's not ready," George said. "But were you ready? I know I wasn't. And I know I worked damned hard and still made mistakes."

Tim paused for thought. He fiddled with his pen while he deliberated.

"Let's see how he does on this investigation, but if he's not ready," he said, closing the file on his desk as though closing topic, "then he's not ready."

"He'll be ready," George said.

"And in terms of these additional resources…" Tim said, pausing as though about to announce the winner of a singing competition. "I have two for you. They work well as a team. They've been in the force for about eight years now, so they have experience on the ground."

"But?" George asked, mirroring Tim's earlier question.

"But they're not readymade, George. You're not going to find another Ivy, not in this neck of the woods. These lot are rough around the edges. They need sculpting."

George nodded, thinking of Byrne and his rough edges. "I think Campbell is the closest thing to an Ivy I'm going to get. I'll take whatever you have."

"Don't make me regret it, George," he said. "I fought for months to create a consolidated major crimes unit here. The area needs it. And whether they know it or not, the public wants it. They deserve it."

"Well, I'm glad that's settled," George said, rising from his chair and starting towards the door. "You won't mind when I put in for more resources then, will you?"

"Just…just make it work, George."

"If you want it to work, Tim," he replied. "Then I'll need the people. If it doesn't work, then you won't need to look any further than this office to know why."

"You'll need to be patient," Tim said, ignoring George's remark. "Major crimes is new ground for most of the officers here. They're used to breaking up fights on the high street and handing out crime numbers. Start them slowly. See if they're up for the job."

George felt a grin forming on his face.

"Oh, don't worry about that," he said. "I've got just the job for them."

CHAPTER TWENTY-FOUR

PC David Maguire sat in the waiting area tapping his foot on the linoleum floor with such zest and for so long that Sophie couldn't take it any longer. She pushed her foot over the top of his and stepped on it gently, supporting the move with a hard, warning stare. David leaned forward instead, putting his elbows on his knees and began tapping his fingers together. Then he ran a hand through his long, red hair and down to his thick beard, rubbing his chin as though it might give him answers like a magic lamp. He was a tall man — the Maguires were built like rakes, his ma always said — and indeed skinny, with sharp, blue eyes and freckled skin.

"I'm not sure about this," he said.

"Oh, are you nervous?" Sophie asked nonchalantly, scrolling through images on Instagram. "I couldn't tell."

"I'm not nervous about..." He nodded at the heavy, steel door in front of them or, more likely, at whatever lay beyond it. "That. I'm not sure about *this*. About joining Major Crimes. I like what we've got now."

"It won't be *that* different," she reassured him for the fifth time that day. "We'll just be working for a different team."

"Yeah, DI Larson, to be precise. Have you heard about him?"

"Only that he's been a copper longer than you or I have been alive," she replied, her West Country accent breaking through.

He crossed his arms and leaned in so that nobody could overhear. "He's a finicky bugger. Old school. No time for the likes of you and me."

She rolled her eyes. "Who told you that?"

"Everyone," he said. "Why does he need us, anyway?" he said. "He's already claimed Campbell and Byrne, God help them."

"I heard they're moving into plain clothes. So, putting two and two together, Larson needs people to do the grunt work: the legwork. Like you said yesterday, the important stuff." She looked up at him earnestly. "*God's* work."

"I didn't say it was God's work," muttered Dave, slumping down, and, to Sophie's despair, he began tapping his foot once more. "I just think people are too obsessed with moving up."

"PC to DC isn't a promotion—"

"Fine, *along* then. I'd be happy being in uniform for the rest of my career. At least I know I'll have a bloody job tomorrow. For all we know, this major crimes team might be decommissioned in a few months. You know they've shut down three major crimes teams in the past six months."

"Yeah, and they've consolidated them," Sophie told him. "Hence the reason why Larson is now here and not in Mablethorpe or wherever he was based." She shook her head at him. "Look, if it is decommissioned, then we'll just go back to what we were doing before. We won't be out on our ear. They'll have to find us something else."

"Yeah, but where?" he said. "Look, I'm happy doing what we do. I know it's not rocket science, but it's good work. It's a solid life. You know what they'll do when we move, don't you?"

"What?"

"Backfill," he said. "They'll have to. Our positions will be filled with officers from God knows where."

"Right?"

"And when this major crimes team proves to be useless, our jobs will have gone."

"Oh, for God's sake, Dave. What's the matter with you? Most people would jump at the chance. Honestly, if we do this for a year or two, we could go anywhere."

"I don't…" he started, then lowered his voice. It was at times like this, when his emotions were running high, that his Irish heritage became unmistakable. "I don't want to go anywhere. I'm happy here. I've a nice house, a nice girl, and a nice, wee garden."

"Well, I do," she told him. "I'd like to go back down south one day."

"Not back to Bristol? I thought your ex-husband was there."

"Not Bristol. London. That's where it's at for me."

"London? The Met? You're not corrupt enough. They'd sling you out for the way you talk." He laughed. "Or for being a bloody do-gooder. If you're not on the take, Sophie, you get nowhere."

"Don't believe everything you hear on the news."

"It's not *what* you hear on the news, Sophie. It's what you *don't* hear. That's what you need to listen to." She stared at him quizzically. "Ah, you know what I mean. Look, I've had my share of moving about. I finally found somewhere I can put some roots down, and now I'm here risking it all with some old codger who everyone tells me is a lunatic."

"He's not a lunatic."

"Well, his wife is. That's what I heard."

"Dave?" she hissed. "She's ill."

"Yeah, and why's she ill, eh? Because of him. He drove her to madness."

Sophie checked around to make sure nobody had entered the little waiting room.

"She has dementia."

"Yeah? Who told you that?"

She shrugged and turned away.

"I just heard it."

"Ah, just heard it, did you? Just like I heard, she was a nut job."

"If you carry on talking like that, it won't be Larson who ends your career: it'll be me," Sophie said. "She's ill. And anyway, it's none of our business. We shouldn't even be discussing it."

"So why are you?"

"Because my nan had it. It's bloody awful, right? It's like you have known this person all your life, then one day she doesn't recognise you. She's gone. She's still there, but she's gone." She calmed herself with a few deep breaths. "Just leave it, will you? And don't talk like that about his wife. It's not for us to know."

She turned away from him and his tapping foot and scrolled onto the next image on Instagram.

"Every rider knows," he muttered, reading over her shoulder, "that they're only as good as their horse. Oh, for Christ's sake, what a load of—"

"My God, you are in a mood today," Sophie said, locking her phone.

"I'm not in a mood."

"I've known you for eight years, Dave. I know when you're in a mood."

"I just don't see the point of it," he huffed. "It's like spending eight years doing a jigsaw. I've found all the edges, separated all the colours, and pieced together the wee horse and cart. Now I'm going to take three random parts and stick them in the fire."

"If that's supposed to be an analogy, it's rubbish," she said. "It makes no sense."

"It makes sense to me," he told her. "More sense than this, anyway." He huffed and puffed and fidgeted. "Where's our man?" David said. "I tell you, this feels like a windup. First job with a team we've never met, and we get given this. *This?*" He waved his hand around the room. "He's got to be having a bloody laugh. And where is he anyway, this fella we're supposed to meet?"

"He's still in the loo," Sophie said, returning to her phone. "And his name is Ian Eva."

"Ian Eva," David said. "Yeah, that's the one. What's taking him so long?"

"I don't know, David. Why don't you go and ask him?" she said, using his full name as a warning that her patience was wearing thin. He took the hint and sat back down, returning to his incessant foot-tapping.

Quite suddenly, the large double doors in front of them opened and out stepped a large woman in scrubs amidst a breath of icy air. Her sleeves were rolled up to the elbow, revealing a mass of random tattoos, and from beneath her neckline was the unmistakable head of a Welsh dragon. When the woman spoke, her strong accent confirmed Sophie's suspicions.

"Now then," she said, striding forward with an outstretched hand that Sophie was reluctant to shake, considering the circumstances. "Pippa Bell. Old George sent you, did he?"

"That's right," Sophie said, shaking her hand anyway. Pippa appraised them both with a keen eye as if waiting for an introduction. "I'm PC Sophie O'Hara. This is my colleague."

"David Maguire," he said, shaking her hand without standing, then returning to tapping his foot.

Pip stared at it until he stopped. Only then did she reply, "I'm ready when you are." She looked around the reception room for a man not wearing a uniform. "Where is he?"

"In the loo," David said.

Pip crossed her arms and leaned against the wall as though taking his absence as an excused moment for relaxation. "So, you're George's newbies, are you? Fresh blood, as it were."

"We think so," Sophie said. "Depends how this goes, really."

"Yeah, we haven't decided yet," David added.

"Well, you could do worse," said Pip. "Don't tell him I said that."

"And how exactly could this be any worse?" David said, making no effort to hide his displeasure.

Pippa smiled at his response as if enjoying his misfortune.

"You're not from round here, are you?" she said.

"What?"

"You're not from round here?"

"No, obviously not."

"Donegal?" she said, her eyes narrowing and her head cocking to one side.

David stiffened and sat upright.

"S'right," he said. "Rossnowlagh."

"Ah, thought so," she replied. "Did some surfing out there a few years back, I did. Froze my tits off." The comment was so far out of their world that both of their mouths hung open in surprise. "And you?" Pippa said, turning to Sophie. "Bath?"

"Close," Sophie replied. "I grew up near Bristol."

"Ah, I'm losing my touch."

"Don't tell me, you used to surf there," Sophie said as a joke.

But the humour was lost on the pathologist.

"There's no surfing in Bristol or Bath," she said as if Sophie was an imbecile. Then she lightened her tone. "Did a stint in Shepton Mallet though, back in the day. Before they closed the prison. Good times." She leaned in conspiratorially and winked. "Plenty of the local brew."

"Well, now we know who we all are," David said, clearly tiring of the woman after just a few short minutes.

"Ever heard of a DCI Freya Bloom?" she asked, to which he shrugged.

"No, should I have?"

"Count yourselves lucky," Pippa said. "You asked how this could be any worse. Thank your lucky stars you're not reporting into her. Wouldn't last five minutes with her, you wouldn't." Sophie smiled. She liked the woman. She liked the thick Welsh accent that fell out of her mouth like treacle. She felt they had a sort of kinship, perhaps some kind of connection via the Severn Bridge. "Look lively," she said, as Ian Eva's footsteps could be heard from the corridor. He entered the reception room, saw them, and then stopped.

"Sorry about that," he said quietly. "I was just..." He trailed off as though too tired to explain himself.

"No problem at all, Mr Eva," said Pippa, stepping forward. She didn't try to shake his hand but instead touched his arm gently. "My name is Doctor Bell. I will be escorting you through the identification today."

Ian Eva nodded, his face pale as though unaccustomed to hearing about his son in such formal language. "You can just follow me now," she said kindly and held open the door as though escorting him into a hotel or restaurant, leaving Sophie and David alone in the reception.

David puffed out. "I don't envy her that job. Not only do you have to cut open dead bodies, but you have to show them to their grieving relatives. How do you think she does it?"

"She probably thinks the same of us. How do we tell people that their loved ones have just died? How do we deal with witnessing some of the worst acts of humanity? At least she deals with people when they're already dead. The worst has happened. She has no responsibility to stop it from happening like we do."

"That's what it's gonna be like, isn't it?" David said. "If we take on this job, we're going to be dealing with the worst kind of people. Murderers. Abusers."

"Probably," Sophie said. "But think of the good we'll be doing. The satisfaction..."

Her motivational rhetoric was cut short by a terrible cry that rang out through the corridor and seemed to bounce off the waiting room walls like a lost soul.

David's eyes widened, and slowly, he turned to face her. "Yes?" he said. "You were saying something about satisfaction?"

CHAPTER TWENTY-FIVE

The double doors opened automatically as Byrne and Campbell approached the hotel. They walked into the reception to be met by a tall, middle-aged, thin-faced woman whose eyes grazed upon their uniforms but whose expression of neutrality gave nothing away.

"Good morning," Campbell said. "My name is PC Campbell, and this is my colleague PC Byrne. We are looking for Melissa Hale. Is she working today?"

She glanced around the reception, which had been designed to reflect that timeless elegance Campbell associated with snobbery and the upper class. The walls were oak-panelled, the carpet was of rich reds and royal blues, and the furniture could have been delivered straight from the set of Downton Abbey, more pleasing on the eye than the backside.

"Melissa?" the woman repeated, checking some paperwork before her. "I'm afraid she's busy. May I ask what it concerns?"

"I can't really say," Campbell said apologetically.

A pair of double doors on the right-hand side of the room opened, and a man ambled through, his head bowed to his phone, offering just enough of a glimpse through the doors for her to realise the restaurant lay beyond. She strode over to the still swinging doors and peered inside, seeing a waiter moving back and forth between tables, ferrying empty dishes and plates to the counter. "She's a waitress, isn't she?"

At this, the receptionist stood up. She was even taller standing, and with her shiny bob haircut, she could have been a villain in a Bond movie. "I'll get her for you," she said. "She's on a rather busy shift right now, so it might be best if you come back later."

"Talking to her now will be fine," Byrne said, and again, Campbell felt that sense of command in his voice. It was as if he had stepped out of a shroud, revealing himself for the first time. Either that, or she was paying him more attention since feeling that strength in his shoulder. He stood still, just as he had in Ian Eva's house, exhibiting a patient authority. The receptionist was clearly less than impressed.

"We're about to serve dinner. I'd prefer it if our guests were not interrupted by the sight of...you two," she said as politely as she could. "Wait here a moment."

She pushed through the double doors and returned not long after with a young, blond woman with large, dark eyes carrying a huge, black tray the size of a car wheel.

"Hello," she said hesitantly, as though unsure whether or not to drop her hostess persona.

"Melissa?" Campbell asked, despite the name printed on her nametag. "Is there somewhere we could talk privately?" She eyed the receptionist, who was pretending to keep herself busy but had clearly tuned into their conversation.

"Margaret," Melissa said, "I'm just going to take five, okay?"

Despite her age and what she'd been through, Melissa carried herself well, and Campbell wondered if Ryan Eva had some part to play in that inner strength. Without waiting for a reply, she let them through another set of double doors off the reception and into what appeared to be an empty private function room. Chairs were stacked against one wall, the shutters had been pulled down to close off the bar, and various pieces of cleaning equipment had been parked in one corner. On the far side of the room, a few tables had been dragged, presumably to allow the cleaners access to the carpet. Byrne tugged a few chairs from a nearby stack, and they sat at a circular table designed for eight or more.

"Melissa," Campbell started, "I understand you met our colleague yesterday. DI Larson?"

She nodded. "Yes, I remember. The old bloke."

"And he explained that we're investigating Ryan Eva's death. Is that right?"

"Yes," she said, a hint of sadness in her tone.

"He mentioned that you told him that Ryan had been to see you before he died?"

For the third time, Melissa nodded, her expression revealing very little of her emotions.

"He came to see me last week. On Thursday. Dad was at work. I was in the house on my own." Campbell repressed the shudder that ran the length of her spine. That was the whole point of restraining orders, to keep filthy perverts away from their victims. It should never have been allowed for Ryan Eva to have turned up on her doorstep. Anything could have happened.

"And what happened, Melissa, when Ryan came to see you?"

"He didn't..." she said quickly. "You know? He didn't try anything."

"Well, what did he do?"

"He just wanted to talk. He stayed on the doorstep. He said he was making amends. He wanted to apologise to me face-to-face and reassure me that I would never see him again."

"Making amends? Did he explain what he meant by that?"

"No, not really," Melissa said. "Just that he'd been thinking that he'd had nine years to think about what he'd done, and he knew it was wrong. He said he wished he could go back in time and change things, and although he could never make it right, he could apologise and reassure me that nothing like that will ever happen again."

"Did he say anything else, Melissa? Anything more specific?"

"No, he just kept apologising. He said that he had been a stupid kid. That he had made a mistake. That he was so sorry."

"How did you feel? Did you feel threatened by him?"

She frowned. "No," she said. "No, I know I should've felt unsafe. I should've called you lot. But I don't know... Something about the way he spoke, the way he stood there. He didn't seem dangerous at all. He just seemed sad and full of regret." She looked at them with large, innocent eyes, young eyes that still saw the best in people, even after everything she had been through. "I thought it was quite brave of him, if I'm honest, to risk his parole to apologise to me face-to-face."

Byrne shuffled in his seat and cleared his throat with a sigh. Campbell shared his discomfort. While it might have seemed to Melissa an honourable act for Ryan to apologise face-to-face, it was not only against the law, but it could've triggered her trauma. It could've triggered his own unreliable reactions to seeing her. It had been far from selfless of him. It had been selfish. To force her to look him in the eye, see him again, and hear his apology.

"Did he ask you to forgive him?"

"No, he didn't say anything like that. He said he didn't have any expectations or agenda. He just wanted me to know that he was sorry."

Campbell hesitated, choosing her next words carefully. "Melissa, I'm glad that you didn't feel threatened by Ryan turning up at your house. But he shouldn't have done that. He served his time for what he did to you, and he should've left you alone to live your life without being reminded of what he did, even if his intentions were harmless. He had no right."

"I know," Melissa said, bowing her head as though she had something to be ashamed of. "That's why I didn't tell my dad. I knew he'd be angry. I knew he'd think that Ryan was there to get me on my own. He wouldn't understand. He's so protective. Too protective."

"Protective, how?"

She shrugged. "I don't know. I guess it's just normal dad stuff. He doesn't let me leave the house on my own. I'm not supposed to answer the door when he's not in. That kind of stuff."

Campbell nodded as though she empathised, even if it sounded far from normal.

"Look, I know that this is very hard to talk about. But we're trying to develop a timeline of Ryan's movements in the days leading up to his death. He came to see you on Thursday..." Campbell hesitated, unsure how to get an alibi from Melissa without putting words in her mouth.

"Did you see him on the Friday?" Byrne asked.

"No," Melissa said, frowning. "Only on Thursday. I was working on Friday, anyway."

"Until when?"

Byrne's voice was steady and calm, without a note of accusation. He sounded genuinely just curious.

She shrugged. "Had a breakfast shift, then Dad came to pick me up about one o'clock."

"Where did you go?"

"Just home."

"And your dad?"

"Dad went back to work."

"And what did you do?"

"When I got home?" she asked. "Not a lot. Showered. Netflix. You know?"

"Did you think about Ryan?" Campbell asked.

"What, on the Friday?"

"Sorry, I should rephrase that," Campbell said. "Did you think of him at all after he visited you?"

She scrunched her nose. "Not really. Maybe a bit, but I've got pretty good at blocking it out. My therapist taught me a few techniques."

Delving into her therapy was way beyond the remits of the investigation and introduced the risk of Melissa relapsing. It was far better to keep the tone objective.

"And can you tell us about your history with Ryan?" Campbell asked. "How did you know him? How did you meet?"

She stared at them both. "Don't you have it all on record? I mean, I had to tell the story a hundred times in court. Surely someone wrote it down?"

"You're right," Campbell said. "I did read the transcript. I know what Ryan did to you."

"You just wanted to hear it from me?"

"We just want to understand, that's all," Campbell said, to which Melissa relented, took a breath, and dug deep.

"We went to the same school. I didn't really know him. My boyfriend, at the time, played rugby with him. Always said he was a bit weird but a good runner. He was the guy on the side lines, you know, the one that they throw the ball to, what're they called—"

"The outside centre," Byrne said.

"That's it," she said, and Byrne smiled back at her, coaxing her on. Then her face dropped as though she remembered who they were talking about and why. "Anyway, that's all I knew about him. Before he started following me, that is."

"Your boyfriend?" Campbell said, remembering reading his name. "Is that Adam?"

"Yeah," Melissa said. "Adam Potter."

"And when was the last time you saw him?"

Melissa laughed. "*Adam?* I don't know, years? Not even sure he still lives around here." Byrne and Campbell shared a look that Melissa picked up on shrewdly. "What?"

"What makes you think he's moved away?" Byrne asked, to which Melissa shrugged.

"Don't know. Haven't seen him, I suppose."

Byrne nodded gently.

"Well, he does," he said. "Live around here, that is."

Melissa shrugged as if the fact mattered very little. And then the fact merged with the direction of the conversation. "You're looking into Adam? You think *he* had something to do with this?"

"We're considering every option," Campbell admitted.

Melissa laughed in denial. "Look, you don't know Adam, but he's not like that. He's a...sweetie. He's...nice."

"We do need to speak to him, Melissa. The last thing we want to do is drag the past up, not when you seem to be doing so well. But the fact remains that he was part of the original investigation, so we need to eliminate him from our enquiries."

"Because he beat Ryan up, you mean?"

Campbell slid a contact card across the table.

"If you see him, call us, okay?"

Melissa took the card, studied it, and then popped it into her breast pocket.

"He didn't do anything, you know?" she said. "Adam, I mean. He wouldn't have done anything."

"What makes you so sure?" Byrne asked. "If, like you said, you haven't seen him?"

Melissa shook her head.

"There's plenty of people out there with reason to hurt people like Ryan," she said as she rose from her chair. "You haven't even scratched the surface."

CHAPTER TWENTY-SIX

"I've been thinking," Ivy said, accepting the whisky glass that George passed her, as was their tradition after dinner. "We're going on about Mark Hale and Adam Potter having a motive for killing Ryan. But what about Melissa? I mean, If anyone has a motive—"

"Please don't tell me you want to drag her down to the station, Ivy. We've managed to avoid a social media catastrophe so far. Let's not fall at the next hurdle, eh?" George let his newspaper rest on his lap, and he removed his reading glasses. Like an old married couple, they had adopted routines, including their evening seating arrangement. Ivy was on the armchair, and George was on the sofa. She had a book that her busy mind refused to begin while he read the paper. George didn't have a TV, which was a pleasant change from having cartoons or mindless soap operas blaring all hours of the day. "The poor girl's been through enough. She was raped, if you recall."

"How could I forget?"

"And then the trial and the therapy. The adjusting to a life as close to ordinary as she could."

"And all the while, resent is building like a...like a volcano," Ivy suggested. "And then he shows himself. He rocks up at her house to apologise. God knows what she thought when she saw him."

"Forget it," he said, snatching up his newspaper. "While we have other leads, we will not be putting her through any kind of ordeal." He flicked the page over, unable to finish reading the piece on the devastation the government was causing with far less of a conscience than he. "Besides, you saw her. She's a sweet little thing. Imagine that getting into the papers or onto Tic-Tac."

"Tik-Tok."

"Whatever," he said. "It's not happening. I couldn't live with myself."

"Come on, guv," Ivy said. "You've been doing this long enough to know that *anyone* is capable of *anything*. Little old ladies can rob banks. Ten-year-old kids can suffocate babies. Sweet young girls can murder their abusers." He set the paper down again, this time closing and folding it. "She's the only person that for sure knew Ryan Eva was out of prison. We're assuming that she told someone, maybe her dad or someone. But she could've kept it to herself. She's a smart girl. She could've...I don't know; hunted him down and killed him without anyone else knowing. She could have followed him. She could have lured him there."

"So, who broke into Ryan's bedsit? Byrne said he saw a man on the CCTV. Edward said it was a man."

"Okay, she didn't break into his bedsit," Ivy said. "That doesn't mean that she didn't kill him on Friday afternoon."

"So now there's a team of them, is there? You just said she did all this alone."

"It's just a theory. I'm not saying that at all. But we're also assuming that whoever broke into Ryan's room also had something to do with the murder. They could've been two completely separate events."

"Well, how would she know that he would be at the wedding rehearsal? The people at the wedding rehearsal didn't even know Ryan would be there."

"Maybe she followed him," Ivy said.

"She doesn't drive. How would she have got all the way out to Skegness if she was doing all this on her own?"

"The same way he got to the wedding rehearsal. She took a bus or got a taxi."

"Oh, right, so she rode on the same bus as him, did she?" George said. "You do know that the bus doesn't go past the mill. It's a fair old walk from the main road at Horncastle to Stockwith Mill. Are you saying that not only did she manage to avoid being seen on the same bus as him, but then she got off at the same stop, in the middle of nowhere, and followed him? Was he blind, Ivy? Did I miss that in the report?"

"Oh...stop being so bloody flippant," she said. "I'm just throwing ideas around. We're missing something."

"We're missing a lot," he countered. "And until we've spoken to everyone else, we leave her alone, alright?"

"Well, somebody must have followed him," Ivy said.

"Well, that I do agree with," he replied. "We need to know how Ryan got to the wedding rehearsal and whether he was followed. If we recognise someone else on the bus or following his taxi, then that's our lead."

"Well, the team are working on it," she said. "Just something to bear in mind, that the only way anyone else could've known that Ryan Eva was out of prison would be if Melissa had told them."

"Well, not the only way," George said. "His parents would've been contacted, no? His mum and dad?"

"Sure, but Ian Eva was at a golf weekend from Friday to Sunday."

"Oh?"

"Byrne got it out of him," she said. "It was one of the things I wanted to talk about."

"And when was this conversation planned for?" he asked.

"Whenever I had a chance," she said. "Whenever your mood allowed me to."

"My mood?"

"Yes, your mood," she told him, then softened. "Guv, you're..."

"I'm what?"

She shook her head.

"I don't know. Different. You're...bitter."

"I'm trying to solve the murder that nearly every decent member of society would have been happy to commit. I'm trying to build a team; I'm trying to keep Tim Long off my back and, by way of proxy, your back, and Campbell's and Byrnes's. Right? I'm trying to keep whatever light the newspapers want to shine on us positive."

"And you're trying not to think about Grace," Ivy said flatly. She might as well have slapped his cheek. His glare was brief, but his disappointment stung more. "Sorry," she said. "I had to say something."

"You're wrong," he told her, reaching for his glass. His thumb traced the cut crystal design, and he held the drink up to the light.

"Which part?"

"The part about Grace," he said, and his voice cracked, so he sipped at his whisky. "I'm trying *not* to forget her."

"Sorry?"

"I'm trying not to forget her," he repeated, then peered at her over the rim. "Can I speak frankly?"

"I wish you would," she replied, hoping to lighten the mood, even if it was only by a degree.

He hesitated. His mouth was ajar, and he seemed to linger on the opening words.

"I...I struggle," he confessed. "I struggle to think about you and your marriage, the team, and work, and...and people like Melissa Hale. I struggle to think about them *and* Grace. It's like, an investigation like this lands on our laps, and all of a sudden, there's no room in my mind for her. Does that make sense?'

"It does," she replied almost instantly. "It's a flaw of the human brain, and if I'm honest, I'm grateful for it."

"Well, that's the difference between you and me, Ivy," he said. "I *don't want* to forget about her. There was a time when she sat at the forefront of my mind all day, every day. Now, it seems she only gets my attention when the cuffs go on, and the charge sheet is handed to the custody sergeant."

"That doesn't make you a bad person, guv."

"I know, but it's hard, you see? I fight for people like Melissa Hale. I mean, for God's sake, I'm fighting for Ryan Eva, a bloody sex offender. Why aren't I fighting for Grace? Why aren't I doing whatever I can to make her life more comfortable? I should be reminding her of years gone by. Of holidays, and cars, and dinners. I should be reminding her of times we laughed and times we cried." He took a long drink, then set the glass down on the sofa arm, rolling it around to swirl the contents. "There's no room," he said, tapping his temple with an index finger. "There's no room in here for her."

Ivy took a sip of her own drink and then set the glass down.

"I didn't realise, guv. Sorry, I thought—"

"Thought what?" he said. "That I was handling it?"

"Well..." she said shamefully. She thought about what he had said and the journey that lay before them. "Guv, can I speak frankly now?"

"Of course," he said, draining his glass and averting his glassy eyes.

"You're the strongest man I know," she started. "And you know what, you're the most compassionate, caring man, as well."

"I'd go easy on the compliments—"

"No, stop," she said. "Just stop with the flippancy. You are."

"Flippant?"

"Strong," she said. "And all the other things I said. Bloody hell, you just talked me down from questioning Melissa Hale. Not because you don't think she has a motive, because she does. And she had the opportunity, too. She had the full MMO guv, but you talked me down. Why? Because you're one of the good ones. You're a decent bloke. And if you want to tell me that Grace isn't at the forefront of your mind, then I say you're a liar. And that disappoints me."

"I'm sorry?"

"You can't tell me that you don't think of her every time you go up to bed, guv. You sleep in her childhood bedroom. I haven't been in there, but I'll bet you haven't replaced the bed, either. Judging by the repairs you did to the bed I sleep in, I'll bet you restored her bed and any other piece of furniture in there. And I'll bet that you think of her every night and every morning. I'll bet that when you drive down these lanes, you think of those times she was in the passenger seat. And when you go to that little tea room in Alford—"

"How on earth do you know—"

"About Willow Tea Rooms? Oh, I know you go there," she said. "I could even tell you what seat you sit in." She smiled sheepishly at him. "The wingback by the fireplace?" She softened again, realising that her tone belied the purpose of her rant. "Look, you can't be everywhere at once. It's nothing to do with age. It's a natural limitation. What matters is that when you do have the time, you spend it with her. Because, trust me, if you give this up to spend more time with her, you might as well book yourself into the room next door. The day you give all this up is the day you have nothing to live for."

"I have her to live for."

"Right, and on those days, when her mind is clearer than others, and when she recognises you, don't you think she's proud? Don't you think she admires you or tells people about how compassionate and caring her husband is and how he changes people's lives?"

"She does mention her husband," he admitted. "She just doesn't know it's me. To her, I'm just some bloke who keeps her company from time to time."

"But she does mention you, does she?"

"She does," he said.

She smiled and leaned forward, resting her elbows on her knees.

"Guv, not a day goes by without you mentioning her. She's a part of you. A part of your life. She always will be."

It was that final statement that really hit home. Jamie had been part of her life, but that was never going to be a forever thing, not like George and Grace.

"Anyway," she said, draining her glass. "If ever you fail to mention her, I'll be sure to. Don't you worry about that."

"I don't doubt it," he replied. He collected the newspaper from his lap and tossed it onto the armchair beside her. She glanced down and read the headline of the quarter-page article.

"Until death do us part?" she read. "Jesus, who thinks these things up?"

"Somebody with far less scruples than you or I," he replied.

"The consolidated major crimes team based near Horncastle is being put to the test in recent months, as Detective Inspector George Larson gets a grip on the third Wolds-based murder investigation in as many months. In light of the body of an unknown man being discovered during a recent wedding, Larson, with more than thirty years experience as a serving officer, had very little to say about the death, except that he and his team are treating it as suspicious. Having called the press conference with so little to share, perhaps he's hoping to control the flow of information in a bid to prevent the devastating scene from going viral..."

She slapped the paper down, unable to read on.

"How on earth have they managed to write a bloody article this size based on what you said?"

"The article isn't about Ryan Eva's murder, Ivy," George replied. "It's about me. They're stirring it up."

"Bloody right, they are. I'll bet it's that bloke who was at the front. The gobby one."

Preventing the devastating scene from going viral," she repeated. "Of course we are. The last thing the couple need is for everyone to start asking questions, let alone Ethan St Claire and his wife."

"What does he mean, viral?" George asked, and Ivy had to laugh. There had to be times when ignorance of modern technology and social media had its benefits.

"It means that the story gets picked up and shared by lots of people, resulting in millions of people seeing it. You know, if I were to post a video of a suspect being beaten up by police officers, that would go viral. People would be all over it."

"It depends on what the suspect did in the first place," he said. "If he was minding his own business, then fair enough."

"That's just it, guv. The public doesn't need to know what happened to form an opinion. They just need to know that officers beat up a suspect."

"Even if he assaulted one of them beforehand?"

"Even if he assaulted one of them," she agreed. "That's what the media does. It edits the information to suit the narrative. By the time the public learns that the officer in question was defending another officer who could be lying on the ground dying, it's too late. His career is done."

"And all because an edited video went viral. That's misinformation."

"That's what they call the news, guv," she said. "Speaking of which, we'll need to get them back to update them. The last thing we need is for this reporter to start making assumptions."

"Actually, I disagree," George said, reaching for the bottle. He topped up his glass and handed it to her. "I think we should play them at their own game."

"Sorry?"

"I'm not speaking to them," he said. "Or, more accurately, I'm not giving them the identity of the victim."

"Because nobody will come forward with any information if they know he was a convicted sex offender?"

"Exactly. What's the opposite of viral?" he asked, to which she shrugged.

"I don't know. Contained?"

"Right. Contained," he said, sinking a large mouthful of whisky. "That's exactly what we'll do. We'll contain it. I'll paint the bastard as a bloody saint if I have to." He held up his glass in a toast. "Let's see what social media does about that."

CHAPTER TWENTY-SEVEN

There was a slight variation to George and Ivy's usual Monday morning routine. George had been up early, as usual, and Ivy had come down late, and as usual, she had tipped her coffee into a takeaway cup to drink on the journey. Just as, whilst driving, George recited the list of the day's tasks, and Ivy added her own where appropriate. The change came when they entered the incident room. Byrne and Campbell had shifted their seats to the whiteboard, which was standard, but DCI Timothy Long was standing in George's spot. And if that wasn't change enough to skew George's organised mind, then the woman who stood beside him was. She was tall enough to see over Tim's head, slim enough that his body concealed hers in its entirety, and dark-skinned enough that her intelligent eyes shone like precious stones. Thick ringlets fell in a fringe over her face, and large, thick, white-framed glasses that wouldn't have looked amiss in the eighties sat prominently on the bridge of her nose. And if they had fallen off, the pearl spectacle chain around her slender neck would have saved them.

"Morning, Tim," George said, removing his coat and placing it on his chair before leaning back on the desk. "To what do we owe the pleasure?"

Ivy, too, settled at her desk and turned to meet the stranger. Byrne and Campbell watched quietly from their front-row seats.

"George, I'd like to introduce you to Ruby Farrant," Tim started. "Ruby, this is Detective Inspector George Larson." Tim beamed at him. "Ruby is a civilian researcher with CID."

"Ah, nice to meet you," George said, offering his hand for her to shake. "The force needs more people like you."

"That is," Tim continued, "until today."

George stared between them both.

"Are you leaving?" George asked her, and she grinned to show two rows of perfectly straight, white teeth.

"She's being seconded," Tim said on her behalf. "To you."

"To me?"

"You said you needed more bodies," Tim said. "I can't give you any more officers, but—"

"No, no," George said, feeling flustered for the first time in a long while. "A researcher?" He turned to appraise her. "My God, you've been sent from heaven, my dear."

Tim leaned in closer to her.

"You'll have to forgive George. He has a way with words."

She stepped forward to shake George's hand, gripped it professionally, and shook it once.

"I don't know about being sent from heaven, but it does give me something to work towards."

At George's prompt, the rest of the team introduced themselves, standing to welcome her.

"While I'm feeling generous," Tim said, nodding at the storage room to the left of the whiteboard. "I'm also going to turn that into an office for you lot. Now that you're up to what? Seven people? You need some proper space."

"That would be great," George said. He met Ivy's eyes briefly, which reflected his own suspicions. "Thanks, Tim."

"You're welcome," he said, then clapped his hands once. "Back to work then. We want this one cleared up quickly, don't we, George?"

George forced a smile, and once more, Ivy replied for him with a, "Yes, guv."

But as Tim started towards the door, George called after him, leaving the others to find a vacant chair for Ruby.

"Tim," he said, catching him up, and they stopped in the middle of the room, where CID operated. "You could've given me a heads-up. I only asked for two PCs."

"Ruby is the best there is, George. She'll be a brilliant addition to your team."

"And I'm grateful, don't get me wrong. We need a researcher. I just wasn't expecting it."

Tim turned around fully and lowered his head. "Look, I've been thinking, and you're right. You didn't have the resources you needed when you got here, and that was my fault. I'd like to make up for it. Now you have them, use them."

George paused, sure there was an insult in there somewhere, although he couldn't quite identify it.

"We did okay, I think. With the resources we had, I mean."

It was Tim's turn to hesitate. "That press conference the other day, George. It really opened my eyes to what other people have already noticed. Like I said, I don't want any drama on this one. And if I need to take Ruby from Horncastle CID to ensure you have the resources to do your job properly, then that's what I'll do."

"Well, it's appreciated."

"Good," Tim replied. "So if this goes belly up now, I'll need to look further than my own office door to find out why, won't I?"

The intent was much clearer that time.

George watched him go, giving himself time to quell the frustration in his chest. It rose almost every time he interacted with Tim Long these days. Then he clapped once and turned around, addressing his rapidly growing team. Ruby had found a chair and was pulling a laptop from the satchel at her feet.

George took his rightful place in front of the whiteboard to add a few much-needed names around the central name. *Ryan Eva*. "Ruby, you'll need to pick up what you can," he said. "Campbell will send you everything we have so far."

"That won't take long," Campbell added, then winked at Ruby.

"Let's talk this through," he said. "Melissa Hale." He wrote the name as he said it. "What have we got? MMO, please."

"We're going after Melissa?" Campbell said. "Why?"

"We're not going after her," George said. "But we'd be remiss to leave her out of the investigation. Ivy pointed out last night that she has more motive than anyone else to kill Ryan Eva. We have to consider her."

"The murder victim raped her nine years ago," Byrne said to Ruby, to which she simply nodded impassively.

"I see," she said.

"And the means," Ivy added. "She knew that Ryan Eva had been released from prison due to a courtesy call from the prison service."

"Which reminds me…" George cut in. He wrote a heading in the centre of the board, tasks, beneath which he outlined the first task, which he said aloud as he wrote. "Find out who the prison called about Ryan's release. I want to know who knew he was out. They keep records of that kind of thing. Byrne, that's for you. Check with the parole service before contacting the prison."

"On it, guv," Byrne said.

"Well, we know two people, at least," Ivy said. "Melissa Hale and Ryan's dad, Ian Eva."

George clicked his fingers at her. "That's an assumption." He moved his pen back over to the *Tasks* column and added another, which he read as he wrote, "Look into Ian Eva's golf alibi. He says he was at a golf weekend from Friday to Sunday. I have no reason to believe he was lying, but double-check it, would you? Byrne, you have the details, right?"

"Yes, guv. And will do."

"Good. Now, Melissa Hale. Opportunity?"

"She has an alibi," Campbell said. "She said she was at work at the hotel until one o'clock. That's when her dad picked her up."

"That still gives them both an hour to get to Stockwith Mill and kill Ryan," Ivy pointed out. "Pippa Bell stated the time of death was between twelve and two."

"What did they do after?" George asked.

"He dropped her home and went back to work," Campbell said. "And she showered and watched Netflix."

"Doesn't sound like an alibi to me," Ivy said.

"Still..." George said, writing a second task on the board. "Get access to hotel CCTV. Check if she's lying about being at work. Then, check ANPR for Mark Hale's car. Find out if he did go to work after dropping her off at home. If either of their stories is anything less than watertight, it's time to bring them in. Ruby," he said, tapping the task with a marker and disturbing the sound of her frantic typing. He had never seen a woman type so fast, not even Campbell. "Could you?"

"Yes, guv," she said simply, without looking up.

"Good." He moved on to the next name, which he gave its own space on the board. "Mark Hale."

"Motive is protecting his daughter from her recently released abuser," Ivy said. "Plus, he was charged for physically assaulting the victim."

"Ah, now, he wasn't charged," Byrne said.

"What?"

"Sorry, guv. We looked closer and Ryan Eva didn't actually press charges; not against Adam Potter, either. The assaults were recorded, but they were both let off with a warning. Ryan didn't want to take them any further."

"Why would he do that?" Ivy asked.

"Maybe he felt he deserved it," offered Byrne.

"Maybe," George said. "Well, for now, it doesn't change anything. The motive is there, and if no charges were made, then it's a fact we can take into consideration but not use as evidence. Understood?"

"Yes, guv," Ivy said, as if he was stating the obvious.

"Good," he said. "Means?"

"Anyone of them had the means to kill Ryan Eva with a hard rock," Ivy said. "It's possible that Mark knew that Ryan had been released if his daughter told him, although she says she didn't. Otherwise, we don't know how anyone knew Ryan was at the wedding rehearsal."

"Not yet," George said. "Which, again, reminds me." He added a third task to the board. "Look into buses from Skegness to Horncastle, and anybody alighting near the Stockwith Mill turn off. If you can't find anything, widen the search to local taxis. I want to know how the victim got to the wedding rehearsal. Road traffic cameras, bus cameras, CCTV, the lot. Once you've found him, look for any familiar faces nearby. We can only assume, for now, that someone followed the victim there."

"I can do that, guv," Ruby said.

George nodded at her. She was already proving very useful.

"Is there another word we can use other than victim?" Campbell asked.

"He is a *victim* of murder, Campbell," George said. "Whether we like it or not. Now, what else? Opportunity?"

"Same as Melissa Hale," Byrne said. "Picked up his daughter at work at one o'clock, took her home, then went back to work."

"Right, we won't know more until we get CCTV and some ANPR data," George said, with a nod to Ruby. "Let's move on." He turned and added a third name to the board. "Adam Potter. Task three," he said, writing it down, "I want a full report on Adam Potter, where he works, who he spends time with, what he does. I'm planning to speak to him today."

"Already on it, guv," Byrne said.

"Motive?"

"Revenge. He was Melissa's boyfriend at the time of the assault and, like Mark Hale, he has a history of assaulting..." Campbell hesitated. "The victim."

"And potentially wanting to win Melissa back," Ivy added.

"After nine years?" Byrne said.

"We don't all roll over and give in, Byrne," Ivy said. "Some of us fight for what we want. Maybe he wanted to protect or impress her."

"She didn't even know he was still local," he said. "When we spoke to her last night, she thought he'd moved away. Said she hadn't seen him for ages."

"In which case, he'll be easy to eliminate," George said, regaining control. "What's his MMO?"

"Pretty much the same as everyone else," Byrne said. "If we're assuming that Melissa told her dad about Ryan's release, then we have to assume that she could have told him."

"Right," Ivy agreed.

"Even if she hasn't seen him for years and thought he'd moved away," Campbell added. The comment was borderline insubordinate, but it was good to see her defend Byrne.

"Did you believe her?" George asked.

Campbell looked at Byrne. "It's hard to imagine she was lying."

"Well, let's find out," George said. He wrote down a few new tasks, making use of the space to get down his thoughts, hoping they might look more organised outside of his whirring mind. *Find out if Adam and Melissa are still friends.* "Use social media, phone records, whatever we can. We need to start corroborating these statements." He jabbed a full stop on the board, then slid the lid onto the marker. "Anything else DS Hart and I should ask Adam Potter when we catch up with him?"

"I have one," Ruby said, who had been silently typing away or accepting her hand of the tasks. George hesitated, rather taken aback. Up until five minutes ago, she hadn't even heard of these people. But then he said, "Shoot."

"You might want to ask how he knows Lucas Coffey."

The whole team silenced, stopped their notetaking, and turned to look at her with blank expressions. So out of context was the name that it took them all a minute to place it. But George was the first to remember, being the only one who had met Lucas.

"The groom?" he said. "At the wedding at Stockwith Mill?"

"Yes," Ruby said with a straight face.

"What makes you think Adam Potter knows Lucas Coffey?"

"Because," she said, turning her laptop to show a florally decorated copy of Nancy Wetherford and Lucas Coffey's guestlist. "Adam Potter was his best man."

CHAPTER TWENTY-EIGHT

"He was there?" Byrne said, his face scrunching into a combination of confusion, frustration, and regret. "He was at the wedding?"

"How did we miss this?" Ivy said to George.

"There were eighty-five people at that wedding," Campbell answered.

"You must've interviewed him," Ivy said.

But Byrne was already at his desk, scrolling through the witness reports he and Campbell had taken on the day.

"Adam Potter, best man," he muttered to himself as he did so. Then he stopped and dropped into his desk chair. "There he is. Best man. Ruby's right." He turned to her. "How did you get that guest list?"

"The bride made it on Canva and shared it on her Instagram, asking for advice on which floral border to use. Nancy Wetherford, right?"

"How do you know that?" George asked, torn between frustration that they had missed such a huge link and admiration at her ability to find it so early on in the team.

"Well, I did a bit of research based on the names." She nodded at the whiteboard. "It was just basic social media stalking. Nothing, really."

Ivy grinned at the potential of their new tool. Ruby Farrant would come in handy, indeed.

"Byrne, read that out." George nodded at Byrne's laptop. "What does that witness report say?"

"Adam was inside with all the guests when they heard Nancy scream. He doesn't have much else to say about it, to be honest."

"He would've been at the wedding rehearsal the day before," George said. "The day Ryan died." He tapped Adam's name with his marker pen. "This is it. This is a connection between the crime scene and Ryan's history of abuse. Adam Potter," he said, tapping his name with the end of the pen, "has the motive, the means, and the opportunity."

"That still doesn't explain how he could have known that Ryan would be at the rehearsal in the first place."

"Maybe he didn't know," George countered. "Maybe Ryan just showed up and caught Adam off-guard. Maybe they fought, and it got out of control. Someone smashed his head with a rock, for God's sake, and left him upstream from a popular wedding venue. It was hardly premeditated."

"Okay, but it still brings us back to the same place. Why was Ryan Eva there? What was *his* connection to the wedding?"

George turned to Ruby. "Do you think you can help us out?"

"Ryan Eva's connection to Nancy Wetherford's wedding," she repeated. "I'll do my best. Can I borrow a desk?"

"You can use any desk you like," George said. "Just get it done."

With that, she picked up her laptop and took it over to an empty desk in the middle of the room. George and Ivy watched her go, then their eyes met, and they both nodded their approval. He turned to the others. "Ivy and I need to go and speak to the Hales about Adam Potter," he said. "You two stay here. I want a full report on Potter ready when we bring him in. And help Ruby look into Melissa and Mark Hale's alibis. But before you do," he said, looking at Ivy. She nodded. The time was right. "We need to speak to you about something."

Campbell and Byrne both stopped writing in their notebooks and gave their full attention to George. He could see the apprehension on their faces, the focus in Campbell's eyes and the twitch of Byrne's Adam apple.

"I spoke to DCI Long earlier," George continued, "and he's given us the go-ahead to grow the team."

"Hence, Ruby?" Byrne said, nodding. "Makes sense to me."

"And two more," George said. "Maguire and O'Hara."

"Dave and Sophie?" Campbell said.

"Oh, so you know them?"

"Yeah, they're alright," she replied. "I'm a bit surprised about Dave though."

"Dave?"

"Maguire, guv," she said. "I thought he'd be in uniform until he retires."

"Plenty of officers are," George said. "The fact of the matter is, we're not the Met. We're a small rural station that just so happens to house the local major crimes team. Opportunities won't come thick and fast. If you want to move on, you have to take what you can get or look elsewhere."

"Are you speaking from experience, guv?" Byrne asked and then appeared surprised when George nodded.

"I am, actually. I made the move to Mablethorpe. Had I stayed here, I could have been sitting in DCI Long's office. Or, I might have stagnated. It's a call you have to make when the opportunity arises."

"What are you saying?" Campbell asked.

"I'm saying there's space for a sideward move." He stared at them both. "Do you remember what I said to you on my first day here?"

"You said that DCI Long had spoken to Sergeant Kerrigan

and that we'd be working with you for the foreseeable," Campbell answered, her voice breathy and muted with anticipation.

George smiled. Even though his memory was not what it used to be, he was pretty sure she had recited him verbatim. "And what did you say?"

"Yes," she whispered as quickly as she had that first day.

"And is that a path you'd still consider, having a few months' experience now?" he asked, still smiling.

"*I* would," Campbell said, exhibiting that same determined urgency with which she answered the phone, replied to emails, and delivered results.

Byrne, on the other hand, didn't reply.

George turned to him. "What about you?"

He shifted in his seat and swallowed. "I like the work," he said. "I do. I love it, actually. And I appreciate your support. I just...I have some work to do..." He glanced at Ivy. "I'm aware of where I need to be, and I'm working on it."

Ivy didn't roll her eyes or dismiss Byrne's trepidation. Instead, she held his gaze, studying every detail of his face.

"Is this because I called you out the other day because you spoke out of turn?" she said simply. "Acting inappropriately in this department can cost lives. We are working with life and death, and if the public doesn't trust us, if they don't think we're taking this seriously when their loved ones are killed, then our jobs become harder, and then nobody wins."

"Is there something I should know?" George asked.

"No," Ivy said, then she leaned forward, still holding Byrne's gaze, which, to his credit, he matched. "If you can't take a little bit of criticism, then you're right. This isn't for you. Major Crimes is a whole different ballgame. It tests everything you thought you knew. About yourself. About society. About humanity. You have to constantly reassess your abilities and decide if you can keep going. It's not a straight line, and it's not easy. And I will not sit here and promise that I will never criticise you again or call you out for making a mistake. Because that's what the job is, and that's how you get better at it. You want something cushier, something lighter, something less challenging?" She sat back, still only with eyes for Byrne, although the words seemed to be hitting Campbell hard enough, too, who watched on with wide eyes. "Then this isn't for you."

George allowed a long silence to let Byrne absorb this information. Then, he offered the softer approach. That's why he and Ivy were such a good team. They balanced each other out.

"If I'm not going to be privy to detail, let me say this," George said. "I want you on our team, Byrne. In my eyes, you already *are* on our team," he said honestly. "Campbell, how about you? You can speak frankly. We're all grown-ups."

"Yes," she said with that same urgency.

"Ivy?"

Her eyes had not moved from Byrne's, who stared back in hope.

"Yeah," she said. "I want you on our team. Of course, I do."

"You're sure?" George asked, to which she grinned and winked at him.

"I'm sure," she replied. "Most people would have got up and walked off after hearing what I just said. The fact that he's still sitting there speaks volumes, guv."

Byrne smiled, and she nodded at him.

"Good, well, that's that, then," George said, clapping once before addressing the two PCs. "You'll need to sit your NIE exams."

"Oh Christ, they're brutal," Campbell said. "I heard one of the CID lot talking about them. It's all legislation and case law, right?"

"Unless you want to carry a crime reference book with you everywhere you go, you'll need to know it all," George replied. "And, of course, there's the advanced interview course, which you'll need to attend."

"The what?"

"It enables you to interview vulnerable or intimidated individuals," Ivy said, to which Campbell puffed her cheeks.

"And there's the CID course. Everyone has to sit that, of course," George added. "The name changes, but it's all the same thing."

"Anything else?" Campbell asked.

"Plenty," George said. "It's not an easy journey. You'll have to develop a portfolio of complex crimes you've worked on and demonstrate an understanding of the CPS—"

"And the IOPC," Ivy added.

"Right," George said. "Like I said, it's a long road, but I think you'll find it rewarding."

"And how long do you think this will take?" Campbell asked. "Roughly, I mean. An estimate."

"Fast track?" Ivy said, looking at George for support. "A year."

"A year?" she said. "Are we being fast-tracked?"

"No," George said. "No, look, this is a small team. I can't afford to let you go for one day a week, let alone two or three."

"We'll have to do this in our own time?" Byrne said.

"Like I said, it's a rewarding career when you get going," George told him. "When you've done that, let Ivy know, and she'll get the changes done on the back end. There's no change in salary, yet, but you won't be working shifts anymore, and I expect you to dress appropriately. Plainclothes means plain clothes. No jeans, no slogans, no logos, no fun. Got it?"

"Right," Byrne said, a little wide-eyed. "When do we—"

"Tomorrow," George said. "Ditch the uniforms. We might as well start as we mean to go on. If DCI Long has anything to say, I'll set him straight." He sat up straight and looked them both in the eye. "Happy?"

"Very," Campbell said.

"Byrne? Happy?"

He nodded, seeming a little surer of his decision.

"You won't regret it," he said, including Ivy in the response. "I'm going to prove I can do this."

"You won't know the ins and outs of my conversations with DCI Long, but when I tell you he has exonerated himself from any responsibility with regard to our success, you can be sure that that means it's me carrying the burden. If this all goes wrong, it's my head on the chopping block. So, for God's sake, don't let me down."

"No pressure, then," Byrne said huskily with an unsteady laugh, which faded when he realised nobody else had cracked a smile.

"Campbell," George said eventually, breaking the moment, "could you start with Ruby on the Hale alibis?" he asked, and with a brief look at Byrne, she rushed over to Ruby's desk. "Ivy—"

"Warm up the car?" she asked, looking between George and Byrne.

"If you would," he said, pulling the keys from his pocket and tossing them to her.

Then he turned to Byrne, who had lowered his head to stare at the floor. George crouched down in front of him, feeling it was important to be on his level - to hell with his knees.

"Listen, son. Can I give you a piece of advice?"

Byrne's eyes slowly rose to meet his.

"Okay," he said, tentatively.

"It's something my father taught me. And I can't promise I always stick to it, but it's served me well in the moments I remember to use it."

"What's that?"

"*Think*," George said, "Before you speak, take five seconds and ask yourself, do I really need to say this? Will it help? Will it make things worse?"

"But I—"

"Ah, ah, ah," George said, stopping him. "Take five seconds."

George watched him carefully as the lad took it in. "One, two, three, four, five." He waited. "Do you still need to say it?"

Byrne thought for a second more, then shook his head.

"Good." George smiled. "Do you know the saying about God giving us two ears and only one mouth?"

"I don't think—" Byrne went to say, but again, George held up his hand. Then, he counted up to five with his fingers. Byrne frowned, then at the count of five, his face relaxed. "So we can listen twice as much as we speak?" he said.

"Exactly," George said, patting his shoulder and leaning down to whisper in his ear. "And trust me, when you're dealing with Sergeant Hart, those five seconds could be the difference between a good day..." He dragged his coat from his chair and then returned to Byrne's ear, resting his hand on his shoulder. "And the worst day you've ever had."

CHAPTER TWENTY-NINE

From a visitor's perspective, the fields surrounding the single, narrow country lane were pretty, glorious, expansive, even. But to the familiar, they held a much deeper and darker meaning. A meaning that, as each day passed, George was relearning. They were places of work, of grit and dust, of history, of family, of lives and deaths, and so much more. Every inch of the Wolds had a story.

He pulled into the Hale driveway and took in the large family home, wondering how many stories the place had to tell.

He knocked twice on the large oak door, then looked around. There was not a car in sight; no sage-green Volvo; no anything.

"He's probably at work," Ivy said, nodding at the empty driveway.

"And Melissa?" he asked. "Do we know where—"

The turning of a key in the lock cut him off. The door opened to the limit of the security chain, and Melissa's face poked through the tiny gap. George wondered if that was how she had spoken to Ryan Eva or if the chain had been added after the assault.

Ivy stepped forward, perhaps assuming that a woman on the doorstep might be less of a trigger to an abuse victim.

"Hello, Melissa. It's me, DS Hart. You remember us, don't you?"

"How could I forget?"

"We just want to talk to you for a bit."

Melissa seemed to relax but remained frustrated. "You came to see me yesterday morning, and then two of your team visited the hotel last night. I had to work late to make the time up. What more do you want from me? I've told you everything."

"I realise that—"

"Do you know how difficult it is to keep going over it again and again?"

"I completely understand," Ivy said with a sigh. "And I promise we wouldn't be bothering you if it wasn't completely necessary. But this is a murder investigation, Melissa, and we need to ensure that we arrest the right person to prevent them from harming anyone else. You understand that, don't you?"

Melissa didn't answer. Rather, she hung her head and closed the door.

Ivy closed her eyes, then glanced up at George as if apologising for taking over and going too hard on Melissa.

Then they heard the rattle of the chain, and Ivy's eyes widened. She stepped back as the door opened fully to reveal Melissa beckoning them inside.

"Haven't got long, mind," she said as George stepped past her and into the hallway with Ivy close behind him.

The house was as impressive on the inside as it was on the outside. The spaces were clean and uncluttered, but it wasn't hard to imagine children's bikes and pushchairs nestled into the nooks, coats slung over the bannister, and muddy shoes scattered across the wooden floor. The style wasn't quite modern, but not quite old-fashioned or dingy. It was somewhere between the two. A hybrid, perhaps reflecting the occupants' combined tastes. For example, in the hallway, a framed, autographed poster of Taylor Swift hung above a cabinet, in which lived an antique ship in a bottle.

Melissa led them through to the kitchen, following the instinct of most people George visited in their homes. She immediately picked up the kettle, filled it at the sink, and put it on to boil.

"Milk, sugar?" she asked over her shoulder, opening a cupboard to pull out three cups and three teabags.

"Just milk for me," George said.

"Me too," replied Ivy.

George perched on one of the kitchen island barstools, hoping to ease Melissa's anxiety. At the same time, Ivy remained standing, hands in pockets, eyes ever watchful. It was these small psychological behaviours that differentiated George and Ivy, yet they worked so well together. George's relaxed posture would be easy to miss without the contrast of Ivy's rigid and authoritarian stance.

"Where's your dad?" Ivy asked as an opener. "At work, I suppose?"

"Yeah, he's down the suppliers. I don't know if he told you, but he owns a brewery nearby. Local beers, you know?"

"A brewery? I hear it's a growing industry again," George said. "The smaller breweries, anyway."

"That's what Dad says. I don't get it myself. They all taste the same to me." She pulled a face. "Like soap."

"You don't drink beer?" Ivy asked.

"I don't drink at all," she said. "Don't really like the feeling of losing control." The statement lingered in the air awkwardly. "Anyway, it's becoming more popular for people of my age. Sober curious, they call it."

"Probably because you can be recorded at any time doing stupid things while drunk," Ivy said, holding up her iPhone. "In our day, embarrassing moments stayed up here." She tapped her head with a finger. "And most of them were forgotten."

"There's that, and health reasons," she said, "I read somewhere that my generation smokes less, drinks less, and eats better than..." She hesitated.

"Us old farts?" George suggested.

"I wasn't going to say that."

George had read something similar and had seen drinking and smoking ruin many lives. Still, he couldn't deny himself a glass of whisky at the end of the day.

"He'll be back any minute," Melissa said, as though in warning. "Dad, that is." She placed two mugs in front of them and stood back in a similar position to Ivy, guarded. "So, unless you want to deal with him..." she left the statement open for interpretation.

"Adam Potter," George said, getting straight to the point. He watched for a reaction but saw none.

"What about him? They asked me about him yesterday, too."

"Who did?"

"The police. The two that came to see me. It was a woman and a bloke. She was a bit uptight, and he was..." She glanced over at Ivy, blushing. "He was alright."

"Ah, Byrne and Campbell, you mean?" George said.

"That's it. They asked me all about him. Don't you lot speak to each other?"

"We do. In fact, we've just spoken to them. But in light of some information that has come our way, I thought it pertinent to speak to you myself."

"What information is that?"

"Do you still talk to him?" George asked, ignoring her question. "I mean, you used to be close, didn't you?"

Again, Melissa frowned. "As close as you can be with a teenage boyfriend. I think we went out for about six months, what? Ten years ago?"

"Have you spoken to him since?" Ivy asked.

"Maybe a few times after we broke up. I mean, this isn't Lincoln, is it? It's not the city. But it wasn't some big whirlwind romance. It just fizzled out. I was going through a few things, as I'm sure you can imagine."

"Of course," George said. "But Adam, about that. He went after Ryan. I heard he beat the living daylights out of him."

Melissa looked between Ivy and George in silence. "Adam has nothing to do with this."

"I'm not saying he does, Melissa. But I'm right, aren't I? Adam *did* assault Ryan?"

"He was a teenager," she said. "He was dumb and angry. We all were. He made a mistake. That doesn't mean that he killed Ryan."

"How do you know, Melissa?" Ivy said. "Like you said, you barely know him anymore."

"I know him well enough. He's gentle, really. He just felt like he should do something, to defend me or whatever. You know what they're like."

"Exactly," George said. "He felt the need to defend you back then against Ryan. How do you know he didn't feel the same need three days ago?"

"Because," Melissa said, getting worked up now, "he didn't even know Ryan had been released. I sure as hell didn't tell him."

"So, to be clear, you haven't seen Adam for what, a few years?"

"No," she said. "I haven't seen him for a few years."

Then she hesitated, and Ivy was the one to pick up a slight tremor between her eyes.

"What is it, Melissa?"

"It's nothing... I just, well, I might not have seen him, but he has been in touch a few times. A message here and there. Usually at Christmas or New Year's, sometimes on my birthday, like he wanted to keep in touch, you know? But I just wanted to move on. To be honest, he always reminded me of that time and how difficult it was." She cradled the mug in both hands and resigned to honesty. "*That's* why we broke up. I just couldn't handle being with him, not after everything that happened."

"So it might not be beyond the realm of possibility," George said, "that Adam still has feelings for you?"

"Maybe..." Melissa said with a nonchalant shrug. "I don't know, maybe."

Hers and George's eyes met, sharing a similar understanding of the possibility. But the sound of a key in the front door broke the moment, and then the door slammed, sending a shockwave through the walls, as though someone had kicked it shut with their foot.

"Honey?" came a voice. "It's Dad. Are you here?"

"Oh God," Melissa said, looking between Ivy and George. "He's not going to be happy."

"Melissa?" Mark called again, an ageless worry sounding in his voice.

"I'm here, Dad," she said, as though used to easing his anxieties. "I'm in the kitchen."

They heard his footsteps on the stairs and above them as he walked across the floorboards. They sipped their teas in silence, waiting for Mark to join them and the inevitable fallout. George enjoyed the moment of peace. But soon enough, Mark's footsteps thudded down the stairs, and he entered the kitchen carrying a laundry basket in both hands.

He stopped in the doorway, and his face said everything that needed to be said.

He dropped the laundry basket beside the washing machine, saying nothing.

"Hello, Mr Hale," George said, pleasantly sipping at his tea as Mark Hale shoved the laundry into the machine.

"What are you doing in my house?"

He tossed a detergent capsule in with the dirty clothes, then closed the door and fiddled with the dial.

"We came to talk to Melissa."

Eventually, he stood and took a breath.

"Hoping to talk to my daughter alone, I suppose? First, you go to her work. That's right, she told me about that. And now you come here while I'm out of the house. Do you have any idea how inappropriate that is?"

"With all due respect, Mr Hale, your daughter is a twenty-two-year-old woman. It's perfectly acceptable for us to speak to her alone. And she has the right to speak to decline us if she so wishes."

He glanced at his daughter, who peered down into her tea.

"Melissa?" he said, to which she simply shrugged.

"It was just a word or two," she said.

He put his hands on his hips, then nodded at the hallway. "I would rather you leave now. If you wouldn't mind."

"Dad, please. It's fine," Melissa said.

"I mean it," he said, stepping up to George, who sat unmoved on the barstool while Ivy straightened. "Get out of my house."

"Dad, can you just stop? I want to talk to them. I want to know what's going on."

"You can't trust them, Melissa. They'll spin anything you say."

"They helped us last time, didn't they?"

Mark scoffed. "Eventually. And they only gave that creep nine years in prison. Now he's free to walk around again, doing whatever he wants." He turned to George. "Do you know what that's like? As a father? To know that he could show up here any time he likes?" Then he turned on his daughter. "And you tell me that they're helping? The only way they could help would be by keeping that freak locked up for the rest of his life."

"Mr Hale, I can promise you, we are only here to help."

"You want to help? Where were you when my teenage daughter had to go through what she did? Eh? Where were you when our family fell apart at the seams? Nowhere, that's where," Mark said, his voice trembling. "Don't make me repeat myself, Inspector. Please, don't force me to be impolite."

"Mr Hale—"

"Get out of my house."

"If Melissa wants—"

"I said *get out*!" Mark yelled. He grabbed George's cup of tea and tossed it across the room to the far wall, where it smashed into fragments and left an inkblot-like tea stain on the pristine, white wall.

George studied the stain and glanced up at Ivy, who was raring to step in.

"I think we've got enough for now," he said, sliding from his stool. From his pocket, he withdrew a contact card and slid it across the kitchen island. "Despite our misgivings and shortfalls, Melissa, we really do want to help." He gave her a warm smile and edged past her father, calling out over his shoulder. "My phone's always on."

CHAPTER THIRTY

"Dad, what the hell is wrong with you?" Melissa said, and George stopped in the hallway, holding up a hand to halt Ivy.

"I don't like coming home to two strangers in my house," Mark said, on the brink of tears, as though his own outburst had shocked him. "God, I shouldn't have left you alone. I should've asked somebody to come and be here."

"What, like a babysitter? Dad, I'm twenty-two. You can't look after me forever. I shouldn't even still be living here. I should have my own place by now, my own life. But you hardly let me leave the house on my own. It's too much."

"I'm just trying to protect you—"

"I don't need you to protect me. I need you to get over what happened. It's like you're obsessed with the past. Like you still see me as a thirteen-year-old girl. But I need to move on, and I have. I've worked through it, Dad. I've come through the other side, but you..."

"What?" he said. "I what?"

"*You* haven't, Dad," she said, and George edged back past Ivy towards the kitchen. Ivy glared at him, gesturing silently at the front door.

"I'm your father, Melissa, and I will protect you as long—"

"You're not *protecting* me, Dad," she said, exhibiting her father's anger. "You're *controlling* me."

George stepped back into the kitchen to find Mark staring at his daughter, unblinking, as though only just processing her words.

"I thought you'd gone," Mark said.

"We're not here to cause trouble, Mark," George said, and Mark rubbed at his stubble irritably.

"Just...just tell me what you're doing here."

"We're here to talk about Adam Potter," George said.

Mark stared at him with an empty expression. "Who?"

"Adam Potter," Ivy repeated slowly, stepping into the kitchen to stand beside George.

"My old boyfriend, Dad," Melissa said. "You remember Adam, he's the one who—"

"I know who he is," Mark said, a little too feverishly, then turned to George. "What does *he* have to do with any of this?"

"When was the last time you saw him, Mark?"

Mark laughed out loud as though George had told the funniest joke he had ever heard. "When's the last time I saw some kid who went to school with my daughter? What do you want, an exact date, or will a year suffice?"

"Whatever you can give us," Ivy said.

"Well, I have no idea," he said, leaning forward as if thrusting the words at her. "I can barely remember the kid."

"He's not a kid anymore, though, is he?" Ivy replied, and she nodded at his daughter. "They're all grown up."

"If there's something you wish to say, Inspector," Mark said, turning to George for a response. "Then bloody well come out and say it, won't you?"

"Can you tell us where you were on Thursday between four and six p.m.?" George said.

His face darkened. "My daughter told you. I picked her up

from the hotel and then went back to work. I was at work when Ryan Eva was killed."

"This isn't about Ryan Eva's death," George said. "Ryan was killed on *Friday*. I need to know where you were on *Thursday*."

"Why?"

George looked at Ivy, who answered for him, deciding to be honest.

"We have CCTV footage of a man entering Ryan Eva's bedsit on Thursday at four-ten."

"You are joking, aren't you?"

George didn't reply but watched as every muscle in Mark's face moved independently, forming all manner of expressions, from bewildered to offended and then mildly amused.

"I was at work," he reiterated. "I have a job. I go to work every day. I come home at six p.m. I was at work."

"And if I called the brewery," George said, "and asked one of your colleagues to corroborate that, would they?"

Mark hesitated but eventually nodded.

"Yes, they would. Go for it. I can give you the number if you need it. Ask them yourselves."

"And if I asked you to come in for an interview," George said, watching the twitches on Mark's face as he struggled to compose himself, "you would oblige, I'm sure? In order to put all this down on record?"

"Yes. I would be happy to help," he replied through gritted teeth.

"And you, Melissa?" Ivy asked.

She looked between her dad and George with worry in her eyes, then settled on Ivy. "If you think it would help."

Mark shook his head at her response as though the last thing he wanted was for his daughter to sit through yet another police interview. "We've answered your questions," he said, his voice shaking as though every word was a chore to control. "Is there anything else?"

"No," George said. "No, I think that's enough for now. Just let me know when you're free to come in, and I'll make sure we're available to meet you."

"Very well," Mark said politely, rising to shake his hand. "Now, please, for the last time, would you get out of my house?"

Mark Hale continued to watch them from the living room window as George and Ivy walked across the driveway. They sat for a while in George's car, and still, he watched them.

"All roads lead to Adam Potter," Ivy said, breaking their thoughtful silence.

"Indeed."

"Do you believe Melissa?" she asked.

"That she hasn't seen Adam in years?" George said.

"Yeah."

"Not for a second," he replied with a laugh.

He unlocked his phone, found Campbell's number, and hit the green button to initiate a call through the car's Bluetooth system.

"Guv," she said, answering as swiftly as always. "I've been trying to get hold of you."

"Did you manage to find Adam Potter's address for me?"

"Oh," she said, and there came the sound of her spinning on a squeaky desk chair and then clicking a mouse. "I'll send it through to DS Hart, but—"

"We just spoke with Melissa and Mark Hale again," George continued. "I can't be sure, but I have a feeling that one of them isn't being as honest as they could be."

"Guv, I—"

"It's time we spoke to Adam Potter to see what he has to say. He's the link here. My guess is that he's involved here, somehow. But who knows? Maybe I'm wrong. Maybe my instincts aren't what they used to be," he repeated. "We're going there now. How's Ruby getting on?"

"Erm, yeah, great," she said. "She's impressive, I'll say that much."

"What about the other two? Maguire and O'Hara?" he asked. "We sent them to accompany Ian Eva to the chapel of rest yesterday. I believe they have some paperwork to finish up before they can commit their time to us, but have they popped in?"

"Oh, erm, briefly," Campbell said, distracted. "They seem pretty happy with the move."

"Good, good," George said. "Well, we'll touch base when we've spoken to Potter. We'll have a lead to go on, or all of this will be one big dead end."

"Okay," Campbell said quickly, as though she'd been waiting for George to stop speaking. "But before you do that, guv, there's something you should know."

CHAPTER THIRTY-ONE

By the time George and Ivy arrived at Ryan Eva's bedsit, CSI had taken over the building, uniformed officers had cordoned off the road, and an army of local residents held their phones in the air, videoing the proceedings.

In the sea of white suits and masks, George struggled to identify Katy Southwell. They ducked beneath the police tape, showing their IDs to the officer at the scene to log, and entered the red-brick building through the white tent that had been erected to preserve the scene. The front door was now hanging on one hinge, leaning against the wall like an old drunk. George bent to study the broken lock while Ivy pulled two pairs of shoe covers from the box CSI had obviously provided.

"Wouldn't be hard, guv," Ivy pointed out without him uttering a single word. He took the shoe covers from her. "A door like this. Lean on it too hard, and it'd snap in half."

"I'm not thinking about *how* it was forced," he said, straightening to slip the covers over his shoes. "But who forced it?" he caught the attention of the uniformed officer at the tent door. "You?" he said. "Was this done by us gaining entry, or is this how we found it?"

"That's how we found it, guv," she replied, and he nodded a brief thanks.

They walked inside and along the hallway, where two local uniformed officers were taking a statement from the delectable Steve. But whatever bravado he had demonstrated before was gone. The man was sobbing into his tattooed hands.

"I want that statement," George said to Ivy, pointing at the interaction. "Make sure it comes my way, will you?"

While Ivy followed his instruction, he climbed the stairs to the ugly carpeted hallway, ensuring he touched nothing with his bare hands. His eyes tracked around to Ryan Eva's room as he climbed, where he expected to find investigator's Tuffboxes, plastic sheeting, and more white-suited individuals poring over the tiniest details.

But Eva's door was as intact as it had been during their previous visit. The main event was taking place in the neighbouring room.

He stopped in the doorway and found Katy Southwell's unmistakably lithe figure in discussion with one of her colleagues, whom George recognised but had never been able to distinguish their gender. In this day and age, it seemed inappropriate to ask, and so he'd always avoided any interaction with them, which Ivy assured him was just as offensive.

The world was a changing place, but some things were just beyond him, and if he was honest with himself, Southwell's colleague was the least of his concerns. What concerned him was the man lying on the bed.

Edward's eyes were wide open, and his mouth was ajar, from which his limp tongue hung.

A surprising pang of sadness caught George off-guard. Like something had stirred in the depths of his stomach.

"Ah, Christ," Ivy said as she joined him and took in the scene.

"Thanks, Pat," Southwell said as she finished with her

colleague. "Now then, Inspector Larson. We must stop meeting like this."

"If only we could," he replied, nodding at the body. "What do we have?"

"Well, Doctor Saint has been and gone."

"Already?"

"He'll send you his report," she explained. "Besides, I wanted to get a grip on the crime scene without you lot treading all over it."

"Strangled?" George said, ignoring the light-hearted dig and studying from afar the bruises on Edward's neck.

"Asphyxiation," she said. "He hasn't been dead more than two hours. Rigor mortis hasn't even set in yet. All the usual signs. Petechial haemorrhages," she said, stepping over to where Edward lay and pointing to the red spots in Edward's eyes. "Facial congestion, oedema, and cyanosis," she said, circling his face with her hand, which was oily, swollen, and a disturbing blue-purple in colour.

"Sounds like we missed the party," George said, annoyed that he had missed Campbell's calls while dealing with Mark Hale.

"We've got a fair bit to do," she said. "Not going to be easy, though. This place hasn't been cleaned properly for years. It's like lifting fingerprints from the door handle of the local dole office."

"At least they should all be on record," Ivy cut in. "A few dozen ex-cons have probably lived here at some point over the past few years."

"There is that," Southwell said.

"Look, before you leave, Katy," George said. "I need a little favour."

"Another favour? Do I really need to remind you that recently, my favours for you, George, have not been so little?"

"Yeah, I know, I know. And I'm afraid this one isn't either, not really. The room next door belonged to Ryan Eva."

"Who?"

"The man who was killed at Stockwith Mill."

"Ah," she said. "You want us to give his room a going over? See if there's anything you missed?"

"You'll notice the lock is broken. Someone broke into his room last Thursday. The day before he died."

Southwell was silent for a few seconds as though processing the information, then patiently, looking around the room, she turned to her colleague.

"Pat?" she said, and the individual glanced up at her. "Pop next door, will you? Fingerprints and fluids. The usual." Pat said nothing but nodded and immediately collected his or her tools in a little tool tray and edged past them.

"Let me know if you find something, will you?" George added, turning back to Edward. "The guy downstairs seemed pretty shaken."

"Yeah, I overheard your lot talking to him," she said.

George smiled. "They're not my lot, Katy. They're local lads."

"I've given them my email to send the statement through," Ivy cut in.

"Did he see much?"

"No, not really," Ivy replied. "But even if he had, would you expect him to tell us, the enemy?"

"No, I suppose not," George said.

"So, who called it in?"

"Oh, it was him who called us," Ivy explained. "He said Edward usually comes down for dinner at half five." She trailed off, looking at Edward's sorry-looking body. "But today he didn't."

"How do we know he didn't do this?" Southwell said. "Seems the type to me."

"Is there a type?" George asked. "You've been spending too much time with us. Apparently, I'm judgemental." He winked at Ivy in reference to her earlier comment.

"Can't get away from it, I'm afraid," Southwell said. "My boyfriend is one of you lot."

"Oh?"

"Jim Gillespie," she explained. "He works under DCI Bloom."

"Bloom?" George said. "I'd be lying if I said that news of her... personality hadn't come this far."

"Ah, she's alright," Southwell said. "When you get to know her, that is. But us standing here gossiping isn't going to help matters, is it?" She pulled her goggles down over her eyes and her mask up over her mouth. "I'll send through what we find." She glanced down at the body and then back at George. "And I have a feeling there's a darn sight more here than there was at the mill."

"You didn't find anything, then?"

"Have you had an email from me?" Southwell asked.

"Not yet," George replied, checking with Ivy, who in turn shook her head.

"What does that tell you, Inspector?" Behind her goggles, she raised her eyebrows, turned away, and bent over Edward's body.

George led Ivy out into the hallway.

"How did nobody hear that door being kicked in and not notice a stranger walking around?"

"Everyone else is at work. He only got home an hour ago. My guess is that Edward was sleeping and didn't even realise what was happening until...well, until it was too late."

"But there was a struggle," George said. "He has blood on his mouth, which suggests he was hit. Whoever attacked him might have blood on his clothes. Maybe scratches to his face."

"Do you think that it's a safe assumption that this is connected to Ryan Eva's murder?" Ivy asked. "I mean, half the people who stay here must have enemies."

"No assumption is a safe assumption," he replied. "The MO is different."

"That doesn't mean anything."

"No, but Eva's murder wasn't planned." He jabbed a thumb over his shoulder. "That was planned. That was intentional. The killer knew which room to find Edward. They knew the door would be locked. Maybe they even knew that everyone else would be out."

"Everyone apart from Steve, you mean?"

He nodded.

"And he seems pretty shaken up," George said. "Although I doubt he's too fussed about Edward's demise. Rather, he's just had a wake-up call."

"It could have been him, you mean?"

"I wouldn't want to come across as judgemental, Ivy," he said with a grin.

"So whoever did this knew where Edward would be, and it's possible they knew the house would be mostly empty,' Ivy said. "So that begs the question, why? Why kill a young lad who, let's face it, was afraid of his own shadow?"

"Well, we don't know what he did to wind up inside, do we?" George said. "He might have been just released, like Ryan. He might've been more like Ryan than we realised if you know what I mean?"

"A predator?" Ivy said. "Oh, for God's sake. This investigation is beginning to leave a bad taste in my mouth, guv."

"Actually," a voice said, and Katy came to the bedroom door. "Sorry, I couldn't help but overhear. The man with the tattoos downstairs said he was here after leaving state care. Treated it like a halfway house before independent living. Not sure if that's any use to you."

"You're in the wrong game, Katy," George said.

"Oh, I'm not," she said with a laugh. "Trust me, every time Jim comes home and tells me about his day, I count my blessings that I stuck university out." She held up the paintbrush and pot of chemicals she was using to dust Edward's body down. "Anyway, sorry to interrupt."

She slipped back from view again.

"State care," Ivy said. "What is that? Foster care?"

"Why would they put him in a house with released convicts?"

"Not everyone here has been to prison, Ivy. There are people from all walks of life. I knew a man once whose wife divorced him. Took the house, the kids, the savings. Wiped him clean," George said. "He ended up somewhere like this."

"That doesn't sound like your usual crowd, guv," Ivy replied. "If you don't mind me saying."

"He wasn't. Before the divorce, he was a law-abiding citizen. Paid his taxes and held down a job, you know?" He took a breath, feeling he was venturing down the path of a tangent. "Anyway, he spiralled. Lost control of his life."

"Surely he got half the money for the house?" Ivy said. "The courts aren't that unfair, are they?"

"Oh, he kept his half of it. But that's only any use when it's sold."

"And the wife didn't want to sell?" Ivy said.

"Had he stayed in his job, he would have been paying the mortgage and bills on a house he wasn't allowed inside. He would have been paying for children he could see once a month, and he would have been keeping a wife who had destroyed him in the lifestyle to which she had grown accustomed."

"So he quit?"

"Quit work and started drinking," George said. "Wound up somewhere like this place. Six months later, he was inside."

"What did he do?"

"Do you really want to know?"

"Well, yes and no," she replied.

"He got drunk and kidnapped his own children," George said, and he watched as Ivy processed the sorry tale, comparing it to the decision she had recently made.

"I suppose the wife called the police on him, did she?"

"I wish she had," George said. "No, she went looking for them. Knocked on his door."

"Oh, God, no."

"And now those children are probably in care somewhere,"

George said. "Not quite the happy ending. They'll be in the system until they're eighteen, and then, like Edward, they'll have to make their own way in life."

"The guy downstairs was in the system, too, years ago," Katy called out, and this time George and Ivy went to the doorway. She looked up at them. "He knew Edward. He was keeping him under his wing."

"Did you take a statement or something?" George asked, to which Katy laughed.

"No, I just listen," she said with a hidden smile that raised her goggles half an inch. "You'd be amazed what you hear when you walk around like a ghost." She waved a hand over her white overalls. "We're like ghosts."

"Wait, you say he was keeping Edward under his wing. How old was he?" Ivy asked, nodding at Edward.

"Him?" Katy said. "Seventeen or eighteen."

George studied the dead young man he had put in his twenties or early thirties.

"Jesus, he was just a kid, which explains why our mate Steve didn't like him hanging out with Ryan Eva," he said. "He was probably just looking out for him."

Ivy shook her head, angry at the system that had led Edward here.

"So let's say he *doesn't* have a list of enemies as long as Ryan Eva," she said, as though the news that Edward might not have been a predator had renewed her vigour. "Maybe this *is* about Ryan."

An idea was forming in George's mind, but it wasn't quite clear yet, like a Polaroid developing before his eyes.

"Edward had *seen* someone breaking into Ryan's room only a few days ago," he said.

"Maybe he was covering his tracks. Edward was a witness. Edward knew what he looked like."

"Hardly," said George. "He only saw him for a second. All he could remember was that he was tall with brown hair."

"If the man that came here was the same man that killed Ryan, maybe he knows we came to speak to Edward. Maybe he knows Edward could help us find out who he is."

George, Ivy, and Katy processed the theory until a shadow fell over them, and Katy peered between them. George turned to find her colleague standing behind them.

"Got something?" Katy asked, and Pat nodded.

The three of them rushed into Ryan's room and gathered around one of Southwell's team crouching at the foot of Ryan's bed. "Look at this," she said, pointing at what George thought was a tiny wood knot on the bedpost.

"Have you swabbed it?" asked Katy, even though George could still not see exactly what was there.

"Am I missing something?" Ivy said.

"It's blood. There's more here," said Katy, pointing at it as though it was obvious. "It's a few days old," she said, inspecting the blood as though it was a painting. "And looks like blood splatter to me. Like someone banged their head against the bedpost."

"Get me an identification if you can, Katy," George said, going to leave the room. "And if you can—"

"Fast track it?" she said, finishing his sentence for him.

"Am I that predictable?"

"Yes, you are," she replied, handing the find over to her colleague with a nod. "Don't get your hopes up, though. It might not take your investigation forward."

"As long as it doesn't take us backwards, Katy," he said. Ivy started to leave, but George just had one more question. He stopped and stared at Edward.

"Not another favour," Southwell said, reading his gestures.

"Did you find a mobile phone?" he said. "In his pockets or anywhere else?"

Southwell shook her head. "There's an empty chip wrapper and a Coke can in the bin," she said. "I'll call you if we find anything else. Why's that?"

"What's up, guv?" Ivy asked from the hallway.

"The MOs are different," he said. "Ryan Eva's murder was spontaneous; Edward's appears to have been premeditated."

"Yet, neither of them have mobile phones," Ivy said.

"Funny, don't you think?" he replied thoughtfully. "Who doesn't have a mobile phone these days? And yet, here we are with two victims, neither of whom have one."

CHAPTER THIRTY-TWO

The first thing George did in the incident room was turn the whiteboards around to the blank side. They needed a fresh slate. He wrote Edward's name in the middle of the board, then hesitated. He didn't even know the boy's surname.

"Higgins," Campbell said as she joined him at the whiteboard. She nodded at the board. "It's Edward Higgins."

When George turned around, Ruby, Byrne, and Ivy had all joined Campbell, too, pens poised and ready for his briefing. The back of the room was already feeling tighter than usual. Although Tim had allocated a few officers to start moving the furniture from the storage space to his left, it was taking time; that room was home to decades' worth of bits and bobs.

"Where's the new lot?"

"Maguire and O'Hara?" Ivy said. "They'll be with us tomorrow. They're still finishing off any reports, so they can focus on whatever we give them."

George checked his watch.

"They were doing that this morning. Let's hope that's a sign of their attention to detail."

"Irish, are they?" Ruby asked inquisitively.

"You'd think so?" Byrne said. "Maguire's from Donegal, I think, and she's from near Bristol somewhere."

"Maybe we should organise a few beers to get to know each other?" Byrne suggested.

"But you already do know them, don't you?" George replied.

"Well, yeah, but you don't. And neither does Ivy or Ruby. I just thought it might be good for team building."

"Let's...let's just get through this investigation. The last thing I need is six hangovers to deal with right now," George said, turning to the board. "Now, I don't think it's too huge a leap to assume that whoever broke into Edward's room is the same person who broke into Ryan's room on Thursday afternoon." He turned to look them in the eye. "But we will need to prove it."

"Did CSI find much?" Campbell asked.

"They're still there," Ivy cut in. "But Southwell did say the place hadn't been cleaned properly for an age. It might be tricky to single out individual prints with enough confidence to stand up in court."

"Correct," George said, regaining control. "He knew what he was doing. He had done it before. Ruby, look at the CCTV from the pet shop. They helped us once; they might be willing to do so again. Campbell will give you the details."

"Do we have a time frame?" Ruby asked, with her pen poised.

"Today," he replied. "We were there an hour ago, and the poor lad was still warm."

Anyone else might have grimaced at George's description, but Ruby had a straight and, so far, unreadable expression. "I'm actually looking right now, guv," Campbell said and turned the laptop around to show a man in a tracksuit and hoody entering Hawthorn Court at the far reaches of the camera's lens. "It's a cloud-based system, and they gave us the login details."

"That's very trusting," Ivy remarked.

"Fortunate is what it is," George said, and he leaned forward to watch as Campbell replayed a section of the video. "That's him. That's our man."

"He waited to get inside last time," Ivy said as the man stepped up to the front door and removed something long from inside his jacket. "What's that?"

"Some kind of jimmy bar," Byrne said.

"Of course it is," George added. "He's been inside once. He knows the layout. He knows there are no cameras inside. He knows exactly what he has to do."

The front door suddenly opened, and with a glance over his shoulder, the man slipped inside.

"What do we think?" George said, pointing at the screen. "Are we confident it's the same man?"

Byrne squinted. "Could be. Similar clothing, at least. Was the other bloke wearing gloves? Anyway, I couldn't say for sure. He seems a bit bigger, maybe, but you just can't tell on these cameras."

"What time is that?" George asked Ruby.

She checked the time stamp. "Three forty-nine. He leaves again at four o'clock."

"Around the same time, someone broke into Ryan's room last Thursday," George pointed out.

"We can't assume, guv," Ivy said. "It's too big a jump. We can't assume that the same person who broke into Ryan's room is the same person who broke into Edward's room and killed him. And we can't assume that whoever killed Edward also killed Ryan."

George didn't reply. He watched as Campbell flicked forward to four o'clock on the timestamp when the hooded man left the bedsit, removing his gloves as he did so.

Byrne's desk phone started to ring. He looked to George for permission, who nodded. Then Byrne stood and walked over to answer it.

"You're right," George said. "We can't make assumptions. We need to evidence it. I'm damn sure that is the same man who gained access to the bedsit last Thursday, and I'm damn sure that whoever it is, they're also responsible for Ryan Eva's death."

"What makes you so confident?" Ruby asked, and George turned to look her in the eye. "I'm curious, that's all."

"We weren't expecting the results so soon," Byrne said, his voice raised to gain their attention.

George checked his watch again. There was no way that Katy's team could have processed the evidence from Edward Higgins' room yet. He turned back to the board, tuning out of their phone conversation and getting his team's attention. He pointed at Edward's name.

"Let's...entertain the idea," he said, avoiding the word *assume* and the shake of Ivy's head, "just for now, that whoever killed Edward did so because he was a witness to that man breaking into Ryan's bedroom. But until we get news back from Katy and some more information from Pip, there's not much we can go on. Is there?"

He looked around the team, hoping one of them would come up with something. But no one did.

"Okay, then moving on." He flipped the whiteboard back to the other side, where Ryan Eva's name was in the middle, and in the empty bottom-left-hand corner, he wrote another young man's name. *Adam Potter*.

"Adam Potter?" Campbell said. "Didn't you go to see him earlier?"

"We didn't have time," George said. "But we did speak to Melissa and Mark Hale, and I'm convinced that at least one of them still has a connection to Adam. But we still need to speak to him, and when we do, I want to have as much on him as possible. So..." he said, looking around the team. "What have we got?"

"I found out his link to the groom," Ruby said.

"Go on."

"Like I said, he was Lucas Coffey's best man. From socials, it looks like they see each other quite a lot. Once or twice a week.

And I found their profiles on LinkedIn. They both worked as project managers for the local council. Before that, their connection runs dry. So, I'm guessing that's how they know each other."

"I also looked at the photo I took of the seating plan at the wedding," Campbell said, handing George a printout. "He's there, on the top table, right next to the groom. He must've had a speech prepared and everything."

"Have you spoken to the photographer?" George said, looking up from the photo. "I'd like to see *evidence* of him at Stockwith Mill on Saturday. I want to know where he was standing, what he was doing, who he was talking to." He jabbed at the name on the board. "And I want to see the look on his face."

"Why's that?" Campbell asked.

"Because, as hard as it is to believe, Campbell, not everyone is a killer," George said. "And when the average person commits murder, it tends to keep them up at night."

"Ah, guilt," Byrne said, covering the phone's mouthpiece with his free hand.

"Not always," Ivy said. "Actually, most of the time, guilt isn't even a part of it."

"What is then?"

"Getting caught," George replied. "And spending the next twenty years inside."

"I'll contact the photographer, guv," Campbell said, pulling out her phone.

"Good,' George said. "And presumably, he was at the rehearsal."

"I would imagine so," Campbell replied.

"Let's not imagine. Let's evidence it, shall we? I want to place him at the rehearsal. I want to match his identity to whoever that is on the video, and I want irrefutable evidence that he's spoken to Melissa Hale since she learned Ryan was out of prison. That will give us an MMO strong enough to bring him in."

"I also read the report, guv, about his assault against Ryan

Eva," Campbell said. "It was pretty bad. Nothing compared to what Mark Hale did to him, but still, he put Eva in hospital overnight with a concussion and dislocated shoulder. I think it's fair to say he had the means to kill Ryan Eva."

George looked over at Byrne, who was frantically scribbling notes into his notebook with the handset pressed between his shoulder and ear as Katy relayed information over the phone.

"Campbell, Ruby," he said. "What did you find on Mark and Melissa's alibis?"

"I managed to access the hotel CCTV footage," Ruby explained. "They took some convincing that Melissa wasn't in any kind of trouble, but we got there in the end."

"Only because you threatened to send half a dozen uniformed officers down there," Campbell added, which raised a guilty grin on Ruby's face.

"Is that true?" George asked.

Ruby shrugged.

"Was that wrong?"

"No," Ivy cut in, glaring at George. "No, it wasn't wrong. But next time, it might be worth running it by one of us. I doubt there's a half a dozen uniformed officers available, anyway. So your bluff might have been well and truly called." She smiled to convey there was no harm done, and Ruby, as ever, remained impassive.

"What did it show, anyway?" George asked. "The CCTV. Is she clear?"

"Well, Melissa Hale was at work that day, but only on the breakfast shift, so she finished at one p.m. Then the camera in the car park shows her being picked up by Mark Hale at about one-ten."

"You're sure it's him?"

"Checked his car registration," she replied. "Green Volvo."

"Okay," George said, and he took a few steps in thought. "Surely he had to leave his job to go and collect her? I know he's protective, but if he does that every day, he wouldn't get anything done."

"She *was* sexually assaulted, guv," Ivy said, and she gave him that look she often did when he'd voiced a faux pas.

"I know," he said. "And I'm not saying that he's wrong by doing so. God knows the pair of them have been through enough. She could've walked home. She could've got the bus. Why, on that specific day, did he choose to pick her up?"

"Sounds to me like you're trying to make your theory fit, guv," Ivy said.

"I'm not trying to make anything fit," he replied. "But it's a theory, and from what I've just heard, it is far from being made implausible."

"There's an ANPR camera just outside Horncastle," Ruby continued. "It shows Mark Hale going through in the direction of the family home and then returning half an hour later."

"Half an hour?" Ivy repeated. "Enough time to drop his daughter at home and then get back to work."

"And then," Ruby continued, darting between screens on her laptop. "The town centre CCTV shows him returning to work, and he stays there until six o'clock that evening."

"Presumably, he then does the journey in reverse?" George asked, to which Ruby nodded. "So, at the actual time of Ryan's death, Melissa is at home, and her father is at the brewery. Somebody follow that up. Ask one of his colleagues. I want a witness of Mark Hale leaving work to collect Melissa and returning to work by two p.m. on Friday afternoon."

"Just because his car didn't leave work until six doesn't mean *he* didn't," Ivy said. "What about phone locations?"

"We can't access location data without a warrant," Campbell said. "All we have to go on right now is CCTV."

"Ruby," George said, "I want you to look into their phone records. See who they texted that day."

"Again, we need a warrant, guv," Campbell pointed out.

"Then request one," George told her. "When we've got the warrant, Ruby, talk to the phone providers."

She nodded. "But that will only show the time and date of any messages and calls and what number they were talking to."

"That'll do, for now," George said. "While you're at it, do the same for Ryan Eva, Edward Higgins, and Adam Potter, won't you?"

"I didn't think Ryan Eva had a phone," Campbell said.

"Well, we didn't find one on his person, but the same could be said about Edward Higgins."

"Ah, right. You think whoever did it took the phones?"

"Which makes me wonder what could have been on the phones," George added.

"Yes, guv," she said, falling into his way of thinking.

While Campbell made her notes, Byrne finally hung up after his long conversation with Katy Southwell and strode back over to the whiteboard. George looked up at him expectantly.

"You won't believe this," he said.

"Save the anticipation, son. Just tell me."

"That was Katy Southwell. She's processed all the glasses from the wedding on Saturday. She's tagged them and identified them according to the guest list. Most of the DNA isn't on the system, but a couple of names were flagged."

"Let me guess," George said. "Adam Potter was one."

"No," Byrne said. "He's not on record. He wasn't charged for the assault against Ryan. But yes, we know which glass is his from the seating plan, in case we do need his DNA."

"Okay," George said, somewhat disappointed.

"But that's not all. There were some DNA matches worth considering."

"Well, that's to be expected," Ivy said. "It's a wedding. Most people in that room would be related."

"No," Byrne said, smiling. "Not just to each other, guv. The DNA matches were to Ryan Eva."

This gripped the attention of the whole team. Even Ruby, who had only been working the investigation for less than a day, looked up at him in shock.

"What do you mean?" George asked. "Ryan was related to someone at the wedding?"

"Not just someone," Byrne said. "Multiple people. There was a partial match with the glass that Katy numbered number thirty-two, which belongs, according to the seating plan, to a Maeve Wetherford."

"The bride's mother," Ivy said.

"Exactly. And that's not all. There was another partial match to number thirty-four, although Katy was unable to identify it from the seating plan. It wasn't a wine glass or champagne flute. It was a whisky glass. She wasn't sure who it belonged to, but it definitely had a partial match with Ryan Eva's DNA."

George stared at Byrne, his heart beating fast as his mind caught up to the information his body already knew.

George cast his mind back to that awful day. He pictured himself at the head of the room, addressing the wedding party. He pictured the catering staff topping up wine glasses and champagne flutes, and one man had ordered a pint of beer.

"There was only one person drinking whisky at that wedding. She was clutching it all afternoon." He looked at Ivy, then back at the board, on which he wrote a name.

"Nancy Wetherford?" Byrne said. "Bloody hell, you're right. She was at the bar knocking them back. I thought she was going to pass out."

George heard him but was lost in thought.

"How does she fit in?" Ivy said quietly, coming to stand beside him.

"Honestly," he replied, checking to make sure nobody could hear. "I have absolutely no idea."

CHAPTER THIRTY-THREE

"We need to know what that link is," Ivy said, running them through the possibilities. "If there was a partial match with Maeve Wetherford, the mother of the bride, and with Nancy Wetherford, the bride," Ivy said slowly, processing, "was there a match with Nancy's father, Rory Wetherford?"

Byrne shook his head slowly, then said loudly and clearly, "No."

Campbell sat back. "Well, that's very interesting."

"So Ryan Eva is related to Nancy Wetherford," Ruby said. "I guess that answers why he was invited to the wedding."

"He wasn't invited," George reminded her. "He wasn't on the guest list."

"Well, maybe he felt that he had a right to be there."

"A partial match," Campbell said. "So that means brother or cousin or?"

"Katy said the match to Maeve Wetherford indicated parentage, and the match to Nancy Wetherford suggests half-sister."

"How does it suggest that?" Byrne asked, and Ivy took the spare pen from the tray beneath the whiteboard.

"Our DNA comes from our parents," she started. "We get fifty per cent from our father and fifty per cent from our mother." She wrote mother, father, and child in a Y-shape, with the child at the bottom, then connected them with lines. "There's more to it than that, but you get the gist." She checked to make sure he was following. "If Ryan Eva's DNA suggests that he and Nancy were step-siblings..." She added in another father to the right of the mother.

"Then he's a child from another relationship," Byrne said, nodding to show he understood. "Because the father is different."

She clicked the cap back on the pen, then reached for the rag to wipe it clean.

"Leave that," George told her. "Let's just let that sink in, shall we?" he turned to Byrne. "Any other matches?"

"I mean, there were plenty. Like you said, it was a wedding. There were matches between the groom and his family, the bride and her family, and other partial matches with other guests. But those were the only connections to Ryan Eva. Just Maeve and Nancy Wetherford."

"Well, she must've recognised him then," Campbell said. "When she saw him in the pool. Nancy must've recognised her half-brother."

"You'd think so, wouldn't you?" George said, almost to himself.

"And the mum," Byrne said. "Surely she would have recognised her own son?"

"She didn't see the body. The only people who saw the body before we arrived were the bride, the groom, and the photographer."

"Well, how's this for a theory?" Campbell said. "Maeve Wetherford had an affair with Ian Eva. The question is, did Rory Wetherford know about it? Or did the child of his wife's affair just turn up on his daughter's wedding day? A man who is quick to anger wouldn't take that lightly. I think that gives him a motive, don't you?"

The question hung in the air.

"The problem isn't finding a motive for someone," George said. "The problem is narrowing down the people *with* motives. This is a lot to work with." He turned to the board, which was beginning to look more and more like a collage; any cohesion between the elements was limited at best.

"Better than our last investigation," Byrne cut in. "We had bugger all to go on until the last minute. And we all know how that worked out."

"It all depends on your perspective," George said. "Yes, we have plenty of people to look into, but it's not just a case of identifying the guilty party." He tapped at the names on the board. "Melissa Hale, Mark Hale, Adam Potter, Rory Wetherford. They all need eliminating."

"But surely if we can evidence the guilty party—"

"If we evidence the guilty party, charge them, and then wait for a trial, their defence team will be all over the alternative options," George said. "The more alternative options we have, the greater the chance of a jury finding them not guilty. If we leave the other names, then that creates doubt."

"A technicality?" Byrne said. "That stinks."

"It is our job to develop a case against the guilty party that finds them guilty beyond reasonable doubt." He tapped at the names again. "These? These are all reasonable doubt."

Byrne shook his head and sat back in his chair.

"Do you have a problem with that, Byrne?"

"It feels like the rules are stacked against us. It's like a dad who plays football with his son, then volunteers to wear a blindfold to give them a chance."

"It's nothing like that," George said. "It's the framework of our legal system. All being well, one of the names on this list will serve a life sentence. I don't know about you, but I'll sleep better at night if there's no doubt of their guilt."

"I suppose," Byrne said reluctantly.

"Ruby, find out what you can on Ryan Eva's past. I want to

know if Rory Wetherford knew about him prior to the wedding rehearsal."

"Can do," she said, as if the task was a breeze when George knew it to be a significant challenge.

"Until we know more, we have to work with the evidence we do have. And right now, that is all pointing towards Adam Potter. We need to talk to him. We need his side of the story and an alibi if he has one. So..." George said, circling the name and encouraging them to get back on focus. "What else have we got on him?"

"He has a motive," Byrne started. "He attacked Ryan Eva before. And didn't you say that he's been in touch with Melissa in recent years? He clearly still cares for her."

"Plus, if we take into account that Adam might have found out that Ryan reached out to Melissa, that would give him extra motivation to act now," Campbell said.

"Good," George said. "So we need to find out if Melissa and Adam are still in contact and if Melissa had told Adam about Ryan's visit to her house. Either way, we've got a strong motive here. What else?"

"Adam would have been at the wedding rehearsal as Lucas' best man. That gives him the opportunity."

"Okay," George said. "So Adam is the only suspect that we know was definitely at the wedding venue when Ryan was killed. Unless we also count Rory Wetherford, and I think we should. Campbell, any news from the photographer?"

"He emailed back but said he still needs time to curate and edit the photos."

"I'm not trying to make a photo album here. Tell him to send everything through, and we can go through them ourselves. Email him back. In fact, no. Call him. I want those photos now." She grimaced a little. "What is it?"

"Well," she began. "You know what they're like. Wedding photographers, I mean."

"Not really, no," George replied.

"You're forgetting," Ivy said, hoping to sweeten George's sour tone. "When the guv was married, the photographer had to bend down and put his head beneath a sheet."

Byrne laughed out loud. "Yeah, and he would have had one of those massive flashes."

"Watch the birdie," Campbell added.

"Are we quite done?" George said. "Campbell?"

She sighed. "It's just it seems like he's reluctant to show us the originals. I suppose it's like us handing a charge file to the CPS halfway through an investigation. It's not our best work. It's not polished."

"I don't care about polish. I'll not be judging his vignette or his depth of field or whether or not he selected the corrected ISO," he said. "I want the bloody photos."

"Yes, guv," Campbell said, retrieving her mobile from her pocket and walking to the far corner of the room.

"So," George said, turning back to the whiteboard. "Means. How did Adam know that Ryan would be at the wedding rehearsal?"

"Like we said," Ivy spoke up, "He didn't, necessarily. If Ryan had just shown up feeling entitled to be at his half-sister's wedding, then maybe he spooked Adam. Maybe it was an act of passion."

"That is what Katy Southwell thought," Ivy said.

"Or," Byrne said, "maybe he *did* know about Ryan's history with the Wetherfords. Maybe someone set it up. Maybe someone invited him to be there that day. Maybe they needed him on his own, out of the house, somewhere there were plenty of distractions. Like we said, for the last seven months, all he's done is travel to work and home again. Maybe this was premeditated."

"I don't know," George said. "Murdering someone with a rock at a busy wedding venue and leaving them in the open in a shallow stream doesn't exactly seem like a well-thought-through crime to me. Why not do it elsewhere and dump him in a field or a ditch?"

Campbell returned with her phone in her hand and sat down at her desk. "He said he'd send them over now," she said over her shoulder. "I had to use the old hindering-an-investigation card, so it shouldn't take long." She clicked on her emails, and after a few seconds, a folder appeared in her inbox.

"Byrne," George said, "get a picture of Adam up on your laptop."

They all gathered around Campbell's desk as she flicked through the wedding photos. Ivy wondered how Nancy Wetherford would feel about her wedding photos being scrutinised by a major crimes team. But five sets of eyes watched on as Campbell scrolled through, searching for a familiar face.

"Stop," Byrne said suddenly, his eyes the sharpest of all of them. "There he is."

Campbell stopped on a photo that was taken before the chaos had ensued. The softly lit field and long shadows suggested it was morning. The guests were gathered around in casual groups as though welcoming each other before taking a seat and waiting for the bride's arrival. In the background, Lucas Coffey was shaking someone's hand, preparing himself to watch his wife-to-be walk down the aisle. Beside him, to the side of the photo, Adam Potter wore a sullen look on his face as he stared down at his phone.

"Hardly in the spirit of things, is he?" Ivy said. "He's bloody texting."

"Maybe he had other things on his mind," George said. "I want to know who he was texting at; what time was it?"

Campbell right-clicked on the image and found the metadata. "Eleven thirty-four a.m."

"Eleven thirty-four," George repeated but was interrupted by a gentle cough from behind them. He turned to find two uniformed officers, a male and a female.

"Reporting for duty, guv," the young man said, clearly hoping to raise a smile.

"Maguire?"

"S'right, guv," he said, his Irish accent a welcome blast of joviality. He stood on tiptoes to see what they were doing. "Oh, who was married?"

"Never mind that," George said. "I'm afraid you're going to have to hit the ground running." He turned to Ruby. "Give them the details for the phone provider and all the suspects' phone numbers."

"You don't want me to do that?"

"No, you're far too useful for that," he said, then turned back to the new pair. "When you get the details, request the necessary warrants, then contact the relevant service provider. I want to know who this man was messaging at that moment. Who that message was to."

"His name is Adam Potter," Ivy said. "He'll be on the list Ruby gives you."

"Right," Maguire replied, then turned to the researcher. "And you'll be Ruby, will you?"

"I am," she replied, then tugged a sheet of paper from her notepad and handed it to him. "Everything you need is on here."

"Grand," he said, then searched for a desk.

He caught Ivy's eye, and she nodded at a free desk for him to use.

"You must be O'Hara," she said, extending a hand towards the remaining uniformed officer. "DS Hart. You'll have to forgive us; we're in the middle of a briefing."

"Why don't you listen in for now," George said. "Pick up what you can."

"Guv," she replied, then sidled over to the team.

"Ruby, see what else you can find on Adam Potter, will you?" George said. "You've got an hour."

"An hour?"

"By which time Campbell and Byrne will have brought him in."

"Eh?" Byrne said. "I thought you and—"

"Voluntarily?" Campbell asked, cutting him off before he said something he would regret.

"Yes, if possible," George said.

"And if not?"

George turned to Ivy for support.

"We've got an MMO, guv," she said. "He was there, he had the means, and he certainly has a motive."

George nodded, then turned back to Campbell.

"If he doesn't want to come in, then we can only assume he has something to hide. Nick him," George said. "Either way, I want a file on my desk in an hour and Adam Potter downstairs in one of the interview rooms."

CHAPTER THIRTY-FOUR

Adam Potter looked different than he had in the photos. The only similarity was that he was a twenty-four-year-old man with styled brown hair. He wasn't dressed in a three-piece suit, he didn't have flowers in his buttonhole, and he wasn't texting on his phone. Instead, he was slumped back in his chair, wearing grubby jeans and a t-shirt, peering around the room, and keeping his eyes anywhere except on Ivy. He wasn't a particularly remarkable-looking man, not good-looking or ugly, but run of the mill, with long arms that suggested to Ivy that when he stood up, he would be rather tall.

They had been sitting in silence for a good ten minutes, Ivy staring at Adam and Adam avoiding her eye contact while the duty solicitor scribbled inelible notes that Ivy thought might only be for show in order to deal with the awkward silence.

She was waiting for George to enter the room with a jovial *good afternoon* and a nice, thick file he could drop onto the table. It was a play. They had played it many times, Ivy sitting there first with a stony silence that suggested there was something to worry about and George coming in later to reassure the suspect that everything was tickety-boo.

Indeed, that was exactly how George entered the room, with a pleasant nod at all three of them. "Good afternoon," he said, as he came in and closed the door. "Apologies for the delay. You know how it is. Nothing's where you need it when you need it."

He dropped the weighty file on the table with a slap, not overly dramatic but loud enough to make an impact.

With a nod from George, Ivy started the recording, and George began.

"This interview is being recorded and may be given in evidence if this case is brought to trial," he started before relaying their location, the date, and time. "I am Detective Inspector George Larson. The others present are..."

"Detective Sergeant Ivy Hart," Ivy said, her eyes still never leaving Adam's face.

"Adam Potter," Potter said when George held out his hand, welcoming him to speak.

"Bekka Mitra, legal counsel," the duty solicitor said without looking up from her note-taking. She was a beautiful woman with wild, curly hair with no true parting and deep, dark eyes. She returned to her note-taking.

George opened the file and spread out some of the papers, looking between them with his hands on his lap as though scanning through an interesting book of art. "Well, well," he said, "where shall we start? What have we got?" He chose one as though at random, holding it up and adjusting his glasses so that he could read properly. "Mr Ryan Eva was hospitalised for injuries to his face, shoulders, arms, and torso from physical assault. The patient required seven stitches beneath his right eye. After further examination, it seems he was diagnosed with a concussion and a dislocated shoulder and was kept in overnight for observation." He gave a low whistle. "Hardly bedtime reading, is it, Adam?" He held up the paper. "Do you know what this is?"

Potter shrugged, but there was a fear in his eyes beyond the nonchalance.

"It is a report of the injuries that Ryan suffered when you physically assaulted him nine years ago."

He leaned forward. "Do you want me to apologise for defending my girlfriend against a nonce?"

"Your ex-girlfriend," Ivy said.

"She was my girlfriend at the time," he spat.

"I'm not asking you to apologise for anything, Adam. I'm merely pointing out that you attacked Ryan once before, which suggested to me that, under the right circumstances, you could be willing to do it again."

"I didn't even know Ryan was dead until I was arrested an hour ago. I have no idea what I'm doing here."

"My colleagues informed you of your rights when they arrested you, Adam. You are here because you have been accused of murdering Ryan Eva."

He threw his hands up. "This is ridiculous. I haven't seen Ryan for years, not since..." He nodded at the file. "That's the last time I saw him."

"I understand," George said. "You were just protecting your girlfriend. Any man would do the same. Wouldn't they, Adam?"

He sat back as though smug. "Any proper man. Yes, they would."

"And do you still feel protective over Melissa?"

He hesitated as though remembering where he was and that every comment could be used against him. "Well, I don't really know her anymore."

"So, no?"

"I suppose not."

"Do you still talk to Melissa?"

"We message now and again, at Christmas and birthdays and that, but we haven't met up in years."

"Have you seen her?" Ivy asked.

"What's that supposed to mean?"

"It's a simple question," Ivy said. "Have you seen Melissa even if she hasn't seen you?"

"Am I stalking her? Is that what you're asking?"

Ivy didn't reply. She didn't need to.

"No," Adam said. "I'm not stalking Melissa. Of course, I want her to be okay. She was important to me. She went through a lot. But like I said, we don't really talk anymore."

"And would you like to?" George asked. "Would you like to be friends with her again?"

Potter shrugged. It was a large, overdramatic shrug, the kind a child might do. "I mean, sure. We got on well. We didn't exactly break up after an argument. She just needed time to…"

"To?" Ivy said.

"To process what happened to her."

"But it's not easy to be friends with your exes, is it?" George said. "That's what I hear anyway."

"I told you. It's not like it ended badly," Ryan said. "We were just young, and she was going through a lot."

"So maybe you could've rekindled things again now that you're older? Now that Melissa has moved on?"

"That's not what I said."

"But it's what you would want, isn't it, Adam? You *would* like to be with her again?"

"I…" He looked to his duty solicitor, who looked up from her notes for the first time and shook her head subtly.

George sat back and joined Ivy in staring at Potter for half a minute before asking casually, "Do you recognise us, Adam?" Again, Potter was preoccupied with looking around the room. "We met the other day, didn't we? You were at Stockwith Mill at Nancy and Lucas's wedding. You must've seen us there. We were difficult to miss. I even gave a speech, remember?"

Potter cast his lazy gaze George's way. "Yeah," he said simply. "I remember you."

"Well, we were there because, as I'm sure you remember, Ryan

Eva's dead body was found floating in the pool of the watermill. So why were *you* there, Adam?"

"I was the best man," he said quietly.

"Lucas Coffey's best man?" George reiterated.

"Who else's?"

"How do you know each other?"

"Through work," Potter said.

"So you're colleagues?" George said.

"Well, yeah. I mean, we were."

"You must be closer than that, though. For him to make you his best man? Surely, you're good friends, no?"

"Well, yeah, obviously."

"No, not obviously," George said. "Nothing is obvious to me. You're going to have to spell it out. How long have you and Lucas been friends?"

"I don't know. Five years? We met working at the council. Lucas moved onto bigger and better things, and I stayed where I was."

"You didn't want to move on to bigger and better things?" Ivy said dryly.

"Not everyone is made for that, are they? Some of us find joy in the little things," he said with a scowl. "I'm happy where I am."

"You look happy," Ivy said

"Were you happy at your best friend's wedding on Saturday, Adam?" George asked.

"What?" He laughed. "Yes, of course I was. Nancy is lovely. Lucas is lucky to have her."

"Really? Because the photographer sent us the images. I have to say, you don't really look too happy. In fact, I'd go as far as to say you were...what would you call it, Ivy?"

"Stressed."

"It's a wedding," Potter said. "There's a lot going on."

"But that's what the rehearsal is for, isn't it?" George said. "To make sure everything goes according to plan on the day?"

"I'm not a wedding planner," Potter said. "But I guess so."

"How did the wedding rehearsal go?" George asked.

Potter frowned. "Why are we talking about wedding planning?"

"We're not talking about wedding planning. We're talking about Nancy and Lucas's wedding rehearsal. How was it?"

He shrugged again, just slightly this time. "It was fine."

"No arguments, no family drama?"

"Oh," Potter said, laughing again to himself. "So that's what you're on about. The thing with Nancy's dad? I've no idea what that was about, honestly."

"If you had to guess," Ivy said.

Potter raised his arms in uncertainty. "Family stuff."

"Who was at the wedding rehearsal, Adam?"

"What? I don't know. I didn't take a register."

"See if you can remember for us," George said. "There can't have been that many."

He puffed his cheeks and looked up at the ceiling.

"Nancy and Lucas, her parents, his parents, me as the best man, and Summer, Nancy's maid of honour."

But before George could continue his line of questioning, the door to the interview room opened. Smoothly and without uttering a word, Campbell walked into the room and silently handed George a file. Then she left as quietly as she had entered.

"Excuse me," George said as he opened the file, processed the information inside, and then put it down as if it were little more than a menu for lunch. "Tell me, were you there for the entire wedding rehearsal, Adam?" he continued.

"What? Of course, I was," Potter said. "Where else would I be?"

"You didn't take a walk? Get some air? It can get quite over-whelming dealing with all those different characters. You didn't take a minute for yourself?"

"No," he said, visibly confused. "I was with Lucas pretty much the whole time."

"And Lucas could corroborate that, could he? He could say that you were with him all day all afternoon. Even, oh, let's say between twelve and two p.m.?"

"Of course, he could. We were all there all day. We didn't have a minute on our own."

George stared at the lad, and Ivy imagined that he, too, was reading between the frown lines on his forehead. She wondered if, like her, he saw some truth in Potter's responses.

George changed tack. He opened the file Campbell had handed to him once more and produced a single photograph. He placed it on the table and turned it around for Potter to see. Even upside down, Ivy recognised it. It was the photo of Adam texting at the wedding while Lucas shook hands with a guest.

"Who are you texting in this picture?" George asked.

He looked between the photo and up at George incredulously. "I have no idea. How am I supposed to know who I was texting three days ago?"

"You're right," George said. "People don't usually remember. See, that's why we go to the service providers and get the information." Potter didn't reply. "And the information we got is that, at the exact time this photograph was being taken, you were texting a specific phone number. Somebody who wasn't at the wedding. Do you know whose number that is?"

"Nobody knows phone numbers anymore," Adam whispered.

"Well, I can tell you," George said. "The number belongs to Mark Hale." George sat back in his seat while Potter studied the image. "Perhaps we can start again, Adam?"

CHAPTER THIRTY-FIVE

"What I'm wondering, Adam, what I find strange," George said, "is why you would be texting your ex-girlfriend's father? It's strange because I asked Mark Hale only today if he had spoken to you recently. And do you know what he said?"

Potter said nothing.

"He assured me that the two of you had not spoken since you were fifteen years old. So I find it strange that you were texting him only minutes before your best friend got married. It must've been quite important for you to be on your phone at such an event. So now, I'm going to ask you, Adam. When was the last time you spoke to, or contacted, Mark Hale?"

At this, the woman who had been silently scribbling notes for the entire interview chose to lean across to whisper in her client's ear.

Adam nodded his understanding and then said, "No comment."

"See, it's not only this one message that my colleague found to Mark Hale. No, there's a whole load of them sent that morning, as well as calls taken and missed in the days leading up to Ryan Eva's death. Can you explain that to me, Adam?"

"No comment."

"Did you kill Ryan Eva?" George asked. It wasn't a question with a hidden agenda. It was designed to provide a platform on which to base a prosecution case.

"No comment."

The response was expected and spoke volumes.

"Did you and Mark Hale work together to kill Ryan Eva?"

"No," he said quickly.

"Did you know that Ryan would be at the wedding rehearsal?"

With a glance at his duty solicitor, Adam returned to, "No comment."

"Did you and Mark Hale orchestrate the murder?"

"What? No."

"I'll ask you again, Adam. When was the last time you spoke to Melissa Hale?"

He shook his head, but it was more of an involuntary twitch. "No comment."

"When was the last time you spoke to Ryan Eva?"

"No comment."

"I thought it was when you beat him to a pulp?" Ivy said, her finger on her notes. "Sorry, there seems to be a conflict of responses."

"Well, yes," Adam said. "Yes, that was the last time."

His solicitor returned to her scribbling as though frustrated with Potter's inability to give a simple 'no comment' answer.

"Did you know that Ryan went to Melissa's house last week to talk with her?"

Adam's fist clenched on his knees, but he said, "No," with gritted teeth.

"She didn't tell you?"

"No."

"Have you ever been to Ryan Eva's bedsit in Skegness?"

"No," he said, his eyes watering now.

"We have CCTV evidence of a man matching your description

who visited Ryan's bedsit around four o'clock on Thursday afternoon. Was that you, Adam?"

He gulped and looked at his scribbling solicitor. "No," he croaked.

"You never broke into Ryan Eva's room?"

"No."

"Did you break in earlier today and murder Edward Higgins?"

Ryan shook his head more and more until his whole body was shaking, and then he threw his head into his hands on the desk. "No," he said louder. "No, no, no, no, no. I haven't bloody done anything."

"Where were you, Adam? Where were you today between eleven and twelve o'clock?"

"I was in town," he said quickly, looking up from his hands, his eyes bloodshot. "In Lincoln. You can check it," he said, pointing at his wallet, which was with the rest of his possessions in a clear plastic bag beside Ivy. "You can check my bank records. I took money out of the ATM beside the bakery on the high street at eleven o'clock. You can check it," he repeated. "You can check my bank records."

George looked at Ivy. "We will be doing that, Adam. But I must say, I'm quite impressed. That's quite a memory you have. To know where and at what exact time you were taking money out."

Adam looked up with those wet, bloodshot eyes, and even though George had not asked a question, he said, "No comment."

"Do you understand how serious this is, Adam?" George asked, closing the files and trying, above all else, to reason with the young man. "We're talking about a murder here. The murder of a man you have a motive to kill and indeed have attacked before. A man who died not far from where you were standing in that photograph at that exact time. It doesn't look good, Adam." He sat back again, letting those words permeate. "Now, is there anything you'd like to tell us? Anything that could help with our investigation?"

Potter said nothing. He bowed his head and fiddled with his hands beneath the table, chewing on his lower lip.

"I see," George said. "Well, we'll be applying for a custody extension, so you'll be with us for a further thirty-four hours." Potter squeezed his eyes closed, and his gullet rose and fell with guilt. "I suggest you use that time to do some thinking," George said, checking his watch. He nodded for Ivy to end the recording. "In the meantime, I shall be going home for my dinner." He rose from his chair, gathered the files, and stopped by the door. "I mean it, Adam," he said. "Think about the future."

"Do I even have a future?" Potter said, his voice thick with emotion.

"That all depends on how much thought you give to what you just told us," George said. "And what you didn't."

"Guv," Ivy said when they were in the corridor and she had closed the door behind her.

"That lad's future is bleak," George said.

"Guv," she said again, ignoring his statement. "I might slip off if it's alright with you."

He checked his watch again.

"There's only half an hour left. I suppose it's fine," he replied, then studied her expression. It was akin to the one she wore moments before visiting Pippa Bell in her mortuary. "You heading home?"

"I think I should," she replied, then averted her gaze. "There's a few things I want to say to Jamie. See the kids and that. You know?"

He smiled at her, reassuring her, he hoped.

"You okay?"

"Yeah, yeah," she said. "Just. Well, I don't know. I'll be fine, I suppose. I just don't know what to expect. All this talk about divorces and kids in care-."

"That's not you," he said. "Not every divorce has to be dramatic, and not all the kids end up in care. You've both got good jobs. They're great kids."

"I know," she replied dismissively.

"Tell you what," he told her. "I'll make a move, too. Come on, I'll walk you out."

"What about Campbell and Byrne? Ruby and the other two are up there, too."

"So call them on your way home," he suggested. "Tell them to prepare for the morning briefing."

"What about Potter?" she asked.

"Ask Campbell to request the custody extension," he replied. "To be honest, I'm beginning to think we brought him in too early. The stakes aren't high enough yet."

"What stakes?" she said, to which he grinned.

"Just an idea I'm working on in here," he said, tapping his temple. He shoved the door to the station yard open and stood back for her to exit. "You going to be okay, Ivy?"

"Honestly, I don't know," she said, mirroring an earlier remark he had made. She turned and strode across the yard, holding her head high. "If I'm not knocking on your door in an hour or two, you'll know it went well."

CHAPTER THIRTY-SIX

George's rear garden had been used as a workshop throughout the summer. He had managed to get the front garden looking choco-late-box perfect, but the rear lawn resembled the Somme, and the beds were more like rainforests. He didn't even recognise some of the weeds that had come through and had even had to look one or two up to make sure they weren't some strange plant that Grace's parents had planted.

There was a balance to be struck, and he was in search of it. Grace adored a nice garden, and maybe seeing the old place how her parents had kept it would invigorate her mind. But on the flip side of the coin, restoring it to the previous standard would require some serious upkeep, daily monitoring, and, above all else, far more knowledge than he could lay claim to.

A car door closed somewhere nearby, and he listened out for the doorbell but heard nothing. He jabbed the trowel into the earth, scooped up the pile of weeds, and made his way across the lawn to the compost heap. It was that time of year when the days began to draw in, which was all the excuse he needed to call it a day. He was pulling off his gloves as he strode across the lawn when he saw her standing at the side of the house with a holdall hanging from one shoulder and a brown paper bag in her hand.

"Takeaway on a Monday night?" he said as she strode around to the back door. "What's the special occasion?"

But she said nothing. She barely made eye contact. Instead, she entered the house and set her bag down.

He took a few minutes to brush the trowel clean and then store it on the hook near the back door, where Grace had always kept it.

The sound of plates was loud in the quiet little hamlet, and the smell of fresh fish and chips was welcome.

"I miss this place," she said, sniffing the salty fish and chips when he entered the kitchen, kicking off his old boots and slipping into his worn slippers. "Thought I'd pick some up while I was on the coast. It's not the same inland, is it?"

"You don't need to convince me," George said. He gave his hands a rinse at the sink, then joined her at the kitchen table, where she was dividing the chips. It was something that Grace had often done; bought two pieces of fish and one portion of chips, and the sight of Ivy re-enacting the charade amused him.

"You know, those new PCs aren't bad," Ivy said. "They handled the meeting with Ian Eva and Pippa Bell just fine, and they've already confirmed that Adam was indeed in town this morning, withdrawing cash from an ATM."

"Is that your way of telling me we're barking up the wrong tree?"

"And they already highlighted a timeline of Adam Potter and Mark Hale's communications from the phone bill," she continued. "They told me they should have a warrant to look at the actual messages by the morning."

"Not bad," George said. "They would've had to hound the judge to get that turned around so fast."

"Yeah, I think they know what they're doing," she said. "I think they'll be good additions."

"Unless, of course, Ruby gave them a helping hand," George said. "She seems to have a knack for getting what she wants."

"Something tells me it had more to do with DCI Long, though, if I'm honest. Two PCs requesting warrants to delve into a suspect's phone records." She scrunched her nose. "That would have been put to the back of the list. I doubt even I could get them to issue a warrant that fast."

"Ah," George said. "Yes, of course. Tim has a lot riding on those two."

"In what way?"

"Well, he's begged, borrowed and stolen resources from various teams to give our little team what it needs to succeed. What does that tell you?"

"That he wants it to be a success?"

George laughed.

"Well, he does, of course," he said. "But there's more to it than that. He's bet on us."

"He's what?"

"He's bet on us," George said again. "He's been pushing for the major crimes team for months. I imagine the DCC and everyone in Lincoln HQ were telling him it wouldn't work. But he insisted. And now we're here—"

"And he needs it to work?"

"Exactly," George said with a smile. "He feigns indifference, of course. But it's something I'll keep in mind."

"I don't get it," Ivy said. "Why does it matter?"

"It's leverage," George told her. "He's got our backs; regardless of what he says to my face, he has our backs."

He cut a piece of fish and forked it into his mouth.

"Can I ask you something, guv?"

"Anything at all, Ivy."

"What's the deal with you and him? I thought you were friends. I thought you were close back in the day. Didn't he help you with the Tucker investigation and everything?"

It was George's turn to pause as though trying to balance his professionalism with his need to expunge his frustrations. And there was no one he trusted more than Ivy. "Yes, we were friends. Definitely close colleagues. We walked the beat together. I think that's the problem. When we were equals, we worked well together, but now that he ranks higher than me, the dynamic just feels like he's trying to exert his control. Even though he doesn't need to."

"I think he feels threatened, guv," Ivy said. "You've come back after all these years, and maybe if you hadn't gone away, that would be you in his office, in his position. I think he knows that."

"That's never what I wanted though," George said. "Hell, I'm sixty..." He stopped himself just in time. "I'm sixty-odd years old with no plans to retire. I definitely don't want to end up in a windowless office in the corner of the building. I always wanted to be in that incident room, at that whiteboard, talking to suspects in those interview rooms. Tim knows that. He knows me. The trouble is, Tim Long is slightly more ambitious than I am. Always has been."

"Does he know about Grace?" Ivy said cautiously.

"No. No one knows about Grace. Only you." He plucked a particularly crispy chip from the plate. "And that's how I want to keep it."

"Can I ask another question, guv?"

"Why don't I tell everyone?" He pushed a chip around his plate with his fork. "I don't know. I think I'm wary of pity. Grace would never want anyone to feel sorry for her. She'd hate the fuss. She just wants to go quietly, you know. Maybe I want to give her that dignity. Or I don't know...maybe I'm just protecting myself."

Ivy just nodded and continued eating. He knew she didn't have an answer for him, but he was grateful to her for making him say it out loud. "How did you leave it with Adam?" he asked.

"I did what you said. I asked Dan Robson to keep him in

overnight. Hopefully, that will make him aware of the gravity of the situation."

George looked up from his dinner and took his own leap in the conversation. "How is Dan?"

"He's fine," Ivy said. Then she added with a grin, "You should ask him yourself."

"You know what I mean," George said, rolling his eyes. "Are you two still...?"

"We were never anything," Ivy said, and George could sense her discomfort. But whether it was because she was lying or simply uncomfortable talking to George about her love life, he wasn't sure. "Did I like the flirting? Did I like the attention? Sure. But I'm not actually going to act on it. He's the custody sergeant, for God's sake."

"I suppose you're free to now though, aren't you? You know, now that you and Jamie are separated?"

She shook her head. "I told you. I'm not ready for that. Certainly not before we're divorced."

"So that's definitely the plan, is it? Divorce?"

"If you're asking how it went tonight, then the fact that I'm here should tell you all you need to know."

"Have you talked to your mum about it?"

"Mum just wants me to be happy." Ivy shrugged. "I'm sure she doesn't exactly approve. But she's seen me be so miserable the last few years; I think she gets it."

"So, no dating?" George said.

"No dating," she said, holding up her water glass in a *cheers*.

"If you're sure, you're sure."

"I am," Ivy said. "The last thing I want to do is jump straight into someone else being dependent on me. That was the whole point. I need time on my own. I need to work out who I am outside of Jamie, outside of the kids. Do you have any idea how nice it is to walk into a house where people don't immediately jump on you? Not question you about where their socks are or if I can make them cupcakes for the school fair? Let me tell you, guv," she said, looking around the large, scantly decorated kitchen, "you have it great."

Even though she didn't mean it that way, George felt a stab of hurt. Something akin to loneliness. Or grief. And he was sure it showed on his face.

"God, sorry, guv," she said. "I didn't mean…I know you would rather Grace was here. I just meant—"

"I know Ivy, and I understand not all marriages are the same." He took a sip of water. "But yes, of course, I would rather Grace was here with me."

A silence developed between them, heavy as a cloud. Memories played like snippets of film in his mind. Off-cuts of larger memories without context. He could picture Grace in that room throughout her life, from when he had first courted her as a young girl to her mother's last days and the weeks that followed when they had closed the house down. But it was the insignificant times that carried the most nostalgia. The everyday habits. The way she couldn't bear to leave the hot chocolate mugs until morning. She insisted on washing them, drying them, and putting them away. The way she untied her pinny and hung it on the back of the kitchen door. He turned in his seat, and there it was. Vacant. Even the way she used to say, "I think I'll head up," every single night as if it was out of character. And how, each time, he would reply with, "I won't be far behind you," and he would pour himself a half-measure of scotch, giving her time to get ready for bed.

"So what did you think?" Ivy asked, dragging George from his thoughts. "Did you believe Adam Potter?"

"It didn't make me any *more* suspicious," George said. "Of course, he's lying about some things, but I don't think we can pin everything on him, especially if Maguire can confirm he was in Lincoln today. I'll tell you what it did do, though. It's made me a hell of a lot more suspicious of Mark Hale." He jabbed a fork in her direction. "He needs looking at in great detail."

"Right, but we don't have anything on him. It's hardly a crime to text your daughter's ex-boyfriend."

"But it's weird, Ivy."

"We need more than weird before we bring Mark Hale in, guv."

"Why? He doesn't have an alibi. He has an MMO. He ticks all the boxes."

"Does he?" Ivy said. "What's his means? He has no connection to the wedding. He didn't know Ryan Eva would be there. Anyway, he was at work all day, and when he wasn't, he was picking his daughter up. He wouldn't have had time to get to Skeggy to see Ryan."

"He has Adam. That's his connection to the wedding. Maybe that's what they were texting about. Maybe Adam saw Ryan there and texted Mark, and Mark came over to Stockwith Mill to..."

"Guv?"

"To tell him to back off," George said. "Maybe it escalated."

"That's a lot of maybes, guv," she said.

"Yes, I know," he replied. "Maybe one day, one of those maybes will become a certainty. Maybe a night on a blue, plastic mattress with nothing but warm water to drink will change Adam Potter's mind."

"Maybe we'll get in tomorrow and find that the others have made a breakthrough?" Ivy suggested.

"Steady on, Ivy," he said, reaching for his phone.

"You're right," she said. "Guv, do you think we should have asked for officers with more experience? I mean, Campbell's okay and the two newbies seem to be switched on."

"You still have doubts about Byrne, do you?"

"He's...inconsistent," Ivy replied.

George found the number he was looking for, debated his idea for a moment, and then hit the green button to initiate a call.

"Where are you off to?" Ivy said as the call connected, and

George started towards the back door, wiping his mouth on his handkerchief.

He considered telling her his idea. But regardless of how much he leaned on her, there were times when he had to run with his instincts without question.

"I'm testing a theory," he said cryptically as he stepped outside, and the call was answered with obvious anxiety.

"Guv?"

"Byrne, sorry to bother you out of hours," George said. "I need you to start early tomorrow." He checked behind him to make sure Ivy was out of earshot. "I've got a little job for you and Campbell."

CHAPTER THIRTY-SEVEN

"Absolute rubbish," Maguire announced when George and Ivy walked into the incident room. The four PCs were all at their desks, and the Irishman was red-faced and animated. "It goes Sean Connery, Daniel Craig, Timothy What's-his-name, Roger Moore, and then the other one."

"Lazenby," Byrne said, sounding as if he was either bored of the conversation or unable to fathom Maguire's ability to remember every actor who had played Bond.

"Right," Maguire said. "Him. He was rubbish. But Connery's the one. It was he who made it. If it wasn't for Connery, we wouldn't even *have* Bond films."

"I think that's unfair," Byrne cut in.

Across the room, a handful of CID officers put their heads down in their work, and Ivy opened her mouth to put a stop to the nonsense. But George stopped her by raising a hand.

"What does this have to do with the investigation?" she asked.

"Nothing," he said. "But just wait a second."

He watched with interest as the conversation grew in intensity.

"Daniel Craig," Byrne said matter-of-factly. "Connery was good, but everyone knows that Daniel Craig modernised the Bond franchise."

"What about Roger Moore?" O'Hara said. "My mum adores him. She'd have something to say about this; I can tell you that much."

"Ah, he might have been okay in that seventies show," Maguire said. "But as a Bond? No, too much satire."

"Do you mean The Saint," Byrne said again in that bored tone. "And that was the sixties."

"Not that one. The other one," Maguire said. "The one with the other fella. The Professionals."

"The Professionals?" Byrne said, sounding surprised. "Bodie and Doyle?"

"Aye, that's the one."

"The one with Martin Shaw and Lewis Collins?"

Maguire appeared perplexed for a moment.

"Right," he said. "That's it."

"You mean *The Persuaders*," Byrne said. "With Roger Moore and Tony Curtis."

"Ah, whatever," Maguire said, agitated at Byrne's obvious superior knowledge. "The fact is that on the list of best Bonds, Moore is nowhere near the top."

"Despite him making more Bond movies than any of the others?" Byrne added. "I suppose the people that made the movies should have come to you for advice, shouldn't they?"

"Look at him," George said to Ivy as the argument unfolded.

"Who? Maguire?" Ivy muttered. "Yeah, he's got a gob on him, hasn't he?"

"Not him. Byrne."

"Byrne?"

"He's like a different man," George remarked. "I always had him down as a bit pathetic."

"He did get punched on the nose during his first arrest with us, guv."

"That could have happened to anyone," George said, and he slowly moved forward between the CID desks. "I think I've had him wrong these past few months."

"What, because he knows about James Bond?"

He laughed once and scanned the team. Ruby held her phone between her head and shoulder, typing away furiously; Campbell was poring over the investigation file, keeping one ear in the conversation, O'Hara had positioned her seat close to Campbell, clearly hoping for an opportunity to help out, and Maguire was leaning back in his seat, fuelling the argument. Byrne, however, had his laptop open and several documents spread out before him, and despite Maguire's red face and loud mouth, was effortlessly winning the argument.

"You failed to mention Pierce Brosnan," Byrne said without even looking up. He handed Campbell a document, then peered up at his laptop.

"Who?" Maguire said.

"Never mind who," George said as he strode into the throng. Maguire immediately set his chair down on all four legs and hurriedly opened his laptop. "Briefing. Five minutes. Get a drink, have a wee, bring a pen and paper."

"Have a wee?" Maguire said, and he peered around at the team. "Have a wee what, guv?"

"Have a wee whatever you want," George replied, laying his coat over his chair. "Just be back here in five minutes." Campbell and O'Hara took the opportunity and slipped out of the room, and Maguire stood to follow them. "Maguire?" George called.

"Guv?"

"I don't mind a bit of banter, but I have two pieces of advice for you."

"Go on?"

"If you do decide to engage in banter during work hours, at

least pretend to be working." He glanced down at the laptop, which Maguire hadn't even logged into.

"Ah, sorry, guv," he replied, grinning his way out of the corner. "What else?"

"Never argue a case against the evidence," George said. "Byrne clearly stated the facts surrounding Roger Moore's competence and Daniel Craig's abilities, yet you insisted on making an argument based on your own subjective views. I hope that's not an indication of your work ethic."

"Eh?"

"I would have enjoyed seeing you find an argument against the facts that Byrne laid out or some kind of poll that supported your views. But you didn't. You just kept on forcing your opinion."

"Aye but, guv... I mean, Daniel Craig or Sean Connery. It's Connery all day long. Craig was just a miserable wretch. At least Connery did what he had to do with a smile on his face."

"And yet you still provide a subjective opinion," George said, and Maguire stopped and held his hands up in defence.

"Alright, alright," he said. "Point taken."

"Good, I hope so," George said.

"It's my fault, guv," Byrne said. "I started it."

"Another of your quiz night topics, was it?"

"Quiz night? Oh no, guv. We were discussing the investigation."

"And somehow that led to the question of who was the best James Bond?"

"It was the suspects, guv," Byrne continued, and he nodded at the names on the whiteboard. "Whoever did it was strong enough to overpower Ryan Eva and Edward Higgins."

"Both of whom were fairly small men," George said.

"But then they also broke the lock on the bedsit," Byrne continued. "Which suggests they had some kind of weight behind them, yes?"

"Yes," George said slowly.

"Now, the footage from the pet shop shows *a man* breaking into the house. Edward Higgins said he saw *a man* at Ryan Eva's door. Which rules out Nancy Wetherford, Maeve Wetherford, and Melissa Hale."

"For Edward Higgins' murder, yes," George agreed. "But not for Ryan Eva's."

"Ah, but both of their mobile phones were taken," Byrne continued. "Suggesting that it was the same person. The same man. So we were discussing which of those men could have A) overpowered the two men and B) broken into the house. Now," Byrne continued, "Maguire reckons that Adam Potter is too small and that Rory Wetherford, who has more weight behind him, is most likely."

"Of course he is," Maguire said. "He's emotionally motivated. He could have crushed both men with one bloody hand and the front door of the bedsit," he continued. "I saw the images that the scene of crime guys sent through. Now that takes some doing, let me tell you."

"But you feel differently, do you?" George asked Byrne. "You think it was somebody other than Rory Wetherford, based on some other factor?"

"I think that we can't simply go on a man's appearance and strength, guv," he replied. "If Rory Wetherford is heavy enough to destroy a front door like that, then why struggle with Ryan Eva in the stream? He could have pummelled him to death with ease." He shook his head. "Ryan Eva put up a fight, guv. Whoever grabbed that rock did so in desperation."

"And this somehow led to the James Bond discussion?" Ivy said.

"I was merely demonstrating that size and strength are not factors here. Sean Connery was overpowered on more than one occasion. But he used his wits to get him through," Byrne said.

"Wits my backside," Maguire said, like a sulking teenager.

They were interrupted by Campbell and O'Hara's return. Each

carried a coffee and were laughing at something that one of them had said.

George took his place at the whiteboard, and Ivy leaned on her desk between Campbell and Ruby.

"So, we followed up on Adam Potter's alibi from yesterday. He was on Lincoln High Street when Edward was killed, so we can eliminate him from the Edward Higgins' murder."

"CCTV confirms it, guv," Ruby added. "Definitely him."

"But that doesn't mean he wasn't involved in the Ryan Eva murder," George said. "While we have him in custody, I wouldn't mind talking to Lucas Coffey again to find out if Potter left the rehearsal at any point. Campbell, maybe you could get in touch with him?"

"Interview him, guv?" she said. "Me?"

"Not an interview," he replied. "Just a chat. See if he's willing to help with our enquiries. You never know; he might say something that will give us another angle to go at Potter with."

"Speaking of Potter," Ivy said. "Are we going in for round two?"

"Not until we have a new angle. I see very little benefit in going over the same questions."

"So, we're just going to leave him in his cell?"

"Unless you can think of a better idea, Ivy," George said, and he waited for a response. "No? Thought not. He stays in his cell until we have a new angle or the custody clock expires."

"I don't know how reliable Lucas Coffey would be given that they're best mates, guv," Ivy said. "We could really do with some evidence that puts Adam Potter by the stream with Ryan Eva."

"That's where we differ," George said, smiling broadly. "You're looking for evidence to charge him and everyone else." He slid his hands into his pockets and softened his tone. "I'm trying to clear them. Potter, Hale, Wetherford. All of them."

"That doesn't make sense," Maguire said.

"I agree, it's unusual," he replied. "But think of it this way. If we can't definitively prove that Potter was there, then perhaps we can prove he wasn't. The same applies to the rest of them. We should, in theory, be able to prove, whether by statement or hard evidence, that the innocent are indeed innocent."

"Which, in the case of your theory, guv, would leave just one suspect."

"One suspect to focus our attention on," he said. "You have to understand that had this murder been in London or a big city, I'd have a dozen or more officers working on it. A few of you would be investigating Potter, a few would be investigating Hale, and so on." He shook his head. "There are seven of us, and with all due respect, only Ivy and I have any major crimes experience. Campbell and Byrne, you're coming on, but you have a long way to go. Maguire, O'Hara, you're what, a few hours into this? I'd be mad to think we can break this using a conventional approach." He smiled at them all, hoping to reassure them. "But break it we will. We just have to use the resources to hand to our advantage. We have to adapt our approach."

"And how do we do that then, guv?" Maguire asked.

George studied him for a moment. Ivy was right; he did have a big mouth, but there were times when that was beneficial. Every team needed somebody to ask questions. If he had a team full of O'Hara's, then they would all be too worried about his opinion of them to ask.

"That's a very good question," George replied. "We talk to people. I've got four officers, all of whom are experienced in taking statements. Taking a statement in a murder investigation is no different to taking a statement for a burglary or a car accident. I've also got eighty-odd witnesses. You ask questions, PC Maguire. You read people. You don't try to catch people out. You take an objective approach."

"Objective?"

"I know, it goes against your natural way of doing things," George said. "We look at phone records. We look for patterns.

We do not have the luxury of bringing every name on this board in for questioning. But we do have DCI Long on our side. If there's a phone number we want to look into or a warrant we need, then we'll get it."

"So we're doing this the long way, then?" Ivy said.

"We're doing this the only way we can," he replied. "Speaking of warrants. How are we doing on that warrant for Adam's text messages? I want to know what exactly he said to Mark."

"They said they'd be in touch in the morning. Maguire gave them my number," Campbell said. "I'll let you know as soon as it comes through."

George turned to Ruby. "As soon as that comes through, I want to know what those messages said." He checked his watch. "Preferably while Potter is still in custody. Meanwhile, Campbell, talk to Lucas Coffey. Go easy on him. You're gathering facts."

"No shining a bright light in his eyes, then?" she replied, to which he grinned and let his silence respond. "Yes, guv."

"And be ready for a call from Pippa Bell," he said. "You and Byrne can attend the post-mortem."

"Sorry?"

"You don't need a certificate to attend a post-mortem," he said.

"No, just a strong constitution," Ivy added.

"Take notes," George said. "Ask questions. Show interest." He eyed Ivy knowingly. "And whatever you do, don't upset her."

"What does that mean?" Campbell asked.

"You'll find out," he beamed back at her. "Oh, and when you're done there, you might as well swing by Southwell's lab. Give her a nudge, will you?"

"A nudge," she replied with a sigh. "Right."

"What do we do until then, guv?" Ivy asked. "What do you want me working on."

"I want you in the interview room," he said.

"I thought we were leaving Potter to stew?"

"We are," he said, and he turned to Byrne. "Did you manage what I asked last night?"

"Oh, yeah," Byrne said. "He's in interview room two."

"Who's in room two?" Ivy asked. "What is going on?"

"Haven't you been listening?" he asked, enjoying how she behaved when things were out of her control. He pointed at the list of suspects. "If we can't prove their guilt, then maybe we can prove their innocence."

"Whose innocence?" she said. "Who have you brought in?"

"Somebody with a motive and the means to have murdered Edward Higgins," he said as he passed her on his way to the door. "Mark Hale."

"Mark Hale?" she said. "We've got him on CCTV, guv. He was at work when Edward Higgins died."

"Yes, so you said," George replied, holding the door for her. "So we shouldn't have any trouble proving his innocence, should we?"

CHAPTER THIRTY-EIGHT

"I hate it when you do this," Ivy said as George marched along the corridor.

"No, you hate it when you lose control," he told her.

"I just don't understand why you didn't tell me," she said, running to keep up with George as he strode towards the custody suite. Her raised voice reverberated off the hard, painted breeze block walls and caught the attention of the Custody Sergeant, who peered through the glazed doors, saw them, and then returned to his work.

"Would you have supported my decision?" George asked.

"No," Ivy said. "No, I would've told you to wait. I would've said that we're not ready to interview him yet, that we should wait because we don't have enough to go on and that *you* have a habit of following your gut over the evidence. For God's sake, guv. You just spent ten minutes telling that lot upstairs that if we can't prove anybody guilty, then we'll prove them innocent and see who's left."

"And that's what I intend to do," he said. "I'm going to lay everything on the table and have him explain."

"Everything?"

"The lot," he said.

"That's a risk," she said. "This isn't a strategy. This is your gut. You're following instinct. You want him to slip up."

George smiled as he came to the interview room door. "Has my instinct ever let you down?"

He went to enter the room, but before he could, Ivy grabbed his arm, not hard but firm enough.

"I'm trying to protect you, guv. It might not have let us down, but your instinct has landed us in some messy situations in the past. And I don't think DCI Long will be too forgiving knowing we have two individuals in custody with verified alibis, and all because your gut tells you they know more than they're saying. Half the people that come through here know more than they tell us."

"Yes," he said regretfully. "Yes, there is that." He pondered the door handle, then looked at her. "Are you finished?"

He pushed down on the handle, and she grabbed his arm again.

"What about evidence?" she hissed. "What about facts?"

"The facts are simple," he replied, pulling the door closed. "Mark Hale has a motive. Adam Potter has a motive."

"You think they did this together, don't you?" she said, her eyes narrowing. "You think that Potter did Ryan Eva and Hale did Edward Higgins."

He grinned.

"Now there's a thought," he said, and before she could reply, he opened the interview room door. "Are you joining me or not?"

Ivy followed him inside and took her seat beside the recorder.

"Good morning, Mr Hale," George said. "How are you doing today?"

"Oh, let me think," Mark said, who, unlike his duty solicitor sitting down calmly, was pacing the room like a caged tiger. "Well, I woke up and went to work, and then you lot came to my brewery and arrested me in front of my staff. How do you bloody think I'm doing?"

"As I'm sure you're aware, Mr. Hill, you are by no means under arrest."

"He told me he would arrest me if I didn't come voluntarily."

"Well, yes, quite possibly," George said. "But thankfully, you saw sense and came to help us with our investigation. Very wise, I must say. And charitable, too."

"Don't butter me up, Inspector," he replied.

George held out his arm, inviting Mark Hale to join them at the table. Only when Mark Hale seated himself with a grumble did Ivy begin the recording.

He announced the time, date, and location, and then introduced himself and Ivy, before beckoning for the legal aid to follow suit.

"Duty Solicitor, Andrew Drinkwater," the little man with short hair and dark skin said. He was dressed in an expensive blue suit with a shiny tie clip that kept catching the overhead lights and spraying a bright rectangle across the walls. From a first impression, he looked more put-together than many of the solicitors George had seen over the years, and he peered over his glasses in anticipation.

George turned his attention to Mark Hale, who, seated beside his groomed legal aid, looked rough. Compared to the first time they had met, only two days previously, he looked like a different man. Where he had been well-groomed and well-dressed, he was now unshaven, wearing a wrinkled t-shirt with a bleach stain on the sleeve. His hair flopped across his forehead, casting a shadow over his eyes that merged with the dark bags that ringed them and made the whites, laced with tiny red arteries, piercing.

"Mark Hale," he said eventually. "Volunteer interviewee."

"Excuse me for saying, Mr Hale, but you don't look your usual self."

Mark scoffed. "Is that why you brought me here? To insult me?"

"Of course not. I just wonder if something's on your mind. Something keeping you up at night, perhaps?"

Mark leaned forward, and as he did so, George noticed several long scratches along his forearms, red and angry.

"Many things keep me up at night, Inspector Larson. Rising taxes, falling trade, greater employee rights, failing employer rights."

"I imagine it's a difficult time for business," George said.

"And then there's you lot turning up at my bloody house and interrogating my daughter."

"Is that the word she used? Interrogating?"

"She didn't need to."

"Do you often do that, Mr Hale? Do you often put words in your daughter's mouth? Do you often take responsibility for her instead of letting her speak for herself?"

"How dare you," Mark whispered in a low growl.

"I'm just saying, Mr Hale. You strike me as a man who would do anything for his daughter." It was George's turn to lean forward so that the men were almost nose to nose. "*Anything.*"

Mark didn't reply but simply sat back slowly and said, "Yes, Inspector. I would."

"Murder, maybe?"

"No," Mark said, and he sat back, crossing his legs. "See, this is what gets me about you lot. You think that we're all bloody lunatics. That none of us can think for ourselves. You don't understand us common people. That's your problem."

"Enlighten me."

He gave the question some thought, then settled on his phrasing and spoke as if he were leading a business meeting, controlling.

"If you lot locked me up, what would happen to Melissa? She'd be on her own. I wouldn't be able to protect her anymore, would I? It would be counterintuitive." He shook his head. "I couldn't do that to her, not ever. So, in response to your allegation, Inspector, I know why you think I did it. But I did not kill Ryan Eva."

"I understand," George said. "And for what it's worth, I believe you."

"Sorry?"

"I don't think you killed Ryan Eva," George said.

Drinkwater scribbled notes as fast as his hand could move, leaving no room to interact with his client.

"So, why am I here?" Hale asked.

"I don't think you were responsible for Ryan Eva's death, but I would like to spread that certainty into another death."

"Another what?"

"Another murder, Mr. Hale."

"Another what?" he said again. "Who? Who the bloody hell am I supposed to have killed?"

Ivy adjusted her seat and cleared her throat as she peered over at Drinkwater's notes.

"You'll be sure to add that we're looking to eliminate your client from the investigation. This is by no means an accusation."

Drinkwater peered over his glasses at her, then at his client, and eventually struck a line through his writing and made the correction.

"Who?" Hale insisted.

"Edward Higgins," Ivy said.

"He was a young man living at a bedsit in Skegness," George added.

"Well, what the hell does that have to do with me?"

"He lived in the bedroom next door to Ryan Eva," George continued. "Yesterday, somebody broke into his room and murdered him in his sleep."

"And you think I did that, do you?"

"I think you could have, yes," George said. "But like I said, we're hoping to strike you from our investigation."

George was amazed it had taken this long for the duty solicitor to speak up, and when he did, he seemed to do so as though slowly waking from a dream. Perhaps he was not as put-together as George had expected.

"If you are accusing my client of murder, DI Larson, then I suggest you make an arrest so we can do this properly."

Mark turned to his solicitor. "That's your advice? That's your bloody advice to arrest me?"

"Believe it or not, you have greater rights when you are arrested."

"I don't want them to bloody arrest me, you—"

"Your solicitor's right," Ivy said, grinning. "We *can* arrest you, Mark."

"Look, I did not kill Edward Hibbins."

"Higgins."

"Whatever. I don't know who he is. I've never been near him. Why on earth would I? I can understand why you would want to question me over Ryan bloody Eva, but this other bloke? Come on."

"We have CCTV footage showing a man of your description breaking into Higgins' bedsit and leaving eleven minutes later. The times match the pathologist's given time of death."

"Oh, so you have proof, do you?"

"Not proof, per se," Ivy said.

Mark scoffed, and his laugh triggered something in George.

"Where were you, Mr Hale? Where were you yesterday afternoon? Tell us that, and we can drop the whole thing."

"I was at work," Mark said. "Like I said, I have a job. But you know that already, don't you?"

"And your colleagues could confirm that, could they? They could say that they saw you at work?"

"I don't brew the bloody beer myself," Mark said. "I was in my office. They probably saw me coming and going, yeah, but I have a private office."

"Well, that's okay," George said. "We will be able to corroborate using ANPR and local CCTV footage," George looked up at him. "Automatic Number Plate Recognition," he clarified. "So we can see you coming and going. Very useful tool, isn't it, Ivy?"

"Sure is, guv," she said.

"What time did you say?" Mark asked, licking his lips. "I was coming and going. Seeing suppliers."

"I will be able to see where you were coming and going," George said. "Don't worry about that." George paused, narrowing his eyes before his next question. "Do you have a cat, Mr Hale?"

"Excuse me?"

"I've been to your house a few times, as you pointed out, and I've never seen one."

Mark Hale threw his head back in exasperation, then brought it forward, saying, "No, I don't have a cat. What is this?"

"Well, I was just wondering how you got those scratches on your arms."

Mark's eyes widened, and he immediately removed his hands from the table. "Work," he said quickly.

"What's that?"

"I got them at work," he said. "The scratches."

"I thought you didn't brew the bloody beer yourself? I thought you had a nice private office where you sit all day?" Mark didn't reply, and just when he went to, George moved on, keeping him ungrounded. "Thank you for providing your fingerprints with our custody officer, by the way. They will be very useful to us," George said politely.

"I have nothing to hide," Mark said quietly.

"Well, that's what I had hoped," George said. "Now, you'll never guess who we had in here yesterday."

"Sorry?"

"An old friend of yours."

Hale swallowed. "And who's that?"

"Adam Potter," George said, as though they were two friends chatting over coffee. "You remember Adam Potter, don't you, Mark? Your daughter's ex-boyfriend. The one you said was too skinny. The one you said you hadn't seen or spoken to in nine years."

Mark didn't reply

"The reason for bringing it up is that we found some messages and calls between you and Mr. Potter."

"You did what?"

"The last one was yesterday," George said, leaning forward. "Now, why on earth would you be texting your daughter's ex-boyfriend, Mark?"

Mark rubbed his eyes with his palms, making them even more bloodshot than before.

"You can see how it looks, can't you?" George said.

"Look, he likes Melissa, alright? I didn't want to embarrass the lad in front of her, but he's been texting me, trying to get back with her. What can I say? I'm a romantic at heart."

George sat back, amazed at what he had just heard.

"Let me get this straight, your daughter's ex-boyfriend contacted you to get back with your daughter. You, a father whose job it is to protect her." He glanced across at Ivy. "I don't know about you, but I avoided my father-in-law like the plague, even after we were married."

"Times have changed, Inspector," Hale said. "Besides, better the devil, you know, and all that."

"Is he a good match for your daughter?" George asked.

"He protected her back then. He protected her against Ryan Eva, and he'd do the same again. I know he would. He's a good lad."

"Oh, we're not doubting that," Ivy said. "Believe me. We saw the charge sheet."

"The charges were dropped," Hale said. "As were mine."

"But no one would protect Melissa like you would," George said. "Would they, Mark? No one could have as strong a grudge against Ryan Eva as the father of his victim."

"Do I have a grudge against Ryan Eva? Of course, I do. Any father would. I'm open about that. I'm honest about it. Does that mean I killed the man? No. It does not. I can't be the only father in this world with a grudge against Ryan Eva."

George was caught off guard by the imagery triggered by those words. He allowed a long silence to gather his thoughts, which had started spinning, first out of control, and then towards a whole new line of train of thought. The silence was so long he could feel Hale and Ivy beginning to wonder what was happening.

"We'll be sure to check those times with your staff," he said.

"What?"

"You're free to go," George said. "All being well, you won't hear from us again." He closed the file before him. "Oh, you don't mind if we send a couple of officers to the brewery, do you? I'd hate to intrude."

Hale's face was a picture of bemusement.

"Do what you have to do," he said quietly.

George smiled his gratitude, then called out. "Guard?" The door opened almost immediately, and a uniformed officer leaned in. "See Mr Hale out, would you?"

"And just like that, it's over, is it?" Hale said as he neared the door.

"I told you," George replied. "It was my intention to prove your innocence." He let the statement settle. "Good day, Mr. Hale."

Only when Hale and the duty solicitor had closed the door behind them did Ivy throw her hands up incredulously.

"Guv? What the hell are you doing? First, you risk our necks by bringing him in in the first place, and then you let him go. Why? What's the plan here?"

"Ivy..." George said, frowning at the table while his thoughts arranged themselves into some semblance of a plan. Ivy moved into his line of sight.

"Guv? Guv, are you okay?"

"Yes," he said, pulling himself from a whirlpool of wonderings. "Meet me by the car, would you?"

CHAPTER THIRTY-NINE

"Guv, where are we going?" Ivy said as George pulled out of the station car park and put his foot down. She reached up for the handle and braced as he rounded a bend far too fast. "Guv?"

But George didn't reply. He was biting down on his lip in deep thought.

"Guv, can you just stop the car, please?" Ivy said, which seemed to do the trick. He glanced across at her, eyes wide as if it had been *her* that had offended *him*. "Stop the car, guv."

She fixed her stare on him until, finally, he checked his rear view mirror and brought the car to the side of the road.

"Do you want to explain yourself, Ivy?"

"Me?" she said. "Me, explain myself? Guv, we sat down last night and spoke about the investigation, and while I admit we don't have enough to make a solid plan, we at least agreed on how we would move forward. Yet halfway through the briefing, you announce that you've had Hale brought in. We'd barely even tried to get him to crack, and you gave up. You let him go. And now we're speeding into the Wolds like it's on fire. Have I done something to offend you?"

"What? No."

"Have I upset you somehow? I don't know. Said something without realising?"

"No," he said flatly. Usually, she welcomed his direct responses, but all they were doing now was adding to her frustration.

"You're infuriating, guv. I thought we were in this together. I thought we shared information. You know, talked through it. I thought that was what we did. I thought," she said, jabbing a finger at her chest, "that when I transferred here with you, things would be as they were in Mablethorpe. I didn't realise I was being demoted to a puppet."

"You're not a puppet."

"Well, what am I, guv?" she said. She turned to look out of the window, but he deserved to see the hurt in her eye. "Do you realise what this move has done to my marriage, guv? Granted, it was on the rocks anyway, but this has well and truly driven a wedge into it. Like a big fat fountain pen being driven through my heart and his poxy solicitor telling me where to sign like it's as easy as signing for a delivery. Well, it's not," she said. "It's not easy. I've lost my house, my husband, my..." She swallowed and breathed. "My kids, guv. I've lost it all, alright? The only thing keeping me going is this. Is..."

"Is?" he prompted her.

"Is you, guv. You're like the bloody father I never had."

"You have a father," he said.

"I know, but he's not like..." She sighed. "It doesn't matter. The point is that I don't feel like my input is being valued here. It's the bloody George Larson show."

"Oh God, can you imagine that?"

"Don't make light of it, guv. I mean it. You bring in Campbell and Byrne, and no matter how many times I suggest Byrne isn't quite right for the team, you insist on him staying."

"He's done well so far."

"Doing well doesn't equate to being a team fit," she said. "And then there's Maguire and O'Hara."

"What's wrong with them? You said they were okay the other night."

"They're fine so far," she said. "But it might have been nice to have been asked."

"And what would you have said?"

"I would have said that we need somebody with a bit more experience. Somebody who has at least passed the exams and is at least capable of conducting an interview without having their hands held. All we've done is make ourselves busier."

"Is that really how you feel?" he asked. There was very little in the way of emotion in his voice, which wasn't unusual for George.

"It is," she said. "I just feel like I'm in your shadow."

"I see," he said. "So what do you want? Do you want to be in the light? Do you want DCI Long breathing down your neck?"

"No, of course—"

"Do you want the media pulling you apart? Every decision you make to be scrutinised, publicised, and...bastardised? Your career to be laid on a knife edge?"

"What? No. Of course, I don't."

"And yet, you feel that being in my shadow, as you put it, is somehow beneath you?"

She stared at him and saw only sincerity in his eyes.

"I don't need your protection, guv."

"I know. You're quite capable," George replied. "But one day, I'll be handing the gig over to you. And when that day comes, I want to be sure that it's in the best shape it can be."

"What are you saying?"

"That life is short, Ivy," he replied, and he stared through the windscreen at nothing in particular. "Time is shorter." She watched him, and as much as she wanted to say something, to probe further, she couldn't bring herself to. "The truth is, Ivy, that every investigation we work on, I realise two things."

"And what are they?" she asked, to which his eyes moistened.

"That you grow sharper with every passing day, and I have grown duller and blunter."

"Sorry?"

"There was a time," he said, "when all I had to do was say the words 'I've got an idea' or 'I have a feeling', and everyone would sit up and listen."

"You're not losing it, guv."

"No?" he said. "But you doubt me."

"I don't doubt you. I just want to be included."

"You've never questioned me before," he said, eying her knowingly. "You doubt me, and that's fine. I'll admit, I've made some pretty wild calls these past few months."

"But you've always been right," she said. "I mean, it's been touch and go more often than not, but—"

"I need you to trust me," he said. "I just need some leash. Some slack, as it were. This one is a mess. We've got too many people to talk to and not enough information to go on, and you're right; I should have consulted you about the additional officers. But I do believe they have a place. They just need to find it."

"Do we have time for that?"

"Campbell reminds me of you, you know? When you were new to this."

"Campbell? Really?"

He grinned.

"And Byrne," he said and gave her a knowing look.

"No way."

"'Fraid so," he said. "It's like looking in the mirror all those years ago."

"Byrne? But he's—"

"Awkward?" George said, and then presented himself with a wave of his hand.

She cocked her head and tried to find the resemblance but failed.

"He's a goof."

"I used to speak before I thought, too," he said. "I made jokes to cover my anxieties. I tried too hard."

"Jesus," Ivy said. "And that's what you see in him, is it?"

"What? No. He's bloody intelligent, that's all. He's logical. Whereas you..."

"Lateral thinker?" she said and then fell in. "Like Campbell? Bloody hell, guv, you've hired younger versions of us."

He laughed aloud and then waited for her to speak.

"What about the other two?" she said. "I mean, Ruby is amazing. And I mean that. From the off, she's been on the ball. But Maguire and O'Hara? We could have had a couple of CID officers."

"Yeah, yeah. And they'd come in thinking they know it all. They wouldn't follow instructions, and we'd be in a mess. And if I have the choice of making a mess, I want it to be my mess."

"So where do they fit in?"

"Well, O'Hara and Campbell get along well. O'Hara looks up to her, I think. There's a healthy relationship to be nurtured there."

"And Maguire? Don't tell me he looks up to Byrne?"

"No, of course not," George replied, and he grinned at her. "But you must admit, with him around, Byrne doesn't look so bad, does he?"

"He's here to make Byrne look good?"

"And knock on doors," George said. "Make coffee, write reports...learn to listen."

"I see," she muttered. "Well, now I know your plan with the team; maybe you can tell me about the investigation? What are we doing? Where are we going? What's the plan here?"

"Oh, I don't really have what you'd call a plan," he said, scrolling through his phone.

Ivy leaned over and watched him find Campbell's number.

"What are you doing?" she asked, and the call began to ring. He winked at her once, and the call was answered.

"Guv?" Campbell said.

"Ah, Campbell," he said, beaming as Ivy shook her head at him. "Get me the address for Maeve Wetherford, will you?"

"Want me to send it across to Sergeant Hart's phone?" she said.

"Yes, she can navigate," George replied. "Oh, and what did we find on Adam Potter?"

"Other than the phone messages between him and Mark Hale, guv, nothing."

"Nothing? There must be something?"

"He's clean so far. I mean, with more time, we could—"

"No, let's not search for something that isn't there. Tell Byrne to get downstairs, will you?"

"Guv?"

"Tell him to release Adam Potter on bail," George replied, and Ivy had to stop herself from asking why. He turned to look her in the eye but spoke to Campbell. "Consider him eliminated from the investigation."

———

"Maeve Wetherford?" Ivy said incredulously. "Guv, we have to go back. We have to keep questioning Mark Hale. Or at least re-question Adam Potter before we let him go."

George didn't reply. He was studying the route, which was only a ten-minute drive.

"Will you *please* tell me what's going on?" she said, feeling petulant.

"It was something Hale said."

"He said a lot of things. Half of them seemed like a pack of lies."

"It was about being a father. That he can't be the only father in this world with a grudge against Ryan Eva."

"Okay, so?" Ivy asked.

"So it made me think. They're probably other fathers out there. Fathers of Ryan's victims."

"You think he did this more than once? You don't think Melissa was the only victim?"

"I think it's strange, Ivy, that Maeve Wetherford's son wasn't on the guest list to her daughter's wedding. I think it's strange that Ryan decided to turn up anyway. And I think it's strange that there was a big family drama at the wedding rehearsal that everyone refuses to talk to us about."

"Nancy," Ivy said, sitting back, her body drained with the realisation. "You think he-."

"It's...a possibility," he said. "The sad truth is that offenders like Ryan Eva are rarely caught the first time. It's one of those crimes that seems to escalate as they hone their powers of persuasion. They grow in confidence. But more often than not, it begins at home."

"Jesus," she muttered, sickened at the imagery his words had conjured.

"Why else would you disown your own son? Why else wouldn't he be invited to his own sister's wedding? Weddings are a time of celebration, of forgiveness," he looked across at her. "Very few things are as unforgivable as...well, that."

They pulled up outside the house, and George gave it a once over. The outside was nothing special. Tidy and respectable and concealing the interior. Much like the owners, he mused.

The curtains twitched once or twice, and the door was opened slowly by a small, red-eyed woman. She seemed smaller than she had the other day when she had been dressed in her fineries. Ivy recalled the red and pink dress that made her look like a strawberry and the oversized, quite distasteful hat. But in her pyjamas and a fluffy dressing gown, she seemed tiny, and that opinionated tone with which she had so brazenly admonished anybody who tried to comfort her daughter was mouse-like, timid, and uncertain.

"Oh, hello," she said,

"Maeve Wetherford?" George said gently, adapting his hyper-proactiveness to her clear despair.

"Aye," she said. "That's me."

George opened his warrant card for her to see.

"I am Detective Inspector Larson, and this is my colleague, Detective Sergeant Hart."

"Yes, I recognise you now. You were at the..." Her voice trailed off. "It was you, wasn't it?"

"One day, I'll be recognised for something of a positive nature," he said, then gestured at the hallway. "Can we come in?"

She didn't give a direct answer. She simply left the door open and shuffled down the hallway in her fluffy slippers. Everything she wore was made of soft cotton or fleece, as though she wanted to douse herself in as much comfort as possible. When she sat on one of the two sofas in the living room, she pulled her dressing gown around her as though it were a duvet and tucked her feet beneath her as if she were settling down to a film.

The house was small and charming but seemed to be in a state of temporary disarray. The curtains were closed, and forgotten cups of tea occupied various surfaces *sans* coasters.

On the sofa beside Maeve Wetherford was a large photo album, the old-fashioned kind that died out with the onset of digital images. It was a large, thick book with some of the photos slipping out from their plastic sleeves. Beneath each one, someone had made the effort to note the date and time and who was in the picture.

"How can I help?" Maeve croaked as though it was painful to be a hostess.

"Mrs Wetherford, as you know, a body was found in the pool at Stockwith Mill on Saturday afternoon. We have now identified who the body belongs to."

This alone was enough to break Maeve, who turned her face away, held her hand to her mouth, and sobbed. Despite the human temptation, it was against protocol for George or Ivy to comfort the woman. Instead, they simply gave her time to collect herself. But when that time grew beyond what George deemed reasonable, he took a long breath and cleared his throat. She dabbed at her eyes with a tissue and then eyed him cautiously.

"Excuse me for saying, but from your reaction and..." He gestured at the photo album. "Would I be right in assuming you know who it was we found?"

She closed her eyes, clenched her jaw shut, and George pressed on.

"You see, Maeve, we've discovered a link between the victim and yourself." He let that statement settle, and Ivy studied the tiny twitches of her facial muscles. "It's a DNA link, which means it's accurate."

"It's Ryan," she said, then dropped her feet to the carpet, leaned forward, and stared down at them. "Ian called me."

"Ian?"

"His dad," she said, which, of course, they had already known, but there was little harm in clarifying facts.

"Maeve, I'm sorry if this is personal, but did you have a relationship with Ian?" George asked.

"A relationship," she scoffed, grabbing another tissue from her pocket. "Why don't we say it as it is? It was an affair. I was already married to Rory. Oh, and he's gone, by the way. He buggered off as soon as..."

"He left you?" Ivy said, to which Maeve nodded.

"I haven't seen him for two days."

"Because you were *grieving*?" Ivy said.

"Can you blame him?" Maeve asked. "All those years, he suspected me of going behind his back. It was all the excuse he needed."

"So you told him?" George asked.

"What was I supposed to do?" she asked, then blew her nose and seemed ashamed of her reaction. "My little boy is dead." She stared them both in the eye as if forcing herself to hold her head up. "I know who he was. I know...I know what he did, but I still love him. I'm his mother."

"Maeve, forgive me, but I need to know exactly what happened in your family. I realise the timing is bad, but we've been trying to piece it all together, and something isn't adding up. It's hindering our investigation. Do you understand?"

She took a deep, shaky breath, her hand shaking as it held her wrinkled-up tissue.

"Ryan was a complicated boy. A difficult boy. Of course, he was," she said, only half answering, only half listening to George's question. "But he was doing his best. He was making amends these last seven months. But he didn't deserve this. Not my little boy."

"How is Nancy doing?"

"Oh, she's upset, of course. Her day was ruined. The day every girl dreams of. It was the first day of the rest of her life." George glanced across at Ivy, and she got the impression there was an inference to her own situation. "They even cancelled their honeymoon. It's a mess. Look at him," she whispered, turning to her photo album and holding up a photo of a little boy holding a young girl's hand. They were standing in front of a seawall wearing shorts and baseball caps and squinting in the sun. "He was such a good little boy. I mean, look at him."

George looked at the little boy in the photo and the question on his lips tasted sickening. But it was one he had to ask. He took his own deep breath.

"There is no easy way to ask this, Mrs Wetherford. So I'm just going to keep it simple." She looked up at him, her eyes dry, as though she had no more tears left to cry. "The crimes that Ryan was convicted of..." he began, and she braced for what was to follow. "Had he ever done that sort of thing before the incident with Melissa Hale?"

CHAPTER FORTY

As so often was the case, verbalising her son's awful story had lifted a burden from Maeve Wetherford's shoulders. For the first time since they arrived, she seemed to truly relax. Nothing either of them said now could be any worse.

"It was a mistake. Me and Ian. It should never have happened," she said. "I didn't realise at the time how much I'd hurt Rory. You don't, though, do you? You don't think about anybody else. You don't think how they feel." She blew her nose again and sniffed. "You never think there might be consequences."

"We're not here to judge, Maeve," George said.

"But you do judge, don't you? It's human nature."

"Did Rory find out?" Ivy asked. "Did he know?"

"We never spoke of it. But he suspected. He was...different towards me." She looked up at the photo on the wall of a wedding where a murder hadn't been discovered. "I don't think he was ever the same, come to think of it. We just, I don't know, established a new normal. Anyway, it didn't last long. I was pregnant."

"Is that when Rory found out?"

"No," she said. "No, when Ian and I went our separate ways,

I..." She sought the right words. "I made a fuss of Rory, shall we say?"

"Made a fuss?" George said.

"Guv?" Ivy warned.

"In the bedroom," Maeve reiterated, eyebrows raised.

"Ah," George replied, then let her continue.

"So, when the news came that I was carrying, well, he didn't question it."

"But you knew?" Ivy asked. "You would have known your cycle."

Maeve nodded. "I did. But it seemed foolish to bring it all up. Ian and me, it was over. We raised Ryan as one of our own, one of Rory's own. It seemed the best for everyone. Then, a few years later, Rory and I had Nancy. This little bundle of joy. We were a happy family, the four of us. They were both lovely children. Ryan was slow to develop. But Nancy was this bright little thing. He always struggled to keep up, even though he was older."

She flicked back and forth through the photo album as she spoke, as though the photos inspired the memories that she relayed to Ivy and George.

"When it happened," she said, "with him and Nancy, that's when Rory knew. I think he always had his doubts, but when that happened...I don't know if he just couldn't believe that any child of his could do that or if he was looking for somebody to blame. But that's when any suspicions he had were confirmed. He threw Ryan out of the house right there and then. He and Rory had always had a difficult relationship. Rory would oscillate depending on his moods. I mean, it wasn't Ryan's fault, but sometimes, when Rory looked at Ryan, all he could see was doubt. It ate away at him slowly but surely. I tried to stop him. I said we could work through it, but he was adamant. He agreed not to go to the police only if Ryan never came near any of us ever again."

"How old was he when this happened?" George asked.

"Thirteen," Maeve replied.

"So, where did he go?"

"Where else could he go?"

"His dad's?" Ivy said.

"Ian came to collect him. Rory had stormed off and said that Ryan needed to be gone when he got back. So I called Ian." She took a deep breath. "I told him who Ryan really was, and that was that."

"And that was the last time you saw Ryan?"

"Almost," Maeve said. "After he went to live with Ian, I wasn't sure I wanted to see him at first. I was angry, of course. But after a few years, I wanted to reach out. But Rory forbade it. Then, the next time I saw my son was in a courtroom."

"When the Hales accused him of abusing their daughter."

"Not the reunion I dreamed about," she said glumly.

"And that was the last time?"

"Yes," she said, looking down at the picture on her lap. "That was the last time I saw my little boy."

"You never visited him in prison?"

"No," she said.

"And did anyone tell you, Maeve, when Ryan was released? Did anyone call you?"

"No. No one, not even Ryan. I think he just wanted to stay away from us. Shame, maybe?"

"It might give you a little comfort to know that Ryan was in the process of rehabilitation. He was holding down a job. His few possessions were neat and orderly. I think he was really trying to make something of himself."

"Why would you say that?" she asked.

"Because Ryan recently contacted Melissa Hale. Did you know that?"

"What?" she said, again holding her hand to her mouth. "No. No, he wouldn't have—"

"He went to her house and, according to Melissa, said that he wanted to apologise properly. That he was making amends. And that she would never see him again."

"Perhaps Ryan wanted to do the same to Nancy," Ivy said. "Maybe he wanted to apologise, to make amends, before her wedding day."

"Do you think that is something Ryan might have done?" added George.

Maeve stared into the middle distance and started to shake her head slowly as though she didn't know what to believe anymore. "Maybe," she said. "Maybe..."

"We met your husband, Mrs Wetherford," George said. "On the day of the wedding. We had a chat with Rory. He didn't seem very happy to be talking to us, if I'm honest. We asked about the fight with his brother at the wedding rehearsal. He was loathe to go into detail."

She seemed to ease at the change of topic and crossed her legs, tugging her dressing gown into place.

"It was, you know...." she said, turning away, back to the memories. "Family stuff."

"Family stuff is often at the heart of our investigations," George explained. "Unfortunately, we need to know."

Maeve hesitated, biting her lip, and looking behind her as though worried her husband might come home at any minute. "It was about Ryan," she said. "He kept it from me until the row a couple of days ago. Rory didn't want Ryan at the wedding, and he didn't want his name brought up in front of me."

"That's understandable, isn't it?" Ivy said. "Surely Nancy didn't want him there, either."

"Of course," she said. "But Rory's brother, he wanted Ryan there."

"What? Why?"

"He said Ryan had served his time. That he should be given a second chance. That he was family at the end of the day, and he had made mistakes, but that it was only right that he should be there. That's how he is, you see? He's the forgiving one."

George caught Ivy's eye, and it was that alone that stopped her from pointing out to Mrs Wetherford how ridiculous a suggestion it was. A victim should never have to interact with their abusers, especially not on their wedding day. What the hell was this man thinking? But she held her tongue, wanting to keep on her side.

"And so this escalated, did it? Between Rory and his brother. They had a fight?"

"It wasn't so much a fight as a brotherly scramble. You know what they're like. They just pushed each other about until some-body split them up, and Rory uninvited his own brother from the wedding. He said his loyalties were in the wrong place. That they should've been with Nancy, not Ryan."

"But Ryan was there already," George said. "At the rehearsal."

"What do you mean?"

"He was there at the wedding rehearsal."

"No, you've got that wrong—"

"I can assure you I have not," George said. "I'm sorry to tell you this but he died during the wedding rehearsal, the day *before* the wedding."

"No," Maeve said, shaking her head. "That can't be."

"Maybe Uncle Pete was going to introduce him?"

"No, I would have seen him."

"Maybe his uncle had invited him to the rehearsal, thinking that it would be okay. That there was a chance the family could be reunited. It's just theory, you understand."

"Why would he do that? Why would Pete invite Ryan?"

"I don't know," George said honestly, and he glanced up at Ivy, wondering if she had any further questions. Ivy shook her head. "Well, we'll leave you in peace now, Maeve," George said, rising from the seat. He looked down at the picture of the little boy holding his little sister's hand and struggled to believe how that boy might have grown up into such a monster, even a rehabilitated one. He put a hand on her shoulder and gave it a squeeze. "We're on your side, Maeve," he said, and she closed her eyes to suppress the tears. "We'll get to the bottom of this."

"Even though he was..." She stopped herself, then swallowed. "Even though people think he was a monster?"

"He served his time, Maeve," George replied. "He deserved better." She smiled at his answer but couldn't bear to look at him as she made to stand. He held a hand up to stop her and nodded at the photos. "Savour them. The memories," he said, and he caught Ivy's eye. "We'll see ourselves out."

CHAPTER FORTY-ONE

The corridor that led to the pathology department at Lincoln County Hospital seemed endless, and Byrne's silence was beginning to irritate Campbell. He had barely said a word during the car ride over. She had barely heard him say a word all day, in fact.

"Are you alright?" she said as they passed the long wall of windows that lined the corridor.

He didn't reply immediately but eventually said, "You know what? I think I am."

"Could have fooled me."

"Oh?"

"You've been quiet," Campbell said. "Something's wrong."

He took a good five seconds to think about it.

"I'm fine," he replied with a grin. "Honestly."

"Have you thought any more about the guv's offer?" she said. "About taking the exams and that?"

"It *is* what I want," he said. "I never really considered it before. I always saw myself in uniform. But, if the guv is giving me this chance, I should take it. I just feel like I have to earn it, you know?"

"I know," she said. "I think we both do."

At this, he scoffed and collected himself, as though he had forgotten to wait before reacting.

"What?" she said with a grin, seeing the old Byrne coming through.

"Come on, Alice. You've been ready for this since day one. I'm surprised you haven't made the move before."

"Because of the same reason as you," she said. "No one gave me a chance before." It was her turn to hesitate. "I don't know if you've noticed, but I can be a bit full-on sometimes. It's like I'm trying too hard or working too hard or something. Too hungry. I've always been like it."

"I hadn't noticed," Byrne said, adding a smile to show he was just joking.

"What I'm trying to say," she said, walking into him with a push, "is that we're more in the same situation than you think. I have to prove to the guv that I can be a team player and not let my ambition run away, and you have to prove that you *have* ambition and that you can handle it. But I have to admit it, Liam. I think you're winning him over."

"Really?"

"I think you're winning everyone over. Whatever it is you're doing, keep bloody doing it."

Byrne hesitated for a moment, grinning to himself.

"I bet you never thought you'd say that," he said as they stopped at the large door to the mortuary.

Campbell laughed, remembering the immature, useless constable she had sent uphill to stop traffic during a storm on the day they had both met DI Larson. "You can say that again," she said.

They stared up at the door in silence, unsure what to expect on the other side. All they had to go on were stories, mythologies even, about the pathologist behind that door. From what Campbell had heard, if anyone was about to challenge Byrne's newfound strong silence and turn him into a blubbering, stuttering mess, then it was the woman they were about to meet.

"Here goes nothing," Campbell muttered and pressed the buzzer.

The door was answered by a large, pink-haired woman wearing a smock that didn't quite cover the dragon tattoo on her chest. She blinked in shock at the sight of them.

"Now then," she said cautiously. "Which ones are you?"

"Campbell and Byrne, Doctor Bell," Campbell said, offering a hand for her to shake, which she looked at, then ignored. "DI Larson sent us."

"George?" she said. "Oh, in that case, you'd better come inside. Busy, is he? Too busy to come see me?"

"It's a complex investigation," Byrne added, much to Campbell's surprise. "We're doing what we can to support him."

"Getting out from under his feet, you mean?" she said, closing the door behind them. She pointed to a row of cupboards. "PPE's in there. Get yourself kitted up, won't you? I'm just finishing up with somebody in here. I'll come and get you when I'm ready."

She pushed through a heavy door, and a blast of cold air rushed at Campbell's ankles.

"Jesus," Byrne said as he tentatively opened the cupboard doors to find them both a gown and mask. "Makes you wonder what she means by finishing up with someone, doesn't it? What do you reckon she's doing? Cutting one open or sewing them up?"

"Or scooping them out?" Campbell suggested, to which he pulled a sickened face. He was about to reply when the door opened once more, and two people emerged from the cold.

"Did you have to say that?" the man said. "You know what she's like."

"I said what I had to say," the woman replied. "I'm fed up with her bullying everyone into submission. And as for you, I would have thought you'd have learned to ignore her by now..." She saw

Campbell and Byrne, then stopped mid-sentence. "Apologies," she said. "I didn't see you there."

"No need," Campbell replied.

The woman tore her gown and mask off and dumped them on the little visitor's couch. The man, however, turned and held his arms up for his colleague to untie his gown strings.

"You're like a child, Ben," she said. She spoke as if she'd been chewed up and spat from an Oxbridge college, but she smelled divine. Whatever scent she was wearing seemed to fill the room. It was floral yet masculine. Unique.

She tugged on his strings and he removed the gown, folded it, and placed it beside hers. He eyed them both.

"City?" he asked, revealing his warrant card and slipping it into his jacket pocket. "You with DCI Cook, are you?"

"Wolds," Campbell replied.

"Wolds?"

"DI Larson," Byrne said. "George Larson. Do you know him?"

They both smiled affectionately at the mention of the guv's name.

"We worked together a while back," Ben said. "We were just helping out, really. How's he settling in?"

"Well, it's been a rough—"

"I read his press statement in the paper," the woman said. "It was interesting, to say the least."

"Interesting, how?" Campbell asked, watching as the woman fixed her appearance in the little mirror on the wall, pulling her hair from her shoulders over half of her face. There was something about her that, even in the few seconds since they had met, irritated her.

"Interesting that he dared to give a press statement with almost nothing to go on," she replied. "Yet he declined to come and see the dreaded Pippa Bell. I'd call that a fishing trip, personally."

"A what?"

"A fishing trip," she explained. "He's hoping a member of the public will come forward with something. The risk is, of course, that in doing so, the guilty party cottons on and does a runner."

"Well, he's very—"

"Busy? Yes, you said." She smiled disbelievingly and beckoned her colleague with a nod of her head towards the door. "Well, good luck. I'm afraid she's in rather a foul mood now. You have him to blame for that." She waited for the door to be opened and then stepped outside into the corridor, leaving the room cold but fragrant.

"Bloody hell," Campbell said. "You know who that was, don't you?"

"Come on, you two," a voice said. Doctor Bell filled the doorway, and the hairs on Campbell's arms rose to attention. She peered through the little window in the door at the two retreating officers. "Ah, met her, did you?"

"We did," Campbell replied.

"Warned you about me, did she?"

"Who?"

"Bloom," the doctor replied, nodding at the door.

"Not really," Campbell said, suddenly finding herself lost for words.

"Right," Bell said slowly as if she was making her mind up about them both. She eyed their PPE and clapped her hands. "Shall we?" She presented the cold morgue with a sweep of her hand. "Don't want him warming up now, do we?"

Edward Higgins' body was laid out much like it had been in the crime scene photographs, as though he was sleeping.

"So, Byrne, was it?" Pip said. "Why don't you start us off? What does George think he's working with here?"

"I thought that was your job," Byrne said after a moment. "We were hoping you'd tell us?"

"Asphyxiation," Campbell said, peeling Pip from her prey.

She turned on Campbell instead. "And why do you say that?"

"The FME declared it at the scene," Byrne said, regaining Pip's attention. "I read the report."

"The signs of asphyxiation were subtle," Pip said quickly, and she took a few steps to one side as though giving a lecture. "It happened quickly. This type of asphyxiation allows a combination of oxygen depletion and an increase in carbon dioxide concentration. But cyanosis was present on all nail beds, fingers, mouth, lips, and gums. Petechial haemorrhages appeared inside the eyelids and the white of the eyes. The skin was congested, wet with moisture." She paused to look at them both. "Are you keeping up?"

"Yes."

"So what does all that mean?"

Campbell stuttered, then went silent, and she imagined Byrne was counting to five over and over again.

"It means that this man was suffocated. Mostly likely with a plastic bag. I don't suppose you've found one, have you?"

"Not yet," Campbell said through gritted teeth.

"There were no fingerprints on his body, but there is some slight bruising on his neck." She retrieved a pen from her breast pocket, slid the sheet from Higgins' torso, and indicated the affected area.

"Doesn't that suggest he was strangled?" Campbell asked, surprised at her own interest and lack of repulsion.

"Well, not exactly." Pip leaned forward and with the end of her pen, identified the large slit she had made in the man's throat. "The trachea is intact."

"The trachea?" Campbell said.

"It's the windpipe," Byrne said, which seemed to impress Pip.

"Medical training?" she asked.

"No, he's just a nerd," Campbell answered on his behalf. "Does quiz nights and game shows and all that."

"Ah, so you're the brains of the operation, are you?" She straightened and eyed Campbell. "Which makes you the brawn."

"It makes me keen to go back to DI Larson with an accurate report that will help drive the investigation, Doctor Bell," Campbell replied. "Nothing else."

Pip beamed at the interaction.

"Put a bag over my head," she said, stepping up to Campbell. Byrne straightened as the two women faced each other. Whatever his newfound confidence, if he stepped between the two of them, he would come off worse than either of them.

"What?" Campbell said.

"Pretend you have a plastic bag and put it over my head."

"Don't be daft. This is stupid—"

"Just...humour me, will you?" Campbell glanced at Byrne, and then reluctantly pulled a make-believe bag over the pathologist's head. "Now, pull it tight."

"Oh, for God's sake."

"Just pull it tight," Pip said. "Christ, have you never played murder in the dark?"

"Not for the last twenty years, no."

"Well, it's like riding a bike. You never forget it."

"I certainly won't forget it," Byrne said, then apologised for interrupting.

Campbell pulled the make-believe handles of the make-believe bag tight at the front of Pip's neck.

"Tighter," Pip said. "I can still breathe."

Campbell stepped closer and pulled the handles tighter.

"Ah, there," Pip said. "Did you feel it?"

"Feel what?"

"My neck. Did you feel it?"

"Well, yes, of course, I was suffocating you."

"But you had to put some pressure on my neck, didn't you? You had to close off the air."

"Well, yeah, but—"

"Now watch this," Pip said, and she brought her hands up to

her face, and pushed a single extended index finger into her mouth.

"What on earth are you doing?"

"I'm making a hole in the bag," Pip explained. "So I can breathe."

"Well, what's the point in that—"

"She means that if he was suffocated with a plastic bag, then he would have had to be restrained," Byrne said, and carefully he lifted the sheet covering Higgins. "There are bruises on his wrists."

"What does that tell you?" Pip said, and Byrne looked away as if picturing the scene.

"They knelt on him," he said. "He was laying down, and they knelt on his arms to pin him down, and then pulled the bag over his head."

"Sure about that, are you?" Pip asked.

"Positive," he replied, then looked away. "I'd know those bruises anywhere."

"Fingernails," Campbell said before Pip could press him further. "If there was a struggle, there might be DNA under his fingernails."

"Only if he scratched his attacker," said Pip. "Not everyone has the instinct or time to fight back."

"In which case, why pin him down?" Campbell said, and Pip beamed at her, seemingly impressed.

"I scraped them and sent the debris to Katy Southwell. What else?" she said with wry grin.

"Toxicology?" Campbell said lamely.

"He wasn't a heavy smoker or a drinker," Pip said. "He's young, but no evidence of lung or liver damage. I found no evidence of drugs in the system, so I think you can rule out that this is drug or alcohol connected. No, what you're looking at here is the victim of a quick and planned attack. It happened before he could think to properly defend himself, and it happened fast."

"So a different MO to Ryan Eva," Campbell clarified.

Pip clicked at her. "Bingo," she said. "Ryan Eva was killed with a blunt object, probably a rock, and then left in the water to drown. There was a struggle longer than this took." She gestured at Higgins' body.

"That's the theory we came up with," Byrne said. "Eva's murder was emotionally motivated and definitely not planned. It was messy. This, however…" he said, looking down at the teenager on the gurney. "This was very much planned." He looked at them both in turn. "The guv was right. We're looking for two different killers."

"Or one killer," Pip said, with a glint in her eye, and her guttural response emphasised her Welsh accent when she finished with, "in two different states of mind."

CHAPTER FORTY-TWO

George slowed as he neared Maeve Wetherford's front gate, until eventually, he came to a stop and leaned heavily on the gatepost.

"You alright, guv?" Ivy said, stopping beside him. It was one of those days that felt like neither season. It wasn't cold or warm. It wasn't bright or dark. And the carpet of clouds that shrouded the county was featureless.

George squinted, trying to focus on the thoughts in his head. "Don't you think it's strange," he said, "that nobody contacted her?"

"What do you mean?"

He turned to Ivy. "Ryan was released, but nobody contacted her. Nobody called her to let her know that her son had been released from prison."

"Well, it doesn't seem like she and Ian Eva were in contact. She probably had asked him not to call her again after their affair. Christ, guv. She called him out of the blue after all those years and told him he had a son—"

"No, not Ian Eva," George said. "The parole team. The prison. Why would they not give his mother a courtesy call?"

"Do they have a responsibility to?" she asked. "I mean, he's not a kid."

"Well, him, then," he said. "Surely he got in touch, somehow?"

Ivy thought about it but didn't seem to have an answer either. George pulled out his phone.

"Who are you calling? Campbell?"

"No, she's busy. They're busy having a baptism of fire with Pip, no doubt," he said, daring to grin. He pressed the newest contact in his phone and waited for the call to be answered.

"Maguire speaking," the voice said, laden with that wonderful accent.

"Maguire, it's DI Larson. I need you to make a call for me."

"Aye, guv," he said. "Who would that be to, then?"

"To Ryan Eva's parole officer. You might need to do some digging to find the right person. Find out who they made a courtesy call to when he was released. They'll have a record. They record bloody everything."

"We've been trying, guv. Over and over. They keep saying they'll get back to us, but you know what they're like. Maybe they will in a week."

"We don't have a week."

"I know, but—"

"Tell them..." He paused as he thought of a consequence.

"Tell them it's part of a very public murder enquiry," Ivy said. "The last thing we need is for the police force and the parole service to be dragged across the news."

"Aye, guv," Maguire said, his smile shining through in his voice. "I'll get back to you."

George ended the call and stuffed his phone back into his pocket.

"Well, he's up for a challenge. I'll give him that," Ivy said. "He's a loudmouth, but he's up for a challenge."

"Enough to work with?" he asked, to which she simply laughed and shook her head.

They started towards his car and climbed in, both in deep thought.

"If Ryan Eva abused Nancy Wetherford before he abused Melissa Hale, that gives us a whole new family of suspects with just as strong a motive," Ivy said, outlining their problem.

"A family of suspects who were all at the wedding rehearsal when Ryan was killed," George said by way of agreement.

Ivy threw back her head. "We've been going after the wrong family. We should've listened to Beatrice Coffey from the beginning. The Wetherfords are the ones to watch."

"Not necessarily," George said. "I still think Mark Hale is up to his neck in something."

"And let's not forget Nancy Wetherford's new husband, Lucas Coffey. I mean, if Melissa Hale's boyfriend was willing to attack Ryan for what he did to her, can you imagine what a husband might do?"

"We don't know that," George said. "We don't even know if he *knew*. The way Maeve Wetherford spoke about it, it was clearly a family secret. I mean, they didn't even go to the police. They just outcast him from the family. He was charged with a whole different abuse case. If they wanted revenge for what Ryan had done to Nancy, then why didn't they do it all those years ago, *before* he had a chance to do it again and ruin somebody else's life?"

"Well, he was a kid," Ivy said. "Just a teenager."

"Right. But now he's a man, and if he was reaching out to his victims, trying to make amends, as he called it, how do we know he didn't do the same to Nancy?"

"You think he reached out to her? Like he reached out to Melissa Hale?"

"I think it would make sense," George said. "Why would he try to make amends with just *one* of his victims?"

"So if he reached out to Nancy, then Lucas could've found out. Or her father, Rory. And that could've triggered them to finally take revenge on Ryan for what he did." Ivy paused. "Even if it was at Nancy's wedding rehearsal," she said, shaking her head.

"Yes, that's where the timing seems to falter a little bit."

"Unless…" Ivy said. "Unless they didn't know he was going to be there. I don't think anyone would've planned to kill another person at a wedding rehearsal. It's not exactly great timing, is it? But what if, like you said inside, Ryan turned up at the wedding rehearsal, using *that* as his opportunity to approach Nancy and make amends."

"Then he'd be a madman," George said. "Approaching a bride before her wedding day reminding her of her past abuse in front of her entire family and new in-laws?"

"Nobody said Ryan Eva was mentally stable," Ivy said. "But how would he even know Nancy was there? That's what gets me. How did he know she was getting married?"

George thought about it, then grabbed Ivy's arm in realisation. "Through the only man who wanted him there. The one who stood up for him, to the detriment of getting uninvited from the wedding."

"Uncle Pete," Ivy said.

"That's why we haven't found Ryan on any bus or taxi cameras. He didn't go there on his own. He went with Uncle Pete under this delusion that the family might be okay with it."

Breaking their line of thought, George's phone vibrated in his hand, and he answered it immediately.

"Guv," came Maguire's rough voice on the other side.

"What have you got for me?"

"I called Ryan Eva's parole team and made sure they knew it's urgent."

"Very good," George said. "What did they say?"

"They gave me the mobile number of his parole officer. He didn't seem too happy that I was interrupting his tennis lesson."

"And?" George said patiently.

"He said they did give a courtesy call to three people before

Ryan was released. One was Melissa Hale. One was Ryan's father, Ian Eva. And one was Ryan's mother, Maeve Wetherford."

"Then why did she lie?" Ivy said, frowning while she listened in. "Why did she say she wasn't called?"

"The parole officer told me," Maguire said. "He said Maeve Wetherford didn't answer the home phone. It was answered by someone else instead, and he promised he would pass on the message."

"No," George said, "surely they wouldn't do that? Surely, they wouldn't just pass on the information. I mean, maybe to a—"

"Spouse?" Maguire said. "Maeve Wetherford's husband."

"Rory Wetherford," George said.

"Exactly."

Ivy looked and listened on, her mouth opening with understanding. "Very good, Maguire," George said. "Thank you. I'll be in touch if there's anything else."

George hung up the phone and looked at Ivy, who looked back at him, trying to process the information.

"So Rory Wetherford *did* know that Ryan Eva had been released," she said.

"Then why wait seven months before doing anything about it?"

"Maybe he didn't know where he was. Just because he knew he was released doesn't mean the parole officer told him his address. He might have spent seven months searching for him or..."

"Or he might have conceived of an event where Ryan Eva could be present," George said.

"What, do you think he lured Ryan Eva to his sister's wedding in order to kill him?"

"I don't know," George said. "It just seems strange that Uncle Pete would invite Ryan along."

"Like an ambush?" Ivy said.

"It's a theory," George said. "Either way, we know Rory isn't afraid to bloody his knuckles. He was willing to disturb his daughter's wedding rehearsal to have a fight with his own brother."

"Might have been a decoy fight, guv. To cover their tracks."

"Still, he's a fighter. How do we know he didn't do the same with Ryan Eva? And it got out of control? Let's look at the MMO. He has the motive. Ryan Eva abused his daughter. He had the means, and he had the opportunity. They were both at the wedding rehearsal that day."

Ivy nodded. "You're right, guv."

Once more, George pulled out his phone and hit redial. They waited in silence for the call to connect.

"I have one more task for you," George said as soon as the connection was made. He glanced at his watch. "Find me Rory Wetherford's work address, would you? I think we're finally getting somewhere."

CHAPTER FORTY-THREE

The lab was a sea of white and grey worktops with a myriad of microscopes, laptops, and machines that Campbell had no hope of identifying. White-coated individuals ambled from bench to bench, seemingly lost in some experiment or other. In an office across the lab, Katy Southwell stood from a desk, pulled open a drawer and began fingering her way through files.

Byrne elbowed Campbell gently.

"That's her. I recognise her from the mill," he said, and they strode across the room, apparently unobserved.

Campbell knocked twice and leaned through the open door.

"Katy Southwell?" she said almost apologetically.

Southwell eyed them both. Then her eyes narrowed as she dug deep into her memory.

"George's team?" she said.

"Campbell." She leaned forward and shook her hand. "And this is—"

"Byrne," Southwell said, clearly proud of her memory. "I take it this isn't a social visit?"

"Afraid not."

"I see," Southwell said, taking her seat and flipping the file open. "Let me guess. George sent you here to add a little pressure, did he?"

"A little bit." Campbell grimaced.

"Which means he's either onto something and needs some kind of forensic evidence to get the CPS to accept the charges," she said, eyeing them with those wide, intelligent eyes. "Or he's got nothing at all and is hoping we can steer him." Her eyes flicked between them. "The latter? Correct?"

"Correct," Campbell said.

"He's eliminating," Byrne said. "In lieu of having a single solid suspect to prove guilty, we're eliminating the pool of suspects-."

"By proving them innocent," Southwell finished, nodding. "A little unorthodox, but I can see his thinking, considering there are only four of you."

"Seven, actually," Campbell said. "We've just taken on a researcher and two more police constables."

"I'd keep that quiet if I were you," Southwell said. "You'll have the likes of DCI Bloom sniffing around, wondering why her team hasn't grown."

"It's more of a necessity than a luxury," Campbell said.

"Well, lucky for you, we're just wrapping up. I would've been calling George within the hour, anyway."

"I'm sure he's grateful for your help," Byrne said.

"Oh, he's grateful. He's one of the good ones," she said. "Unlike this one." She gestured at the file she had opened and rolled her eyes. Campbell leaned forward and read the post-it note affixed to the front page.

"DCI Bloom?"

"At least George has the decency to send his team to see me. All her team does is hound my phone until we've got the job done."

"We just met her," Campbell said.

"Oh?"

"At the morgue. They were just finishing up as we got there. She seems...charming."

"Charming. I'll pass that on," Southwell said. "Anyway, I'll talk you through what we found, seeing as you're here."

The office space was small, but the three of them managed to squeeze behind Katy's desk and view her screen. She brought up some information on her laptop, which meant little to Campbell without Katy's translation.

"This is the toxicology report that Pip sent over. As she might have mentioned, there was no alcohol or evidence of drugs in Edward Higgins' system. In fact, correlating with Pip's autopsy, I'd say he kept away from the stuff entirely."

Campbell eyed the report. It just looked like a bunch of numbers to her.

"Then this," she said, "is the material we extracted from beneath Edward's fingernails."

Campbell looked at her hopefully.

"Nothing, I'm afraid," said Katy. "I was hoping for a DNA trace, but no such luck."

"That doesn't mean he didn't fight back," Byrne said. "What about the fingerprints on the door handle to Edward's room? DI Larson said you dusted the entire place down."

"Nothing," Katy said, then added. "Sorry. They must have been wearing gloves."

"He was removing them, remember?" Byrne said. "In the CCTV."

"In her report, Pip mentions a plastic bag being used as a means to suffocate Higgins," Southwell said, pulling up another document and scrolling through it. "If we had that, we might be able to do something. The killer may have even removed their gloves, in which case their prints would be on the plastic."

"He must have taken it with him," Campbell said. She shared a worried glance with Byrne. It wasn't exactly the breakthrough they were hoping to bring back to the team.

"Moving on," said Katy, no doubt sensing the tension. "I processed the blood we found in Ryan Eva's room. The one found on his bedpost. Somewhat unsurprisingly, it matches Ryan Eva's. We were, however, able to date it. Four days."

"So Ryan hurt himself four days ago. What would that have been? Thursday?"

"From the angle of the blood spatter, I'd say there's a good chance he fell against the bedpost. It's impossible to tell from what part of the body the blood came from, but it was a nasty fall of some kind. Hard enough to break his skin or graze him. Of course, given the injuries to his body after the attack, it's now very difficult for us to isolate a particular injury to the fall."

"Okay," Campbell said, nodding, once more understanding the information but not understanding how it might further their investigation. "So, if we're not able to identify any DNA from the material from beneath Edward's fingernails, we can't be a hundred per cent sure that whoever broke into Edward's bedroom was the same person who killed him."

"We can assume so. But no, we can't be sure, and if I might add, a defence team would highlight this as reasonable doubt. Even if you managed to identify the person who broke in, there's a chance a jury could fall for it. Happens all the time."

"Great," Campbell said. "Anything else?"

At this, Katy smiled as though she had been saving the best information for last.

"What?" Campbell asked, her heart rate quickening.

"I do have something else. I can tell you exactly how the locks were broken. They were done so in the exact same way, both to Ryan Eva's door on Thursday and Edward Higgins' door. It's easy enough to bust through an old internal door like this. All you need is something to lever the door. A crowbar or something."

"He had a jimmy bar," Byrne said. "The bloke in the CCTV. He used to gain access to the house."

Southwell nodded.

"There's strong evidence in the damage to the wooden door frames that both doors were broken with the exact same tools."

"Okay," Campbell said, leaning back to process what that meant. "So you think the same person that broke into Ryan's room broke into Edward's yesterday?"

Katy shook her head back and forth as though not wanting to commit either way. "Or they coordinated. One learned from the other. My guess..." Katy hesitated as though unsure whether to say something that might sway their investigation based on a theory. Then she committed. "You're looking at two different break-ins using the same method, possibly carried out by two different people."

"You don't think it's the same person?"

"I said it's a possibility," Katy said, pulling up yet another report. "We also have the remnants of several footprints."

"Footprints?" Byrne said. "The crime scene images showed carpet. How would you get footprints?"

"Well, it's hard to depend on them fully due to the volume of traffic, who came and went and when exactly. But, using a tool called an electrostatic dust lifter, we were able to identify several individual footprints inside Edward's room. We eliminated known samples, such as Edward himself, DI Larson and DS Hart, plus our own team, of course, and we were left with one recent print that we cannot account for. We then performed the same test inside Ryan Eva's room, and again, there's a print we can't account for."

"Bloody hell," Byrne said.

"Well, before you get too excited, it's worth noting that the accuracy of these findings can really only be used as indicative. It's not like DNA, but it does prove useful, and we were lucky in the sense that the carpet in both rooms hadn't been vacuumed for... well, a long time."

"Remind me to hoover up the next time I murder somebody," Byrne said, which earned him a surprised look from Southwell.

"For example," she continued. "The rogue print found in Edward Higgins' room was a size eleven. But the print found in Ryan's room was a nine."

"What about the tread?" Byrne said. "Can't we identify the make of the shoe from the tread? Isn't there some kind of database?"

"You're right, there is," Southwell said. "But in both instances, the tread is shared by several manufacturers, all of which sell millions of pairs of shoes. We could invest time into it, but the chances are it'll either amount to nothing or be dismissed as evidence." She paused. "But there is something we can use."

"Go on," Campbell said.

"Like I said, there were no fingerprints on Edward's door, suggesting whoever broke in used gloves. But that's not true of whoever broke into Ryan's room."

"You have the fingerprints of whoever broke into Ryan's room?" Campbell clarified.

"Yes."

"And you're saying this person is different?"

"That's exactly what I'm saying. You're looking at two different break-ins using the same method. Whoever killed Edward is not the man who broke into Ryan Eva's bedroom a few days earlier."

"The man?" Campbell said. "How do you know it's a man?"

"Because he was nervous when he broke into Ryan's room," Southwell said. "He left traces of sweat on the brass."

"Sweaty hands?" Campbell said, almost laughing at the sudden breakthrough.

"And seeing as Ryan didn't return to his room—"

"Because he died," Byrne said, egging her on to reveal more.

"The prints and the sweat remained intact."

"And you've identified him, you say?"

"We matched the samples to one of those taken from the wedding glasses," Southwell said, and she clicked on her mouse to reveal the final page of her report, on which a single name stood out.

"Bloody hell," Byrne muttered aloud. "The guv is not going to be happy."

CHAPTER FORTY-FOUR

"I have to say, Mr Wetherford," George called across the howling wind, "you're a hard man to find."

George climbed the last section of the hill, reaching the crest, where the wind was fierce but worth enduring for the glorious three-hundred-and-sixty-degree view of the Wolds. It looked like a patchwork quilt flung haphazardly to create the peaks and troughs. Standing at the top of the hill, leaning on a fence post, a tall, burly man with a thick, dark beard and receding hairline gazed across the hills where fifty-odd sheep were grazing as George might peer into his garden, lost in thought.

"I'm not hiding," he grumbled back. "If that's what you're inferring."

"I wasn't inferring anything," George explained as he closed in. "It's just that when we visit people's places of work, it's not often we have to pack a bag and don our walking boots."

"You could have just called," Wetherford said.

"We did," George said. "Your phone's off."

Lazily, he tugged his phone from inside his olive gilet.

"No signal," he replied and turned the screen for them to see. "You alone?"

George took a break to catch his breath and rest his aching knees. He wasn't one for hiking these days.

"I left my colleague back at the farm talking to your employer." George grinned. "I got the short straw."

The whole time George was talking, Rory Wetherford had hardly offered him a glance but remained focused on the sheep in the distance. But when eventually he spoke, his gruff tone matched his rugged appearance.

"I'm not one for office work," he said. "Never have been."

"I'm here to talk to you about the incident at your daughter's wedding, Rory," George started.

"Oh, aye?"

"I don't need to recap the details, but I should add that since that day, the investigation has been elevated to a murder investigation." If the revelation was indeed news to Wetherford, then he disguised his surprise well. "We identified the body," George continued as he stepped closer to the man, coming to lean on the fence beside him. "It was Ryan Eva."

Wetherford nodded slightly, but his gaze never once wandered from his sheep.

"And I have to inform you that until we can prove otherwise, you are deemed a suspect."

"A what?" Wetherford said the statement too powerful for him to ignore. "A suspect?"

"Until we can prove otherwise," George restated. "So, if you don't mind, I'll need a few minutes of your time."

"Mind? Of course, I mind. Who the hell do you think you are coming up here and telling me I'm being investigated?"

"Nobody said you were being investigated, Rory," George replied. "And if you have nothing to hide, then I'm sure we can settle this quite quickly."

"Here?" Wetherford said, and he nodded at the sheep, who looked cosy enough in their windproof fleeces. "Supposed to move them into the next field, aren't I?"

"I promise I won't take up much of your time," George said. "Anyway, don't you have dogs for that sort of thing?"

Wetherford looked at George with something like disdain, then eventually relented.

"Two minutes," he said. "That's all I can give you."

"I've just been to see your wife," George said, and Wetherford immediately hung his head, either in regret for walking out or for agreeing to talk to George at all.

"Oh, aye?"

"Said she hasn't seen you in days." Wetherford said nothing. He jutted his chin out and swallowed. He didn't appear dishevelled or dirty in any way, so presumably, he wasn't sleeping in his pickup. "Where are you staying, Rory?"

"Does it matter?"

"Technically, yes," George replied. "Until we can eliminate you from our investigation, yes."

"Think I'm going to run, do you?"

"We can do this at the station if it's easier. At least I'll know where you are."

"And you've been talking to Maeve?"

"I have, but I'm not in the habit of getting involved in other people's marriages if that's what you mean." He looked earnestly into Rory Wetherford's eyes to cement his point.

"Pub down the road. Got some B and Bs out back."

"There are lots of pubs down the road," George replied.

"The White Horse," he said. "I did some work there a few months back. Landlord owes me a favour." He looked George up and down. "Do you need to check that? In case I'm lying?"

"I don't think so," George said. "What was the argument about, Rory?"

"You what?"

"You and your wife. Why were you arguing?"

"What happened to not getting involved in—"

"Unless it's pertinent to my investigation," George said.

"Which, in this case, I think it is. Was it Ryan? Is that who you were arguing over?"

Rory scoffed. "Our son?" he said. "He was a monster. She should be glad he's dead. Glad he's out of our lives."

"You're not helping your cause, Rory."

"My cause?" he said. "You know by now what that bastard did, eh? What do you want me to do, mourn? Good bloody riddance, that's what I say."

"We have an account of Ryan's history, yes," George said. "And for what it's worth, I am sorry you had to endure that. I can't begin to imagine."

"Ruined us, it did," Wetherford said. "It was all we could do to...to find some semblance of normality. To keep Nancy in school, to stop our lives from coming to a complete standstill. I thought it was over. I thought that was it. We could get on and, I don't know, be a normal family. On the surface, anyway. But, oh no. He had other ideas, didn't he? Couldn't help himself. Has to go and ruin her wedding day. The one day she'd been dreaming about. Bastard."

"What was he doing there?" George asked. "At the wedding rehearsal, I mean. Why was he there? Was he invited? There was no mention of him on the guest list-."

"He weren't invited. Course he weren't."

"So how then? How did he even know about the wedding?"

"I don't know," Wetherford snapped. "Alright? I don't know."

"What about your brother? Is there a chance he wanted him to be there? Is that why you fought at the rehearsal? Because he wanted Ryan to be at Nancy's wedding."

Rory shook his head. "Can you imagine having your brother who...did that to you, turn up at your own wedding? What the hell was he thinking?"

"Why didn't you just tell me?" George asked. "Why didn't you tell me when we spoke at the mill that that was why you were fighting?"

"I told you it was family stuff. It's nothing to do with you. It's nothing to do with anyone. Do you think I wanted anyone to hear me talk about *that* or *him* on Nancy's wedding day? You only have to mention the bastard's name and she starts bloody shaking. Even after all these years. Course, it didn't help when the Hales brought it all to light, splashing it all over the papers."

"Melissa Hale was assaulted, Rory."

"It's private. It's Nancy's business. No one else's. And the sooner we can bury it, the better," he said. "For all our sakes."

"I'm going to be honest with you, Mr Wetherford, because I feel like you're a man who appreciates honesty." Rory turned his face to the breeze, closing his eyes as if the wind was cleansing his mind. "Somebody broke into Ryan Eva's bedroom on Thursday, and I believe that person may have been you."

He laughed, a loud, booming laugh that carried from the top of the hill across the valleys by the same breeze that toyed with his remaining hair. "I didn't even know that Ryan Eva was out of prison until my wife told me about it."

"You sure about that, Rory?" George asked, to which the larger of the two shrugged.

"Course."

"You see, it's that statement that I find a little perplexing."

"If you've something to say, Inspector—"

"One of my team spoke to the parole board, Rory. You received a call from Ryan's parole officer seven months ago. The call was logged as being intended for your wife. But you took the call, didn't you?"

Wetherford didn't reply. He just stared out across the hills.

"And you didn't tell her, did you?" George pressed.

Again, Wetherford said nothing.

"So I'll ask you again, Rory, why didn't you tell your wife that her son was out of prison?"

Rory continued to look to the hills as though they might answer for him.

"Have you ever had a wedding in the family, Inspector?" he said eventually.

"That wasn't my question."

"I'm asking you," he said. "Have you?"

George sighed. "Only my own," he said. "And my sister's, a long time ago. But I have to say they were both quite low-key compared to how weddings are today."

"Well, then you should know that weddings these days are madness. They bring up all types of family issues. People get wedding fever. Ever heard of it?"

"I have," George admitted. "I haven't given it much thought."

"Well, they go crazy. The infected. Thinking about what they'll wear, how they will look, how their family will present to the other family, where they'll stay, who'll have the dog, how they'll get to the hotel afterwards, and God knows what else. It's a social minefield. The last thing I wanted was to throw another spanner in the works in the months leading up to Nancy's wedding. To tell my wife that her monster of a son was back on the streets. It would have been carnage," he spat. "You want me to be honest? Then I'll be honest. It was all I could do not go after him, alright? I had to stop myself from finding out where he lived to keep him the hell away from my family. My wife cares about what other people think. She might pretend that she doesn't, but she does. It would've killed her. The risk of her son ruining her daughter's wedding. I couldn't do that to her. I love her. You understand? I did it out of love. Sometimes, you have to lie in a marriage. Sometimes, that's the only way to keep the people you love safe."

"And is that what you did, Mr Wetherford? Did you kill Ryan Eva to keep your family safe?"

Rory turned to him, and for the first time, he squared up to George.

"Now, you listen to me. I did not break into Ryan's sad, little hovel, and I did not kill him the day before my daughter's wedding."

"What about Edward Higgins? Do you know who that is?"

A look of confusion washed over Wetherford's face, and he returned to his fence post.

"I have no idea who you're talking about."

"Edward Higgins is — sorry, *was* — the man who lived next door to Ryan Eva. The man whose body I witnessed only yesterday," George said. "Murdered in his own bed."

"And why would I have anything to do with that?"

"That's what I'm trying to find out," George said. "But by your own admission, Mr Wetherford, you are prepared to take care of your family at all costs."

Rory took a deep breath in and out and turned back to the fields that were clearly a source of comfort to him.

"Do you know what I like about this job?"

"I can imagine why," George said, with eyes only for Wetherford, trying to see past his weathered skin to the man inside.

"I like being outside. I like being in the fresh air, feeling the wind on my face and the sun on my arms. I have absolutely no intention," he said, turning to George with a sneer, "of spending any amount of my life locked inside a dark, cold prison cell." He turned to face George again. "Especially for something that I didn't do."

"I hope for your sake that's true," George said.

"What do you want from me?" he said. "What do you want me to say?"

"Well, for a start, I'd like to know where you were yesterday."

"What time?"

"All day," George said, to which Wetherford puffed his cheeks and shook his head.

"Up here, mostly."

"Mostly?"

"Yeah, mostly," he said. "When I weren't up here, I was down there." He nodded at the lower field.

"And I suppose your employer can confirm this, can he?"

"I don't know," Wetherford said. "He pays me to take care of his sheep. So that's what I do. I don't clock in and out if that's what you're asking."

"If I find out that you were involved, Rory, then you can rest assured that I will see justice serve its course," George said slowly so that the inference couldn't be misunderstood. "Don't let me catch you out on this."

Rory shrugged. "I won't," he replied.

"You won't what?"

"Let you catch me," Rory said, and for the first time, the grimace he had worn until now broke into a grin.

George stepped closer to the man, turning towards the view so they stood side by side. "Do you know how this works, Rory? How we eliminate suspects from an investigation?"

"Enlighten me," Wetherford said.

"Have you ever heard of an MMO?" George asked, then proceeded before Wetherford had a chance to respond. "It stands for means, motive, and opportunity. An individual with the means to commit the crime, the motivation to do so, and the opportunity becomes what we call a person of interest." He gestured at the hills and the farm beyond. "If your employer can't verify your whereabouts, then until we know otherwise, you tick all those boxes. That's not a good position to be in, Rory."

"You'll need more than that," Wetherford said.

"Oh, I agree. We'll need certifiable truths," George said. "DNA, fingerprints, witnesses."

Wetherford nodded.

"I needn't worry then," he said, turning his attention to the sheep.

"Don't plan any trips away, Rory," George said, and he leaned in close. "Leave that little pleasure to me."

CHAPTER FORTY-FIVE

"You know he'll do his nut when he finds out we've been here?" Byrne said. "You heard what he said. Go to the post-mortem, then the lab."

"He didn't say not to come here, though, did he?"

"Eh? Well, no—"

"So why would he be upset?" Campbell asked, and she gave him a winning smile as she climbed from the car.

Two women on the far side of the street stopped to see what was happening, making no attempt to hide their intrigue.

"Because this isn't part of his plan," Byrne said as he caught up with her. "For Christ's sake. We should at least give him a call."

"I just want to have a look," she said, quietly dismissing his concern.

Someone had hastily repaired the front door, presumably until fitting a more permanent arrangement. Campbell gave it a nudge, but the door didn't move, so she tried again.

"Well, we tried," Byrne said, and he started to back away when they heard a sound from inside. He stopped, and they watched as the door opened a crack, and half a man's face came into view.

"PC Campbell. Lincolnshire Police," Campbell said, holding up her warrant card. "Can I have a word?"

The door closed again, and the security chain rattled before it was opened fully. It revealed a man in tracksuit bottoms, a grubby t-shirt, and tattoos along the lengths of his arms.

"Thought you lot were done," he said.

"Not quite," she replied, leaning in to peer up the stairs. "And you are?"

"Steve," he replied. "Steve Clarke."

"You live here?"

He pointed along the hall to a downstairs room. "And before you ask, yes, I've given a statement."

"It's okay," Byrne said. "I've read it."

Campbell turned to look at him, surprised. "You have?"

"The local lot interviewed him," Byrne explained. "Maybe we should just get inside, eh?" He gestured at the two women, one of whom was holding their phone up to video the action, presumably for social media.

Campbell stepped inside, ushered Byrne in, and then closed the door.

"We'll just be a moment," she explained to Clarke, and she started towards the stairs, seeing for herself what Southwell had meant by the lack of cleaning.

At the top of the stairs, the two rooms in question were evident by the police tape that had been pulled across the doorways.

"This must have been Higgins' room," Byrne said, peering inside. "I recognise it from the photos."

Campbell came to his side and let her eyes drink in the scene.

"What is it?" Byrne said, and she stared at him.

"What's what?"

"What's on your mind?" he said.

"I was just wondering," she replied. "What it must have been like."

"What, being murdered?" he said, with one of those nervous laughs.

"Yes," she said flatly, and his laugh came to an abrupt halt. "He would have been lying on that bed right there."

"Bloody hell, Campbell. This is a bit morbid."

"Whoever did this jammed the jimmy bar between the door and the frame and then eased it open. Applying just enough pressure for the wood to crack. They would have taken their time, or else Clarke would have heard."

"Wouldn't he have been worried about anyone else hearing him?"

"The guv said that most of the occupants were out. They have to work, don't they? Part of their parole terms."

"Edward wasn't on parole. He was coming out of state care."

"Exactly," Campbell said. "He knew that. Just like he knew that the room next door was empty."

"No, Southwell reckons it's too different people."

"Yeah, two different people who might have conspired," she said. "Picture the scene. Higgins is lying on the bed. You break in, hoping you haven't woken him. What do you do?"

"I don't know," Byrne said. "Stick the bag over his head, suffocate him, and then leg it, I suppose."

"No, no, no," she said. "Did he have the bag already, or was it in the room?"

Byrne gave it some thought, then shrugged.

"If he had it on him, then that pretty much gives us what we need for premeditated murder."

"Right," Campbell said. "So he pulls it from his pocket, then steps over to the bed, then climbs on top of him, kneeling on his wrists to stop him fighting back."

"That would have woken Higgins up," Byrne said.

"You're damn right it would have. But he would have been powerless to do anything. His legs would have been thrashing about, maybe trying to kick whoever it was off of him."

"Must have been terrifying," Byrne said. "He would have called out."

"So the killer covered his mouth," Campbell continued. "He didn't have the bag with him. He reached for the first thing he could find."

"The bedside table?"

"There was a chip wrapper in the bin," Byrne said. "And a drinks can. He probably got a bag of chips for his dinner the night before."

"And he left the bag beside the bed," Campbell continued. "The killer dragged it over his head, held it tight at the neck—"

"Which caused the bruising," Byrne added.

"Then what? His life was snuffed out. He stopped thrashing and kicking. If you were the killer, what would you do?"

"Run," Byrne said.

"Not if it was premeditated," she said. "He meant to kill Higgins in his sleep. He hadn't expected him to wake up. The bag over the head was an adaptation. He was thinking on his feet."

"So?"

"So, he wasn't panicking. He'd planned it all. The only deviation from the plan was the bag, and that's only because Higgins woke up," she said. "He walked. He didn't draw attention to himself. He walked normally."

"Well, yeah, we saw him leave on the CCTV footage. We know he walked normally."

"What do you do with the plastic bag when you're done?" she asked, to which he puffed his cheeks and exhaled loudly.

She turned from the doorway and started back down the stairs. Byrne followed close behind, mumbling to himself, but she wasn't listening to his griping. She had an idea.

"Which way did he turn?" she said.

"Eh?"

"Which way?" she said. "When he came out of the house, which way did he turn?"

"Right," he said, as if the answer was obvious.

She strode along the pavement, checking in hedges, gardens, and anywhere that litter might have been caught.

"Campbell?" Byrne said, chasing after her. "Come on. We've been long enough. We've still got to get back."

"What if he had a car?" she said, ignoring his plight.

"Well, then he would have turned left out of the house, being as that's the direction from where he came."

"Unless he parked up somewhere around here and did a lap of the block?"

"Right," Byrne said, and for the first time, he was supportive of her angst. "If anyone had seen him park up, they would have seen him walk in the opposite direction. They wouldn't associate a stranger parking his car with the incident. Dozens of people must park up around here to avoid the parking charges at the seafront. Especially coming into the summer."

"But he'd be conscious of the bag," Campbell said. "He wouldn't want it in his pocket or in his car, for that matter. It wasn't part of the plan."

"He'd need to adapt," Byrne said as something moved in the corner of his eye. A crisp packet bounced along the pavement on the far side of the road, carried by the wind. "It's an onshore wind."

"A what?"

But it was Byrne's turn to ignore Campbell and let his own imagination run wild. He crossed the road and followed the crisp packet.

"Byrne?" she called after him. "Liam, what are you doing?"

He started up the street, jogging to keep up with the packet. Reluctantly, she gave chase, half walking, half running to stay close. By the time she had closed the gap, he was coming to a stop at a chain link fence at the edge of a primary school. He was staring at the fence and the crisp packet, which was stuck like a fly in a web, fluttering for futile freedom — along with several other discarded wrappers, packets, and rubbish.

And a single plastic bag.

CHAPTER FORTY-SIX

"Ruby," George said as he thrust his way through the spread of CID desks into their little appointed area. "What are you working on?"

"Well, I was just—"

"Forget about that," he said, cutting her off. He snatched up a marker and circled a name on the board.

"Rory Wetherford?"

"I want his phone and bank records," he said.

"What's the urgency, guv? Did you learn something?" Campbell asked.

"No," he said. "And that's my point. Before I spoke to him, I believed him to be an angry, protective father who would do anything to protect his daughter."

"And now?"

"And now I believe him to be an angry, protective father who would do anything to protect his daughter and who had the means, motive, and opportunity to murder Edward Higgins."

"What? He didn't have an alibi?"

"He said he was in the fields where he works," George replied.

"On his own?"

"I spoke to his employer," Ivy cut in. "He comes and goes when he wants. He gets the job done and he's reliable. So they don't bother to keep tabs on him."

"Alright for some," Byrne said, then winced at speaking before he'd thought.

"What about you two?" George said. "How did it go with the delightful Pippa Bell?"

"Oh, not bad, guv," Byrne said, which wasn't one of the answers he was expecting, and made his disappointment evident with a hard stare. "I mean, she had a lot to say. About Higgins, guv."

"Well, I rather hoped she wouldn't discuss the weather, Byrne. Come on, lad. Pull yourself together."

"We established the cause of death, guv," Campbell said, saving Byrne, whose face was reddening like a ripe plum. "And we have a theory."

"Oh?" George said, plunging his hands into his pockets.

"There were bruises on Higgins' wrists. Pip seems to think the killer knelt on them to stop him from fighting back."

"That's not a theory—"

"And we agree, guv," she said. "We think the killer had intended to kill Higgins. We think it was premeditated."

"Hence the gloves?" George said.

"We also think that the bag wasn't part of the plan. It's plausible that the killer had intended to strangle Higgins, but he woke up. With his arms pinned down, what else could he do apart from kick out and scream?"

"And so you think the killer reached for a plastic bag?"

"We think the killer reached for whatever was in reach," Campbell said. "The report said there was an empty chip wrapper in the bin, which we presumed was his dinner the previous night."

"Right?"

"And a drinks can."

"Okay."

"But there was no bag," she said. "You know what those places are like. They give away a plastic bag nearly every time you buy something. He got a can of drink and a bag of chips from the chippie up the road, and what, carried them home in his hands?" She shook her head. "Not likely."

"Possible," George said.

"But unlikely," she insisted. "So we had a look around."

"You did what?"

"We had a look around, and we, well, Byrne found it."

"Found what?"

"The bag, guv. Well, *a* bag."

"You found a plastic bag?" he said, deflated. "Where exactly?"

"The wind had blown it along the street. We think the killer dumped it to get rid of it before he drove off."

"He wouldn't have wanted it on his person, guv," Byrne said.

"A bag?" George repeated. "You found a plastic bag."

"That's right. It was stuck to a chain link fence. Looks like one of those places where rubbish just seems to collect."

"The school up the road from the bedsit?"

"That's right," Byrne said.

"You found a plastic bag, what, two hundred yards from the house?"

"Something like that," Byrne said, nodding.

"And about four hundred yards from the chip shop?"

"Yeah, give or take."

"And you somehow want me to believe that this is the exact bag the killer used and not some piece of garbage somebody tossed away, presumably once they had finished their chips," he said. "What were you doing there, anyway? I didn't ask you to go there."

"No, guv, but we just…" She eyed Byrne, then changed tack. "I wanted to see the crime scene. It's not Byrne's fault. It was my idea. I made him come with me."

"You made him?"

"I was driving, guv," she said.

"And what was that about Wetherford not having to report to his employer? You need to earn that kind of freedom." He straightened and composed himself. "I'll deal with this later. With you later," he said.

"Guv, I'm sorry, but I think we've..." Byrne started as George was trying to get back on track.

"What?"

"I think we've actually got the bag," he said. "There was a receipt inside."

"For a bag of chips?"

"And a can of coke," Byrne said, but before George could respond, Byrne added the final touch. "The time and date corresponds with when Higgins got his dinner."

"Sorry, what?"

Byrne turned his laptop around for the team to see.

"This is the CCTV from the pet shop the night before Higgins was killed. Look, he leaves his house at half-seven, gets some chips and a drink, and carries it home in a plastic bag."

"But there was no bag found at the scene, guv," Campbell said.

"And the time on the receipt matches this exactly," Byrne added.

"Where is this bag?" George asked.

"We dropped it off at the lab," Byrne said.

"You picked it up?"

"I did," Campbell said, and she pulled a pair of latex gloves from her pocket. "We haven't compromised the evidence."

George turned away from them, stared at a blank space on the board, then took a deep breath and faced them once more.

"Well done," he said, then held an index finger up to make a point. "I don't agree with you running off like that. But, if that bag turns out to be *the* bag, then you've done a fine thing, the pair of you."

"And if it doesn't?" Campbell asked, to which George forced a smile.

"Just pray it does," he told her. "Now, listen closely." He tapped at Maeve Wetherford's name on the board. "Ryan Eva was the illegitimate son of Maeve Wetherford and Ian Eva. Rory Wetherford, meanwhile, was suspicious, but his paternity was never questioned verbally. It was only when they caught Ryan..." He paused, not wanting to sour the air with the graphic explanation, "Assaulting his sister, did they realise there was something wrong with him. Rory lost the plot and kicked him out. Maeve arranged for Ryan to go to his father's. His real father's that is. Nobody heard a peep about him until the Melissa Hale case came to light. Scroll forward a few years, and Ryan Eva is due to be released. The parole board notify his next of kin, his mother, but who answers the phone?"

"Rory Wetherford?" Maguire said, speaking up for the first time since George and Ivy had returned.

"Quite right," George said. "Now, he doesn't do anything with this information despite admitting to me that he wanted to pay Eva a visit. But he refrained from doing so. Scroll forward another seven months. It's his daughter's wedding. His brother Pete wants Ryan to come. Reading between the lines, I am assuming that neither Uncle Pete nor Ian Eva knew about the assault on Nancy Wetherford. So why wouldn't he push for his nephew to be at the wedding? As far as he is concerned, Ryan served his time, and he learned his lesson. Pete and Rory argue at the rehearsal. Pete is asked to leave." George made a series of squiggles and dotted lines to illustrate the tale. "Then we have an indeterminable gap, during which time Ryan Eva is killed, and his body floats down into the mill pond."

"So we don't have anything on him regarding the Ryan Eva murder?"

"We have nothing," George admitted. "And unless somebody can fill in the gaps, we can't even eliminate any of them."

"Guv," O'Hara said, raising her hand.

"Go on, and please don't put your hand up."

"Are you suggesting that you're leaning towards this being a family-based crime?"

"I suppose I am. Yes."

"So, what about Mark Hale and Adam Potter?"

"Try as I might to put Mark Hale at the crime scene, O'Hara, I just can't do it."

"That fits with my findings, guv," Ruby spoke up.

"Go on."

"You asked me to look into Mark Hale's alibis, and I did. We called his colleagues at the brewery," she said, giving credit to Maguire and O'Hara for helping, who nodded at her in reply.

"They confirmed that they saw Mark Hale at work in his office between four and six p.m.," O'Hara added.

"I requested their CCTV, which was sent over by the manager, and it confirms it." Ruby looked up at George. "Mark Hale was at work when somebody broke into Ryan Eva's bedsit."

"What about Friday?" he said. "During the wedding rehearsal?"

"Same again." She grimaced. "He was at work all day, including during Ryan's estimated time of death. Confirmed by both colleagues and cameras."

"That's good work," George said, nodding. "We're eliminating. That's what we're trying to do. We're moving forward."

"But there's more, guv," Ruby said, and though she remained passive, George thought he might have seen a slight glimmer in her eye. "Neither Mark Hale's colleagues nor the cameras were able to confirm that he was at work when Edward Higgins was killed."

George's elation was short-lived.

"So, Mark Hale couldn't have killed Ryan Eva," George said aloud. "But we can't rule him out of Edward Higgins' murder."

"And Adam Potter couldn't have murdered Edward Higgins, yet he was perfectly placed to murder Ryan Eva," Ivy added.

"And Rory Wetherford," Maguire said without invitation, "could've done them both. What a conundrum."

"We can place Potter at the scene, though," Ivy said. "That's got to narrow it down. Rory Wetherford and Adam Potter were the only ones who were definitely at the wedding rehearsal."

"And Potter was the one who broke into Ryan Eva's bedsit," Byrne said, and George stopped and replayed that sentence in his mind.

"Sorry?"

"He was the one who broke into Ryan's bedsit on the Thursday," Byrne said again. "Katy Southwell found his fingerprints on the bedroom door handle, along with traces of DNA from his sweat."

"His sweat?"

"He was nervous, guv," Campbell said. "She also managed to extract some footprints from the carpet."

"Yeah, apparently because the carpet was so filthy, they were able to use an electrostatic dust extractor to identify several pairs of shoes in both rooms. Once they'd eliminated your shoes and Sergeant Hart's, the scene of crime team, the FME, and the rest of it, they were left with one pair in each room that they couldn't identify."

"The same shoes?"

"Size nine in Ryan's room and size eleven in Edward's."

George stepped back, wrapping his head around the news.

"And she's sure Adam Potter's DNA is on the door handle, is she?"

"Adamant, guv," Byrne said.

George turned away and took a few steps, feeling six pairs of eyes boring into the back of his head.

"Edward saw a tall, brown-haired man," George said. "It fits Potter's description. Can we do anything with the CCTV?"

"It's too far away, guv," Ivy said. "It might be enough for us to get an idea, but it would never stand up in court."

"But it looks like him?"

"And about five million other men in the UK, yeah," she said.

At this point, Byrne's desk phone rang, and with an approving nod from George, he went to pick it up.

"I want to talk about motives," George said. "It's all well and good us placing these suspects at the scenes, but unless we can give a good reason, it means nothing."

"Jesus, whoever wanted to murder Ryan Eva had a clear motive, eh?" Maguire called out.

"Oh really? And what is that motive?" Ivy said.

"Well, he's a..."

"He's a what? Reformed criminal?"

"He's a nonce, sarge," Maguire said. "Sorry if that's not politically correct, but there it is. Fella assaulted his own sister, for God's sake. How old did you say she was?"

"I didn't, and you don't want to know," George said. "And if you could refrain from voicing subjective opinions, Maguire. They aren't useful. If anything, they're divisive."

"What about Higgins?" Ivy asked. "The only reason I can think of for anybody killing him is that he saw whoever was breaking in."

"Right, but we've established that the person who broke into Ryan's bedsit was not the same person who killed Edward Higgins," George said, turning to the board. "Who do we have? Mark Hale does not have an alibi for the time Edward Higgins was murdered. However, why on earth would he murder Edward Higgins just because he might have seen his daughter's ex-boyfriend from nine years ago breaking into Ryan's room? It's not strong enough." He turned to Ruby. "How are we getting on with those text messages between Potter and Hale?"

"Nothing," she said. "We can see that they spoke; we just can't see what they said."

"So, no progress then?" George said. "All we've managed to do is somehow make this more complex."

"We can put Adam Potter at the scene breaking into Ryan's bedsit, guv," Ivy said. "He matches Higgins' description; his DNA was on the door handle, and he has a rock-solid motive. He's in love with Melissa Hale."

"He was," George said. "Nine years ago."

"Ah, that's tosh," Maguire said.

"Excuse me?" George said.

"It's tosh, guv. Sorry, but it is," he replied. "She was his first love. Do you remember your first love?"

Grace's image was never far from the forefront of his mind, and she came into view in a melee of memories.

"What are you saying, that he never quite got over her?"

"Or under her," Maguire replied. "Sorry, but yeah. Jesus, I was with this lass, Cara. Together, all through school, we were. Right up until we went to college, and then bam. She met an older fella with a car and a job, and I was out on my ear."

"And that was that, was it?" Byrne asked.

"Ah, I used to see her in town from time to time. And I tell you, my heart used to just melt."

"Is there an ending to this forlorn love story?" Ivy asked, and Maguire realised the tangent he had ventured down.

"I'm just saying that it's not beyond the realms of possibility that maybe, just maybe, he might still carry a flame, you know?"

"As much as I hate to admit it," Ivy started. "Potter is looking very promising."

"No," George said. "No, it doesn't add up."

"His DNA was found on the door handle, guv," she said. "We've got him there, bang to rights."

"No, we haven't," George cut in. "We can place Potter breaking into Ryan's bedsit, yes. But Ryan was killed at the wedding rehearsal the next day. What we can assume, however, until further information comes to light, is that Edward was killed because he saw Potter breaking into Ryan's room."

"So why was he breaking in?" Maguire said.

"I thought he was alibied for the Higgins murder," O'Hara said.

"He is," Ruby said. "ATM withdrawal."

Hot bile rose like lava in George's chest, and he swallowed the bitter aftertaste.

"Guv?" Ivy said.

"Just..." he started. "Just give me a minute to think."

He perched on the edge of his desk, his eyes closed to the world around him, and Grace's image came before him. How easy it would be to fetch her from that place, scoop her up, and take her home. Sod the world.

"Guv?" somebody said.

"I asked for silence and silence I shall have," he said, opening his eyes to find the culprit.

It was Byrne, and he was holding the phone's handset in the air.

"That was the custody sergeant," he said hesitantly. "Adam Potter is downstairs, guv. He's handed himself in."

"Handed himself in?" George said. "For what?"

"Well, that's just it," Byrne said. "He claims to have killed Ryan Eva."

CHAPTER FORTY-SEVEN

Without greeting Adam Potter or the duty solicitor sitting beside him, George and Ivy entered the interview room, took their respective seats, and Ivy began the recording. First, George said the date, time, and location.

"This interview is being recorded and may be given in evidence if this case is brought to trial. I am Detective Inspector Larson. Others present are..."

"DS Ivy Hart." There was a long pause, and then she added, "Come on, Adam, you know the drill by now, surely?"

"Adam Potter," he mumbled.

"Michael Pedroza. Legal Aid," said the duty solicitor, an older man with large ears and spiky, grey hair that appeared abuzz with static. He wore a traditional wool suit marred only by the addition of a sickly green tie with golf clubs in place of dots.

"Adam," George started, genuinely curious as to what the lad had to say, "for the benefit of the recording, you have confessed to the murder of Ryan Eva, a crime for which you have been previously arrested and bailed. Would you like to tell us what happened? What's changed your mind?"

The young man's eyes were wide and bloodshot as if he hadn't slept in days. His dark hair, which had been at least messy before, was now laden with grease. But by far, the most noticeable change was the nervous twitch he had developed — a series of hard blinks every minute or so, as though he was blinking away memories he would rather forget. He looked across at his duty solicitor once, who nodded for him to continue.

"I killed him," Adam said quietly.

"Sorry, could you repeat that a little louder?" George asked.

"I did it," he said. "I killed him. I killed Eva."

"Well, okay," George said. "We're going to need a little more detail if you could. Shall we start at the beginning? Can you tell me what exactly happened? When did you last see Ryan Eva?"

"I went round to his house," he said.

"When? What day was this?"

"Thursday."

"Last Thursday?" George said, to which Potter nodded. "How did you know where Ryan lived?"

Adam wiped his eyes on his sleeve, breaking already, even though they had only just begun what was looking to be a lengthy interview.

"Mark told me."

"Mark Hale?" George clarified. "Mark Hale told you where to find Ryan Eva?"

"Yes," Adam said, staring down at his clenched fists. "He found out where Ryan lived. He let me know where it was."

"Why would he tell you, Adam? Why would he tell you where Ryan Eva lived? Had there been some kind of conversation leading up to that, or did he contact you out of the blue?"

"Because...he had asked me to keep an eye on him." He looked up at George. "He called me. Out of the blue. Said he'd got my number from Melissa's phone. He said that Ryan Eva was out of prison."

"How did he know?"

"Melissa told him, I suppose."

George shared a look with Ivy, but neither of them said anything, and George gestured for Potter to continue.

"He said he wanted to make sure Ryan came nowhere near Melissa now he was out. But he couldn't do anything without worrying her. He asked me if I still cared about her. I guess she had told him that I'd been in touch."

"When was this?" Ivy asked.

"Months ago," Adam said.

"How many months?" she pushed.

"I don't know," he said. "Six? Seven? It was when Eva got out. He asked me if I still...you know, had feelings for Mel."

"And what did you say?" George asked. "When Mark Hale asked if you still cared for his daughter? What did you tell him?"

"I told him the truth. That I'd never stopped caring about her."

Maguire's little romantic anecdote came to mind, but George pushed it away, praying that he wouldn't have to be there when Maguire heard this part of the interview.

"Mark told me that if I still cared about her," Adam continued, "then I could help Melissa by keeping an eye on Ryan and making sure he didn't come anywhere near her."

"So that's what you did. Is it Adam? You kept an eye on Ryan Eva to make sure Melissa was okay?"

"I just wanted to keep her safe," he said.

"Why?" Ivy said, her voice holding the kind of judgment that George had kept to himself. "She's not your girlfriend, Adam. Why are you so protective of her?"

"She *was* my girlfriend," he said defensively.

"Yeah, a decade ago," she said, and George shot her a warning look.

"That doesn't mean I stopped caring for her, does it? That doesn't mean I don't want her to be safe. You have no idea how messed up she was after what Ryan did to her. How it affected her. And do you know what? It affected me as well. How do you think it feels when the one person you're supposed to look after gets..." His voice trailed off. "I failed her. Alright? I should have been there."

"Nobody's blaming you, Adam."

"Well, I am. You didn't see what she had to go through."

"I've read the reports and the statements," Ivy said. "I've seen the evidence. Believe me, I probably have a better idea than you do."

"How often would you keep an eye on Ryan?" George said, moving them along. "In the last seven months?"

"Every couple of days or so," Adam said, turning his glare at Ivy back to focus on George and letting it soften.

"Every two days? For the last nine months, you followed him around?"

"Not all day," he said. "I still go to work. But I'd check in on him. Get to know his routine. Make sure he wasn't going anywhere near her."

"Still, between work and..." George tried to find an alternative word to *stalking*, "*following* Ryan, you can't have done much else. What about your social life? Your hobbies?"

"I knew this would happen," Adam said seriously. "You're making it sound like I waited outside his house. I didn't. I just checked in on him. Made sure he was where he was supposed to be when he was supposed to be there. I got to know his routine, that's all. I just...I just wanted to make sure he was where I could find him if...you know?"

"If he went after Melissa?"

"Yeah. Those places aren't forever homes, you know? People move on, and the last thing I wanted was for him to move on and disappear into oblivion."

"It sounds like you saw Melissa as your responsibility," George said. "And that protecting her was a mission, of sorts, for you. Does that sound fair?"

Potter sat back as though he was finally being heard. "I love that girl. Always have."

"And did he?" George asked, knowing the answer. "Did Ryan ever get close to the Wolds?"

"Not at first," Adam said, then his face darkened. "But when he did, I wasn't there. Again..." His voice cracked. "I missed it. I was at work. I went to his house after work, but he wasn't there. I can usually see him in the window. But the light wasn't on. And only later I found out that he had been to see Melissa. I should've been there... I should've stopped him."

"So when did you find out? When did you find out that he had gone to see Melissa?"

Adam took a deep breath and exhaled slowly.

"I waited for him. I couldn't take it. I needed to know where he was. I knew he'd been to see Melissa. I knew it in here," he said, pounding his chest with his fist. "He *never* broke his routine. I needed to know for sure."

"And this was on Thursday?" George said. "When you waited for him?"

Adam nodded his head.

"For the tape, please, Adam," George said.

"*Yes*," Adam said. "On Thursday. I went to see Ryan. He wasn't there. I went inside the house. Someone had just left, and I ran in before the front door closed. I went up to his room, and I waited for him. I just wanted to talk to him. That was all. I just wanted to find out where he'd been."

"Why couldn't you ask Melissa?" George said. "Why couldn't you ask her if Ryan had been to see her?"

"She didn't know what I was doing, did she? We kept it from her," Adam said. "Mark said it was best for everyone if Melissa didn't know I was involved. Anyway, she doesn't know me. Not really. She probably thinks I'm a lunatic after..."

"After what?" Ivy said. "After the last time you saw him? When you beat the living daylights out of him? Do you think she might be on to something?"

"Okay, okay," George said with a knowing look at Ivy. "So you waited for Ryan. Then what happened? I assume he came home?"

Adam swallowed. "Yes. Around five-twenty."

"And you were already in his bedroom?"

"Yes."

"You'd broken in?" George clarified.

Adam nodded, again exhibiting some warped sense of chivalrous pride. "I used the tyre lever from my car's tool kit."

"And that's what you used to break in, is it?" George asked. "You prised the door open?"

"The lock was rubbish, and the wood just splintered. It wasn't hard."

"Then what?"

"Then I just looked around. He didn't have much stuff, barely anything, actually."

"What did you expect? He'd been in prison for nearly a decade," Ivy said.

"I thought he might have pictures or something. Of her. Melissa."

"I didn't see any pictures," Ivy said.

"Because there weren't any. I don't know what happened. The longer I was there, the angrier I got. I pictured it, you know? Hitting him. Hurting him." He looked up at George. "So I hid."

"You hid? How long for?"

Adam shrugged. "An hour? Maybe more?"

"Where?" Ivy asked. "Under the bed? The room is tiny."

"No," he snapped, as though offended at the absurdity. "Just behind the door. Eventually, I heard his footsteps outside. The rattle of his keys. I could sense it, you know, him realising the door was broken. He came into the room slowly and turned on the light. And I closed it behind him."

"He must've been shocked to see you," George said.

Adam allowed himself a twisted grin. "He was." Then his face softened, and he frowned. "But in a way, he wasn't. Like maybe he'd expected it. I guess people like him have to, right? Someone was going to get him one day."

"And did you talk to him?" George asked.

"I asked him where he'd been, and he told me it was none of my business. I told him that when he broke his routine, that was my business."

"And what did he think of that?" George asked. "You, knowing his routine?"

"Well, he didn't get angry. He just got nervous and asked me to leave."

"I guess he was used to it," George said thoughtfully. "After all those years in prison. People knowing his routine was probably the least of his worries." Then, he refocused on Adam. "Then what?"

"I said I wasn't leaving until he told me where he'd been."

"And?"

"And...he just sort of gave up. He just admitted it. He didn't even lie. He said that he'd gone to see Melissa Hale to apologise and set things right. To make amends, he called it."

"Go on."

Adam's jaw clenched as he relived the memory. "It was the *brazenness* with which he said it. He wasn't even ashamed. It just made me realise that he had learned nothing from all those years inside. He was just the same. Then, something just rose inside me. I don't know. A fire? Rage? I lashed out. I only hit him once. I punched him in the face and..." Potter paused, closed his eyes, and let the tears begin to roll down his face. Any misplaced honour that he felt about his behaviour was quickly being replaced by guilt and shame like the freezing ocean forcing air from a sinking ship. "And he..."

"He what, Adam?" George pressed.

"He fell." Adam's voice shattered. "He fell back and hit his head on the bed, and then he just stopped. Stopped moving. Stopped breathing." George looked at the duty solicitor, who had done nothing to stop his client from confessing to murder but simply watched on, mouth open as though watching a reveal on a TV show.

"Did you check his pulse?" Ivy asked.

"What? No. I didn't want to touch him," Adam said. "But I knew. Of course, I knew," he said, hitting his fist into his chest once more. "Then, at the weekend, when you found that other fella, I figured that somebody had done something in revenge to somebody else."

"Who?" George asked. "Could you explain that for me?"

"I don't know. Ryan's family, maybe? His dad. I don't know. Maybe he thought somebody else had killed his son and just lost it. He's a nutter, you know?"

"Who's a nutter?"

"Ian," Potter said. "Bloody lunatic he is. Last thing I need is *that* madman coming after me."

"So, you thought that Ian Eva had found out about Ryan and had gone after somebody?"

"The whole family's nuts," Potter said, jabbing his temple with his index finger.

Ivy opened her mouth to speak, but George rested his hand on her arm to quieten her.

"Look, I'd seen he was in a state. You know?"

"Who, Ian Eva?"

"No, Rory. His face was like a beetroot."

"When?"

"At the rehearsal. And the wedding, come to think of it. His face was all red, and his eyes were bloodshot, and he was untucked, you know? His shirt." He gestured at his own shirt as if to illustrate his remark.

"As if he'd been in a fight, you mean?"

"Right," Potter said. "He did not look the proud father at his daughter's wedding. Something was definitely up with him. So, I put two and two together. I figured you lot had found Ryan's body and told Ian and that...I don't know...he was keeping it from Melissa until after the wedding. She would have been devastated."

"So, piecing all that together," George said. "If you saw Rory looking..."

"Messed up," Potter said.

"Messed up," George continued. "Then, presumably, you thought that he'd had a fight with Ian Eva."

"Right," Potter said. "Couldn't see him anywhere, though. I expected to see some guy with a black eye or a bloodied nose or something."

"And then we turned up?"

"Right," Potter said. "You lot turned up, and then I realised why I couldn't see anybody with a black eye."

"But surely he would have told his daughter. Surely, she would have found out."

"You think he'd ruin his daughter's wedding day? Jesus. You really don't know him."

"You think highly of Rory Wetherford if you think he could keep that kind of secret."

"He might be a nutter, but he loves Nancy," Potter said. "Look, you have to understand. I figured that Rory would get the blame for Ryan and that, I don't know, somehow I'd get away with it. I didn't *mean* to kill him, for God's sake."

He dropped his head into his hands and sobbed.

"All you saw was an opportunity, is that right?" George asked. "You thought that we'd arrest Rory, and he'd be blamed for Ryan's death as well. Meanwhile, you just carried on sipping champagne."

"I avoided you at the wedding. I spoke to one of the uniformed lot. Gave a statement, you know?"

"A false statement?"

"Well, no. Not really. I didn't lie, did I? As far as I was

concerned, you were there because of whoever it was that Rory had gotten hold of."

"I'm keen to understand," George said, moving the topic on. "What did you do after you'd hit Ryan Eva and he was lying on the floor?"

He looked up at George. "I legged it, of course."

"And did anyone see you, Adam? At the house? Did anyone see you at all?"

"Yes, one bloke," Adam said. "It was right when I arrived. I was jimmying the door when some scrawny little fella asked who I was.

"Scrawny fella?"

"Yeah, about my age. Looks like he could do with a decent meal."

"About your age?" Ivy asked, to which Potter shrugged.

"Something like that."

"He was barely eighteen," Ivy said quietly.

"What did you tell him?" George asked, staying on track.

"Nothing, really. Only that I was a friend of Ryan's," he said, looking between Ivy and George as though confused by her statement. "He seemed to buy it. I didn't see him again."

"And did you tell anyone? Did you tell anyone what you'd done?"

Adam crossed his arms on the table and threw his head into the cavern they created. He replied, and to George's immense frustration, his voice was muffled and unintelligible.

"Say it again, son," George said urgently. "Come on, we're nearly there. You've done well. Hold it together, alright?"

Adam sat up, removing his face from his hands, shaking. As he looked at George, any suggestion that he had ever acted out of valour or chivalry had escaped his demeanour entirely. He looked like a little boy.

"I had to tell somebody. So I told Mark. I called him," he said, loud and clear, as if just saying the words were both condemning him and freeing his soul.

"You told him what you'd done to Ryan Eva?" George asked, and Potter nodded. "What about the other man? The one who saw you? Did you tell Mark about him?"

"Yeah, of course," Potter said. "I told him everything."

"And what did he say?" George asked, to which Potter shook his head.

"Nothing," he said. "He said nothing at all."

CHAPTER FORTY-EIGHT

"So when do we tell the poor bastard that he didn't, in fact, kill anybody?" Maguire asked.

"Poor?" Ivy said. "He..." She lowered her voice to a hiss. "He assaulted someone. He *could* have killed him."

"Aye, he assaulted a nonce. But he didn't actually kill anyone." Maguire hesitated. "Did he?"

The entire team, all seven of them, had gathered around the whiteboard in an impromptu team meeting, trying to dissect Adam Potter's interview to see where it left them.

"No," George said. "He didn't. Pip confirmed that Ryan Eva was killed between twelve and two on Friday afternoon, not at five-thirty on Thursday afternoon. Whatever Adam did to Ryan on the Thursday, it didn't kill him."

"So why does he think he did?" Campbell asked.

"That might have been my fault," George said, allowing a grin to run free for a moment. Letting them know he had a playful side wouldn't hurt. "I didn't tell Adam where or when Ryan was killed. He assumed that he'd killed him on Thursday. He was on a roll, you know? I didn't want to break his flow."

"That's mean," Campbell said.

"That's police work," George replied. "Interviewing is ninety per cent listening. You'll do well to remember that."

"What a bloody idiot," Maguire muttered, earning himself a glare from Ivy and a few wide-eyed stares from the team. "Not the guv," he said. "Potter. I mean...come on, confessing to a murder you didn't do? You've got to be some kind of imbecile, right?"

"He doesn't seem in a healthy mind space," Ivy added.

"What do you mean?" asked Ruby, who for once was more preoccupied with the breakdown of Adam Potter's interview than she was with the research.

"The way he talked about protecting Melissa Hale," Ivy said, shaking her head. "It was like he was on a quest. Like she was a princess who needed rescuing. He's delusional. Living in some daydream."

"It's easy to do," Byrne said, then faltered, not having thought first. "Not from experience, I..." He gathered himself. "I just mean, in this day and age, with everyone so available on the internet, social media stalking and whatnot, it's easy for young people to get obsessed with someone they don't actually know."

"You're a young person," Ivy said. "Doesn't mean you indulge in fantasies about women you barely know, does it? Doesn't mean you stalk your ex-girlfriends."

"Well, no, I just mean—"

"I know what you mean," Ivy said gently. "And it's a good point. I just don't think we should excuse Adam's behaviour too much, that's all."

"So that was the blood spot on Ryan's bed?" Campbell asked. "It was Ryan Eva's from when Adam attacked him?"

"Yes," George answered. "Potter said he punched him just once, and he fell and banged his head on the bed. It fits."

"And then Edward saw him? When he left Ryan's room?"

"Not when he left the room," Ivy said. "When he entered the room. It seems Edward Higgins just took his word that he was a friend of Ryan's and let it be."

"I hope my neighbours would be a little more diligent if some nutter came round my house," O'Hara said.

"He thought about it enough to mention it to us," Ivy said, to which George raised his eyebrows and nodded.

"If you watched the CCTV," Campbell said to Byrne, "then you must've seen Ryan re-entering the house just before Adam attacked him?"

"I must've," he agreed. "But like I said, you can't identify anyone on those things. The CCTV is old, I mean proper old. They're just blurry shapes."

"So then what?" Maguire said. "Potter went back a few days later? And finished the lad because he had seen him?"

"Impossible," Campbell reminded him. "Potter had an alibi for Higgins' death, remember? CCTV has him taking money out of an ATM on Lincoln High Street."

"You're both right," George said, impressed at Campbell's understanding of the situation. "Somebody did go back to kill Edward because he had seen Adam that day."

"Answers the question, doesn't it?" Byrne said. "About why anyone would kill Edward just because he witnessed them breaking and entering."

"What do you mean?" George asked.

"Well, they didn't kill Edward because he witnessed a burglary. They killed Edward because he witnessed the man who had just killed Ryan Eva."

"But he didn't kill Ryan Eva," Maguire said, frowning. "We just established that. Keep up, Byrney."

"But he *thought* he did. And that would be enough motive for someone to go after Edward. Clearly, someone wanted to protect Adam. To stop him from going to prison for what he thought was murder?"

"Exactly."

"Wait," Maguire said, still catching up. "But what about Edward? Who would care enough about Adam Potter to actually kill a man?"

"Somebody with just as much to lose," George said. "Somebody who was just as culpable."

"His best mate?" Campbell said as her phone began to ring. "The groom. What was his name?"

"Lucas Coffey," George said and nodded for her to answer her phone. "No, it's not him. He's a wet lettuce who gets pushed around by his mum."

"Well, who then?" Byrne said. "Guv, you look like you know who it might be."

"I have an inkling," he said, glancing at Ivy. "But I'd rather not follow my gut on this one. I want to know for sure before we bring anyone in."

George took a moment to absorb the whiteboard, applying his theory to the gaps to see if such hypothetical strings might connect it all together.

All of a sudden, Campbell hung up the phone with a vigour that George at first mistook for frustration, but from the way her face lit up, he realised it was, in fact, accomplishment.

"That was quick," he said as she walked back over.

"It didn't take long for Katy to relay what we need to know."

"And what's that?"

"Two things," she said, the delight evident in her features. "One. She fast-tracked the bag for us."

"And?"

"Analysis from the swabs taken from Higgins' body shows that the grease inside the bag is a perfect match to what she found on his face."

"Jesus," Ivy said. "I wasn't expecting that."

"Fingerprints?" George said. "On the plastic? Tell me there were fingerprints."

"He had gloves on, guv," Ivy said. "Remember?"

"I can do better than fingerprints," Campbell continued.

"DNA?"

Campbell nodded and grinned.

"That's the second thing. Saliva. Only a few drops, but enough for her to use."

"Well, of course, there was saliva," Maguire cut in. "You'd be spitting bloody feathers if some lunatic pulled a plastic bag over your head."

"Not on the inside," Campbell said, her gaze not once leaving George's.

"Maybe he turned it inside out?" Maguire said as if the answer was obvious.

"In which case, the receipt would have fallen out," George said on Campbell's behalf. He reached behind him, collected a pen from the little tray beneath the whiteboard, and held it for her.

"Circle it," he said, gesturing at the list of names on the board. "Circle the name."

CHAPTER FORTY-NINE

He opened the front door with trepidation and tentatively stepped towards them as two liveried cars followed George's onto the driveway, the first with Byrne and Campbell, the second with Maguire and O'Hara.

"What the hell is all this?" he said as soon as George climbed from the car.

"Ah, Mr Hale, I was hoping you were home," George said, maintaining pleasantness for as long as he could before the sparks began to fly.

"I just picked my daughter up from work. Not that it's any of your business."

"Melissa's inside, is she?" George asked, and he gestured for Ivy to take a look.

"Hey, no. Don't you dare go in my house," Hale said, stopping her with a firm grip on her forearm.

She wrenched her arm free and glared at him.

"Mr Hale," George advised, "Don't make this any worse for yourself."

"Make what worse for myself?" he spat. "Are you going to explain what's going on here?"

With a sweep of his hand and a gentle click of his fingers, George brought Byrne and Campbell into play.

"Mark Hale," Byrne began, "I am arresting you on suspicion of murdering Edward Higgins. You do not have to say anything, but it may harm your defence if you do not mention, when questioned, something which you later rely on in court. Anything you do say may be given in evidence."

His face paled as Byrne read aloud his rights.

"Do you understand, Mark?" George said as Campbell snapped the second handcuff into place.

"Understand? No, I bloody well do not."

"There'll be plenty of time for us to explain at the station," George replied.

"You'll explain right now," Hale spat. "Who the hell is Edward Higgins?"

George took a step forward, close enough that he only had to breathe the words.

"Adam Potter confessed to the murder of Ryan Eva," he said, and Hale closed his eyes in disbelief. "Edward Higgins is the name of the man who witnessed him breaking into his bedsit."

"Dad?" a voice called out from the front door of the house, and the quintet turned to find Melissa there, gently being held back by Ivy. The look on her face spoke volumes. "Dad?" she said again.

"Go back inside, Melissa," he said. "There's nothing to worry about."

"But, Dad," she said, breaking free from Ivy's loose grip and running across the drive. "What's happening?"

"Nothing, sweetheart—"

"We're taking him to the station, Melissa," George told her. "We just need to ask him a few questions."

"What? Why? What's he done?"

"Nothing," Hale said.

"Oh, I think you can afford your daughter a little more

honesty than that, Mr Hale," Ivy said as she joined them and regained her grip on Melissa's arm. "Why don't you tell her why we're arresting you?"

"She doesn't need to know," he said, then turned to his daughter. "I'll be home soon. Just stay inside, eh? Lock the door."

"What, no?" she said and sought a response from George. "What's going on? Don't treat me like a child."

George took a few moments to deliberate, then nodded slowly.

"Your father has been arrested on suspicion of murder, Melissa."

"What?"

"I can have somebody come and sit with you if—"

"I don't need a babysitter. I need my dad," she said.

"In that case, I'm afraid I can't help." He nodded for Byrne and Campbell to lead Hale away.

"Murder who?" she said, stopping them. "Who is he supposed to have murdered?"

"Just leave it, love," Hale said.

"Edward Higgins," Ivy said. "He occupied the room next door to Ryan Eva."

"Why him? Why my dad? What does this have to do with him?" She gazed lovingly at her father. "This is him, isn't it? This is all about him. Ryan. He had nothing to do with Ryan dying. He wouldn't do that. Would you, Dad? Tell them. Tell them you didn't do it."

Hale forced a smile, but it was weak and unsustainable, and it faltered until only a grimace remained.

"They're right," he said eventually. "Adam killed Ryan, love."

"Dad—"

"And someone saw him."

"But Dad—"

"And..." He hesitated. The next words would seal his fate. "And I was part of it."

"No," she said, shaking her head.

"There are messages," he said. "On my phone and presumably on Adam's, too. I couldn't risk it, love. I couldn't risk anything coming back to us."

He nodded down at his pocket, and Byrne slipped his fingers inside, retrieved the phone, and handed it to Ivy.

"It's locked," she said, and she showed Hale the screen asking for a security PIN.

"Melissa's birthday," he replied sadly.

"Of course, the awful truth is that Adam Potter didn't actually murder Ryan," George said.

Hale's brow furrowed.

"What?" Melissa said. "But you just said—"

"Potter didn't kill him," George said. "He hit him, yes. And he thought he'd killed him. But Ryan didn't die until the following day."

Hale's knees buckled, dragging Byrne and Campbell as they fought to hold his weight.

"So Edward Higgins didn't need to die," George added.

"Oh, Dad—"

"I was protecting you," he said. "From Ryan Eva. I knew that if he was out, he could get to you. I couldn't let that happen."

She shook her head and held his arms, stroking them as though both comforting her father and savouring the feel of his skin for the last time for a long time to come.

"Dad, he already came to see me. On Thursday. When you went back to work. He was here."

Mark Hale's head snapped up. "What?"

"He came to talk to me. To apologise. He didn't do anything," she said quickly, seeing the panicked look on Mark Hale's face. "He said he just wanted to make amends."

"Why didn't you tell me?" he said.

"Because I knew what you'd do," she told him, her voice high and succumbing to tears.

He smiled up at her, his eyes wet with regret.

"You know me too well," he said.

"Take him away," George said, and he stood to one side so that Campbell and Byrne could haul Hale to his feet.

"Like I said, Mark…" George called out as Byrne and Campbell manoeuvred him into the back of their car. "Anything you say will be used against you in court. So I'll take all that as a confession."

"No," he said, looking over his shoulder anxiously. "Melissa. Someone stay and look after Melissa."

"Dad, I'm fine," she called after him. "Just stop talking. Stop giving them stuff to use against you."

"Stay safe," he cried. "Lock the doors. I'll come back for you. Don't answer the door to anyone. I promise I'll be back." But George watched Melissa, her head shaking silently, knowing that her father was not coming home today, or any time soon, that she was alone and would have to fend for herself.

"It's ironic, isn't it?" Ivy said as they returned to George's car. "The only person she needed protecting from was her own dad."

"I can protect myself," Melissa called out, having clearly heard the remark.

"Good," Ivy said, turning to her. "Because all his *protection* has done is made your life a hundred times worse. Remember that."

George gave the girl a sympathetic glance, wondering what her future held.

"Can I give you some advice, Melissa?" George started.

"No," she said, shaking her head bitterly. "No, you can bloody well go to hell. All of you."

CHAPTER FIFTY

"What do you think she'll do?" George asked as he turned out of the driveway, catching one final look at the old house in the rear view mirror. "If she stays, she'll be ostracised. You know what people are like."

"I hope she moves on," Ivy said in the passenger seat next to him. "I hope she moves far away from here and starts her life all over again."

"Her life should be on track by now, not starting from scratch," George said. He checked the clock on the dashboard and pondered his next move.

"At least the interview will be short," Ivy remarked.

"Oh, I think we can leave that for now," he replied. "It's late, and I'm done in. Give him a night in a cell to gather his story."

"What about the team?" Ivy asked. "Once they've processed Hale, what do you want them working on?"

"Well, Maguire and O'Hara are still bound to shift timings," he said. "Why not get them to find the elusive Uncle Peter? Maybe Ruby can help them? I'm afraid to say that I feel we've let Ryan Eva's case slip. I've been so preoccupied with linking

Higgins to him that it's, what, four days on, and we've still got nothing."

"We've eliminated Potter and Hale," Ivy said.

"Ah, don't fall for it," George told her.

"Guv, they thought Eva was dead."

"Right, and what a good alibi that is. They couldn't have killed him because they thought he was dead. Try proving anything against that."

"Now you're venturing into the world of bizarre and ludicrous," Ivy said.

"All I'm saying is that we need to keep an open mind," he told her. "Hale, yes. But Potter? It's the perfect crime. He shows up at Ryan's house, makes sure he was seen, makes sure he left a physical mark."

"And so we automatically exclude him from the actual murder."

"It's worth bearing in mind."

"I think you're crediting him with too much intelligence," Ivy said. "The only person I know who could have come up with that—"

"Is a cynical old sod like me?"

"I wouldn't call you a sod, guv," she laughed. "Cynical, yes."

"You know, normally, I'd be heading home to pour myself a large scotch in preparation for the days ahead." He glanced over at her. "Putting the investigation into some semblance of an order for the CPS. But the truth is, we've still got an entire murder investigation to work on. Hale's case will have to wait."

"You can still have a scotch, guv," she said. "I'd happily cook dinner. You never know; a bit of a reset might do us both good."

"No," he said. "No, I think I'll go for a drive. I need some time to think."

"Guv, have a night off, for God's sake."

"Rory Wetherford," he said, ignoring her. "What do we have on him?"

"Honestly? Nothing," she replied.

"Well, let's play devil's advocate. Assuming Potter and Hale are telling the truth, then we can eliminate them from Eva's murder. Which leaves?"

"Rory Wetherford," Ivy said.

"But no evidence against him," added George.

"Nancy Wetherford," she tried.

"Strong motive," George said, "but unlikely. Why would she ruin her own wedding day?"

"Lucas Coffey? Wanting to protect his new wife, maybe?"

"Same motive," George said, "but same unlikelihood. Again, why would he ruin his wedding day?"

"I don't think anyone *wanted* to ruin that wedding day, guv. I think they acted out of passion, out of emotionality. The more I think about it, the more likely it seems that no one knew Ryan was there at all. No one except Uncle Pete. And when Ryan turned up, someone saw him and they just lost it."

"We need to talk to Uncle Pete," George said. "We need his bloody last name first. I'm not referring to him in a formal interview as Uncle bloody Pete. Talk to Nancy. It's been a few days now. Long enough for her to have come to terms with her memorable day. We can do that first thing, assuming they haven't gone on their honeymoon."

"Nancy's mum said they cancelled it, remember?"

"Right, when you speak to the team, have Ruby get the address," he said. "And I want their workplaces, too. We're already days behind on this. I'm not delaying it any more."

"Guv, just relax," she said, then sighed loudly. "Why don't you go and see Grace?"

"Sorry?"

"You haven't seen her since Saturday. Go and see her. Take your mind off things. You're always telling me to make memories. Go and make some with her. Take her somewhere. For dinner, maybe."

He battled internally with what he wanted to say and then finally gave in.

"Memories..." he began, and his mind wandered to Grace. "Memories are all I have, Ivy." He laughed once at how ridiculous it sounded. "You know, I can see Grace right now." He tapped his temple. "In here. She's never more than a blink of an eye away. In a heartbeat, I can see. On our wedding day, back when I was getting to know her." He laughed again. "I can even remember her at school. On Sundays, I used to gobble my dinner down as fast as I could and then run all the way to Bag Enderby so I could see her when she came out of Sunday school."

"You didn't do Sunday school yourself, then?"

"Ah, I was never religious," he said. "Had a respect for the church. Most people did back then. But not like Grace and her family. They were devout. What I'm saying is that she's right there whenever I want her. And do you know why? Because she's important to me."

"Just like Ryan Eva?" Ivy said, and he nodded.

"Not as an individual," he said, getting that point across. "But as an investigation. As an open thing, I have to deal with. He's unfinished business."

"And is Grace unfinished business?"

He opened his mouth to ask her to rephrase the question but stopped himself. She had every right to ask.

"Grace is a business that will never be finished," he said. "Not while she's how she is."

He stared ahead at the road and blinked away the rogue tear that belied his strength.

"I'm going to call in," Ivy said, pulling her phone from her pocket. "Byrne and Campbell can go and pick Wetherford up. Do we know where he's staying?"

"The White Horse," George replied. "In a B and B out the back. And tell them to take bags and gloves. I want every scrap of his clothing."

"Right, and the others can all hunt for Uncle Pete," Ivy replied. "I'm going to cook us something nice, and you—"

"Please," he said, too tired to be lectured.

"You can go and see her, guv. See Grace," she said. "And if you don't..."

"Yes?" he said, daring her to threaten him and keen to see what with exactly.

"I'll tell the team you're actually a softie," she said playfully.

"You wouldn't?"

"I would," she said. "Although, I doubt they'd believe a word of it."

"Do you know what I keep coming back to?" he said.

"Guv, if this is about the investigation, I'm not listening. Not until tomorrow."

"Whoever fought with Ryan Eva would have been wet," he continued. "Not only has nobody mentioned anybody arriving late or slipping off from the rehearsal, but nobody mentioned anybody being wet or muddy either. It rained, for God's sake. How on earth did they pull that off?"

"I'm not listening, guv."

"Unless they had a change of clothes," he added. "But then who takes a change of clothes to a wedding rehearsal?"

"You really are a stubborn old—"

"Somebody who travelled there," he said, answering his own question. "Somebody who was staying the night to be at the wedding the next day."

Ivy said nothing, but he could tell he had piqued her interest.

"Which rules out Rory Wetherford, of course," he continued.

"Unless he and his wife had already argued," Ivy suggested. "And his bags were already packed and in his car."

He grinned, both at adding a piece to the puzzle and for breaking Ivy's resolve.

"Well, that's cheered me up," he said as Ivy started the call to

O'Hara. "I shall go and see Grace with renewed purpose." He grinned at her. "And with any luck, tomorrow night, I might be able to pour myself that drink."

CHAPTER FIFTY-ONE

George drove through the Wolds and enjoyed how the hills opened up the closer he got to the coast. The land grew flatter and easier to navigate. The ribbon-like road stretched out like it was unravelling. And he could smell the salty air Ivy had spoken of through his car window. He longed for the vastness of the sea and the perspective it offered. But before he could drive straight to the coast, he pulled into the car park that was quickly becoming a second home.

He walked into the reception to be met by the constantly friendly Miss Dowdeswell.

"Hiya, George," she said, and then her expression seemed to freeze, as if she'd seen something on his face but was too polite to say. She opened the visitor register and slid it across the desk along with a British Heart Foundation pen. "How are you? Good day?"

He smiled at her impeccable manners and poor acting skills.

"It's been a rough few days, Mrs Dowdeswell. But you know what they say. Life is a balance, which means that I'm owed some joy."

"I think we're all overdue some of that," she replied as he

signed the book and slid it back to her, making a point to hand her the pen.

"Is she okay?" he asked tentatively, knowing that one day he would ask that question and be given the beginning of the end.

"She's in a good place today," she replied. "She's out in the sunroom."

"The sunroom? Crikey. I've been outside most of the day, and I haven't seen the sun once."

"She's painting," Mrs Dowdeswell replied with a laugh. "Go on with you. I'll send someone through to fetch you some tea."

"That would be lovely, thank you," he told her. He made his way across the reception and out into the glazed sun room.

He stopped on the threshold and drank in the view. She was utterly lost in her work, adding tiny dots of burnt orange and amber to a scene so familiar to him that it could have been a self-portrait. An old church occupied the left-hand side of the two-by-one canvas. The foreground, which she was working on, was a grassy patch and a rough lane that led to the focal point — an old cottage with a glorious flower bed and tall trees behind it. It was an autumn scene, hence the fallen leaves she was delicately adding, and the sky was darkening. Not quite dusk, but late enough in the day for lights to be on. But only one light had been switched on, and the window glowed brilliantly against the earthy tones that comprised the rest of the painting.

And it was this window she began working on as he stepped up behind her, being careful not to disrupt her flow — something she used to scold him for. She loaded a fan brush with graphite grey, with which she deftly created a figure in that glowing window: a young girl resting her chin on her hands, gazing out at the same view George enjoyed every single morning.

"That's wonderful," he said softly, in case he startled her.

She turned to face him as much as her wheelchair would allow.

"Oh my goodness," she said. "I didn't see you come in."

"I was watching you work. You're a real artisan."

"Oh, stop it," she told him, collecting up the tiny brush with the burnt orange. She lightened the mix on her palette with the tiniest touch of white, then set to work adding in leaves in areas that, until those lighter leaves were added, he had thought to be complete. But it wasn't until she had added them that they made sense. She could see things — art, spaces, designs — that others simply couldn't.

"My George used to watch me paint," she said, and his heart sank.

For the briefest of moments, he had thought that today just might be the day.

"Did he?" he found himself saying. He made a show of crouching beside her and gazing out of the window into the dying day. "I can't see it."

"You can't see what?"

"The church," he said. "Did you make it up?"

"Oh, you," she said, then she hesitated as if she was suddenly unsure of herself. "I don't know. I just thought of it. Pretty, isn't it?"

"It's gorgeous," he replied. He wanted to tell her that he knew the place. He wanted to tell her that she would fall in love with it. He wanted to say that he knew the girl in the window. He opened his mouth and...

"Grace?" he started.

"Hmmm," she said, leaning back to take the painting as a whole piece.

"I was wondering."

"Hmmm," she said again. Then she stopped painting, dropped her brush into the glass of water she kept beside her, and waited for him to speak. "Yes, dear?"

"It's just..." he said. "I was wondering if I could have it?"

"Have it?"

"The painting," he said. "I have the perfect place for it."

"It's not worth anything," she said.

"It is to me. It's quite something."

"Well, I suppose—"

"Unless you wanted to keep it. You know, hang it on your bedroom wall."

"Oh no. I have dozens of them," she said. "But it's not dry. It'll take a few days."

"I'll be careful with it," he told her. "I wonder. Would you sign it for me?"

"That'll make it worth even less," she said, taking up her fan brush once more and using the graphite to place those two initials in the bottom right-hand corner. *GL.*

"Can I get you some tea?" somebody called, and a nurse entered, paying almost no attention to Grace's work. George was about to ask for tea when Grace spoke.

"Not for me, thank you," she said. "I'm quite tired." She smiled up at the girl. "Would you mind pushing me back to my room?"

"Of course," the nurse replied, turning Grace towards the door. George longed to reach out and give her hand a squeeze or to flick her hair behind her ear. Just like he used to do. But she stared dead ahead as if he wasn't even there.

"Goodbye, Grace," he called out as they passed through the door into the reception.

"Bye, dear," she called back, and in one long, drawn-out heart-beat, she was gone.

CHAPTER FIFTY-TWO

"That was Sergeant Hart. She wants Maguire and me to find Uncle Pete," O'Hara said, placing the phone into the receiver. She turned to Ruby, who was sitting at a desk nearby. "She said you can help us."

"Okay," Ruby said without looking up.

O'Hara waited a few seconds more, craning her neck to see what Ruby was working on.

"What's that?"

"This?" Ruby began, closing the file and placing it at the bottom of a tall heap. "This is what eighty-five handwritten witness statements look like."

"Christ."

"And this," Ruby continued, pulling a fresh file from the top and opening it to her right, "is me typing every one of them into a fresh witness statement form."

"Got your work cut out, then?"

"I certainly have," Ruby replied.

"So?"

"So, what?"

"So, did you hear what I said about Sergeant Hart?"

"Ah," Ruby said, her eyes never once leaving her screen.

"With regards to Uncle Pete?"

"Oh, I heard," Ruby said.

"Oh, good. Today, or..." O'Hara left it open for Ruby to fill in the blanks. "It's kind of urgent."

"Is it now?"

"Sorry, have I offended you?" O'Hara said. "Did I say something wrong?"

"It's nothing you *said*," Ruby replied.

"Something I did, then? Like what?"

"It's nothing you did, either."

"Oh, for God's sake. Just tell me what it was, and I'll apologise."

"There's no point apologising if you don't mean it, is there? You either know or you don't."

"Well...I don't," O'Hara said. "So there's not a lot I can do about it."

"Fair enough," Ruby said, flicking to the next page.

"Oh, just bloody tell me, will you?"

"I just expect a certain level of common bloody decency, O'Hara," Ruby told her. "It's simple."

"Decency?"

"Manners," she said. "Look, do you wonder why I treat DI Larson with respect?"

"He's a nice bloke," O'Hara said.

"Right, he's a nice bloke."

"And Sergeant Hart?"

"She could do with smiling a little more, but she's alright."

"Right, but I still treat them with respect, do I not?"

"I suppose."

"And you?"

"Me?" O'Hara shrugged. "I'm nice. I think I am, anyway."

"Two words," Ruby said. "I'll help you when I hear two words from you."

"Eh?"

"I'll give you a clue. One of them is usually used by the requester to the requestee as a demonstration of the forthcoming appreciation, the pre-favour. The second is usually used by the requester to the requestee as a demonstration of appreciation after the favour."

"I have no idea what you're talking about."

"Oh, for God's sake," Ruby said. "*Please*."

"Please, what?"

"Use the word. Please," Ruby said.

"What word? What word do you want me to use, Ruby?"

"I want you to use the word, *please*. Literally, the word I want you to use is *please*."

The floorboard in the corridor creaked, and the doors burst open, signifying that somebody had come into the incident room, as opposed to the doors bursting open and then the floorboards creaking, which would indicate that somebody had left. Maguire shuffled behind O'Hara, dumped a plastic bag onto his desk, and then began emptying the contents.

"What?" he said, looking between them. "What is it?"

"It's nothing," O'Hara said.

"No, come on. Something's happened. Don't tell me the guv's called in?"

"No," Ruby said. "The guv hasn't called."

"Ah, well, that's good," he said, and he carried on emptying his bag. "Right then. I've got a Ginsters slice, an egg mayo sarnie, or a chicken and bacon wrap. Then, for afters we've got a Twix, a Toffee Crisp, or a Kit Kat." He presented his haul proudly and then snatched the Kit Kat. "Actually, that one's mine." He smiled up at them. "What'll it be then?"

Nobody uttered a word.

"Come on," he said. "Ruby, can I interest you in an egg mayo sarnie?"

"Is it gluten-free?"

"What? No, of course not. Why on earth would I buy that muck?"

"Because I'm celiac?" she said. "I don't eat gluten."

"Oh God, really?" he said, and she nodded slowly. "You're not one of them, are you?"

"One of what?"

"One of those who needs their own menu. Christ almighty," he said. "You know, human beings have been eating normally for literally millions of years. Then the whole world decides to go woke, and the next thing you know, you can't even pop out for a meal without somebody making the process harder than it needs to be."

"Human beings?"

"Yeah, you know. Us." He pointed his way through the circle they made. "Homo sapiens."

"Are you for real?" Ruby said. "I'm allergic to gluten. Do you know what it means?"

"Yeah, right. I mean, I always thought vegetarians were bad enough, but compared to the old GF club, they're easy."

"Maguire, gluten is poison to my body."

"Alright, alright," he said. "So you don't eat bread. I suppose you could have the wrap."

"Gluten," Ruby said.

"What? No way. What about the Twix?"

"It contains biscuit," she said.

"Yeah, of course. It's a Twix, for Christ's sake."

Instead of responding, Ruby closed her laptop, took a deep breath, and dropped it into her bag. Calmly, she pulled on her jacket as she stood, collected her bag, and started towards the door.

"Where you off to?" Maguire asked.

"I don't need this," she replied.

"What do you want me to do? Go and buy some celery or something?"

"Just..." she started, then exhaled again to calm herself. "Just forget it."

"Your loss," Maguire said, tugging open the egg mayo sandwich wrapper.

"And for the record, Maguire," Ruby said. "Homo sapiens? Three hundred thousand years."

"Eh?"

"Enjoy your gluten," she said, and she stormed off. The doors burst open, and then the floorboard creaked.

"What was all that about?" he said. "Jesus. She's highly strung. Won't last long in a place like this, I tell you."

"Sergeant Hart called," O'Hara said. "She wants us to find Uncle Pete."

"Uncle Pete? Ah, that's a shame. Ruby would have been a great help. She'd have found him in a heartbeat."

The phone on Campbell's desk began to ring, and O'Hara reached across to answer it as Maguire cracked open a can of Sprite.

"Campbell's phone," she said.

"I'm looking for DI Larson," came a voice.

"He's not here, I'm afraid." Maguire looked over curiously, running his tongue around his teeth. He took a long drink, then burped quietly. "Can I help? I work in his team."

"I wanted to ask how the Ryan Eva investigation was going?"

"Okay..." O'Hara said. "And who's calling, please?"

"Do you know when he'll be in?"

"Erm, tomorrow, probably. It's late," she said. "Sorry, I didn't get your name."

He hesitated. "I'm Nancy Wetherford's uncle," he said quietly. "Pete."

O'Hara waved madly at Maguire to get his attention and then pointed at the phone.

"Are you there?" Pete asked.

"I'm here," she said, pulling a piece of scrap paper towards her and fumbling in Campbell's pen pot for a pen that worked. "Sorry, I just need to take your name, please?"

"I just told you."

"Oh, sorry. Your last name."

She shrugged at Maguire to indicate she hadn't a clue what to say to him. Maguire stood, pulled his phone from his pocket, and opened the recorder app. He hit the orange button to record and set it down quietly beside the desk phone. O'Hara then directed the call to loudspeaker, noting that the number he was calling from was withheld.

"I just wanted to know where you are with it," he said, ignoring the question. "You know, if I could help at all?"

"Are you calling from a payphone?" O'Hara asked.

"Why do you ask?"

"Oh, no reason. It's just that we don't see them much these days. Most people have mobiles, don't they?"

"I suppose."

"But you don't have a mobile phone?"

"What can I say?" Pete said. "I'm old school."

"It would help us to have your contact details," O'Hara said tentatively. "In case we need to be in touch in the future."

"I'm in touch right now," he said. "Whatever you have to say, you can say it to me now."

"Well, we have been trying to get in touch with you. So, if you have time, we have some questions."

"Go on," he said.

O'Hara swallowed. She felt like she was walking a thin tightrope between proving herself to DI Larson and not spooking the caller.

"Well, one of the things we're trying to understand is why you were arguing with Rory Wetherford at the wedding rehearsal," she said and waited for a reply she didn't receive.

"I'm not sure how that would help you."

"It's just a question that DI Larson wanted us to ask," O'Hara said, as Maguire gave an emphatic and encouraging nod. "You wanted your nephew to be at the wedding, didn't you? Is that right?"

Uncle Pete paused for a while on the other end of the phone, and when he eventually spoke, there was a sadness to his tone.

"He's family. It's only right that he should have been there."

"Well, according to your sister-in-law, Mr..." O'Hara stumbled. "Sorry, what was your last name again?"

She waited.

The line clicked, and then a dial tone ensued.

"Crap," O'Hara spat. She set the phone down in the cradle, then picked it up to slam it down a few times. "I messed it up."

"Ah, come on. You did grand."

"He's gone," she said. "We had him on the phone, and he's gone."

"Ah, but he called in. What does that tell you? Tells you he's thinking about it. Guilty as sin, that one. Mark my words."

He reached over and collected his phone to end the recording.

"Don't play that to anyone," O'Hara said. "The last thing I need is the guv hearing it. I'll never be allowed to speak to a suspect again. I'll be the bloody tea girl."

"Ah, don't be so hard on yourself," he said, and he replayed the recording. O'Hara reached up to grab the phone, but he held it high above his head.

"*I just wanted to know where you are with it,*" came Pete's voice. "*You know, if I could help at all?*"

"I shouldn't have kept on about his last name," O'Hara said. "I should have just dropped it."

"Shh," Maguire said, holding the phone to his ear. "Did you hear that? Tell me you heard that."

"Heard what?"

Irritated, he scrolled the recording back a few seconds and let it play, cranking the volume up.

"There," he said. "You must have heard that."

"Jesus," O'Hara whispered. "I know where he is."

Her eyes wandered to her desk, where the keys to the car they had used to go to Hales' house were lying.

"No, oh no," Maguire said.

"Come on," she said. "We've got him."

"Well, then call Sergeant Hart. Have her go."

"What? By the time anyone else can scramble, he'll be long gone."

"I am not going to Skegness. Did you hear Larson tearing a piece out of Byrne and Campbell?"

"Yeah, until he realised they had something."

"But what if we don't have anything? What if he's gone?"

"Which is why we should go now," O'Hara said. "Think about it. We call Hart, and she calls Larson. Everyone speeds over to Skeggy, and he's gone. Who looks like a pair of idiots? You and me. Whereas if you and I go, and we don't find him, nobody is any the wiser."

"We can't just go for a jolly to Skeg-bloody-ness in a police car."

"We'll take my car then," she said, checking her watch. "Come on, the shift's over. We're into overtime."

"Absolutely not."

"This is our chance, Maguire," she pleaded. "We've been on the team two days, and we bring in the man everyone's been looking for."

"We can't just go and nick him," he said. "We don't have a warrant for one thing, and we can't bring him back in your car."

"Well, we'll talk to him, then," she said. "Come on. He can't put the phone down when we're standing in front of him."

"I don't know," Maguire said.

"Tell you what," she said. "If we don't find him, I'll get you an ice cream."

"An ice cream? You think I'm going to risk my bloody career

for an ice cream? I told you this was a bad idea. I could have been happily sitting in a nice warm squad car driving around Horncastle, about to finish my shift, if I hadn't listened to you. Not considering if I go against a direct order."

"Was it an order?" she said. "Who says we can't go to Skegness in our own time?"

"No," he said.

"Okay, last offer," she said, seeing a crack in his armour. "If it all goes wrong, I'll take full responsibility."

He bit down on his lower lip, considering the offer.

"Full responsibility and an ice cream."

"Done."

"Double cone. None of those single cone cop-outs."

"You're on," she said, snatching up her coat. "Don't look so worried. What could possibly go wrong?"

CHAPTER FIFTY-THREE

The glorious aroma of home cooking reached George the moment he climbed from his car. Carefully, he opened the front door and heard Ivy humming to the radio. It was one of those new tunes that, no matter how hard he tried, he simply couldn't get into. They just lacked memorable melodies. It seemed to him that more effort was put into the beat than the hook. But she seemed to enjoy modern music, and with a busy mind like his, blocking the radio out was as easy as pie.

He crept through the lounge to the stairs and was on the first step when she heard him.

"That you, guv?"

He cringed.

"Hi, Ivy. I'll just get cleaned up."

"I'll serve up then," she said. "Shepherd's pie. Hope that's okay."

"Sounds lovely," he called back and rushed up the stairs as fast as his old legs would allow.

Safely inside his bedroom, he closed the door behind him and held the painting up into the light. He'd tried to steal a few glances of it during the drive home, but parts of it were still wet, so he'd had to prop it upright in the passenger footwell with an old carrier bag he'd found in the boot. He'd been dying to see it, and now he was seeing it; he was itching to see it hanging.

And he knew just the spot.

When the room had been Grace's childhood bedroom, a wooden cross had hung from an old flathead screw about head height adjacent to the door. Since taking over the house, George had used it to hang his weekend hat, which he now discarded with his free hand, then positioned the canvas.

It was perfect-more than perfect, in fact-surreal. Like a Pink Floyd album cover, with the house, the church, and the window, through which was a picture of the house, the church, and the window.

And the little girl.

That was the key to it: Grace. It warmed him to know that he could see her forever more. And if one day, like hers, his memory faded, then he could always remind himself. The day he looked at the painting and wondered who the girl was, that was the day to put an end to it all.

He held that thought for a moment.

"Guv?" Ivy called from downstairs. "I'm serving up."

"Coming," he called back, then lowered his voice, speaking directly to Grace. "Back in a bit, love."

"How did it go?" Ivy asked when he entered the kitchen. She slid two plates onto the table with little ceremony. She had actually laid the table, but the standards were far from ideal. The cutlery hadn't been laid out neatly as he would have done. Instead, they appeared to have been dumped roughly before the two seats they used. The shepherd's pie looked great, and she'd managed to crisp the top like Grace used to, but it would have been nice to wipe the edge of the plate from where she had spilt some of the meat and sauce while serving.

Still, her company was unrivalled compared to the alternative.

"Oh, you know," he replied, taking a small mouthful from the edge of the plate, where the food would be cooler. "She was in high spirits. That's all I can ask for."

Ivy sat cross-legged on her chair with her fork in one hand, elbow on the table, and the other hand on her lap. The knife lay askew and redundant, close to a foot from her plate.

"So, she didn't recognise you then?" she asked.

George forked another mouthful.

"Wine," he said. "Let's have some wine." He rose from his seat and collected two glasses and the bottle of white he'd had in the fridge for a while.

It was only when he'd poured two glasses and taken a drink that Ivy pressed further.

"One day, you'll look back fondly at your visits," she said. "I know it's hard now. But give it time."

There was a hidden meaning to her words, which he picked up on almost immediately. One day, Grace would lose her fight. There would be no more visits, and that was a far worse prospect than visiting somebody who failed to recognise him after a lifetime of marriage. "Don't stop going, guv. Make all the memories you can."

"Are you speaking from experience?" he asked.

"Sorry, I didn't mean to preach."

"Perhaps you should think about making some memories with your children," he said, revealing a rarely used harshness. "And your husband."

"That's not fair."

"No?" He drank some more, then settled. "Sorry. There are some similarities between us, Ivy. But our worlds are oceans apart. I would give anything to have her back. Anything. And you?"

"I'm walking away?" she said.

"I can't know what you've been through, you and your husband. But I do wish you'd reconsider. If he's willing, then I wish you'd give it another go. Sleep in separate rooms if you have to. Get to know each other again."

"Don't you think I've tried that?" she said and set her fork down, collected her glass, and sat back as if she was done eating. "It's not like I haven't tried. Do you honestly think I'd give my kids up without a fight?"

"But how's it going to work?" George asked. "With a divorce, I mean. Will you see them?"

"I suppose that all depends on what the court rules. Our case is slightly different in that I'm the breadwinner. He works for the RNLI, so he has more flexibility. He can pick the kids up from school and do all that, so it looks like he'll get custody. I shouldn't really complain. You hear about dads going through the same sort of thing all the time, don't you? They get to see their kids once a week or once a fortnight."

"Once a month in some cases," George said.

"Right. And they still have to hand over half their pay cheques. They still have to move out and start again in places not too different to the bedsit Ryan Eva lived in. I should count myself lucky. At least I have this place until I can find somewhere of my own."

George topped their glasses up, drank, and then set his own fork down.

"Actually, I wanted to talk to you about that."

"About living here?" she asked, and a look of disappointment washed over her face like a bad smell had wafted into the kitchen. "Guv, I need —"

"I'm not asking you to leave," he said, easing her growing concern. "But I'd like the house to myself this weekend. There's something I'd like to do." He smiled weakly and drank some more. "No, that's not right," he said thoughtfully. "There's something I *need* to do."

CHAPTER FIFTY-FOUR

"Where is it?" Maguire asked O'Hara as they ran into Skegness train station. Unlike many other stations dotted around rural Lincolnshire, Skegness was a heaving melee of chaos. But compared to any London station, it was insignificant. With just four operational platforms, it served the local community, feeding travellers into the larger national networks via more significant hubs such as Nottingham, Lincoln, and Newark.

"I don't know. I haven't been here before."

A train must have arrived shortly before, as a few dozen people were making their way from the platforms.

Maguire studied the signs but saw nothing that would help them. He ran to the ticket desk and joined the front of a short queue.

"Excuse me," he said, catching the attention of the woman behind the screen and smiling a brief apology to the man being served. "I need the payphone."

"Payphone?" she said. "There's no payphone here, is there? I thought they took them all away."

"There's one left," Maguire said, hoping his urgency would be at least slightly infectious. "I just need to know where it is."

She eyed his uniform.

"Well, I suppose you can always use mine," she said. "I can buzz you through if you like."

"No, I don't need to make a call. I just need the payphone."

"You what?" she said, her face contouring in confusion.

"It's out on the concourse," another lady said who was second in the queue, and very likely hoping to make the train that had just arrived before it left again. "Near the toilets, I think. But I don't think it works."

"Oh, it works, alright," Maguire said to her, stopping briefly to look into her eyes. "Thank you."

The toilets were signed well enough, and being a small station, it took them less than a minute to find it while going against the flow of people. They jogged and slowed as they approached the phone, which was, as the lady had indicated, near the toilets. But there was nobody loitering nearby.

"When did the last train leave?" Maguire said, and O'Hara began a search on her phone. "Was he coming into the station from somewhere, or was he leaving for somewhere?"

"Fifteen minutes ago," she said, holding her phone up. "Left for Nottingham."

"So, he's on his way to Nottingham? Where does it stop? Maybe he's going to get off at one of the smaller stations?"

"Unless he *was* coming into Skegness?"

"No, that train hasn't been here long enough."

"The one before it was an hour ago," she said, reading the timetable online.

"Too long," Maguire replied. "We left the incident room what, thirty minutes ago? That means he would have been hanging about for half an hour before calling us. No, he's on it. He's bloody toying with us."

"Maguire," O'Hara said, but he was checking the sign on the wall.

"Jesus, have you seen this? It stops at Havenhouse, Wainfleet, Thorpe Culvert, Boston—"

"*Maguire*," O'Hara said, a little more forcefully this time.

"He could have got off on any one of them," Maguire said, turning to face her. But she wasn't looking at him. She was staring at one of the benches a few metres from the phone box. He followed her gaze. "What's that?"

"What does it look like?" she said.

"A plastic bag," he replied. "Somebody left it, do you think?"

"Not just somebody," O'Hara said.

"Oh, come on. Hundreds of people come through here."

He started towards it, but she grabbed onto his arm.

"No," she said. "No, don't touch it."

"Eh? Don't be daft."

"I mean it," she said, gripping his arm even tighter. "We just don't know. He could have...rigged it or something."

"Rigged it?" he said incredulously. "To blow up?"

"Shut up," she hissed, checking around them nervously. "But yes."

"Listen, if anybody knows anything about exploding bags around here, it's me," he said, pointing at the bag. "And that's not going to go bang."

"How the hell do you know? You don't. We should call it in."

"Oh, behave yourself, will you? It's just a bag." He pulled his arm free and took a step closer.

"Maguire?" she said. "We should at least evacuate the station."

"You must be off your head," he said. "We're not even supposed to be here. Imagine the blast the papers will have. Cops cause chaos for commuters in fake bomb scandal."

"Imagine the papers if you're wrong," she countered. "Cops kill dozens due to negligence."

He hesitated and eyed the bag.

"I'll just take a wee look," he said.

"Maguire?"

"A look. That's all. I won't touch it. I'll just take a peek inside."

"Do not touch it," she said, her face as stern as ever he could remember.

He approached it casually but took a few steps around the bench to get the best view inside, peering into it without the few passengers who were making their way to the waiting train becoming intrigued.

"Oh, Christ," he said, slowly, gazing up at O'Hara, whose eyes widened in horror.

"What is it?"

"Just stay there," he said, then backed the order up with a look she couldn't argue with. "In fact, go back a bit."

"Maguire?"

Slowly and delicately, he nudged the rim of the bag open, then called out to her again.

"Don't come any closer," he said.

She was dumbstruck. Frozen to the spot in terror.

His hand was inside the bag and making slow and cautious movements. He gripped hold of the item, then carefully reversed the movement, trying not to disturb the plastic.

"You're mental," she hissed at him.

"Just hold on," he said calmly. "I know what I'm doing." He looked up at her. "On three."

"What?"

"One, two—"

"Maguire!"

"Three."

CHAPTER FIFTY-FIVE

It was always slightly unnerving to find an empty incident room, Ruby thought as she flicked the lights on. The old fluorescent lamps buzzed, and the tubes flickered once or twice, then burned brightly. Having worked first of all in Lincoln HQ, where teams worked shifts that spanned the clock face, being alone was an alien sensation. Oddly, it was perhaps one of the safest places to work, being that an intruder would have to get through at least three security doors and up to the first floor without being seen. But still, she preferred to have all the lights on.

Besides, she wouldn't be there for long. At the desk she had claimed for herself, she scooped the stationery from her pen pot, separating those items she had supplied herself, such as the nice pens, highlighters, and the little ruler, from those she had taken from the stationery cupboard, such as the cheap pens that dried up within a few days.

In the top drawer of her desk, she rummaged through the odds and ends, most of which had been left by the desk's previous occupant, but found nothing that belonged to her. All that remained was the framed photo she liked to keep wherever she worked.

Oddly, nobody had even commented on it.

She felt the vibration of her phone from inside her coat, and she pulled it out and answered it on loudspeaker.

"Alright, Dad," she said.

"Hey, love," he said, then hesitated, indicating that he didn't actually want to ask the question she knew he was going to ask. "I was just wondering if you'll be long?"

"No, not long," she told him. "I'm just packing up now. Give me half an hour, yeah?"

"You okay?" he asked. "You sound a bit down. Rough day, was it?"

"Something like that." She sighed and then gave in. He'd have to know sooner or later. "It hasn't worked out, Dad."

"What?"

"The new team. I'm not sure if I can do it."

"Why? What's happened?"

"I...I just don't get on with them."

"I thought you said he was nice. What's his name? George?"

"Yeah, he's alright. But he's hardly here. It's the rest of the team. I just...I don't know. They're not my people." She tried to sound upbeat but knew her dad would see through it. "I'm going to see if I can go back to what I was doing."

"Can't you stick it out?" he said. "Who are these others?"

"Oh, they're nobody. It's not about who they are; it's the fact that I'll be stuck with them. Don't you think it's better to get out before things settle? Give DI Larson time to find somebody else, you know?"

"Oh, love. Will they have you back? Wouldn't they have filled your spot by now?"

"I don't know, I can try," she said. "Listen, can you give Frankie some dinner for me, please? Get him ready for bed. Tell him I won't be long."

A pang of guilt thumped in her chest when she rose from her chair. Larson's desk was immaculate, except for a whiteboard marker he hadn't put away. Obliged from guilt, she collected it up and set it down in the tray.

"I've done dinner for you," her father said.

"Oh, lovely. What is it?" she called out, imagining him at home doing his best to stay busy.

"It's a surprise," he said, to which she gave a laugh.

Surprises were his thing. She could recall a dozen times he had picked her up from school and told her there was a surprise waiting for her when they got home. The surprises themselves could range from a tub of ice cream for pudding to a new pair of shoes. It was usually around payday, at a time when every penny he earned had been accounted for before he'd even earned it.

"Maybe it'll be the pony I always wanted," she said with a laugh as she studied the whiteboard, deciphering the information. Larson's handwriting was neat enough. It was just the volume of disconnected pieces that made it complex to read. She had seen many a whiteboard in her time. They'd had smart boards in Lincoln HQ, allowing the SIO to connect their laptop and display images, then write over the top. But this was a rural station, and the chances of the SIO in this team embracing technology were slim to none, even if they did have it available.

"Dad?"

"Yes, love?"

"I just want to finish something," she said. "You know me, I don't like to leave a job half done."

"I understand," he replied, with a hint of sadness in his tone. "I'll put the pony in the stable, shall I?"

She laughed again.

"Thanks, Dad."

"Drive safe," he finished and ended the call, leaving Ruby alone once more.

She drew a horizontal line across the board, then, with a series of vertical lines, she split it into sections, labelling each section with a day: Thursday, Friday, Saturday, Sunday, and Monday.

She referred to the notes Larson had made and used the paperwork on Maguire's desk to fill in a few blanks. She drew crosses to mark places on the timeline. In the Thursday section, she placed a cross at around five p.m., labelling it with *AP assaults RE*. In Friday's section, she placed two crosses — one at midday, the other at two p.m. — then labelled them *RE time of death*. Lastly, in Monday's section, she marked ten a.m. and labelled the cross *MH attacks EH*.

She took a step back to study her work, and then immediately stepped forward to add some more information. She wrote the list of suspects' names beneath each day, then crossed out those who were alibied.

And then she saw it. The anomaly. It was significant enough to capture her attention. The problem was whether or not it was significant enough to call Larson or Hart.

Maybe they would see it in the morning. Maybe they'd see it before they had even realised that Ruby had gone. Perhaps Larson would notice her framed photo was gone and know that she wouldn't be coming back.

Perhaps he would smile in gratitude. However he showed it, he would be grateful. He was a kind man, and kind men tended to stand out from the crowd.

Maguire's desk was a mess, as was O'Hara's, and as much as she loathed herself for doing so, Ruby made an effort to tidy the paperwork, which appeared to have been spread out purposefully. There was no way anybody could work like that, surely.

It was when she was scooping O'Hara's paperwork together that she saw it on Campbell's desk. The notepad. No competent officer would leave that lying around. Notepads were everything. She remembered when they had been used solely to support investigations, but in more recent years, the notepad was evidence of an officer's behaviour when their professionalism was questioned.

Campbell was diligent enough to keep hers on her at all times. It must have belonged to someone else.

It took a few moments for the words on the pad to ring true. The writing was hurried and scrawled but legible.

And when the words did ring true, when she connected the dots, there was no questioning their significance.

CHAPTER FIFTY-SIX

It was only right that George do the dishes, considering the effort Ivy had put into making dinner. But still, she insisted on drying them. George had retuned the radio on the window ledge. The piano intro of *Trois Gymnopédies No. 1, Lent et douloureux,* played softly.

George laughed at the irony, and Ivy peered at him inquisitively.

"What?"

He smiled at her.

"Slow and painful," he said.

"Sorry?"

"*Lent et douloureux,*" he said. "The music. It means slow and painful."

"Unlike Ryan Eva's death," she said. "Or Higgins', come to think of it."

"I wasn't referring to them." He forced a smile.

"She's not in any pain, guv. You should be thankful for that."

"No. No, *she's* not."

He handed her the pan she had used for the mash. She took one look, then handed it back.

"Reject."

"Sorry?"

"It's dirty, guv," she said, and he saw what she meant. A slight ring of encrusted mash loitered halfway up the pan. "How do you think Byrne and Campbell are getting on, anyway?"

He took a breath and imagined the scene. After a day in the hills, Wetherford would be returning to a little room, instead of his family home. His mood would be less than optimal.

"I think it'll be an experience they won't forget."

"Or thank you for."

"Oh, if I were looking for thanks," he said, "I'd be in another line of work. I'd be a postman or something. Providing a service people appreciate. But hopefully, they learn enough that one day, when they have to knock on the door of a miserable and difficult wretch, it'll be easier."

"Easier? I'm not sure if it gets easier."

"Well, their skin will be thicker, anyway. That's the trick of it, isn't it? Not to let them affect you. To do our jobs, keep our heads down, and go through the motions until all the possibilities have been exhausted and we're left with just one."

"What about the others? Do you think they'll find Uncle Pete?"

"I doubt it. If he wanted to be found, he would have given us a means to contact him," George replied. "No. He'll show up when all this is over. That's the thing about families. It doesn't matter how bad the fallout is; you're still connected. There's always that link." He shook his head sadly. "If they think that Ryan's death is a line in the sand, then they're wrong."

He pulled the plug from the sink and, using the dishcloth, wiped the sides as the water emptied.

The sink was still half full when his phone began to vibrate in small circles on the kitchen side. Ivy handed him the tea towel to dry his hands, and then he glimpsed the caller's ID and answered, routing it to loudspeaker for Ivy's benefit.

"Campbell," he said, eyeing Ivy, and she waited with bated breath. "How was our friend Mr Wetherford?"

"No idea, guv," she said. "He's gone."

"He's what?"

"He's gone," she said. "Not here. No car. Nothing."

"Well, he could be out somewhere. Is it worth waiting?"

"That's what we thought. But Byrne had a word with the landlord, and we managed to get inside the room. All his stuff is here. The shower's wet, and the bed looks slept in."

"So, he's clean and didn't make his bed?"

"No, he's been in bed, guv. There's a half-eaten kebab on the floor as well."

"So, maybe he popped out."

"Halfway through dinner?" Campbell said. "It's all over the floor. It's like he left in a hurry. Who else knew he was here?"

"Nobody," George said. "He only told me to stop me dragging him in."

"Phone call," Ivy cut in again. "Maybe his wife called him? Maybe there's a chance they could patch things up?"

George eyed her, making the connection to her situation, but said nothing.

"We thought the same," Campbell said. "We managed to get hold of Ruby, and she got in touch with the network provider. It looks like he spoke to his wife about thirty minutes ago."

"Ruby's still in the office?"

"I suppose she's typing the statements up, guv," Ivy said. "I asked her to do it, but I didn't say she needed to work late."

"Alright," George said. "Let's not jump to conclusions here. If he's gone to see his wife, then I'm not sure us turning up on the doorstep is going to be conducive to them repairing their marriage. Let's give them the night. Try again in the morning."

"You sure, guv?" Campbell asked. "We can be there in fifteen minutes."

"I'm sure," he said, and he eyed Ivy again. "Marriages are a sacred thing. Sacred, delicate, and volatile."

"You said his things were there," Ivy said, making a point of ignoring George's hidden undertones.

"Yeah, everything," Campbell said. "Even his toothbrush."

"Go through his clothes."

"Ivy, we can't," George said. "We don't have a search warrant."

"We've got a warrant for his arrest," she countered. "That's enough, and you know it."

"What are we looking for?" Campbell asked, and they heard the sound of a long zip as she accessed a suitcase or a holdall.

"Wedding clothes," Ivy said. "He wore a grey suit to the wedding, so presumably, he had another for the rehearsal or a smart pair of trousers or something. Check his dirty clothes."

"Gross—"

"Wear gloves," George said. "You do have gloves, don't you?"

"I do," Campbell replied.

"You're looking for signs that he was in the water fighting with Ryan Eva," Ivy said. "Anything. Any kind of dirt on the knees or elbows."

The noise from the search was infuriatingly void of signs that they were onto something. They heard Byrne's voice in the background and Campbell's disappointed responses.

"Nothing," Campbell said. "There's a bag of washing here—"

"How many pairs of underpants are there?" George asked.

"What?"

"Count the underpants," George said. "If there's less than a few, then he's had his laundry done since the rehearsal."

"I did not sign up for this," Campbell said, presumably to Byrne, and then a few moments later, she came back on the line. "There're loads, guv. Nine or ten."

"And the trousers?"

"There are jeans and a pair of tan chinos, but no suit."

"He could have had it dry-cleaned," Ivy suggested.

"We're not looking for the suit," George said. "The man works outside. When I saw him, he was wearing jeans and boots. I doubt he has much call for chinos in everyday life. If those chinos are clean, then I think it's a good sign that he was not scrambling in the stream with Ryan Eva."

"We can't be sure," Ivy said.

"We can't be sure of anything," George said. "But given the lack of evidence, I suggest we let him and his wife talk. You never know; he might even be in a better mood tomorrow."

"After spending the night with his wife, you mean?" Byrne said, and George could almost hear him grimace at speaking before thinking.

"I'll ignore that," George said. "But yes. Let's leave it for now. Put things back as you found them. There's no point letting him come back to a mess. Not when he could be in a position to help us."

"Will do, guv," Campbell said.

"And one more thing," George said before the call ended. "Well done. The pair of you, I'm impressed."

"Thanks, guv," Campbell replied, and he ended the call.

"What did I tell you?" George said to Ivy as he slid his phone back onto the kitchen counter. "In the case where proving one's guilt is impossible, proving them innocent is the next best thing."

He snatched up the dishcloth once more and returned to cleaning the sink while Ivy finished drying their plates. He made a show of spraying disinfectant once he had rinsed the sink, more to let Ivy know how he liked it to be left. It was subtle, but he thought she might pick up on his standards, and there would be one less barrier to their time together.

But no sooner had he sprayed the sink than his phone began its second pirouette.

"Christ, so much for settling in and relaxing," he said. "I told you we should have sent them all home."

Ivy held the towel out for him to dry his hands again, which he did briefly before answering his phone.

"O'Hara," George said. "Burning the candle at both ends, are we?"

"Guv?" she said, her voice trembling with panic.

"What's happened?" he asked. "What's wrong?"

"It's all my fault," she said. "Something's happened. Something terrible."

CHAPTER FIFTY-SEVEN

"Well, where is he now?" George said as he and Ivy climbed into his car. The headlights cast a yellow glow over the scene depicted in Grace's painting, but the similarities were lost to his racing mind.

"He was gone, guv," O'Hara said as George edged out of his driveway, and the call transferred to his Bluetooth system. "He'd left by the time we'd got here. We think he's on his way to Nottingham, but there are so many stops—"

"Just stop," Ivy said, talking over her while George concentrated on navigating the winding lanes from Bag Enderby. "Talk us through it from the start."

"Well, we were in the incident room," O'Hara said. "A call came through on Campbell's phone, so I answered it in case it was important. Turns out it was him. Uncle Pete."

"He called in?"

"Yeah. I tried to get him to give me his last name, sarge, but he was having none of it. He just wanted to speak to the guv. I think I...I pushed him too hard." She quietened for a moment. "He hung up."

"So, how the hell did you end up in Skegness train station?" Ivy asked.

"Well, Maguire recorded the phone call on his mobile. When he played it back, we heard the tannoy thing announcing a train."

"So, you just upped and went, did you?"

"I know it was wrong," O'Hara said, "and it wasn't Maguire's fault. It was my idea, and I convinced him to come with me."

"Why didn't you call me?"

"Well...in case I was wrong. I didn't want to waste your evening."

"I bet you wouldn't have had any trouble telling me had you actually found him, though, would you?"

"I'm sorry, sarge," she said. "I just wanted to make a good impression."

"Let's not worry about any of that now," George said, hoping to avoid the team splitting in the middle of an investigation. "The question is, what do we do about it? We can't have a team go to every station from Skegness to Nottingham. He could have got off at any one of them."

"He left a bag, though," Campbell said. "We found it on a bench by the payphone."

"A bag? What kind of bag?"

"Just an old Tesco bag. From years ago, by the looks of it."

"Please tell me you didn't open a random bag you found in a train station, O'Hara," Ivy said.

The silence that followed echoed with guilt.

"We did sarge," she said.

"You bloody idiots," Ivy told her. "Do you realise what that could have been?"

"It was my idea," Maguire said, speaking up for the first time.

"I don't care whose idea it was. You should have evacuated the station and called it in. There's a procedure for this exact scenario—"

"And I take full responsibility," he said. "But the thing is, we found something inside it."

"So, I'm guessing it wasn't loaded with explosives," Ivy said.

"Never mind, never mind," George said. "We'll go over that later. What was in the bag?"

"There's a picture, guv. An old photo of Rory and Maeve Wetherford with some other chap. I'm guessing it's him, anyway. The age is right, but we don't know what this Pete fella looks like. He wasn't in any of the wedding photos."

George came to a stop at the T-junction before them. Turning right would lead them to the main road, from where they could head into Horncastle in one direction or Skegness in the other. He checked the rear view mirror for headlights. The lanes were dead.

"When did the train leave?" he asked.

"Twenty minutes ago," Campbell said. "I looked it up on the—."

"He's not on it," George said.

"But, guv, he must have—"

"He's not on it," George said. "What else was in the bag?"

"Not much. A half-eaten sandwich, the latest Kevin Banner novel, and his address book. The photo was tucked in between two pages."

"Which pages?" George asked, and O'Hara took a few moments to check.

"Guv, it doesn't matter. Nobody uses address books anymore," Ivy said. "If the photo's old, then he probably put it in there when it was taken bloody decades ago."

"The man doesn't have a mobile phone, Ivy. He's called us twice from payphones. He's a technophobe."

"Guv, I found the page," O'Hara said. "It's Rory Wetherford's. His brother's address."

The information rolled over in George's mind, reminding him of the tumbler they used to use to select lottery numbers. He filtered out the huge error the two officers had made. He shoved Ivy's situation to one side. He picked out Edwards Higgins, Mark Hale, and Adam Potter. And as much as it pained him to do so, he placed the memories of Grace safely out of the way until all that remained were the bare facts.

"He thinks Rory killed Ryan," George said, indicating left and turning out of the T-junction.

"What?" Ivy said.

"He's going there."

"We don't know that, guv," Ivy said. "And even if he is, it might not be as bad as you think."

"He was luring me away," George said, prolonging the verb in the hope that his lecture-like tone might drive the point home. "Why do you think he called from *that* payphone? Why do you think he let them hear the station announcement? Why do you think he left the bag? If those two had followed procedure and locked the station down, all of us, the entire team, would be in Skegness now, red-faced and explaining to an angry bomb disposal team why we dragged them halfway across the county for an empty plastic bag containing an old address book, a half-eaten sandwich, and a poxy mystery novel. We'd be all over the papers... again." He shook his head. "No, he thinks his brother killed Ryan Eva, and he's gone to get revenge."

"Guv, we don't know that—"

"He was crazy enough to start a fight at his niece's wedding rehearsal. Who knows what he'll bloody do now the wedding's over?" He glanced over at Ivy. "And now his nephew is dead."

CHAPTER FIFTY-EIGHT

"The lights are on," Ivy said as they drew up to the Wetherford house.

"Rory's pickup is here, too," George replied.

Ivy's door was open before the car came to a stop, and she was out of it before George had even disengaged the drive. Age dictated that he was unable to meet Ivy's speed and agility, and by the time he had reached the front door, she had already knocked twice and was peering through the letterbox. George made a beeline for the side of the house, and Ivy caught up, then ran ahead to the back garden, where light from the open back door spilt onto the patio. The scene was surreal, and the light was inviting, while the fields behind the house seemed to breed impenetrable darkness.

"Slowly," he said to Ivy as she stepped through the door, gesturing with both hands palm down.

She nodded, and carefully, they entered the house. The kitchen smelled of curry, an alien aroma in rural surroundings. A large pot was on the stove, and the contents bubbled furiously. George reached out to twist the hob off and brushed away the childish thought that he was glad not to be tasked with scrubbing the seared curry from the pot.

Ivy pointed at herself, then upwards, and then at him and down. He shook his head.

"Stay together," he whispered, then beckoned her forward into the hallway. She paused at the doorway to the living room and peered through the crack between the frame and the door. Then, with a little less trepidation, she leaned inside the room and shook her head.

George closed his eyes and listened. Outside, an owl called to its young. Inside, the wall-mounted boiler kicked in, no doubt striving to replace the heat spilling from the back door.

There was one more door from the hallway, and George placed his ear to it but heard nothing. He gripped the handle, noting the Chubb lock. He nodded to Ivy for her to be ready, then turned the handle.

A blast of cold air greeted him, along with a darkness akin to the fields beyond the rear garden. He fumbled inside for a light switch on the wall, and his hand grazed something hanging. He groped for it, felt the string, and then tugged.

A single fluorescent light dinged into life, then ticked in the silence as the tube warmed. In a few seconds, it had settled into a low buzz, casting a dim light over the garage.

"Jesus," Ivy said. "What happened here?"

Someone had pulled a stack of boxes onto the floor, spewing their contents — paperwork, photographs, and all those things deemed of value to families.

Leaving the light on, George backed out of the space and glanced up the stairs. Ivy followed his gaze and started forward, but he gripped her shoulder and shook his head.

"Me first," he whispered as he edged past her. Avoiding the centre of each step, he made his way up the stairs, eyeing a single door beneath which light poured. Again, he listened to the door but heard nothing. "Ready?" he whispered, to which Ivy nodded.

Slowly, he turned the handle and then eased the door open. Light spilt onto their feet, and inch by inch, the scene came into view. A wall of built-in wardrobes, two of which bore full-length mirrors, offered George and Ivy an early glimpse at what lay behind the door. A king-sized bed stood with its four pillows in disarray. Most of the duvet had been cast onto the floor, and only a single corner clung to the mattress as if it had fallen and was groping for purchase to pull itself up.

George felt the bedsheet with the back of his hand and glanced back at Ivy.

"Warm," he hissed, then gestured for her to check the rest of the upstairs room, which lay in darkness.

George took the scene in. He wandered around the bed, careful not to touch a thing. On the far side, beside the window, was an armchair. It was the type that one might sit on to remove or pull on socks or slippers in the evening and the morning. Perhaps even read a book beside the south-facing window.

But nobody had sat in it tonight. Tonight, it was little more than a place to discard clothes. Or, more accurately, he thought, noting a pair of women's briefs on the floor close by, a place to fling clothes as each garment was torn off in frantic lust.

Ivy re-entered the room a few moments later, startling him. She shook her head to indicate the rooms were empty. Gently, George pulled one of the curtains open and peered down into the night. The streetlights were on, revealing a handful of cars, and aside from his own, any one of them could have belonged to Peter.

"What are you thinking?" Ivy asked. "Where could he have taken them?"

"We know that he's driving," George said. "He came all the way from Skegness." He turned to her. "We just don't know what he drives. Rory Wetherford's truck is outside the house, so he would have been forced to park outside somebody else's house."

"I could run a check on the plates," Ivy said, to which George saw little other option.

"Let's go down," he said. "See if Ruby's still in the incident room, will you?"

"It's a bit late for her, guv."

"She was there a while ago, and I very much doubt she's typed up eighty-odd statements yet. I don't care how efficient she is; nobody is that quick."

He edged past her and descended the stairs, listening in case the trio had returned.

"Ruby? Is that you?" Ivy said, coming down behind him. "Don't worry about that. Listen, I need—"

She stopped and sighed, and George grinned at her rolling eyes, indicating that Ruby clearly hadn't sensed the gravity of the situation.

"Ruby, don't worry about that right now. I need you to check some number plates for me."

George stopped at the garage door and then stepped inside. The photos had been kept in manila envelopes neatly stacked in a plastic crate that was now cracked. He pulled a glove from his pocket, and instead of pulling it on, he simply used it as a barrier to avoid leaving fingerprints as he spread a few out before him.

One photo was of two children in a past summer, laughing in swimwear as somebody out of shot sprayed them with a hose. The next image was of a Christmas dinner. The family wore party hats, and the carcasses of spent crackers lay like shrapnel between the plates and dishes.

"It's okay," Ivy said. "Maguire and O'Hara have called in." She stopped again as Ruby spoke over her. "Look, how they leave their desks is not really a priority right now—"

George returned to the image of Nancy and Ryan in the summer sun. From the patio and the shed, he deduced it was the garden through which they had entered the house. The laurel hedge that ran the length of the garden had been neatly clipped, disappearing some eighty metres away into the line of trees that ran along the back gardens. Presumably, the trees were growing on the banks of a dyke dug to prevent the water-logged fields from flooding the houses.

There was so much joy on those two faces. They were at that age when sibling rivalry had yet to take hold. Best friends. Partners in play.

The horrors that came with the job were sometimes too great to bear, and he stood to disassociate himself from what had been to what might be taking place right now.

"Guv?" Ivy said as George peered around at the rest of the garage, hoping the boxes of tools and cans of paint on the shelves might numb the sharp pang of disgust that soured every breath. "Guv?"

He glanced up at Ivy, eyebrows raised in anticipation.

"Ruby thinks she's found something," Ivy said, then routed the call onto loudspeaker.

"Guv, I'm sorry," came Ruby's voice. "I know you're busy, but I think you need to know this."

Something caught George's eye — a steel cabinet mounted on the wall beside the door to the house.

"Go on," he said as he stepped over to it, noting the cabinet door was ajar.

"I found the notes that O'Hara must have made during a phone call. None of it makes any sense, so I got hold of the tech guys and had them locate the number of the last incoming call to Campbell's phone."

"Wasn't it withheld?" he said as he nudged the cabinet door open.

"They can get around that," Ruby explained. "Turns out it was a payphone in Skegness. That's all they could give me. So, I did some digging, and there's only one left."

"In the train station?" George said.

"Yeah, but that's not all. I took it upon myself to get onto East

Midlands Railways. They were really helpful. They managed to get me the footage from the cameras on the trains."

"Which trains?" Ivy asked.

"The last one in and the last one out," she replied. "Either side of the phone call."

"Hold on," George said, and he urged Ivy to see what he had found.

"A gun cabinet," she said, her eyes widening. She raised the phone and spoke to Ruby. "Hold on, Ruby."

"An empty gun cabinet," George corrected her. He swung the door wide open to reveal the two brackets designed to clamp onto a gun's stock and barrel.

"Guv?" Ruby said. "I saw him on the train. He had a plastic shopping bag, and you should have seen the look on his face when he came into the station. It was haunting."

"Whose face?" Ivy said. "Who was it?"

But before Ruby could answer, a gunshot boomed through the night and nesting birds scattered from their roosts.

"The garden," George said.

They ran to the back door, where they stopped and peered out into the night.

"Guv?" Ruby said. "Is everything okay?"

"I'll call you back, Ruby," he said. "We're going to need an ambulance and as many uniformed officers as you can find." He stepped out onto the patio, peering into the depths of the dark garden. "And we need them fast."

"Wait," Ruby said before Ivy could end the call. "There's something you need to know."

CHAPTER FIFTY-NINE

There was a spot on the grass just a few feet from the patio where, once upon a time, two children had laughed and clung to each other, writhing beneath a hosepipe's spray.

But where there was light, there was now darkness. Where the unseen heat had beaten down, a cold mist rose from the earth. And where the bare feet of those children had trodden prints into the grass, the grass now parted in two lines that ventured further than the kitchen's light reached.

"Guv?" Ivy said quietly, but he dismissed her with a shake of his head and an irritated wave of his hand. Slowly, he crouched and studied the parallel lines that every so often broke, only to resume a foot or so later. George stepped onto the grass. "Guv, we need to wait—"

"There's no time," he said as he ventured further onto the grass towards the line of trees in the distance.

"Guv?"

He turned on his heels.

"I am not letting anybody else die," he hissed, then softened. "It's unnecessary."

She glanced back at the house, torn between right and wrong, between procedure and morality. George started once more towards the trees and heard her footsteps behind him, then felt her beside him. The light from her phone cast an eerie glow over her face, and just as she was about to turn the torch app on, he stopped, placing a hand over the screen.

"No," he whispered. "Not this time."

The danger was all too real. Lighting the way would give Peter an advantage they could ill afford to lose.

The garden narrowed near the trees, or perhaps it was a trick of George's mind, as with every step, the chances of retreat grew smaller. He expected to hear voices, murmurings, or even distant shouts from somewhere way off in the fields. But all was still. Even the owl had found some other tree from which to hunt.

There was no fence to mark the edge of the property, the dyke served that purpose, and before that, the trees spindly lower limbs reached into those empty places in search of light so that he had to pull them apart as if he were opening two gates, and then step into the void.

And then there was light.

Not light from the heavens, or the kitchen, or even the moon. But light from an old lamp that had been cast onto the ground on the far side of the dyke.

Six white dots glowed. Three pairs of eyes. Two pairs were deep in the dyke, where the lamplight lit the bare white flesh of two human forms that lay sprawled in the few inches of water.

The remaining pair was at eye level with George, somewhere close to the lamp. But there was one other element from which the lamplight reflected along its length.

And it was pointed at those two sodden, sorry souls.

"That's far enough, Larson," a voice called, and George placed it immediately, having heard it once before.

"Pete," George replied. "Or should I call you Ian, Mr Eva?"

"I'll let you decide," he said.

George took a step forward, and the gun swung towards him, giving George a dim view of the double barrel.

"That's it. No closer. I've told you once."

"What are you doing, Ian?"

"I'm finishing it," he grumbled. "I'm doing what I should have done long ago."

"Murder your brother?"

"He's not my brother. Not anymore, he's not. My brother wouldn't have killed his own flesh and blood."

"Rory? Maeve? Are you hurt?"

"They're fine," Eva said, the shotgun levelling with George.

"Let them go," George told him, to which Eva laughed. "Rory, can you get up?"

"They can stay where they are," Eva spat, and he turned the gun on them. "He's about to learn a lesson. They both are."

"And what lesson is that?"

"What it's like to lose somebody they love," Eva said sadly.

"I heard a shot," George said, delaying whatever plan Eva had for as long as he could. "You've one left." He glanced down at Rory and Maeve. "There are three of us."

Ian Peter Eva stepped forward out of the shadows and into the lamplight.

"I don't intend on running," he said. "You're here to take me away."

"Well, then let's go," George said.

"Not before it's done. Not...not before I'm done."

"Two then," George said. "You need two."

"I only need one."

"Well, then I'll go," George said.

"You'll stay right there, Inspector Larson. You're here to witness this." He stared across the eight-foot dyke. "You can tell *this* to the papers."

"You don't have to do this," Rory called out, and the shotgun was positioned on him in an instant. There was no wavering despite the weight of the gun, which demonstrated competence.

"You've said enough," Eva told him. "You...you had it all and threw it all away. What about me? What about what I wanted? They're just playthings to you, aren't they?"

"Ian, don't do this," Maeve called out, her voice trembling with the cold. "He's done nothing."

"He killed my boy," Eva spat, and there it was. The truth, and it was as good as pulling the trigger. Rory Wetherford was unmoving, but even in the low light, his expression was evident. "Always knew, though, didn't you, Rory?"

"Rory, don't listen to him," Maeve said.

"You can shut it, you slag," Eva said. "You're the reason we're here. You're the reason Ryan was here. You brought him into the world when I told you to put an end to it."

"How could I?" she whined. "How could I end it? He was all I had to keep us together. Rory and me."

"He was no bigger than an apple at that stage."

"He was a life," Maeve shouted at him. "A life." She shook her head. "I could never—"

"And me? What about me? I had no one."

"What we did was a mistake," she told him. "We agreed it was a mistake. But Ryan was the only thing I had to keep my marriage together." She reached for her stomach and revealed the rope around her wrists.

Suddenly, Rory attempted to roll away, but Eva dropped down onto the dyke's bank and kicked him back. The ropes around their wrists and feet explained the parallel lines through the grass, and George could only imagine the horrors Eva had subjected them to thus far. She turned to her husband, reaching for him with bound wrists.

"Rory, I'm sorry. I'm so sorry."

"Shut it," Eva said, and he kicked her back into the water.

Then, with a hard kick to his stomach, he spoke to his half-brother. "Come on, Rory. You know what has to be done."

"Ian, stop," Maeve pleaded.

"She needs to die, Rory," Eva said. "You know what you need to do."

Rory Wetherford was silent. His worst fears had come true. The suspicions his imagination had taunted him with for all of those years had finally come to life.

"Rory, I'm sorry," Maeve pleaded.

"Do it, Rory," Eva said, and without lifting his eyes from the naked couple in the dyke, he addressed George. "Watch carefully, Inspector."

"Ian, this is ridiculous," George told him. "Put the gun down. Look, they're freezing—"

"And how did Ryan feel, eh? My boy? How did he feel?" His grimace strengthened. He reached up for the lamp and held it above the naked couple, letting the shotgun hang over his other arm. He cast the lamp down to the water's edge and re-aimed. "You can watch her die, dear brother. Or you can do it with your own bare hands." He pressed the muzzle between Maeve's breasts. "Just like you did to Ryan."

A shadow moved in the trees beyond the dyke, where Eva had been standing before he climbed down to his prey. And with the lamp now at the water's edge, Ivy moved in, slowly and cautiously, stopping at the shadow's limit, from where she could launch into action.

"Do it," Eva screamed at his brother, and he kicked him between the legs. "Do it. Show me how you did it. Show me how you killed him, Rory."

"Ian, no," Maeve said reaching out for her husband, only too aware of the shotgun's position.

But Rory said nothing. Had he been planning to defend himself, his eyes would have darted from his wife's to his brother's. But they didn't. He stared at her. Through her. And his face was a picture of misery.

Eva grinned, clearly recognising the progress he was making.

"Let's address the real cause of the issue, shall we?" he growled, and he dragged the muzzle from Maeve's chest, slowly creating a path across her stomach and coming to a stop between her legs. "Let's not beat around the bush, as it were." His amusement was evident, but nobody else laughed. "Do it, Rory. I want to see her suffer as Ryan did."

"Rory? No. No, don't do this," Maeve whined. As naked as the day he was born, Rory rolled onto his knees and then straddled his wife. "Rory, no." She shook her head wildly until Eva pressed home the weapon, and she visibly shook.

"Taking notes, I hope, Inspector Larson."

"Just put a stop to this," he replied. "It's gone far enough."

"Oh no," he said. "No, we're only just beginning."

"Tell me one thing, Maeve," Rory cracked, the first words he'd said since learning the truth.

Maeve Wetherford must have known exactly what he would ask as her face crumpled and tears ran from her eyes.

"Nancy?" Rory said, letting the threat of his bound hands finish the question.

Maeve wailed, far louder than any beast George had heard. But the cry came to a croaking halt when Rory gripped her throat. Eva was invigorated by the scene that played out before him. He moved the muzzle from Maeve to the back of Rory's head.

"Come on, Rory. You know what to do. She destroyed us all. She did this. It's her. She's done all this. Do it," he said, his excitement growing, and Rory's lithe muscles tensed in the lamplight. "Do it. I want to see the bubbles. I want to see the terror in her eyes, just like when you did it to Ryan."

"But that's where you're wrong," George called out, and

shotgun turned on him. But that was okay. Ivy crept forward from the shadow; she would be on him in a heartbeat.

"What?" Eva said. "What did you say?"

"Your brother didn't kill Ryan," George said, which came as a surprise, even to Maeve.

Rory held her tight but remained where he was, holding her face just inches from the water.

"Oh, no. You can't play games now, Inspector," Eva said.

"It's not a game," he said. "I can assure you. Am I interested in who fathered who?" he said, shaking his head. "No. It's none of my business. Am I guided by what Ryan did?" Again, he shook his head. "Ryan was a man who had paid the price for his crimes. But do I think that either of these two killed him?"

"He did it," Eva spat. "He killed him."

"He couldn't have," George said. "And I can prove it."

CHAPTER SIXTY

"Lower the gun, Ian," George said.

"Talk," Eva said.

George held his stare, very aware of the man's finger on the trigger and his state of mind.

"Your boy?" he started. "Ryan?" He shook his head. "He wasn't held under the water."

"What?" Eva's face screwed up in disbelief.

"He wasn't drowned, Ian. He was hit on the head."

"You told me he drowned. The two officers. They came to my house. They told me he drowned."

The gun visibly shook in his hands.

"He was hit on the head," George said, hoping to calm him down. "With a rock, we think. He was knocked unconscious. That's how he drowned."

"You're lying."

"You saw him, Ian. You saw his body. Do you remember his face?" George said, and Eva nodded. He turned and stared down at his brother and his sister-in-law. "Your brother didn't kill Ryan."

Ivy stepped up behind him, placing one hand on the barrel.

Eva startled at her appearance but relented when he saw there was no escape. She passed the weapon to George, who broke it, allowed the remaining cartridge to fall to the ground, and let the weighty shotgun hang from his arm.

Ivy tugged Eva's hands behind his back and slipped on the handcuffs, her face grimacing as she pressed down to ensure they were tight.

"Now we know who you are," she said. "Ian Peter Eva, I am arresting you on suspicion of false imprisonment, conspiracy to murder, and endangering a police officer's life. You do not have to say anything, but it may harm your defence if you do not mention, when questioned, something that you later rely on in court. Anything you do say may be given in evidence. Do you understand?"

"You're making a mistake, darling," he growled back at her, and she forced her knee into the back of his leg, dropping him into the water at Maeve's feet. She held him there with a boot on his chest, then nodded for George to continue.

"Let her go, Rory," George said.

He thought the father of one might follow suit, but he didn't. The look on his face suggested he had no intention of allowing his wife to leave that dyke alive.

"Do it, Rory," Eva said, thrashing beneath Ivy's boot. "*She* did this."

With one eye on Eva, George sought a beginning to the sordid tale.

"You always suspected, didn't you, Rory?" George said. "In your heart, you always knew."

"I told you before," Wetherford said. His gentle tone belied his frame and his position. "It's none of your business. Stay out of it."

"But you always suspected. Not just that Ryan wasn't yours," George said. "But about your wife and your brother."

"I told you to stay out of it—"

"You knew your brother was there. You didn't let her out of your sight, did you? You didn't trust her. Or him, for that matter. And that's why I know it wasn't you," George explained. "You see, everyone we spoke to, who was at the rehearsal, said the same thing. Nobody saw anything. Nobody disappeared for a short while. Nobody popped to the loo. At first, I thought that somebody must be lying. Somebody must have seen something. That, in turn, led me to believe that everyone was in on it. But how can that be?" George said, laughing in the hope of somehow easing the tension. "Lucas Coffey's parents loathe you all. The idea of even being related to you through marriage disgusted his mum. Would she cover for something one of your family did?" He shook his head for effect. "Would she hell."

"It changes nothing," Rory said, tightening his grip, forcing his wife's head beneath the surface. "It's over."

Maeve Wetherford thrashed in the water. Twice, she fought hard enough to surface and take a breath, but each time, he forced her back down.

Ivy looked up to George, ready to intervene, but he raised a single hand to quell her ambition.

"Your life is only just beginning," George said, and Wetherford eased off enough for Maeve to splutter and take in air. "Can't you see that? This is your time now. Ryan's gone. It's over."

"To hell with Ryan. He was a monster, and he deserved what he got. But Nancy? Nancy was *mine*. She was always mine." He stared down at his wife. "You've taken twenty years of my life, Maeve. You robbed me of my life, my daughter..." His thumbs caressed her throat, a sign he was capturing one last memory. "My future."

He leaned forward, and the muscles in his back tensed as he prepared to finish her.

"Wait," George said as Maeve closed her eyes, taking long, deep breaths while she could. "You still have her. You still have those memories you made."

"Memories," Wetherford scoffed. "They're all fake. Lies, the lot of them."

"They're memories," George told him. "And you should keep them. You should cling to them, Rory. The only thing that matters is who raised her. Who Nancy calls her father. Who she loves."

"Does she, though?" he snapped, then stared down at his wife. "Does she? Does she know the truth?"

Maeve shook her head, wide-eyed.

"No," she whimpered, breathless. "No, she doesn't know."

"So, make more memories, Rory," George said. "You still have her, and while you have her, embrace it. Embrace her. *You're* her father. You. You deserve those memories."

He blinked away the tears that were pooling in his eyes.

"If you do this, that's it. You've lost her forever."

"And her?" Wetherford said, nodding at his wife. "What about her?"

"Whether or not you choose to tell your daughter the truth, Rory, is entirely down to you. That's none of my business," he said. "But don't you think it's for Nancy to decide how you all move forward? All that matters is that the one person who has stayed by her side for all of these years remains there. Just think about that."

Rory's grip relaxed, but he held his hands still as if contemplating his next move.

"And him?" he said. "What happens to him?"

George gestured for Ivy to get Eva out of there. He reached out a hand as she dragged Eva to his feet, and together, they hauled him up the bank.

"That's for the courts to decide," George said, speaking to Rory but staring Eva in the eye. "Threatening a police officer with a shotgun carries a lengthy sentence, but perverting the course of a murder investigation, that's another story."

"Move," Ivy said and nudged him forward into the garden. Then she called out to the support that had arrived. "Over here."

George stepped down into the dyke and into the water. He slipped from his coat and held it up for Wetherford to cover himself, then extended a hand to show he meant no harm. "There is one thing I'd like to know."

Unabashed at his nudity, Wetherford stood over his wife, who rolled onto her side and curled into a ball.

"Go on," he said as George helped the freezing man into his coat.

"Uncle Pete?" George said. "Why did you call him Uncle Pete?"

Wetherford watched as Ivy led Eva out of the trees and into the garden, beyond which a melee of flashing blue lights was illuminating the distant street.

"You were right," Wetherford replied, and he peered at George as if they had somehow bonded over the tragedies. "I always knew." He thumped his chest and tightened his lips. "Deep down, I always knew the truth would come out one day. I suppose calling him Uncle Pete was my way of making it easier. He wasn't my brother if that makes sense. He wasn't Ian. And if he wasn't my brother, then it might be easier to walk away when that day came."

"You'd walk away from it all, would you?"

"If I had to," he replied.

"And now? Now you know the truth? Now you can put all this behind you?"

Wetherford pondered the question, glaring at his wife.

"Now I can live my life," he said.

Psychiatry was far from George's expertise, but there was a logic in there somewhere, made clear only with a healthy amount of empathy. And George had oodles of that.

"What'll happen now?" Wetherford said. "To me, I mean? Am I..."

"Under arrest?" George said, and he gestured at the two uniformed officers that Ivy had returned with after depositing Eva. "We'll need you to come to the station to give a statement," he said, meeting the man eye to eye. "But like..." He hesitated to say the name. "Like Uncle Pete said, I was there merely to witness what happened. And my statement will reflect that."

Wetherford's smile was fleeting and rare.

"Thank you," he said, then reached up for two uniformed officers to pull him up. Two female officers took their places, one of whom was holding a blanket to cover Maeve Wetherford's modesty. "And her? What'll happen to her?"

George looked down at Wetherford's wife, who, with the arrival of half the station's officers, now covered herself as best she could with bound wrists, quite unable to move.

"Let's let Nancy decide her fate, shall we?" George said, and he beckoned the two female officers down to help her.

It was only when the dyke was void of life and all threats of violence had ceased that Ivy reached down to help George out.

"How long did you know?" she asked. "That it wasn't Rory who killed Ryan, I mean."

"Oh, I didn't. Not for sure, anyway. But it always niggled me that nobody disappeared or went missing."

"So, he *could* have done it. That's not proof, is it? That's your interpretation of events."

"Yes and no," he said. "Ian Eva wanted to see Rory do exactly what he thought he'd done to Ryan."

"He was going to drown her," she said, to which George nodded.

"Whoever killed Ryan Eva hit him with a rock. They didn't hold his head under the water. They didn't grab onto his throat."

"That doesn't prove that Rory Wetherford didn't do it."

"Doesn't it?" George said innocently.

"I don't get it," Ivy said. "We're no closer to getting a conviction for Ryan Eva's murder."

"And do you know why they didn't hold his head under the water?" he said.

"Go on," she urged.

"Did you see how much strength it took for Rory to do that to his wife?" he said, and he turned to face the house. "We've always been close, Ivy. We just haven't known it until now."

CHAPTER SIXTY-ONE

The flashing blues washed over the old house and lit the surrounding hills and fields for what looked like miles.

George knocked twice, then stood back. Beside him, Ivy stood with her head cocked, intrigued as to the outcome. Behind them, six uniformed officers, including Maguire and O'Hara, waited patiently for an instruction.

"Stay here," George called out to them, seeing no need for stealth when the entire area was bathed in blue.

He waved for Ivy to follow him around to the back door, where he stopped and tried the handle. To his surprise, the door opened. The kitchen was cool, and a few LEDs blinked in the darkness, identifying the various appliances George had seen during his last visit. He groped for the light switch and then stepped inside. There was an empty feeling to the place–a sorrow.

Or maybe it was guilt.

"Should I...?" Ivy said, and she started towards the great hallway until George held his hand up to stop her.

"All in good time," he told her. He strode over to the kitchen worktop, felt the weight of the kettle to ensure it had been filled, and then ignited the hob. "Guv?" Ivy said, a bemused expression forming on her face.

He moved across to the breakfast table, dragged a chair out, and took a seat. Slowly and slightly unsure of herself, Ivy walked over to him and did the same.

To her credit, she said nothing, trusting his judgement, which was a relief. The pieces of the investigation were in a state of flux in his mind. The last thing he needed was questions to blur his reorganising of the facts.

It took a minute or two for the water to begin raging. The kettle shook violently on the hob and tiny droplets of hot water escaped from the spout.

But then it happened-low at first, like the hum of a distant insect. As the pressure grew greater, a thin plume of steam rose into the air, and that low hum intensified into a shrill whistle.

Ivy rose from her chair and started towards it.

"No," George said, and again, she peered at him like he had lost his mind.

It was one of those sounds that, by the very nature of its source, one rarely gets to hear in full. From the low hum, it had worked its way through the octaves to something akin to a soprano. George expected it to rise and rise, plumbing new depths of sound, but still, there it hung, swelling and warbling with unimaginable fury.

Ivy screwed her face up with the discomfort.

"Guv?" she said, and again, he held up his hand, asking her to be patient.

And his patience proved itself with the next thirty seconds when Melissa Hale stood in the kitchen doorway wearing a heavy, flannel dressing gown.

"What on earth?" she said, storming over to the hob. She lifted the kettle to a different hob, turned out the flame, and then glared at them both. "What the hell are you doing in my house? How did you get in?"

"Your dad told you to lock the doors," George said calmly. "Why don't you take a seat?"

"You didn't answer my question."

"But you'll answer mine," he replied as she peered through the window at the circus on the driveway.

"What is this?"

"I'll be honest with you, Melissa. It's been a long day, a long night, and my feet are wet," he told her. "The sooner we get this over with, the better."

"Get what over with?"

"There are six uniformed officers on your driveway, all of whom would be more than willing to drag you out of this house in handcuffs and throw you in a cell until the morning," he said, then lowered his voice. "Sit with us, talk for a while, afford us some honesty, and we'll see about letting you get dressed first."

She tugged her dressing gown around her as tight as it would go.

"Now sit," George told her, leaving no room for argument.

With her head held high and exercising her right to grievance, she pulled one of the chairs from beneath the table, dropped into it, and folded her arms. "The kettle was for coffee if you wanted some."

"It's too late for coffee."

"Hot chocolate, then."

"Hot chocolate is for bedtime," she said. "Am I going to bed anytime soon?"

George rocked his head from side to side by way of letting her down gently.

"Why don't we start from the beginning, eh?" he said.

"What beginning? If this is about my dad, then we should probably start with when Ryan Eva attacked me—"

"How about last Thursday?" George cut in before her tongue ran away with her. "When Ryan Eva attacked you."

"What? He never. I told you—"

"I know what you told me, Melissa. And very convincing you were, too."

"Are you calling me a liar?"

"Not if you can prove I'm wrong," he said, and the rally came to an end. The look on her face said all he needed to know. Sadly, he would need to hear the words spill from her lips for it to mean anything. "He got to you again, didn't he? He attacked you."

"Don't..." she started, and he reached out a hand. She stared at it but hugged herself, and that was understandable.

"Do you want to know what I think happened?" George said, and Ivy listened as hard as Melissa Hale was listening. "I think you knew all along that Adam Potter and your father were keeping tabs on Ryan, didn't you?" She stared at him; her expression as cold as ice. "And I think that when Ryan came here last Thursday, apologising was the last thing on his mind. Nine years is a long time to replay events over and over. To grow bitter. To imagine what he would do when he saw you next." George spoke softly; there was little need to demonstrate power or put her on the back foot. The conversation would be her making. Whatever happened afterwards, the conversation would let fly the lies. "It's not for me to go into details about it, Melissa, and I wouldn't ask you to go through all of that. Not here, not now. But I'm right, aren't I?"

"Even if he did, I don't see what difference it makes. He died."

"No thanks to you," George said, and she glared at him briefly, then let it slide. "And he didn't die. He was killed. Murdered, Melissa."

"Well, then he deserved it," she spat, stifling the emotions that were in the trenches of her eyes, like soldiers waiting for the whistle.

"I think you messaged Adam, Melissa."

"I haven't spoken to him——"

"I think you messaged him. A text message."

"Well, get my phone."

"Oh, we will," George told her. "All in good time." He smiled sadly at her waste of a life. "Your father's too."

"Sorry?"

"Your father's phone," George said. "You're not daft, Melissa, are you? You'd read the messages on your dad's phone. You knew what they were doing." He shrugged carefree. "All it took was one message to suggest that Ryan needed checking. You knew that Adam would go round there."

"But Adam didn't kill him. You said he didn't kill him."

"No, but you let him believe he did, didn't you?" George said. "In fact, I'm beginning to question every single thing we've learned during this investigation." He leaned forward and lowered his voice. "And every arrest we've made, Melissa."

CHAPTER SIXTY-TWO

"Adam's a good man," Melissa said, almost pleading with them.

"Too good for you," Ivy said, catching up with George's theory.

"The thing is, you weren't invited to the wedding, were you?" George said. "Why would you be? You don't know Lucas or Nancy. But you know Adam." He laid his hands flat on the table. "I can only imagine that Adam messaged your dad some time to tell him that he wouldn't be available to check up on Ryan. Am I right, Melissa? Is that how it happened? Is that how you knew about the wedding?"

She shook her head gently.

"The hotel did the catering," she said, her voice monotone. "A few of the girls were talking about it." She inhaled long and hard, then let it out slowly. "I knew that Ryan was a good friend of Adam's. I'd seen him online. I knew Adam would be there, so I put my name down to work."

"You were at the wedding?"

"No. Not in the end, no. I went there to have a look the day before the wedding. My manager needed a few boxes dropping off, so I volunteered. It's not far from the house."

"So, you dropped the boxes off—"

"A man arrived and parked by the mill pond while I was carrying the boxes inside. He was one of the bride's uncles, I think. He went up to the ceremony field, and I fetched another box. It's weird. I was hoping Ryan would be there. People don't see you, you know? When you're just delivering stuff or serving stuff. You're invisible. And then, I suppose, he grew impatient. I came out of the building to get the last of the boxes, and he was just standing there on the little bridge near the water wheel." She stared down at her hands and bit down on her lip. "Even after all those years, he was still the same. The way he walked. The way he crept, spying on the rehearsal, checking to make sure nobody was watching. He was a monster."

"Did anybody see you, Melissa?" George asked, and she shook her head. "Not even him. He was halfway up the footpath by the time I caught up with him." She gazed up at the wall behind George as if meeting him eye-to-eye was too painful. "I picked up the first thing I could find, and I just..." Her voice trailed off. "I just hit him. He must have heard me because he turned around as I got close. I remember his eyes. They were as wide as dinner plates. But I had to go through with it. I couldn't stop. I...I just hit him."

"You didn't struggle?" George asked.

"Not really, no. I had to roll him into the stream."

"Why?"

"Why?" she said, with a laugh that faded as fast as it had arrived. "I couldn't do it. I tried, and I tried, but I couldn't do it."

"Do what, Melissa?" George asked, and she stared straight at him with a sigh.

"I couldn't strangle him. He was unconscious, but I just couldn't get a grip. I thought I'd be able to. I dreamed about how it would feel. You know? Thursday night. After he'd..." Her face twisted in repulsion, and she shook her head. "In the end, I had to hold his head under the water. It took ages. I could hear them all laughing in the field. I felt sure one of them would find me."

"How long?"

"I don't know," she said. "A minute. Something like that. Longer than it looks on the TV. He kept kicking and twitching."

"And when you were done?" George asked.

"After that, I dragged him into the tall grass so nobody would find him for a few days."

"When we'd then suspect Adam of murdering him?" George said. "He told us he called your father and told him everything. He told him how he'd hit Ryan and how he'd fallen. He told him that he thought he'd killed Ryan, and he told him about Edward Higgins asking him who he was." George caught her eye, and she turned away, unable to look him in the eye. "I asked Adam what your father said. If he'd offered any advice." Melissa closed her eyes and swallowed hard. "That was you on the phone, wasn't it? You answered the call. You knew Adam would go there because you sent him. So, you made sure you were never far away from your father's phone."

"I didn't mean for anybody to get in any trouble. I just wanted..." she started, then altered what she was going to say. "Do you know what it's like? Have you any idea of what it's like to...be overpowered? To feel powerless?"

"To feel powerless, yes," he said. "But no. You're right; I have no idea what you've been through. And I'm in no position to judge."

"What does that mean?"

"It means that I will leave the judging to a jury," he told her, and then he nodded for Ivy to finish it.

"Melissa Hale," she started. "I am arresting you on suspicion of murder. You do not have to say anything, but it may harm your defence if you do not mention, when questioned, something that you later rely on in court. Anything you do say may be given in evidence."

"Do you understand?" George asked, as for the second time that evening, Ivy used her handcuffs.

"What'll happen to me?" Melissa asked softly.

"That depends on your cooperation," George told her.

"I'm cooperating, aren't I?" she said. "I've told you everything."

"Nearly," he said.

"What do you mean nearly?"

"I read the evidence against Ryan Eva from the first time he attacked you," he replied, keeping his voice calm and controlled despite the bile rising in his throat from just being in the same room as her. "There were statements and witnesses. There was DNA evidence, which was enough to put him away on its own."

"So?"

"And then there was a piece of evidence that I very nearly overlooked," George said quietly. "The senior officer had worked with the mobile phone provider to place Ryan at the scene at the time of the attack."

"Right?" she said, stretching the word out tentatively.

"If I were to call some of our colleagues in here," George said, "and if I were to ask them to search the house, shall I tell you what I would find? Or at least, what I think I would find?"

Melissa glanced at Ivy, who seemed to be the only one not quite following.

"There were two victims, Melissa. Two. One drowned, the other suffocated. He had a plastic bag pulled over his head. The difference meant that, for most of this investigation, we've been looking at two separate crimes. Two killers, Melissa. But you couldn't strangle Ryan, could you? You didn't have the strength. So, when it came to murdering Edward Higgins—"

"No—"

"When it came to murdering Edward Higgins," George said again, silencing her futile argument, "you used the bag. You knelt on his arms, and you pulled the bag over his head, and you held it there until he stopped writhing beneath you." George rose from his chair and made a show of tucking it beneath the table. Despite the mood, there was rarely a cause for poor manners. "I think my officers will find three mobile phones," he continued. "The first belongs to Ryan. But of course, it'll be useless. You'd have wiped the messages and the calls."

"What messages?"

"The message you sent to him inviting him here on Thursday," George replied, to which Melissa offered no argument. "The second will be Edward Higgins'."

"What—"

"Which you took to make sure he hadn't told anybody about what he'd seen the previous Thursday. You turned them both off, of course, so they couldn't be traced back to here."

"And the third?" she said.

"The third?" he replied with a laugh. "Well, that's yours, of course. We'll find no messages to Ryan Eva or Adam Potter. And if we retraced your whereabouts through GPS, we'd find it was here while you were at the wedding rehearsal."

Melissa offered no argument, which in itself was as good as a confession.

"The sad part is that when we arrested your father, Melissa, you had every chance to own up right then. But you didn't. You don't deserve him."

"My dad is my everything," she said.

"So, when he realised what you'd done when we were out on your driveway accusing him of your crimes, Melissa, why didn't you say anything? He's your father. He'd die for you. Going to prison isn't even testing the limits of what he'd do. You're a coward. You've tried to pin the blame on everyone else, Melissa."

"He's my dad," she said. "He loves me."

"You know, some people don't even have a dad," George said. "Some people who deserve one, and who need one, have to go without. And here's you abusing the privilege." George nodded to Ivy. "Get her out of my sight."

Ivy nudged her forward towards the front door. "Oh, and Ivy," George called out, waiting for his sergeant to stop.

"Guv?" she said.

"Call the custody sergeant, will you? Release Mark Hale," George said. "Tell him I will not be pressing charges, but if he tries to pervert the course of justice once more, I'll see to it he spends the next five years inside." Finally, Melissa met George eye to eye, a look of sheer hatred in her eyes. "Then he won't even be there to watch you being sent down, Melissa. You wouldn't deny a loving father that memory, would you?"

CHAPTER SIXTY-THREE

"Well, that's it," Ivy said as she re-entered the kitchen. The flashing blues had long ceased to disturb the night, and George had allowed himself a few moments to reflect on the future. Not Melissa Hale's or Rory Wetherford's, but his own. It felt indulgent to do so, but he deserved it, he thought. She placed three clear plastic bags onto the kitchen table, each containing a variety of mobile phones. Two of them were switched off. The other showed a wallpaper image of Melissa Hale and her father, cheek to cheek. She took the seat opposite him, where Melissa had been sitting. "I've called a team in to have this place closed up."

"Good," he said quietly, savouring the image of Grace before the investigation shoved her to one side again.

"What are you thinking?"

"Me?" he said, and he laughed to himself. "None of us are infallible, are we?"

"Guv?"

He took a moment to straighten his words into some semblance of order.

"We couldn't prove anyone guilty. Not with the information we had. So, we proved people innocent."

"It was the right thing to do, guv," she said. "I'll admit it. I didn't really believe in it at first, but I see it now."

"That's just it," he said. "You believe in me. Like I believed Melissa Hale. I should have questioned everything."

"We did look into her, guv."

"Yeah, we looked into her. But we didn't look too hard, did we? We were too busy with Wetherford and Potter. We let our judgment guide us. Our bias."

"I thought you said using your gut was a good thing."

"Not that kind of judgment," he said. "Unconscious judgment."

"Unconscious bias, you mean?"

"Whatever," he said. "She told us that Ryan had been here, and all he did was apologise. Did any of us stop to question it?"

Ivy shrugged guiltily.

"Why not?" he said. "Because she's the victim of a crime?"

"And because we learned that Potter had been the one to break in."

"Right, but did either of us question who sent him there?" George said. "Did any of us question her father's guilt? Of course, we didn't. There were no alternatives. The only alternative was that somebody had got to his phone, and heaven forbid that we point the finger at a sweet young girl who's been through more in her short life than anybody should ever have to go through."

"So, there is some pity in there somewhere, guv?"

"Pity?" he said. "Pity? I feel for her and what she's been through, but do I pity her? No, I do not. She relinquished any pity she might have deserved when she lured Ryan Eva here."

"See. That's the bit I don't understand, guv. It's not making sense. Why would she lure him here?"

"Why? Because of what he did." He jabbed a finger at the three phones. "Mark my words, when the tech team have finished with that, we'll see a deadly trail of manipulation and cowardice.

She lured him here to do what she set out to do. If things had gone to plan, Nancy Wetherford and Lucas Coffey would have had a day to remember. For the right reasons, I might add. But when things go wrong, that's when it spirals. When she couldn't overpower Ryan Eva, she offered herself on a plate. There was only one way this was ever going to end, and the poor victim would use everyone who loved her as pawns in her terrible, terrible plan."

"So, she sends Adam Potter to see him."

"Right. She sends him there, and he tells her what he's done. As far as she was concerned, he was done with. So, when he turned up at the wedding rehearsal, what could she do but finish it herself?"

"Guv, I think that's a bit strong. The girl must have been distraught."

"Distraught my backside," George said. "She lured him to his death, remember? You've got to stop empathising with her. You'll fall into the trap every single time. Yes, she was assaulted, and yes, it must have been beyond awful. But bad enough to kill two men and condemn two more to a lifetime in prison?"

"I suppose not," Ivy said. "Do you think she'll play ball? Or do you think she'll amend her statement once she's in the interview room?"

"Well, that's when we'll see her true character," he replied. "She can send her father to prison for a crime he didn't commit, or she can hold her hands up and cling to the one man she cares about the most."

"And the Higgins thing?" Ivy said. "How did you know it was her?"

"The phones," he said. "It's been on my mind since the very beginning. Two crimes. Two killers. Both of them tried to cover their tracks by taking the victim's phones?" He shook his head. "No chance. I hadn't made the connection until we were sitting here. And then it all made sense." He pointed to the front of the house. "It wasn't until she came out that Mark Hale actually submitted to us. And even then, he didn't exactly confess. He just took the attention away from her. At no point did he say what he'd done and why."

"Because he didn't exactly know?"

"Precisely," he said. "If we were to interview him and ask him exactly how he'd killed Edward Higgins, we'd get a rudimentary explanation with little to no detail."

"But what about the DNA?" She said. "There were drops of his saliva on the bag."

"Ah," he replied. "Were there?"

"Well, yeah. That's what the team said."

"They said tiny droplets," he told her. "Just enough to take a sample. Just enough to get a partial match."

"Partial match?"

He grinned at her. "We'll need to have Katy Southwell run the test again now that we have Melissa Hale's DNA. My guess is that hers will be a closer match to the sample found on the bag than her father's."

"And if it isn't?"

"It will be," he said.

"But there's a chance it'll be Mark Hale's," she said. "Guv, the CCTV showed a man breaking in, not a girl in her twenties."

"No, the CCTV showed an individual wearing a hood, and as Byrne has quite rightly suggested, the individual in question cannot be identified. Put a big coat on Melissa Hale and pull the hood up. Does she look like a girl?"

"Guv, it's a leap."

"And then there's the bus," George said. "The bus that blocked the view of Ryan leaving his house. Who's to say that another bus wasn't blocking the view of Melissa arriving? Who's to say she didn't ride that bus."

"They don't have cameras on those older models," Ivy said. "Ruby checked."

"So, can we rule Melissa out?"

"I suppose not," she said.

"Remember, it's not always a case of finding positive evidence, but sometimes a lack of evidence and circumstance can be just as powerful."

They each pondered the night's events in their own way. But it took just a few moments of silence for Grace to re-enter his mind.

"I was thinking," Ivy said. "You said you wanted the house to yourself this weekend."

"I'm sorry, Ivy, I—"

"No, it's fine," she said. "I'll make myself scarce."

"Will you go home?" George asked. "I'm sure Jamie will be pleased to see you. Not to mention the kids."

"Actually, I thought I'd look for a place of my own," she replied. "Only somewhere small."

"Ivy—"

"He doesn't want me back, guv. And I shan't beg." She nodded as if convincing herself of the statement. "It's time I grew up and faced up to it. I can't live with you forever."

"Well, you're always welcome—"

"And I appreciate it," she told him. "But I don't want to outstay my welcome. I'm not sure if I could handle being thrown out by the only two men I…" She hesitated. "Twice in one year," she said. "I'd rather keep as much dignity intact as I can."

There was a knock at the front door, and it swung open to reveal Maguire and O'Hara.

"Guv?" Maguire called.

"Through here."

They entered the kitchen with more than a little trepidation, and George's unrelenting stare ensured it remained that way for as long as possible.

"We've come to keep an eye on the place until Mark Hale gets back," Maguire said. "He's being released now."

"In which case, we'll get out of your hair," George said, rising from the chair and encouraging Ivy to follow suit.

"Guv?" O'Hara said as he reached the hallway door. He knew one of them would have to say something, and he was glad it was her.

He turned, raised his eyebrows in anticipation, and waited.

"We're sorry," she said.

"Oh?"

"We shouldn't have gone to Skegness without your say-so."

"Mmmhmm," George agreed.

"And we should have followed procedure," Maguire added.

"Ah," George said, and he nodded at them both gratefully before turning towards the front door.

"Does that mean we're off?" Maguire called out. "Don't we get a reprimand or something? Or are we to go back to what we were doing?" The fresh air hit George like it was the first breaths he'd ever taken, and they were glorious.

"Guv?" Maguire called as they strode across the empty driveway towards his car. "Guv, do we report to you tomorrow, or what?"

It was only when Ivy and George were safely in his car and the doors were closed that she spoke.

"What are you going to do, guv? It warrants a warning, you know?"

George sighed.

"If I followed up on every officer who ever broke the rules in pursuit of the truth, Ivy," he said, as he started his car, "I'd have to add hypocrite to my growing list of flaws and foibles. And quite frankly," he said, winking at her, "I'm saving the last spot on that list for something else."

"Oh yeah?" she said with a laugh. "And what's that then?"

"Lonely," he replied without hesitation.

"You're not lonely, are you? You've got me."

"No, no, I'm not," he muttered. "But perhaps I should be." He looked across at her, forcing a smile. "Then I can be a lonely, cantankerous, contrary, miserable old man."

"And that's better than a cantankerous, contrary, miserable old hypocrite, is it?"

"Oh, by far," he said. "Nobody likes a hypocrite."

CHAPTER SIXTY-FOUR

The sea air was as rich as any George had savoured, and the change of scenery was as good as a rest. And rest was becoming a commodity within his team.

He reached up and rang the doorbell, then took a step back, feeling a pang of guilt stir in his stomach like thick, hot and sticky treacle.

In the three days since they had brought the investigation to a close, the energy he had enjoyed only a week before had nosedived. Even Maguire's witty rhetoric had dulled. Although George was slowly warming to him.

Three days of writing reports, collating more than ninety statements, and conducting interviews had resulted in a file three inches thick, ready to present to the CPS. The evidence against Melissa Hale mostly included forensic evidence that, as he had intended, proved the innocence of those other individuals with the means, motive, and opportunity. But including the two-hour interview during which she had not only confessed to both murders but had admitted to luring Ryan Eva to her home with the intention of murdering him, admitted to framing Adam Potter, and perverting the course of justice by allowing her father to take the rap for Edward Higgins, her fate had been well and truly sealed.

That's how it was sometimes, he thought. If she had only managed to overpower Ryan Eva on that fateful Thursday, then she could be looking at a single life sentence. People might have even empathised. They might have pitied her. She could have been out in ten to twelve years. Instead, the universe had a different idea, and if he was a betting man, he would confidently wager that she served a minimum of thirty years.

He'd heard a man in a hotel bar once tell him that it was his thirtieth wedding anniversary.

"Congratulations," George had said, raising his glass.

"Congratulations? I'd get less time for murder," the man had grumbled.

He'd downed his drink and returned to staring into the mirror behind the bar, leaving George to ponder the sentiment.

The door on which he had knocked was suddenly yanked open, and Jamie Hart peered down at him, recognising him in a heartbeat.

"Hello, Jamie."

"Now then," he replied and leaned on the doorframe, folding his arms as he waited for George to explain the reason for his visit.

"I thought it was time I came to see you," George started.

"So, I see," came the reply.

"It's about Ivy. Look, I battled with whether or not I should come—"

"And you lost, did you?"

George lost his flow but regained some of his momentum.

"I don't like to interfere—"

"But you're going to?"

"No," George said. "No, actually, I'm not."

The statement caught Jamie's attention, and he straightened, tucking his hands into his pockets.

"Alright then."

"I thought I'd tell you about myself," George said, to which Jamie laughed out loud. "I've been married for longer than you've been alive, Jamie."

"Well, aren't you the lucky one?"

"And I haven't had a conversation with her for the last eight of those years."

"So, you never separated?"

"We never had an argument," George said.

"So, you just live side by side, do you? One of those couples who exist together but never cross paths?"

"No," George said. "No, but if I'm honest, the point I'd like to get across to you is this. If I could talk to her. To Grace. My wife. There are so many things I'd like to say. I'd tell her how infuriating it is when she leaves her shoes by the back door for me to trip over them." Jamie's brow furrowed. "I'd tell her that rising at seven o'clock in the morning is not an early start. She's missed half the day. I'd tell her that, yes, it does grate on me when she makes us late because she isn't prepared."

"What on earth are you going on about—"

"And I'd tell her that she makes the best damn shepherd's pie I've ever tasted. I'd tell her that I love the way she makes the bed. I love the way she folds herself into an armchair and cradles her hot chocolate in both hands."

"George, I'm not sure if I'm the right person—"

"But I can't," George said. "I can't. Because she doesn't know who I am. For the past five years, she thinks I'm...I don't know... some bloke who comes to visit his wife but spends more time with her. She talks about me *to* me as if I'm somebody else."

"I'm sorry to hear that, George," Jamie said. "I truly am, but—"

"So, when I see Ivy so upset, and I'm sorry, but when I hear one side of the conversations you two have, it kills me." George looked up at the man on his doorstep and heard the kids playing somewhere deeper in the house. "I love your wife, Jamie. Like the daughter I never had. I love her dearly. And, well, like any good father does, I try to steer her."

"Ivy isn't exactly manoeuvrable," Jamie said, and just for a second, they agreed on something, although the sensation George felt was akin to betrayal.

"We could never have kids," George said. "I don't know if it was me or Grace, but what does it matter who? We had to accept it." Jamie listened intently, reasonably, and with far more calm than Ivy gave him credit for. "I just don't want to see her lose everything," George said. "If it's something she's done, and you can't seem to find the words, then maybe I can help."

"Sorry?" Jamie said, genuinely confused.

"Like I said, I don't want to interfere, and if there were no children, then maybe I wouldn't. But she needs a chance, Jamie. I know deep down that she can make things right." George took a breath. He'd said far more than he had intended and had strayed way beyond the boundary he had set himself. "For what it's worth, if you hit me, I'd understand."

"Yeah, right," Jamie said. "Hit a copper? Not a smart move."

"I deserve it, though," George replied, and he took a step back towards his car. "Look, I'm sorry. I shouldn't have come. I just want to see her have a chance at saving what she's got. You never know what tomorrow holds, Jamie."

"You're right there," Jamie said, and he lingered on the doorstep as George nodded a farewell and climbed into his car. He pulled the door closed and hit the ignition button, then sat back, closing his eyes with the madness of it all.

"What the hell were you thinking, George?" he whispered to himself.

A tap on the window roused him from his self-loathing, and he opened his eyes to find Jamie staring down at him. He lowered the window, fully expecting to be on the receiving end of Jamie's wrath.

"I hope you find some happiness, George," Jamie said.

"Sorry?"

"I do," he said. "It took some doing for someone to come and..."

"Interfere?" George said.

"Well, you said it," Jamie replied. "I hope that someday your wife remembers. Even if it's fleeting, I hope you're there to experience it. To experience her, just one more time." George studied the man's eyes. "My nan had it," he said. "Dementia, right?"

"Right," George said. "It's awful."

"It's the worst," Jamie added. "And for what it's worth, I admire you. I admire anyone who can do what you do despite your own challenges."

George smiled weakly. "I'm off to see her now," he said, and he stared through the windscreen at the sand that the wind had strewn across the road. "I'm taking her home for the first time in...in I don't know how long. I'm hoping it'll jog some kind of memory. The doctor said it could help, but..."

"You're wrong, George," Jamie said softly. "I'm sorry, but you've got it all wrong."

"Am I? You don't think it'll help?" George asked. "To be honest, I'll try anything right now—"

"About Ivy," Jamie said, cutting him off, and he licked his lips, steeling himself. "It's her that walked out."

"Sorry? But she said that—"

"*She* walked out on *us*, George," he said. "We'd have her back in a heartbeat if she'd only change her mind."

CHAPTER SIXTY-FIVE

He had lived the moment a hundred times or more in his head. And each of those times had produced a different result to the time before. Yet, not one of the scenarios his imagination had conjured bore any resemblance to what had played out before him, as George turned into the little lane that led to the old church on the left and the house beside it.

There seemed to be very little in Grace's expression that demonstrated recognition of any kind. She seemed charmed, of course. But then, Bag Enderby had that effect on everyone who visited the tiny cluster of houses.

He slowed as he passed the church, and as she smiled up at it, he reminded himself that, aside from a few outings to the beach and half a dozen hospital appointments, this was the first time she had been out of the home in God knows how long.

"Here we are," he said as he pulled into the little driveway. "Now, you stay there, and I'll get everything ready, alright?"

"Oh, what a wonderful garden," Grace replied, her voice not dissimilar to that of a schoolgirl.

Recognition had been the primary objective, but in the

absence of that, appreciation was a close second. At least he had achieved something.

It took George longer than he had anticipated to drag the wheelchair from the boot and unfold it. But he got there in the end, and when he eventually opened the passenger door, she was still gazing up at the old house. At first, he wondered if he had made a mistake in bringing her to her old home, but then he saw it. Only a hint of recognition was evident in her glazed eyes.

"Shall we?" he said, holding a hand out to assist her. It was with purpose that he left her there for a few moments longer while he fetched her overnight bag from the rear seat. Time for those seeds of memory to sprout.

And it was those seeds he was hoping to nurture over the course of her stay so that by the time he took her back to the home, they might have taken root.

"Lunch is ready and waiting," he told her as he wheeled her towards the front door. He unlocked the door and shoved it open; then, after a bit of jiggery-pokery, he managed the wheelchair up the step and across the threshold. "I thought we'd have some soup."

"Oh, did you make it yourself?" she asked. "You are good. My husband couldn't boil an egg."

That hurt. But he breathed through the blow and cleared his throat.

"I must admit, I had some help."

He closed the front door and removed his jacket, then wheeled her to the armchair he had positioned beside the fire. Not for the warmth, specifically, as it was too early in the year to light it. But it was the best view of the church, aside from her old bedroom, and it was far too early to be carrying her up the stairs. She knew the drill better than he. He helped her stand, then she shuffled her feet into position, and he lowered her into the armchair.

"Now then, how about a nice cup of tea before we eat?"

"Ooh, that sounds lovely."

It was all part of the plan, and he'd laid out what he needed on a tray before he'd left — the teapot with a fresh bag of loose tea, the little sieve she used to use, and, of course, the tiny milk jug. He'd even found one of her favourite teacups in the Mablethorpe house.

While the kettle boiled, he smelled the soup Ivy had made for him, then lit the burner to warm it through.

He chanced a glance through the kitchen door into the living room, and just as the view of the church seemed to entrance her, he found himself captivated by what he saw. Ever smiling, she seemed at home. She was at home, of course, but there was something in the way she relaxed in the chair-not as a visitor, but with familiarity.

Eventually, he carried the tray through to the living room and set it down on the coffee table.

"Shall I be mother?" he said, and she narrowed her eyes. Only briefly, but he was sure he saw it. It was one of those little sayings he used to say when they had guests. It was never planned so, but he would often perform the tea-pouring duties while she fetched and carried the tea and any biscuits they had.

From the corner of his eye, she watched him pour, using the sieve to catch any tea leaves. Everything he did was from memory and designed to stir something inside that fragile mind of hers: the way he tapped the sieve three times and then hurried it to the waiting saucer, the way he poured the milk to the edge of the cup and not the centre to avoid adding too much, even the way he folded the tea towel and laid it over the pot to keep it warm.

"There," he said. "You must be parched."

"Yes," she said, a little distant. "Yes, it was quite a journey."

"There's a downstairs loo now," he said, pointing to the back of the house.

"Now?"

"Sorry?"

"You said now."

"Yes, well, there wasn't one before. I had it put in. The stairs can be ever so cumbersome."

She smiled at him innocently and sipped her tea.

"Ooh, that's hit the spot."

George was reminded of being in an interview with somebody he didn't just suspect of being guilty of whatever crime it was but that he knew was guilty. He had just wanted to blurt it out and get it off his chest. However, strategy dictated that the information should come from the interviewee naturally. There were rules against putting words in the mouths of suspects. And yet he so longed to ask if she recognised the church, or the house, or if the floor he'd painstakingly restored was familiar.

"I'd better check on the soup," he said, setting his cup down.

He was halfway to the kitchen when he heard it, or at least he thought he'd heard it.

"Thank you, George."

"Sorry?" he said, clinging to the doorframe as his heart began to thump wildly. "You said something."

She craned around to see him.

"No, dear. I don't think so."

They lingered there, and he could have sworn there was a look in her eye that suggested she knew exactly what she had said and that he hadn't imagined it.

"I'll just..." he began, then slipped into the kitchen, where he leaned on the worktop to recover. Tears fell from his eyes, and his throat seemed to close up so that he was forced to take huge gulps of air to satiate his body's needs.

It was just beginning, he told himself. There was plenty of time for her to let slip some more of those tantalising endearments.

And even if that would be the only time she ever called him by his name, he would cling to it.

He ladled the soup and had to carry them one at a time to

hide his shaking hands. He set the first down on the little dining table and then fetched his own. The places had already been laid, with the spoons, a jug of water and two glasses. So, with lunch set, he returned to her. Her teacup was empty, and he made a show of carrying the tray to the table for them to finish it while they lunched.

And then he came to stand before her, the wheelchair at the ready.

"Shall we?" he asked.

She was still. Her eyes were closed, and her hands lay on her lap.

"Grace?" he said softly, bending to tuck a loose strand of hair behind her ear.

And then he realised.

"Grace?' he said again, with a little more urgency this time. He dropped to his knees before her, took her hands in his, and let the tears stream down his face. "Oh, God, Grace. Oh, dear God."

He kissed her hands and rubbed them against his cheek, if only to savour her touch one last time.

And then he rested his head on her lap and caressed each finger, memorising the touch of her skin and recalling those times he had touched them before. The first time they had held hands back when they were courting. The time she had sprained her wrist and he had bandaged it tightly, so she could at least hold a paintbrush.

And the time he had stood before her in the church across the road and slipped her ring on her finger.

The ring he felt now. The ring she still wore.

He dragged his head from her lap to stare at her. She was at peace. She was at peace at last.

And for that, he just couldn't be sad. Never again would she have to return to the home, stripped of her dignity, and for that, he was grateful. The last word she had spoken had been his name.

Not in casual reference to her husband during a conversation with a third party. But to him. In recognition.

And for that, he was warmed.

"Sweet dreams, my Grace," he said aloud. He held both her hands in his, leaned forward, and placed a gentle kiss on her forehead. The last kiss, as sweet as the first and every one since. "I won't be far behind you."

The End.

PROLOGUE - THE DEVIL INSIDE HER

The Deadly Wolds Mysteries - Book Four

It was strange, Lily thought, how everything could change in the blink of an eye — her marriage, her life, the weather.

The fog had descended abruptly, swaddling her like death's embrace, unwelcome and bone-chilling. It was the same fog they had spotted from the bottom of the hill, falling like a spectre, its long arms reaching, begging for touch.

Finally, it had enveloped them all.

She had only just reached the road, breathless with adrenaline. Marie was still behind her somewhere, or maybe to the side, or up ahead, she thought, twirling on the spot, abandoning all sense of direction. She needed to find help. Someone. Anyone. Marie needed her. She shouldn't have left her alone, not in that state.

But she couldn't be too far away, surely.

"Marie?" she called, her voice swallowed by the fog.

As Lily stared into the ivory veil, a fresh fear gripped her, a vision of headlights emerging like the mirrored shine of a predator's eyes in the darkness, growing larger and closer. And just as her fear escalated, it manifested. Lily heard the growl of an engine, and before she could even react, a dark car sped past on the other side of the road, a menacing, ebony shape in the darkness; its headlights on full beam only just penetrated the gloom. The snarl of its engine dissipated in the thick, sound-consuming fog. She doubted it had even seen her.

She felt exposed, alone on the road. She spun, no longer knowing which way was up, let alone the right way to go.

"Marie?" she cried again, panic rising like mist off a lake. "Cecelia? Franky? Violet?"

She longed for the sound of Violet's derisive comments, Cecelia's angry retaliation, Franky's sarcastic replies. She longed for the sound of Marie's ragged breathing as she struggled with the slight incline. But more than anything, she longed for that deep, safe voice in her ear that had always told her everything would be alright.

"Jordan," Lily whispered, as she often did in times of need, as an atheist might utter a prayer in desperation. "Help me." She knew he couldn't help her, not anymore, never again. But she begged for him anyway. "Jordan, please."

She felt her way along the tarmac, aware of the steep drop to one side of the road, the way one might tentatively feel for the bottom stair in the darkness. Until a few seconds ago, the long, steep slope into the forest they hiked alongside had offered an unparalleled view of their serene surroundings. The height from the ridge had been a gift, a vantage point from which to take in the valley, the crisscrossing hedgerows, ripening leaves, and gliding kites that soared above the Wolds.

Then, the morning fog had been an aesthetic detail, an aspect of beauty adding drama to the scene.

Now, it was damn well dangerous.

Of course, a sheer drop in the Wolds was nothing compared to other areas of the country. Few places in the Wolds fully allowed for treacherous pitfalls. That's why they'd chosen this place; they thought it would be smooth sailing, a long week of easy hiking. Well, that and Franky had wanted to show off the outstanding natural beauty on hers and James's newly bought doorstep. But they had underestimated the erratic nature of British weather, a deceptively cruel and unforgiving mistress. The drop along which they had been walking had been significant enough to want to avoid, offering a fifty-feet tumble to the bottom that would, at the very least, break an ankle. That's why they had crossed the road, to follow the hiking path on the bank on the other side.

"Marie?" she called out, hearing the fear in her cry.

Gone were the days when she would meet danger head-on. When she and Marie would walk home across London after midnight and accept free cocktails and lifts from strangers into the city.

"Marie, are you alright?"

But the fog was too thick to carry sound.

She tapped the ground with her foot but struggled to identify the material beneath it. It didn't feel smooth, like tarmac, but many of the smaller roads nearby were stony and muddied by the wheels of tractors and four-by-fours. It felt similar to the hiking path on which they had been walking. But she couldn't be sure that such a vehicle was not about to run her down. Lily held up her hand, hoping to find something, someone to ground herself, a tree, a fence, a friend, but her fingers only moved through a wispy, white nothingness.

She felt like she could be dreaming, so disorienting was the greyness surrounding her. She yearned for the crisp, white skies they had enjoyed only a few minutes earlier, the promise of the sun behind the clouds. She yearned for the yellow Viking-helmet logo they kept an eye out for on signposts, the one showing them the way forward.

Then a stick broke, not a flimsy twig but a solid stick beneath a heavy hiking boot. It *cracked*.

Lily spun. "Marie?"

A figure emerged through the fog, slowly, carefully, feeling its way towards her.

"Oh, thank God," she said. "Marie, you're walking. Are you okay now? Where are the others?" The figure continued its trajectory, more certain than Lily — she could see that now — of where it headed, with stronger, more decisive steps. "Careful now," she said. "That drop is here somewhere. We're back on the road."

She turned around, searching for the edge of the drop, squinting through the wisps. But ever-so-slowly, the fog was clearing; she could make out strange shapes although she could not yet identify them. She thought she could see it, the slope off the road, a safe distance from where they stood, metres away. She sighed with relief.

But her breath was cut short.

From behind her, the figure had lurched. She felt it step up behind her, uncomfortably close, and wrap an arm around her neck. She laughed at first, thinking it a game, a childish prank to scare her. But the grip tightened when she laughed.

"Marie?" she choked.

But it wasn't Marie. It couldn't possibly be.

"Stop," Lily said, panicking, gripping the arm that held her tight. Her nails scraped against a raincoat's nylon sleeve, creating a sickly, squeaky sound. "Please."

But with each protest, the grip only tightened, so she couldn't speak, so she couldn't breathe. She tried to pull at the fingers wrapped in thick gloves that held fast. The figure's breath grew ragged and exerted in her ear, quickening like a lover's as she fought back. She tried to scratch but found no bare skin. She tried to scream but found no air. She tried to stamp on the feet of her assailant, but her efforts were too weak to penetrate their heavy, leather boots. Her vision blurred and darkened, and the blood drained from her face as though her fear was a fever. She blinked, and warm tears of dread dropped onto her cold cheeks.

Dreamy images merged with reality. The trees seemed to tremble like cold commuters on a train platform; the sky swelled like a snowy tidal wave about to consume her. Whether she imagined it or not, she believed the fog was lifting, and through it, the drop grew clearer, closer. Suddenly, that drop seemed like a haven. A promise of reality. A sheer fall to shake her from this spectral grip around her throat. If only she could reach it, throw both of them forward, maybe then she'd have a chance.

She felt life slipping away, falling into a panicked sleep.

So Lily lunged forward with what little strength she had, and, caught off-guard, the figure's grip weakened for the first time. She managed to thrust them forward a few metres closer. The drop was within reach. A single step. If only she could...

"Cecelia!" she screamed, using what little breath she had. "Marie, Franky, Vio-"

But the figure pulled her back by the throat, its grip increased ten-fold. Its fingers squeezed around her windpipe, focusing its impact, knowing time was running out. The fog was lifting. Its cover would soon be blown. The figure moaned in her ear, a genderless, inhuman moan, exhausted with the exertion of killing her.

Then, in the chaos, Jordan's face swam across her vision. Lily reached out to touch it, and instead of her fingers falling uselessly through the wisps, she felt his skin beneath her fingerprints, the stubble of his cheek, the bone of his jaw. A new will emerged, a yearning that surpassed fighting for her life — the desire to join him, to lie beside him once more.

She stopped struggling.

She closed her eyes. The figure continued to squeeze, and deep within Lily Hughes's ebbing consciousness, she sensed herself turn limp. She sensed a final breath escape her lips. She sensed herself dying. She sensed herself being pushed forward, then flying, falling, tumbling, rolling, breaking, splintering, failing.

She didn't reach the bottom. The pain faded, as did the light, and she was lying in her husband's arms — warm, calm, and at peace with the world.

ALSO BY JACK CARTWRIGHT

The DCI Cook Murder Mysteries

A Winter of Blood

A Secret to Die For

The Wild Fens Murder Mysteries

Secrets In Blood

One For Sorrow

In Cold Blood

Suffer In Silence

Dying To Tell

Never To Return

Lie Beside Me

Dance With Death

In Dead Water

One Deadly Night

Her Dying Mind

Into Death's Arms

No More Blood

Burden of Truth

Run From Evil

The Deadly Wolds Murder Mysteries

When The Storm Dies

The Harder They Fall

Until Death Do Us Part

The Devil Inside Her

AFTERWORD

Because reviews are critical to an author's career, if you have enjoyed this novel, you could do me a huge favour by leaving a review on Amazon.

Reviews allow other readers to find my books. Your help in leaving one would make a big difference to this author.

Thank you for taking the time to read *Until Death Do Us Part*.

Best wishes,

AUTHOR

COPYRIGHT

Printed in Great Britain
by Amazon

57438158R00270